DRAMA KING

THREE KINGS SERIES BOOK #2

PENNY REID

DRAMA KING

THREE KINGS SERIES BOOK #2

PENNY REID

WWW.PENNYREID.NINJA/NEWSLETTER/

COPYRIGHT

This book is a work of fiction. Names, characters, places, rants, facts, contrivances, and incidents are either the product of the author's questionable imagination or are used factitiously. Any resemblance to actual persons, living or dead or undead, events, locales is entirely coincidental if not somewhat disturbing/concerning.

Made in the United States of America

Print ISBN: 978-1-942874-87-4

DEDICATION

For Cyrus.
You know what you did.

POTENTIAL TRIGGER WARNINGS

Potential trigger warnings: Accidental drug interactions. A drunk person (female) getting aggressively handsy with a sober person (male). Childhood abandonment. Walking in unexpectedly on someone naked. Mobs of fans / inappropriate touching / groping in a crowd. Discussion of the death of a parent / drunk driver accident. Car accident in snow. Death of wild animals. Snowstorm / getting stuck in snow. Hypothermia.

ACT 1: THE SONG

CHAPTER 1

BATHSHEBA

"Quickly, bring me a beaker of wine, so that I may wet my mind and say something clever."

— ARISTOPHANES

~Late June~

Am I . . . drunk?

Returning my half-drained glass to the table without taking another sip, I removed my attention from the six-foot-four, two-sixty, brown-haired, brown-eyed white man at the bar (conceal carrying beneath his ill-cut black suit) and squinted at the bottle of wine sitting at my one o'clock.

The bottle drifted to the left without actually moving and the room gave a slight spin.

"Ugh." Dropping my gaze and blinking rapidly, I tried again with the knife and spoon next to my empty dinner plate. They also drifted without moving. I winced. Light chatter and the delicate clinking of utensils connecting with dishes faded as I worked to correct my swimming vision.

No use. I'm drunk.

The bottle of wine was still two-thirds full. A waiter had uncorked it in front of me approximately twenty-five minutes ago while offering assurances that "my date" would be here within a half hour. The mystery man—known to me only as Mr. Black—had apparently called the restaurant and sent the bottle as an apology for his tardiness. I was told he hoped "his date" would consider staying until he arrived.

Just so y'all know, I wasn't Mr. Black's date. I was a decoy date, doing a favor for my good friend Ryaine O'Rourke and posing as her body double one last time. I didn't mind. She'd wasted enough of her life and nursed too many broken hearts thanks to Hollywood stud duds. But given my sudden and surprising state of inebriation at present, completing this evening's mission seemed doubtful.

I sighed, slurring to no one in particular, "Well, that's just fine and dandy." I'd washed and fixed my hair for this, and the dress had been steam pressed for the occasion. What a waste.

Originally, I hadn't planned on drinking any of the apology wine, but sitting in this here restaurant, in this here booth, on this here numb backside of mine all by myself was just as exciting as a mashed potato sandwich with a saltine salad. Before I'd touched the wine, I'd spent ten minutes staring at the uncorked bottle. And that's not to mention the hour I'd already waited for Ryaine's blind date. After all that waiting, I could see no harm in having a glass.

To be clear, her date was not an hour and twenty-five minutes late. He was only twenty-five minutes late. I'd been an hour early. I'm that person who always arrives in advance everywhere and every time and for everything. The more anxious I felt about a situation, the earlier I arrived. I needed to scope out the exits, the layout of the furniture, the flow of foot traffic, proximity to hospitals and fire stations, how close to maximum occupancy the establishment operated, etc.

Consider it an occupational hazard, even though I wasn't necessarily here tonight in a professional capacity. I no longer worked for Ryaine as of two weeks ago and she wasn't paying me to do a background check or pull together a dossier on this guy. She'd asked—pleaded, actually—and I'd accepted. I loved and cared about her. Which, ultimately, was how I'd talked myself into drinking the free apology wine.

How was it possible to be more than tipsy but less than drunk on a mere one and a half glasses of wine? *Maybe it's the antihistamines?*

Screwing up my face, I plucked my clutch from the booth at my side and dug around for the prescription paperwork provided by the pharmacist this afternoon. I unfolded it, trying to remember if I'd ever had alcohol and taken Benadryl before. Maybe that one time at that barbeque where I'd helped move that beehive? Yep. I'd had two beers, three stings, one oral tablet, and had felt perfectly fine.

Ignoring the man I'd been eavesdropping on sitting at the table to my right and his alarming overuse of the word *groovy*—chin-length gray hair, salt-and-pepper beard, white skin, five-foot-eight, one hundred fifteen pounds soaking wet, I reckoned—I used every ounce of my brainpower to focus on the printed information sheet.

"Possible serious, fatal interactions: MAO inhibitors . . ." Reading out loud but at a whisper, I went through the full list of interactions—potentially fatal to mildly problematic—squint-blinking at intervals. I ended up reading it six times before I found *alcohol* buried in there between opioid pain relievers and marijuana. "Well. There you go."

Swallowing around the odd, heavy feel of my tongue, I took a deep breath, methodically refolded the info sheet, and tucked it back in my purse. Alcohol had been listed under what to avoid, so I didn't think I needed to go to the hospital. Steadying myself, I reached for my water and drank half the glass. Maybe I could just go home and sleep it off.

"Mademoiselle, would you like the cocktail menu?" The waiter from before had suddenly reappeared and spoke from my left. This was a good thing since I'd need his help moving the table.

I'd had two options upon my arrival: claim the chair facing the booth, which would place my back to the room, or opt for the booth side, which necessitated that the table be pulled out before I could sit and then be pushed back in once I was settled. I'd chosen the booth, obviously. At five-foot-two, I had squeezed myself into and out of many tight spaces. But I wasn't sitting with my back to a room. Ever.

"No, thank you." Not trusting myself to roll a turnip let alone move a table covered in plates and glasses and an uncorked bottle of free wine, I gestured to myself and the booth. "Could you help me move the table, please? I'm afraid I must skedaddle—I mean, I must depart."

"B—but mademoiselle." The waiter seemed agitated, so I squinted at him. And what do you know, he looked just as agitated as he sounded. "You cannot leave. Your *Mr. Black* arrived a few minutes ago. He's just there with Ana Ortega and Tom Low, as you see. But he finds himself entrenched, which I'm sure is understandable given . . ."

Tom Low? Ana Ortega? Those were some serious hard-hitters, the types of high-profile Hollywood A-listers I hoped the studio would assign to me as clients when I reported to my new job tomorrow. I'd already received a packet on my first assignment detailing my cover story, travel expectations, and so forth. But the only identifying details on the client had been the person's height, weight, and age: six-foot-one, one hundred eighty-five pounds, twenty-nine.

Shifting my squint to the front of the restaurant—a chic yet bottlenecky design that didn't allow for proper traffic flow and was a blatant fire hazard —I spotted a few bodies making a fuss at the entrance, giving each other air-kisses. Sure enough, Tom Low, Ana Ortega, and a cluster of fancy-looking folks plugged the walkway by the maître d' stand.

One man with his back to me seemed to be at the center of the fawning tsunami. Other than taking note of Tom Low and Ana Ortega, I skipped over the rest without categorizing them by physical attributes, as I always do. My drunken vision wouldn't allow it and it didn't matter. I needed to leave.

Plus, *really!* If this Mr. Black guy Ryaine's agent set her up with had arrived a few minutes ago, why was he over there giving air-kisses and not over here meeting the date he'd left waiting for almost a half hour? And didn't that just tell me everything I needed to know. Ryaine didn't need another attention-hungry sycophant for a boyfriend, she'd dated enough of those already.

"Is there a back door?" I asked, trying to gently shift the table forward, not waiting for him to help because chaotic, possibly nonsensical thoughts were now flitting through my head like, *What if the studio assigned me to Ana Ortega or Tom Low or one of the other movie stars by the maître d' stand or in this restaurant?* I didn't want to be seen drunk the night before my first official day at the studio. Nor did I want folks thinking I was Ryaine, she didn't need any more party-girl press.

"Mademoiselle. Please." The waiter made a huffing noise and gripped the table. The wine bottle rocked back and forth. He grabbed it at the neck. "Please. Just give Mr. Mal—Mr. Black time. I do not think you will regret it."

I let my hands drop from the table and gazed up at the waiter. Even through the lens of my intoxication, the man's anxiety seemed out of place, which made me suspicious.

"Don't take this the wrong way, but why do you care whether I stay or go?" I sat back and crossed my arms. "You have a line of people out the door wanting to eat here." I'd passed the line on my way in. I'd never heard of this place before, but apparently it was very popular.

The waiter seemed to sigh through gritted teeth. "Listen. I want to meet him, okay?" His faux French accent suddenly dropped, becoming generic American.

"You want to meet my date?"

"Yeah. I have a script I want him to read." His eyes flickered away and then back to me. He leaned forward. "This could be my big chance. Are you two . . ." The waiter's gaze searched mine, seemed a little desperate. "He said it was a blind date on the phone when he called about the wine. You've never met him before? Do you think you could help me?"

I stared at the not-French waiter, having trouble keeping up with my sluggish thoughts, but maybe I got the gist of this guy's intentions? He wanted to give a script to my blind date and couldn't do that if I up and left, and he wanted me to help him.

I huffed. The *audacity.*

Speaking and thinking at the same time, I shook my head. "This town is absolutely crazy."

The waiter flinched, blinking, and straightened away.

"No. Y'all are nuts. Seriously." I let my elbow hit the table and leaned forward. "I've been here for three months and every time I go out with Ryaine, she can't go anywhere without someone asking her for a favor."

"Ryaine? Ryaine who? Ryaine O'Rourke?" He seemed to rock back on his heels. "Wait. Are you . . . are you her?"

"I am not her, and I wouldn't want to be her. Folks she doesn't even know approach that poor woman on the street asking for things. Like you and Mr. Black. You don't know him, and look at you"—I gestured to my waiter with a sweep of my hand—"over here plotting to ask the unsuspecting guy a favor on a blind date." Unthinkingly, I picked up my wineglass again. "Shame on you. Don't you think he's a little nervous?"

"Nervous?"

"Yeah. Nervous. It's a blind date, isn't it? Folks get nervous on blind dates where I'm from."

The waiter squinted at me. "Where's that? Alabama?"

"Texas. So, what? Y'all don't get nervous here?" I curled my lip. "Actually, it wouldn't surprise me if y'all don't get nervous on blind dates. This place is like Wonderland. Up is down, down is up, and the Walrus and the Carpenter are looking for oysters."

His mouth opened and closed, but then he turned his attention from me, something or someone at the periphery of my table cast a shadow over my dinner plate and drew his notice.

I went to take a sip of the wine but then remembered myself just as a deep voice coming from the direction of the shadow said, "Ms. White?"

Feeling bleary-eyed and suddenly tired, I glanced up. Forced to do a double take, because I did not trust my vision, the double take yielded the same result as the first haphazard glance. I sucked in a startled breath. I stared at the man, dumbfounded.

Cyrus Malcom. *Well, I'll be . . .*

I hadn't seen Cyrus since he'd briefly dated my stepsister during their senior year of high school. And now here he was, looking taller and broader and so ridiculously attractive to my bibulous gaze, the man looked fake.

Maybe it's because I'm drunk? No one looks this good in person.

"Cyrus? What are you doing here?" I croaked, setting my wine down and gaping openly at his sudden presence.

Green eyes the color of emeralds flickered over me, the side of his alluring mouth shaped in his signature curvy smirk, which was framed by dark stubble, the hint of a beard that was too artful and maintained to be a mere five-o'clock shadow.

"Excellent. I see my reputation precedes me," he drawled, his deep, velvety, haughty voice sending a shiver down my spine.

I blinked at him, my confusion persisting. What was Cyrus doing in Los Ang—*He's a movie star now, dummy.*

Ooooooh. That's right. I'd forgotten.

I wasn't a big fan of comic book film adaptations, they all seemed the same to me—backstory, training montage, bad guy, someone dies, big fight, another montage, another big fight, an emotional reveal, a super big fight where you wonder briefly if the hero will win, hero wins, a happy ending— and so I generally skipped them. But I was aware that Cyrus Malcom had landed the titular role in one of the biggest comic book franchises a few years ago, jettisoning him from virtual nobody pretty boy to overnight movie star.

But that's not how I thought of him. I thought of him as the first son to the hoity-toity old money society family in my hometown, ex-boyfriend of my stepsister, and dichotomously both a supercilious snob and a huge flirt.

He wouldn't know or remember me unless I drew him a chart, I felt certain of that. I'd been twelve when he'd dated my eighteen-year-old step-sister, and I think we only met two or three times in that capacity. I'd been too young to be on his radar.

But here he was, standing at the corner of my table, his gem-like eyes glittering from beneath thick, black, perfectly sculpted eyebrows; equally thick dark hair cut short on the sides, much longer on top, and coiffed to perfection; the sharp angles of his square jaw and the little cleft to his chin would've given him an air of old Hollywood if not for the stubble adorning both.

"Monsieur Black," someone said in a French accent, tugging my attention to the left. The waiter was still there, greedy little eyes focused on Cyrus as he gestured to the chair facing me. "Please. Allow me to bring you the menu."

Dumbly, though not quite as dizzily inebriated or tired as before, I watched Cyrus Malcom claim the seat across from me, his back to the room, his eyes never seeming to leave my face as he nodded politely in the direction of the waiter. "Yes, please. Thank you," he said smoothly, something about his cadence striking me as elegant.

Unlike me and most folks in our hometown, Cyrus had never possessed a southern accent. He and his brother, Titus, had been sent off to a boarding school in some European country for several years during elementary school. They'd both returned with a blend of intonations that reminded me of tea and crumpets and cashmere sweaters and gold pocket watches on chains and other fancy shit.

"Thank you for staying." His hand slid down the front of his suit jacket and tie. Making no attempt to hide his inspection of me, the smirky smile loitered around his full lips. "Was the wine to your liking?"

"I—It was good, yes." I gave my head a little shake. This was so surreal. *Cyrus Malcom is Ryaine's blind date . . .*

What a small world.

Thank goodness I'd volunteered to come in her stead. She would've been half in love already. Ryaine was infamous in our college friend group for falling hard and fast in love at first sight. Cyrus had been awkward in his early teen years, a late bloomer who'd looked younger than his peers until sixteen or so. He'd returned to town after the summer of his junior year having pole-vaulted over the hump of puberty.

Cyrus had been super handsome at seventeen. But now he'd grown so attractive, the man was borderline addictive to look at. Good thing I didn't have an addictive personality.

Giving my head another shake, I closed my eyes to block out the radiance of his physical exterior and attempted to find the words I'd planned to say before mixing prescription antihistamines with alcohol.

"I'm, uh, I'm not who you think I am." Blinking to focus as I opened my eyes, I was careful to keep my attention on the candle flickering in the center of the table.

"I know who you are. You're Ryaine O'Rourke."

My eyes cut to his. "John told you who you were meeting?" John was Ryaine's agent.

Cyrus's lips curved further, revealing a dimple in his scruff, and I stared at it, startled. A dimple? When had he developed a dimple? Had he surgically added it?

"But I must say"—his forehead furrowed a little, a quizzical look—"you look different in person. And your accent . . . I thought you were raised in Massachusetts?"

The room gave a slight spin and I breathed in and out. "John didn't tell Ryaine your name." I needed to go.

"What did he tell you?"

"He told Ryaine you'd be called Mr. Black, but s-said it was a psydo—a pyso—you know." I closed my eyes and gripped my forehead. I couldn't think when I was looking at his ridiculously perfect face. *Focus.*

"Why are you referring to yourself in the third person?" His question sounded hesitantly amused.

I snapped my fingers belatedly. "Whatever it's called. Move the table. I'm stuck back here."

Cyrus made no move to help with the table and so I glanced at him again.

Wide eyes stared back at me, rapidly filling with incredulity. "Wait. Are you . . . are you drunk?"

CHAPTER 2

CYRUS

"What heart, what soul, what bollocks could long endure this plight, having no one to shag in the middle of the night?"

— ARISTOPHANES, *LYSISTRATA*

J harbored no ill will toward drunk people. Drunks could be fun on occasion, depending on the situation, the music playing, and my attire. But as I'd just endured hours of LA traffic after visiting a colleague at his posh rehab facility down in Palm Springs, I wasn't necessarily impressed by Ryaine O'Rourke's spifflicated state.

At the very least, she could've waited for me.

"I am. I am drunk," she admitted, nibbling on her full bottom lip. "But to be fair, even though you sent me this here unsolicited bottle of wine, it's totally my fault."

"Your fault?" I asked, abruptly distracted, unable to decide which was more worthy of my attention: her easy, shame-free acquiescence of responsibility, the disorienting and unmistakable Texan accent that reminded me of home, or how both seemed to enhance her level of intrigue by a factor of ten.

I thought she was from somewhere up north. Huh.

I'd spotted Ryaine upon my arrival but had been unpleasantly waylaid. My fault. I'd been preoccupied and frustrated with myself for being late—

once again—and hadn't adopted appropriate evasive maneuvers with Tom Low and Ana Ortega as they approached.

They'd appeared overjoyed to see me. I seriously doubted this was the case. I'd recently landed a role Tom had been in contention for, and Ana still wasn't happy I'd recommended Vera Rodrigo over her for the Demon Redeemed franchise.

"Yes. It is my fault I'm drunk," Ryaine said, her palm hitting the top of the table, the suddenness of the sound making me blink reflexively.

"I'm sure you had a good reason." My attention lowered to the flawless skin of her neck and shoulders, bared in an absolutely delectable and reckless green strapless dress. Whoever her stylist was deserved an A+ gold star.

Perhaps the evening can be salvaged.

In my vague recollection, Ryaine both did and did not look like the movie and magazine version of herself, but this disconnect was to be expected given the nature of her breakout role. Based on the healthy fullness of her cheeks and figure, she seemed fully recovered now, but she'd played a woman dealing with a severe eating disorder in the film. Reportedly, she'd shed thirty-five pounds for the part, and was now on the award season short list.

The Academy loved physical transformations, one of the many reasons I'd never be nominated. Losing weight or rapidly gaining it was such an effort.

Though I'd initially felt put out by her boozy condition, I was an open-minded sort. I could withhold judgment for now and encourage her to switch from wine to water.

But then she said, "Exactly. I have a rash."

My gaze lifted from the neckline of her dress and I choked on my surprise. "Pardon me?" What were we talking about? Had I missed part of the conversation?

She cupped her hands around her mouth and repeated louder, "I HAVE A RASH."

Chagrined, I glanced at the patrons to our left and right, offering a pacifying smile to the startled woman gaping between me and Ryaine O'Rourke. The woman's eyes hadn't sparked with recognition, so I lied, "Please forgive my sister. She's a performance artist. We're all so proud."

Hammering a smile in place, I moved my chair directly next to the booth where Ryaine sat and leaned close, searching her eyes, studying her pupils. "Are you on drugs?" I whispered.

"I am," she whispered in return, nodding. "That's what I'm trying to tell you. I have a r—"

"Yes." My artificial smile faltered, amusement and alarm fully yielding to intense irritation. I may have been hunting for a real connection over the last year, but not of this sort. "You have a rash. Please, share no further details. I am not a medical professional and shan't be held accountable should your protected health information be used inappropriately."

I'm going to disembowel John.

The only reason I'd reluctantly agreed to this tête-a-tête was because of my agent's badgering. He'd recommended utilizing his rising-star client list for a mutually beneficial arrangement, a reliable *plus one,* as it were. After my last disastrous, fizzled affair, he'd offered to vet the candidates for me, to find a compatible colleague with temperament and goals similar to mine. He'd promised someone *real*, someone I could trust. My taste in romantic partners usually sent me careening into trouble. Of note, fun trouble is still trouble.

"Well." Ryaine grinned, turning her wobbly head away and seeming to search the seat of the booth. "Glad we got that all cleared up."

"Is it cleared up?" My eyebrows pulled together with concern, again surveying her exposed clavicle, upper chest, shoulders, and arms. I'd need to help her out of the restaurant and I didn't wish to touch anything contagious. "Do you need me to take you to a walk-in clinic?"

She attempted to tuck her purse beneath her arm, trying and failing at least three times before she finally managed. "No, no. I'm good. I'll call a taxi and be on my way. Be sure to tell John how awful of a time you had and, furthermore, that you do not wish to see Ryaine again in the future."

I flinched back, squinting at her anew. "Wait . . . are you actually on drugs? Or is this an act?" She'd been rather superlative in her breakout role. Could she be having one over on me?

"I am actually on drugs," she slurred, yanking the purse from under her arm, opening it, and pushing a piece of folded paper at me. "Read for yourself. Prescription strength Benadryl and wine do not mix. The doctor warned me to read the info sheet, but I should've taken her warnings more seriously. Like I said, my accidental inebriation was totally my fault, but it all worked out, so no harm, no foul."

Nonplussed, I stared at her. "Benadryl?"

"Yep. I never got hay fever this bad back home. But for some reason"— she shrugged, it was adorable—"California makes my immune system go haywire and I get a rash. Oh! Hay fever, haywire—hah!"

"You—your rash is hay fever?"

"That's right."

"And the drugs are—"

"Prescription ana-ana-histamines. Whew. Did I get that right?"

"You did beautifully." For the first time in what felt like eons, an unpracticed smile claimed my mouth.

I glanced at the bottle of wine I'd sent to the table. She'd imbibed one glass, perhaps a little more. Prescription antihistamines. Hay fever. A drug *interaction*.

A finger waving in front of my face brought my attention swiftly back to hers. "No more dimple, please." Her gaze had fastened to my cheek. "I've learned my lesson, and now I need to go."

"What lesson?" I asked softly, unused to being completely enchanted so quickly.

"Always read the drug info sheet. I wasn't planning on drinking. Truth be told, I've never been drunk before." Her accent thickened, bringing to mind the country roads and big-sky sunsets of my youth. "But you sent that bottle of wine and I had a glass and now here I am, acting like my Uncle Spit at a Sunday dinner."

I grinned.

She pointed at my cheek. "No more dimple."

Disregarding her order, I captured her hand. Her skin felt exquisitely soft, except the pads of her fingers were calloused. *How odd.*

"You have an uncle named Spit?"

"That's what we call him on account of the way he sprays his words. My daddy says he wasn't born, he was squeezed out of a bartender's rag. And he's so country, he thinks a seven-course meal is an opossum and a six-pack."

A laugh burst out of me, taking me by surprise. She was amazing. This had to be a character.

"Are you in character right now? Or what is with the accent and southern colloquialisms?"

"I'm from Texas. This is just me. I'm too drunk to be anyone else."

I could've sworn she was originally from New England. This had to be a character. *And yet . . .*

"The wine." Studying her, the bleary, unfocused quality to her eyes, my grin diminished. I glanced at the bottle. *The wine I'd sent.* Ryaine was truly experiencing a drug interaction, I felt certain of that.

Her hand in mine twisted, clutched my fingers. "I assure you, despite what y'all's agent thinks, Ryaine and you would not be a good fit."

I lifted an eyebrow. "Are we referring to ourselves in the third person again? In that case, Cyrus thinks we should try our fit later, when Ryaine hasn't mixed antihistamines with a glass of wine and doesn't insist on taking her method acting to levels even Jared Leto would find alarming."

Her grip tightened. "No, I—I mean, Ryaine is wonderful, but her judgment is impaired. She'd fall for you like an anvil dropped off a skyscraper."

To stem my smile, I pressed my lips together. This woman was so wonderfully weird. I'd gone from completely enchanted to hovering on the precipice of swiftly smitten. Eccentric women were, admittedly, a weakness. In my opinion, beautiful women were not uncommon, but a beautiful woman who danced to the melody of her own harpsichord—the more peculiar and idiosyncratic, the better—the deeper in trouble I typically found myself.

Case in point: all my arrests were due to my insatiability for an eccentric woman. Most involved nudity.

"Ryaine would fall for me like an anvil dropped from a skyscraper?" I heard my voice drop as I worked to entrap her lovely, expressive, olive green eyes, bleary as they were. "Why?"

"Come on." Her tone turned flat. "You've seen yourself. Plus you're smooth as gelato. And that dimple? How is that thing even legal?"

I laughed again, likely flashing the aforementioned dimple.

But she wasn't finished. "I think John had it wrong when he set the two of you up because Ryaine is the falling-in-love type and you're the breaking-hearts type. She doesn't need another guy in her life who says pretty words but lacks substance."

"Ouch. What makes you think I lack substance? Is it the dimple?" I placed my free hand over my heart, anxious to see what she would say next.

She squinted, showing me just how much she believed her words made any impact at all, and said, "I know you," as though knowing me were an accusation.

"You really don't," I whispered, my gaze distracted by her mouth. She had the most bitable lips.

"Yes, I do." Ryaine gave her head several sharp nods, but then abruptly stopped to squeeze her eyelids shut. "And now I need to go because I really am drunk."

Ah. Yes. Drunk. Pity.

"Should I call a doctor? I know someone who makes house calls. I could

—" I stopped myself, clamping down on the impulse and clearing my throat for good measure.

This was how it always started, me wanting to be of service, tripping over clumsy attempts at chivalry. As utterly magnetic as this woman was, I wouldn't be making the same mistakes. Again.

Disentangling our fingers, I slid my palm from her wrist to her elbow. "You shouldn't drive. Let me call you a car."

"Like I said, I'll call a taxi."

"One of the agency's cars makes more sense."

Pulling out the table so she could stand, I helped Ryaine to her feet, steadying her by placing my hands on her shoulders. My eyebrows jumped once I caught sight of her shoes and I made the executive decision to tuck her under my arm and firmly against my side. They were three and a half inches, at least, and yet the top of her head barely came to my nose. No wonder she was in this state. I wondered at her alcohol tolerance even without the prescription drug interaction.

"It's fine. A taxi is fine."

"I must insist."

She huffed and grunted, puffed and grumbled, sounds that hearkened to mind the bull back home my mother had named Rodeo. I grinned at the thought.

"Come. Allow me to call a car from the agency. Just to be safe. It would make me feel better."

Ryaine swayed heavily against me, then finally growled, "Fine. Happy?"

"Exceedingly." She had no idea.

"Mr. Black, are you leaving so soon?" The server from earlier appeared at my side, his hands curled around a thick bundle of papers.

Oh. Sigh.

"I'm afraid so. Put the wine on my tab. And if you clear a path for us, you can reach out to my agent at ARC—greedy fusspot by the name of John Williams, like the composer but without the talent—he'll get that script to me." I lifted my chin toward the papers in his grip, then turned my shoulder to him and reached for Ryaine's hand to offer added support.

Immediately, our server rushed to part the sea of bodies.

She snuggled closer, her eyelids drooping tiredly. "Thank you, Cyrus. You're nicer than I thought you would be."

I gave her a squeeze and whispered so that only she could hear, "You're welcome, *ma petit taureau.*"

✳

I didn't personally know or recognize the driver the agency had sent over to collect Ryaine. He looked new. Thus, I insisted on accompanying her home to ensure she remain unmolested and unphotographed. Ryaine sat behind the empty passenger seat while I straddled the middle with my arm around her shoulders. Encouraging her head to rest against my chest rather than press her forehead against the window, her hand braced over my heart.

However, when she fell asleep in short order and her body grew lax, the hand over my heart slid down the front of my torso and landed heavily in my lap. I tensed, glancing up at the driver and finding his eyes on me.

Carefully plucking the appendage by the wrist and moving it to her lap, I gave the driver a tight smile. He returned it, his gaze flicking back to the road. In reaction to the quickly approaching yellow light he almost hadn't noticed, the man slammed on the brakes, necessitating that I hold Ryaine's head to keep it from whipping forward.

"Sorry," the driver said. "Sorry about that."

"No worries," I said, pushing soft strands of hair away from Ryaine's lips, the locks having fallen in her face due to our driver's inattentiveness.

When I glanced up, I found him watching us again in the rearview mirror, the car unmoving, the light now green.

"You're Cyrus Malcom, aren't you?" His voice held a hint of awe.

"I am." I pointed toward the windshield.

He didn't take the hint. "Who is that? She looks familiar."

"This is my cousin, visiting me from Texas," I lied smoothly since I did not know this person and couldn't be sure he'd keep Ryaine's inebriation to himself. "And the light is green."

He flinched, shifting his focus back to the road. "Oh. Sorry."

"Think nothing of it." Irritated with him, I cupped her cheek to keep her head in place as the driver followed the curve leading onto I-5, his speed well over the limit.

But just as he merged with traffic, Ryaine stretched her arm and—with absolutely no warning—fully palmed me over my pants, giving my cock a firm, single rub. I sucked in a breath, drawing the driver's attention.

"Everything okay?"

I nodded, praying he couldn't see the location of her hand. "Fine and dandy."

He gave me a narrowed, confused-looking squint and then returned his attention to the road. As soon as he did, I abandoned her cheek in favor of saving the dignity of her fingers. Unfortunately, her head now unsupported, fell forward while I inhaled a steadying breath, commanding my blood flow to alter course. Alas, to no avail. The beast had awoken by the errant stroke of its head and now I'd be left to deal with its demands, just as soon as I made it home.

Ryaine made a soft sort of snort as I threaded our fingers together and once more removed her hand from my groin. Then her head lifted sharply, her eyes flying open, and—I don't know why, so don't ask—I froze.

She blinked several times, her intelligent eyes narrowing. "What are you doing?" she mumbled, her gaze scrutinizing.

"I—"

"I've never dreamt of you," she said, tugging against my hold. I immediately released her hand. She brought it to my face and her thumb stroked over my bottom lip. "You're so handsome."

I smiled. Of course I smiled. An eccentric, gorgeous woman calls you handsome, you smile. That's what you do.

But then I remembered we were not alone, and I glanced at the rearview mirror again. Unsurprisingly, the world's nosiest driver watched us instead of LA freeway traffic.

Clearing my throat, I arranged my features into something I hoped looked familial and said, "Thank you."

A puff of air left her lips. "Oh. This is nice." Her words were dreamy and her hand smoothed down my shirtfront. "Kiss me."

I grimaced, refusing to look at the man in the mirror again. He was watching, and listening, and there wasn't a damn thing I could do about it. "Uh, I'm afraid that's impossible, my dearest."

"Anything is possible." She pressed herself more insistently forward. "This is my dream."

"Oh, no. I assure you, this is very much r—*real!*" The end of my sentence burst forth a full octave higher than my usual voice as that lovely hand of hers had returned to its favorite place.

I grabbed it and whispered directly in her ear, "None of that, naughty girl. I like my women sober and capable of consent. Behave."

As I leaned away, I saw she was smiling. It looked a little sad. "I'd never do anything like this outside of a dream. I'm boring."

"You are the opposite of boring." I kept my voice just above a whisper. "I can't wait to know you." My heart quickened unaccountably at the thought. I didn't understand it, but I didn't fight it either.

Ryaine bit her luscious lower lip, pulling me from my musings, and I watched helplessly as she pulled it through her teeth before saying in a seductress's voice, "You are so sexy."

"Why, thank you. You're exceptionally—ah-ah-ah!"

Her chin jutted forward, chasing my mouth, and her wayward hand tugged against my hold. Before I could firm my grip, she did some quick magic and had captured *both* of my hands in one of hers. This time my breath was sharp as she gave my cock a wonderfully demanding stroke over my pants, sending an equally sharp spear of white, hot pleasure to the base of my spine. A garbled mess of jumbled protestations mixed with an appreciative, instinctive growl rushed from my lungs and throat. Her movements stilled. In the very next second, her touch felt more exploring than sexy.

"You're huge, Cyrus. Fuck," she said on a breath that morphed into a moan. "I want it."

Involuntarily, my eyes cut once more to the mirror and I almost laughed at the horrified stare that met mine. "I was joking earlier," I said to him, smiling through a grimace. "This isn't my cousin."

"Sure." He clearly didn't believe me. But this man's disgust was the least of my concerns. I could no longer salvage the situation or save face while drunk Ryaine seemed intent on unfastening my pants.

Ah well. The man would likely forever think that Cyrus Malcom preferred to keep it in the family. C'est la vie.

Abandoning any effort to convince him otherwise, I managed to twist my wrists and almost entwined Ryaine's fingers with mine. But then her hand found the buckle of my belt. Never let it be said she wasn't persistent. I grit my teeth.

Shoving her away wasn't an option. I didn't want to hurt her. I wanted to protect her. She clearly didn't understand what was happening, where she was, or what she was doing.

"I'm very impressed by your agility and determination, dear Ryaine. But now it's time to stop." *Damn.* I hadn't meant to use her name. I hoped the driver hadn't heard me.

"I'm not Ryaine," she panted against my mouth, attempting to repeat her earlier trick—the one where she'd magically trapped my wrists. I was wise to her now and kept my longer fingers diligently locked around her much smaller ones.

"Of course you're not. You're, uh, my cousin." Also panting, I rolled my eyes at myself. Her octopus-like maneuvers and craftiness were giving me a frazzled workout. It felt like she had no less than eight arms.

"Call me Beth." Her lips bumped against mine despite my best efforts.

The woman was much stronger than she looked. Strong and skillful at wrestling, even drunk.

"Then, Beth, please stop." I tipped my head back, evading her mouth. "Because you are not asleep, and this is not a dream, and I'd really like to see you again, and I do not wish for you to be embarrassed or avoid my calls because of one and a half glasses of wine mixed with Benadryl."

Finally, *finally,* her frenetic movements slowed, then stilled. Breathing heavy, she leaned away until her back connected with the door. "You want to see me again?"

"Yes." I nodded once to emphasize the word. "So, please, let me hold you until we make it to your place."

Her hair was wild around her face. She looked magnificent. "What happens when we get to my place?"

"You go to sleep, I leave, and then you call me as soon as you're rested and more yourself. And no apologies allowed." I reached forward to gently tuck her hair behind her ears.

Her hesitation was palpable.

I opened my arms. "Come on. You can sleep now, if you wish. I'll wake you when we arrive."

Her eyes drifted, and she blinked as though to focus them, but did move forward. "Okay. I doubt I'll remember any of this anyway."

I pulled her close again, pressing her cheek to my chest as the car swerved suddenly to the right, and then straightened.

I glanced up at the rearview mirror once more. Our driver's eyes were on us and he looked absolutely appalled.

Don't do it. Don't do it . . . I was going to do it.

Why not? The man already believed the worst. At least I could find some amusement for myself in the situation.

Ensuring each of my words were carefully enunciated, I said, "That's right, come to your cuz. I got what you like. Such a good girl." Then I winked at him.

He flinched, his stare cutting back to the road as he seemed to sink down in his seat. It was a struggle to hold in the laughter. Perhaps tomorrow TMY will have a headline about me being an incest aficionado. My publicist would just *love* that.

"I don't want to forget. I need to—to always know and be aware," Ryaine slurred, and I gave her back all my attention. "Stop all threats, no matter what." She cut a hand through the air, and I caught it before it could fall—once more—in my lap.

Setting it deliberately on her own lap, I patted the back of it once before twining my arm around her body. Hopefully, if I held her tight enough, that errant hand wouldn't wander.

"It's why I do what I do," she continued, her voice scarcely audible.

I didn't follow her meaning, so I asked, "Threats are why you're an actress?"

"I'm not. I keep people safe." A hint of vulnerability—or something close to it—snuck into her tone. "I keep people safe now."

The sound of the words, how she'd said them with such passion, ignited something in my chest. "You like keeping people safe?" I murmured against the top of her head.

Ryaine yawned. I felt her body go limp in my arms. This time, thankfully for my sanity, her talented fingers were curled in her own lap, nowhere near mine.

I breathed out relief and pulled the scent of her perfume into my lungs. And then I felt myself smile. Again.

CHAPTER 3

CYRUS

"Let each man exercise the art he knows."

—ARISTOPHANES

"Y ou're late." Lenore Wood, Halina Wraithington's capable administrative assistant, eyed me over the stack of papers she currently held perpendicular to her massive desk.

I paused just beyond the hallway to the elevator, halting at the edge of the large waiting area. An antique handwoven carpet of deep, rich reds, blues, and golds covered the floor, several whiskey-colored leather club chairs were scattered about, a beautiful, tufted velvet green sofa sat primly against the far wall. Each of the white walls featured an original Ed Mell painting of the desert and sky—his favorite subjects and perhaps also his muses—which I coveted but would never attempt to buy. The colors would clash with my décor.

This room was stunning, but my favorite thing about it, by far, was the giant leaded glass window, fifteen feet tall and at least that wide, which sat directly behind Lenore. One of the only preserved parts of the studio's art deco past.

"Am I late?" I glanced at my watch, feigning surprise. "I should get a new watch." An empty suggestion. I would never get a new watch. This one had belonged to my father, passed to me upon his death. I loved this watch.

23

"There's nothing wrong with your watch except that you should set it a half hour early. You're always late." Lenore's sharp gaze swept over me. "You're in a good mood. What's happened? Valentino having a sale?"

Despite not hearing from Ryaine yet this morning—or Ryaine through John, since neither of us had each other's number and I'd neglected to leave her a note when I took her home—I was in a good mood. Last night I'd been smitten. In the light of day, I was more than that. I was curious. I was *interested.* And not just because the woman was eccentric and stunning with a keen fashion sense and wonderful comedic timing.

The main part of our unconventional date on repeat in my brain was her statement, "I keep people safe."

What had she meant by it? Or had the words been part of her bizarre commitment to method acting whilst drunk and on prescription drugs? I found I desperately wanted to know.

"Cyrus?"

I removed my sunglasses from where they perched on my nose and tucked them in the inside breast pocket of my suit. "Why wouldn't I be in a good mood? The sun is shining, it's a beautiful day."

"It's LA. The sun is always shining."

"Scarcity or surplus of quantity does not diminish or improve quality."

Lenore gave me an eternally patient look and cocked her head toward her boss's door, Halina Wraithington, VP in charge of talent relations at World Wide Studios (WWS if you're into acronyms). This entire floor was dedicated to talent relations, and Halina oversaw it all. "She's ready for you."

"Is she? Is she ready, Lenore? Can anyone truly be ready for me?" I paired an eyebrow raise with the jest.

Lenore chuckled, a sound which never ceased to delight. As far as I could tell, I was the only one who could make her laugh. Mostly, she scowled.

"No one else lingers out here with me when they could be in there"—she tilted her head toward Halina's office again—"making demands and having their ego stroked, especially when they're already late."

"Maybe I want to butter you up." In no hurry, I sat on the edge of her desk and picked up a framed photo. "How are the kids? Did your oldest hear from NYU?"

"I'm not a biscuit to be buttered, and—yes—he got his acceptance letter last week. Thank you again for writing that letter."

"You're welcome." I placed the photo of her youngest son back on the desk's surface, winking at her. "Biscuit or no, you look like a snack today. I love red on you."

She laughed again, shaking her head like I was a naughty boy.

"You're so odd. Garrison says hi, by the way. Wants to know when you can manage another spa day." Garrison being her husband and spa day being exactly what it sounded like. In my opinion, more men needed to take a spa day, see to their atrocious cuticles and neglected feet.

"Tell him to call Craig, he'll get it on the calendar. And you love my oddness, don't pretend otherwise."

"Obviously. We all do. You are the most lovable and our favorite, is that what you want to hear?" Lenore, leaving her papers behind, stood and walked around her massive desk. "If I don't use a code name for you when scheduling meetings, this whole area is packed with people milling about, wanting to bask in your charisma."

"Can I help it that I am beloved by all?"

"I'm not sure you can help it. But please go in before someone wanders out here and I have a mob on my hands. You were supposed to have a full hour before the others showed up, but it's looking like all you'll get is fifteen or twenty minutes because you were late."

"What others?" I asked.

I'd been late because I was always late; no matter how good my intentions, an accurate sense of the passage of time evaded me; barriers erected themselves between me and my scheduled meetings; emergencies always popped up at the last minute. Admittedly, I was also easily distracted, thrown off course by anything novel and interesting or unexpected or beautiful. In this way, and several other ways, I wished I were different.

This morning I'd overslept, unable to settle after taking Ryaine to her apartment. The place hadn't been anything like I'd expected— exceedingly small, not in the best part of Hollywood yet obviously professionally decorated in an interesting blend of art nouveau and minimalism —but I didn't stay to snoop after I saw her safely tucked inside her bed. I wanted her to invite me over so I could snoop with her blessing. I wished I'd left a note with my number.

That said, I couldn't help but notice she didn't appear to own a coffee table.

When Craig woke me this morning for our run, I'd almost begged off. And I certainly hadn't remembered to ask Craig about today's meeting upon completion of our six miles.

"The *others* are why you're here," Lenore grumbled.

"Remind me what this meeting is about again. I can't seem to recall. Craig entitled it as 'regarding an entourage' on my calendar."

Circling behind me, Lenore placed a hand on my back, pushed me off her desk and forward. "All will be revealed if you go in and see Halina. Go."

"Couldn't you just—"

"Go." With one last gentle shove, Lenore sent me on my way.

I glanced at her over my shoulder and found her standing with her arms crossed, feet braced apart. Her determined expression only slightly ruined by her small smile. Holding my hands up in surrender, I faced Halina's office door and strolled forward.

Knocking once, I waited for her to say "Come in" before opening the door.

Halina glanced up from her computer. "You're late." Today she wore her pink silk shirt which meant she'd likely paired it with a dove gray pencil skirt.

"Am I late?" I shut the door behind me and meandered the perimeter of her office. "I had no idea. Is this a new painting?" I searched the canvas on the wall next to the door for a signature but couldn't find one.

"Cyrus, I need you to focus. This is important." Halina stood and walked toward me in her dove gray skirt. "I told Craig to have you here on time today. That personal assistant of yours is useless."

"Craig does his best. Don't be upset with him. I'm a terrible burden." I turned from the painting and watched her walk to the sitting area by the immense window dominating her large office.

"I'd offer you something to drink, but we don't have time for that." Halina claimed a spot on the white leather sofa. Like all type A personalities with razor-sharp intelligence and a mountain of ambition, she perched on the edge of the seat rather than lean back against the soft cushions. Someone had made those cushions, it was a shame she didn't use them.

Gesturing that I should take the chair across from her, she said, "I'll have to get straight to the point."

"Are you sure we couldn't be fussy for a minute?" I pouted, shoving my hands in my pockets. "You know how I hate getting straight to the point. How's Lawrence? The kids?"

I respected Halina, and I liked her. We had a strong business relationship based on mutual trust, flirting, and inappropriate jokes. If she didn't work for the studio, we'd likely be better friends.

"Fine." She pressed her lips together, not smiling. "You look well."

I rocked back on my heels. Her terseness was not a good sign. Typically, she didn't care if I was late. Typically, she loved my visits. *Typically.*

"Thank you," I said carefully. "I am well."

A bit of the tension in her forehead cleared and she studied me for a beat. "Wait. You're in a good mood. Why are you in a good mood?"

"Why does everyone keep saying that to me? I'm always in a good mood. I bring joy and light to all I meet."

"I wasn't aware *joy and light* was another phrase for indiscriminate philandering."

Whatever was on the tip of my tongue fled my brain and I snapped my mouth shut. And then I grinned. She also smiled.

This was more like it.

Back on familiar ground, I lifted a single eyebrow. "Vicious lies. You know my philandering is anything but indiscriminate."

She looked like she was trying not to laugh at my response. "But you're smiling."

"Don't I usually smile?"

"No. You smirk—not in a bad way. You always look like you're thinking of or remembering a joke, but it's definitely not usually a smile." Her forehead wrinkled again and her amusement waned. "And I'm glad you're in a good mood because I don't necessarily have the best news."

"Ah. So now we're getting straight to the point." Dutifully, I strolled to the chair across from her and sat, undoing the button of my suit jacket and leaning fully against the back cushions. God gave us cushions for a reason.

"Yes. I'm afraid we don't have much time since *someone* was late."

Refusing to be cowed by the reminder of my dependable tardiness, I picked a piece of nonexistent lint from my pants at the knee. "What is it, then? Did Fergus drop out as director on the *Brutal Desert* project?"

"No, no, it's nothing like that. It's nothing related to any of your contracts or projects. *Brutal Desert* is still full steam ahead, preliminary shooting begins next week. They're expecting you after the press tour for *Asmodeus Falls* concludes in November."

Asmodeus Falls was the second film in the Demon Redeemed franchise, wherein I played the titular character based on the comic books of the same name, published by DarkLens. The role had launched my middling career from B-list to A+. The premise of the comic had been interesting on its own: one of the seven princes of hell is lured away from darkness by an angel when they make a bargain for his soul. He loses and must serve her for an age.

But when I'd researched the actual origin story of the demon Asmodeus —the Persian, Jewish, and eventually Christian derivations—its ninth century BCE origins had been most fascinating, and ultimately why I'd taken the role.

"How are the junkets going, by the way?" Halina asked, her gaze assessing. "Everyone behaving themselves?"

"Splendidly." I faked a grin. Not everyone had behaved themselves. "Harry Lorher asked me if I shave my balls."

"Oh God." Halina's eyes drifted closed and she seemed to be gritting her teeth. "Why is he allowed to participate?"

"He's allowed to participate because his website is a haven for DarkLens comic book fans." I shrugged. "He's a necessary evil."

"What did you say to him? When he asked?" She visibly braced herself.

"I told Harry I don't shave, I wax." I studied my cuticles. "I then offered to wax his balls should he ever grow a pair."

A strangled laugh burst out of her, though she didn't look amused. "You didn't."

"I did."

"Cyrus—"

I cut her off with a sigh. "It's Vera I'm worried about." Vera was my leading lady in the Demon Redeemed franchise. "He asked her about her shaving habits as well, and that's when I ended the interview."

"What? Why didn't anyone tell me about this? Should I talk to Monty?" Halina reached for her phone.

Monty was the WWS director in charge of scheduling the press junkets and ensuring the actors' comfort with the process.

"First talk to Vera," I suggested. "Ask what she wants to do. We should follow her lead."

"I will." Halina nodded, typing something on her phone.

"I'm fine doing the Lohrer interview on my own for the third film, if she wishes to be spared."

"He shouldn't be asking you those questions either, Cyrus. He—"

I waved a hand through the air, suddenly impatient. "Why am I here?" I didn't want to discuss Harry Lorher or his balls.

"Fine. Let's move on." Her gaze grew examining, but eventually she said, "The higher-ups have decided your current security team isn't a good look."

"My current security team? What are you talking about? What's wrong with my team?" I liked my team. I'd grown comfortable with my guys. We weren't exactly friends, but we watched football together on Mondays and had started a wine tasting club on Thursdays. I'd hoped, with more time and prodding, they'd talk to me about real things instead of just sports and red wine tannins.

"Nothing is wrong with them. It's just, you being photographed surrounded by men who are taller than you and twice your size isn't a good look when we've all been hustling to paint you as the machoest of men."

"Macho men can't have tall guards?"

"Macho men don't have any guards because they don't need guards. Asmodeus certainly doesn't."

"Asmodeus isn't a man. He's the fictional demon prince of lust who manifests fire and brimstone at the snap of his fingers, can bring anyone to orgasm with a single look, and uses pleasure via touch to melt brains. His wingspan is sixty feet." I'd enjoyed playing the part of a tragic, morally dark-gray superhero more than I'd anticipated. A demon pulled from hell by angels after losing a bargain for his soul to heavenly forces, forced to do good and rescue damsels in distress—what's not to like?

"Exactly, and that's the image we're going for. Big. Powerful. A little terrifying. Tough and fierce. And having you photographed with men who are bigger and burlier—"

"Hey now." I pointed at her. "Size doesn't matter."

Halina rolled her eyes. "You're incorrigible."

I smiled, enjoying her predictable reaction, but let me be clear about something: I was never not going to make that joke. Judge me all you like, you *puritans*, but I've read the Bible. And so it says in the book of Michael, Third Letter to Dwight, *Let ye who has never replied with* "That's what she said" *cast the first stone.*

"You like it," I said with a shrug.

Her expression flattened. "You wouldn't get away with saying those kinds of things if you weren't so cute."

I gave her my cutest smile and turned my dimpled cheek toward her.

Pressing her twitching lips together, she sallied forth. "Anyway. You must see, being photographed with your current team makes you look small in comparison. It gives off the wrong vibe, sends the wrong message."

"Yes, I do see." How boring. Leaning my elbow on the arm of the chair, I set my index finger along my cheek and propped my chin on my thumb. "You want to replace my very competent guards with shorter versions? Thus, when I'm photographed during press tours or events with my security team, I'm the tallest."

This would be a blow to my social calendar. Thursday wine club was my favorite night of the week.

"Not precisely. Your new guards won't just be shorter, they'll be female, and shorter, and not obviously bodyguards."

I blew out a confused breath. "I don't think I follow."

She glanced at the wall clock to my left. "Your new team will be working undercover, each of them posing as part of your entourage. As far as the media and everyone else is concerned, you'll have two secondary stylists in addition to your current team, two more personal trainers, and two additional personal assistants."

"You're giving me six female guards? All pretending to be part of my nonexistent entourage?" I had a team of professionals who already filled these roles, but they weren't my entourage. "And you want them to be with me at all times?"

Other than my two bodyguards during press tours and fan events, no one had ever followed me around town or anywhere else.

She cleared her throat. "You've got the gist of it. Your new team will be here soon and will start immediately."

I stiffened. "They . . . what?" I would be meeting my new security team *now*?

And why did this news make me feel like I'd just stepped inside a cage? And why did my brain also wonder how Ryaine O'Rourke might react to me being surrounded by an entourage of six women?

Halina had the decency to look guilty. "I'm sorry I couldn't give you more notice, but you arrived late. They've all been painstakingly vetted, and I believe you'll be impressed. If you agree, you'll meet your new team, and then you will all—as a group—circle back at your house for orientation."

"Orientation?"

"Yes. We've given them each a project packet, don't worry"—she lifted a hand as though she expected me to protest—"your name is not attached to the materials, just in case you opt out. Obviously, I hope you won't. But they'll need to see where you live, where they'll be staying for overnights, become familiar with your security system, sort out the schedule, and so forth."

I couldn't keep up, I was still preoccupied by whether and why these changes were necessary. "But this—this makes no sense. Why six instead of two? And why will they follow me everywhere?"

"You need, uh, to have more and tighter security," she said, and I didn't miss how her lashes fluttered and she glanced at her knees. "So instead of two guards working in day shifts, and only during press tours and the like, we'll need at least two with you at all times."

I watched her with growing suspicion, she still hadn't answered my main question. "Okay, but why? Why do I suddenly need round-the-clock security?"

"This is what I wanted to talk to you about, why I asked you to come so early before the others arrived." Her gaze found mine again. "After you meet your new team, you should stay so we can discuss this."

"Discuss what?" Her lack of forthright answers concerned me more than anything she'd said so far.

"Cyrus . . ." Her shoulders rose and fell with a deep breath. "Ever since the press tour for *Asmodeus Falls* kicked off, the number of concerning fan mail sent to the studio has increased. As well, our tracking of social media and fan message boards leads us to believe that twenty-four-hour security is warranted."

Parsing through her words for a hidden meaning, I thought and said in tandem, "Are you saying I have a new stalker?"

Prior to this meeting, I was aware of seven stalkers. Four were in prison for crimes unrelated to me. The other three hadn't done anything dangerous to me and didn't have a history of violence, per se. But they did send creepy notes and photos. One woman worked as a florist in a grocery store and liked to send me flowers daily, always to the studio since my home address was a closely guarded secret. Sometimes, she'd put dead rodents in the arrangements, but there was no evidence she'd killed them herself.

Regardless, I had restraining orders against all seven of these individuals.

"No, Cyrus. It's not one person that's moved the needle on this, it's an alarming uptick in fervor from all your fans. The excitement for this film is exactly what the studio wants to see, but it's also focused on you specifically." Her words sounded rushed as she checked the clock again. "In many peoples' minds, based on their social media posts, you and Asmodeus are one and the same, and they have a para-social relationship with you both. And not like we've seen in the past. This feels extreme, and we'd rather be safe than sorry, especially given how the film ends."

I frowned, absorbing this news.

The film ended with me betraying Vera's angelic character, a shocking departure from the original comic book source material. Our director and I had discussed potential fan backlash for the story decision, but it was the right move for the franchise. It allowed the studio to introduce more characters and therefore spin-off movies and tv shows. It also set up the third film for Asmodeus, a new redemption arc, and tons of opportunities for studio merchandising partners.

It wouldn't make fans happy in the short term, but I believed the payoff for them in the end was worth it. After all, filmmaking was called *the business* for a reason.

Restless, I stood and paced the length of her office. The addition of an undercover bodyguard entourage to my current publicized existence felt like a huge intrusion. Yes, I was used to being photographed while going about my day, followed by photographers, but this was different.

The ability to move about freely in public in LA, grabbing an impromptu bite to eat near my house, running along the beach if I so chose, going to the convenience store on my own—these minor freedoms felt essential.

And assuming she agreed, what happened when Ryaine and I had our second date?

"What about my current team? Will they be reassigned?" I didn't want my guys to be out of a job. "And do they know this change had nothing to do with me?"

"Yes. Both Brody and Kamar will be reassigned by the studio. And if it's important to you, I'll make sure they know this was a studio decision and you had no idea."

"Please do. Thank you." Tugging on my bottom lip, I stared out the window, deciding I would also call them, reiterate that I wasn't to blame for the reassignment. *I hope they won't be too upset . . .*

"I'm sorry."

Without turning, I waved Halina's apology away. "It's not your fault."

"Yes. But I could've given you more of a heads-up."

I glanced at her sharply. "Why didn't you?"

"Because I worried if you were given time to think about it before meeting the team, you'd turn down our offer of round-the-clock security."

"Is that what this is? An *offer*?" A dry laugh tumbled out of me. But she was correct. I didn't enjoy letting people down, disappointing them, or delivering bad news. Once I came face-to-face with these new people, the chances of me opting out were negligible.

"It is an offer. You can say no. But I would strongly urge you to—"

A knock at the door cut her off mid-urging, and Lenore poked her head in a second later. "Sorry. I tried to give you as much time as possible, but they're all here and I didn't like making them wait."

"It's fine." Halina stood, her eyes on me. "Please, bring the team in."

Inhaling a deep breath, I worked to wipe my expression of agitation, arranging an unruffled, polite smile of welcome instead. If I would be in close proximity with these people for the next few months, I wanted to make a good first impression. Perhaps they could join the Thursday night wine club.

The women filed in one at a time, each dressed in some variation of office-professional attire, nothing noteworthy or exciting. If one or more of them were going to pose as my stylist, then we'd have to—

Tensing, I blinked once, then twice at the last woman to enter the room, and not because she was the only one attired in something more thoughtful than whatever had been on sale at Kohl's two seasons ago. But of course she wore what appeared to be a classic Oscar de la Renta floral print, cotton summer dress paired with brown strappy stilettos, because the last woman who'd entered the room was Ryaine O'Rourke.

I smiled at her in question and mouthed, "What are you doing here?"

She stared at me, eyes wide, her lips parted slightly, all the color draining from her face. I hoped she wasn't embarrassed about what had happened in the car. I'd have to soothe her fears.

But . . . why was she here?

"Cyrus, I'd like you to meet your team." Halina, not seeming to notice Ryaine's presence, strolled over to the first woman who'd entered and gestured to her. "This is your team lead, Wren St. James. Wren has served as team lead for—"

"Wait a minute." Smiling uncertainly, I glanced between Ryaine's sheet-white face and Halina's confused one. "Is this a joke?"

"Is what a joke?" Halina seemed honestly perplexed by my question.

Fine. I'd spell it out.

I pointed at Ryaine, but I addressed Halina. "You're telling me that Ryaine O'Rourke is one of my undercover bodyguards?"

CHAPTER 4

BATHSHEBA

"You should not decide until you have heard what both have to say."

— ARISTOPHANES

So far, this had been the most bizarre morning of my entire life. Even stranger than that time my cousin Carter had eaten mushrooms during a camping trip and insisted he had a tail. Then it turned out he sorta did—something called a vestigial tail—and, well, that's a story for a different day.

Anyway.

Given how anxious I'd felt about this morning's meeting, one might've thought I'd been outside the studio gate at the butt-crack of dawn, and that certainly had been my plan. That's not what happened, though.

Exhibit A: I woke up in my apartment. Waking up in my apartment wouldn't usually be a weird thing except this morning I woke up wearing my couture Vera Wang green velvet. It was my favorite dress. I typically treated it like it was made of sugar glass, and I saved it for whenever I wanted to impress. And I'd apparently slept in it.

And that brings me to exhibits B through W: Upon realizing I'd slept in my most precious dress, the events of the previous evening rushed into my brain like water from an overflowing toilet: the restaurant, the not-French waiter, the bottle of apology wine, Cyrus Malcom appearing out of thin air, me telling Cyrus Malcom I had a rash, me telling Cyrus Malcom that Ryaine was prone to falling in love, and me climbing all over Cyrus Malcom in the back of an SUV. Things got a little spotty after that, but I did recall him carrying me up two flights of stairs to my apartment and then leaving.

The first thing I did after groaning into my pillow was call Ryaine and leave a voice mail telling her a short version of what had happened. I hoped she wouldn't be too mad at me. The second thing I did was refuse to dwell on the events or beat myself up too much. If my spotty memory could be trusted, Cyrus Malcom had been a gentleman. I'd need to send him a note of apology and explain Ryaine was not to blame in the least for my horrifying behavior.

Exhibit X: Just as I finished leaving the voice mail for Ryaine and making a mental note to send Cyrus Malcom an apology, my phone dinged with a text message from my ex-boyfriend, leaving me as confused as a goat on AstroTurf.

SANTINO

Hey girl. Miss you. I might be out in LA next month for work. I'll have a car, no need to pick me up. Should I stay at your place or do you want to stay at the hotel with me *kiss emoji*

I squinted at the strange message and reread it several times. *Is he for real?*

I'd dated Santino for two months prior to my move across the country. He was an analyst for the CIA with a fondness for bespoke Italian suits. Despite not feeling any spark initially, I was willing to attempt lasting happiness with him based on our compatibility on paper. We had a lot in common, were the same religion, believed friendship was the basis for any solid, enduring relationship, and he'd insisted that we keep things going long distance. He'd seemed fully committed when I left and I was just beginning to feel the warm and fuzzies with him my last few days in DC.

My dad and stepmom had always said enduring relationships took work, and I was prepared to do the work.

Santino's text messages and phone calls had tapered off after my move. I hadn't heard from him in over six weeks, despite me messaging him no less than daily up until five weeks ago. I'd been willing to put in the work to see if this could be something real. Apparently, he wasn't. I wasn't upset about it, necessarily. On the one hand, I was grateful he'd shown his true colors before I'd invested any more of myself, and even when we'd been in contact, he hadn't crossed my mind as often as I'd expected. I'd resorted to setting reminders on my phone in order to send him daily texts.

On the other hand, I did miss the photos he'd send of himself in bespoke Italian suits and his mom's homemade pasta. His mom had been a super nice lady.

Now, to my mind, six weeks without him sending me any messages meant we were broken up. Whereas apparently in his mind, six weeks was an appropriate amount of time to have zero contact with somebody and yet still be actively dating them.

I guess I still had a boyfriend I needed to break up with.

While I contemplated his message, my gaze drifted to the time in the upper left-hand corner of the phone screen and I gasped. I had less than an hour to shower, change, and beat my way through LA traffic before my very important studio meeting. I did curse at this point, and I did move like the fire of hell was nipping at my ankles—deciding to forgo the shower—but I didn't panic. I wasn't the panicking sort. And since I'd laid everything out yesterday for today's meeting, including the info packet on the assignment and my brand spankin' new studio security badge, I was out the door in less than six minutes.

Exhibit Y: I cruised right through LA traffic. In fact, I encountered barely any traffic, and I began to wonder whether something catastrophic had happened based on the lack of cars clogging the road. Not one to look a gift horse in the mouth, I wrangled up a smile for the man at the guard station as I pulled into the studio lot and handed him over my badge, ID, and the name of the person I was scheduled to meet, Ms. Wraithington, the VP in charge of talent relationships, Building A.

I'd only met the woman once, about a week ago as I was interviewed for this particular assignment. She'd been low on details, but that hadn't bothered me at the time. It bothered me now. Perhaps if I'd arrived several hours early, I wouldn't have felt so entirely unprepared and off-kilter as I walked into the main studio offices and punched the call button for the elevator.

The ride up was just long enough for me to calm my heart and regulate my breathing. By the time I made it out of the elevator and down the short hall to the waiting area, I'd managed a smile and nodded at each of the folks sitting in the club chairs—five women, all about my size and shape, but with various shades of skin, eyes, and hair—then turned my attention to the stern-looking woman behind a ridiculously gigantic wooden desk. I'd met her once before. I doubted she'd remember me.

"Hello, ma'am. I'm—"

"You're Beth Ryan. I'm Lenore Wood. We've been expecting you." She stood as she looked over her spectacles at me, then turned her attention to the room at large. "Now that you're all here, a few words before we go in."

Coming around her desk, she told us basically what I already knew from the packet provided by the studio last week: we would be guarding a very high-profile person as part of a team of six female undercover security guards; duty shifts would run twelve to eighteen hours at a time, potentially longer if necessary; we'd each get two or three days off a week; we would be staying on-site with the client both here in LA and when traveling for press tours or other events; the client's residential security system was state-of-the-art.

Ms. Wood then introduced us to each other. I forced myself to pay careful attention as I was determined to learn everyone's names immediately.

"Wren St. James is your team lead and hand selected each of you for this position. You are here because she requested you after going through all available security specialists employed or under contract by the studio. Do you want to say a few words, Wren?"

Wren St. James. White skin. Five-foot-four. Estimated one-twenty to one-thirty pounds. Estimated midthirties. Blue eyes. Chin-length hair dyed in ombre style from black at the roots to ash-colored at the tips.

Wren stepped forward. "Thanks, Lenore. I'll hold my comments until we're at the client's residence, as I consider him to be part of our team and he needs to hear my spiel just as much as the rest of you. Let's not worry about in-depth introductions until that time."

A clue. We'd be guarding a "him." The height and weight detailed in the packet had tilted the likelihood-scale in that direction, but I didn't like to assume.

She went on. "Some of you have worked with me before, so you know how I operate. For those of you who are new, please don't hesitate to come to me with any concerns."

"Thank you, Wren." Ms. Wood barely cracked a smile before turning to her right and introducing the remaining members of the team by name. I scrambled to connect their names to their physical appearance:

Kristina Barlowe. Medium brown skin. Five-foot-five. Estimated one-twenty to one-thirty pounds. Estimated . . . midtwenties? Hazel eyes. Shoulder-length curly dark brown hair.

Nicole Miller. White skin. Five-foot-five or slightly less. Estimated one-thirty to one-forty pounds. Estimated early thirties. Medium brown eyes. Long wavy bleach-blond hair.

Mindy Camen. White skin. Five-foot or slightly more. Estimated one-twenty to one-thirty pounds. Estimated midtwenties. Medium brown eyes. Long curly dark brown hair.

Tamra Lo. Light brown skin. Five-foot-five or slightly less. Estimated one-ten to one-twenty pounds. Estimated midthirties. Dark brown eyes. Long medium brown hair with blond highlights.

Wren, Kristina, Nicole, Mindy, Tamra. I repeated their names in my head as Ms. Wood gestured to each of us and filled in our roles. We would all be posing as a member of his entourage. My assignment was as a stylist. The other team members were assigned similar roles—Nicole was another stylist, Tamra and Mindy were personal trainers, and Wren and Kristina were the two assistants.

After Ms. Wood finished announcing the undercover appointments, she glanced at her watch, fiddled with it, then said, "Let's head in so you can meet Mr. Malcom."

I was in the process of mentally kicking myself again for being the last one to arrive when Ms. Wood had said the name, *Mr. Malcom*, and my brain officially froze. My heart stuttered. All the air felt like it had been sucked out of the room.

Oh God. She can't mean—I couldn't be that unlucky, could I?

Short answer, Exhibit Z: Yes. Yes, I was that unlucky.

"You mean Cyrus Malcom?" The team member named Mindy stared wide-eyed at Ms. Wood. "Asmodeus from the Demon Redeemed movies?"

Ms. Wood flinched subtly and seemed to struggle for a stretch before finally nodding. "Yes. Cyrus Malcom and Ms. Wraithington are just through here."

My stomach swooped and I clenched my jaw. The ground beneath my feet felt suddenly unsteady and I felt my aspiration rate increase along with my heartbeat.

Well. Isn't that just a yellow jacket in the outhouse. I'd never used an outhouse. I'd grown up in an apartment for the most part, but I'm sure you catch my drift.

I needed to think. But first, I needed to calm down.

Sucking in a low, slow, quiet breath through my nose, I dug deep for focus and cleared my mind. Possibly, there was no reason to worry. Mr. Malcom had been a gentleman last night. I'd told him I wasn't Ryaine, I'd—wait . . . *Did I tell him I wasn't Ryaine?*

Yes. Yes, I did.

Much of the car ride to my apartment was still a blurry haze, but I did recall explicitly telling him I wasn't Ryaine. I'd told him to call me Beth. Nevertheless, he'd undoubtedly be surprised I was here.

Unless he already knows!

Unless they already shared our names and employee profiles with him and he was currently expecting me because he'd seen my photo. Which they would. Right? It's not like they would assign a bunch of strangers to such a big deal celebrity without giving him the opportunity to learn about us first.

Hold up. Did he know last night?

My stomach swooped again. Was it possible that he'd known last night that I'd be one of his guards? I didn't know how to feel about that possibility and I hadn't made up my mind by the time we'd formed a single-file line to enter Ms. Wraithington's office and then suddenly—

Cyrus Malcom was standing by the window, a perfectly tranquil expression on his face. He quietly acknowledged each woman in front of me as they lined up along the wall closest to the door until he got to me. He started.

A crack in his affable façade. A slight narrowing to his eyes. A confused but not displeased curve to his mouth as it formed the soundless words, "What are you doing here?"

Oh God. *Oh God oh God oh God.*

He didn't know I was one of his guards.

Ms. Wraithington was speaking, but I didn't hear what she said because I was too focused on not getting sick all over the carpet. Feeling the blood drain from my face, my stomach swooped for a third time even as I told myself it was okay. It was okay because at least he knew I wasn't—

"Wait a minute." He looked from me to Ms. Wraithington, his expression one of suspicion. Or confusion. Or a mix of the two. "Is this a joke?"

"Is what a joke?" Ms. Wraithington seemed put off by his interruption.

But then he lifted a hand toward me, his eyes locked with the VP of Talent Relationships. "You're telling me that Ryaine O'Rourke is one of my undercover bodyguards?"

WHAT?!

My heart jumped to my throat. No. No, no, no. *How could he—but I'd— I'd specifically—*

Ms. Wraithington laughed lightly and I forced myself to listen to what she said. "Oh, no. This is Beth Ryan. The similarity is striking, I grant you, but that's to be expected since Beth provided personal security for Ryaine until just recently when the studio took over her security management. I believe Ryaine hired Beth specifically because of the resemblance, a body double."

I felt all eyes in the room turn to me except Cyrus's. He held very still, and his gaze remained firmly latched onto Ms. Wraithington, as though he were trying to untangle her words.

The VP's eyebrows lifted slowly when Cyrus continued to silently stare, and she spared me a glance before adding, "Beth is a new hire, but I assure you she comes highly recommended, not just by Ryaine, but also the firm where she worked in DC. Everyone in this room has been thoroughly vetted, Cyrus. Again, I assure you—"

"Of course," he said suddenly, sounding a little winded. Licking his lips, he nodded. "Of course. Please. Continue."

"Thank you." Ms. Wraithington gave him a perfunctory-looking smile.

Cyrus returned it with a stiff-looking one of his own, then glanced down at the carpet. I felt like crying.

He'd thought I was Ryaine last night, the whole time. He'd thought I was Ryaine when I walked in. I didn't know what to do. How could I guard him now? How could he ever trust me? And now I'd need to quit my dream job before they fired me, before he told them I'd pretended to be Ryaine— except I didn't. Or I hadn't meant to. I wasn't a liar. I'd meant to tell him from the start that I wasn't her, that I was there as her friend to weed out—

"Let's continue." Ms. Wraithington set a hand on Wren's shoulder. "To start, how about if each of you introduce yourself, give some background as to your education and experience."

Cyrus nodded, but then turned away to face the window, giving all of us his profile.

I heard Ms. Wraithington sigh just before Wren cleared her throat and spoke. "I'm Wren St. James. I've been with WWS as a security team lead for seven years. I graduated magna cum laude from University of Pennsylvania in criminal justice after completing three tours in Afghanistan in the army reserves."

My chest tightened painfully, for obvious reasons, but also because Wren sounded like a badass and I would miss out on working with her for drinking one and a half glasses of apology wine. But I wouldn't cry. I'd suck it up and take it on the chin because that's what I did, that's how I'd been raised.

By the time each of the other team members had given a brief overview of their history and career, I felt a fair bit numb, but mostly resigned. Based on Cyrus's posture, the rigid line of his jaw, the way his eyes kept narrowing at intervals as he stared out the window, I felt certain of his anger. But I'd figure it out. And when the time came, I'd walk out of here accepting whatever fate had in store. I would not fall apart, and I would not make excuses.

Thus, when it was my turn, I lifted my chin and spoke clearly and calmly. "I'm Beth Ryan. I graduated from Northeastern University in criminal justice, magna cum laude. I entered and graduated from the police academy in Boston after college, accepting a position with private industry to provide security on teams assigned to US senators and members of Congress. After five years, I accepted a new position with Ryaine O'Rourke as her personal bodyguard and—"

"I'm curious, how did you meet Ryaine?" Cyrus asked, his gaze still focused out the window.

The question caught me off guard since he hadn't asked the others any questions. But then, none of the others had—in his mind—impersonated Ryaine O'Rourke during a blind date last night.

"I met Ms. O'Rourke in college, sir."

He blinked, then turned and leveled me with a dispassionate stare. "You met Ryaine in college."

"That's right, sir," I said evenly, meeting his stare head-on and refusing to be cowed.

"And were you her body double in college?"

Despite accepting this situation, I considered his question carefully, determined to give the most honest answer possible without yielding to the urge to explain myself, not even a little bit.

"Yes, I was, sir. But not in a paid capacity."

Stare still impartial, he said, "Explain."

"My resemblance to Ms. O'Rourke and our friendship meant that I did not mind standing in for her during uncomfortable or unpleasant situations that arose from time to time."

"What sort of—"

"Cyrus," Ms. Wraithington cut in, her tone impatient. "What does Beth's resemblance to Ms. O'Rourke have to do with anything?"

Here it comes.

I wouldn't react when he spilled the tea. I would thank everyone for their time, apologize for the untenable situation of my own making, give my notice, and then leave. That's what I'd do.

So when Cyrus's left eyebrow ticked up along with a slight hitching at one side of his mouth, a mischievous glint behind his eyes, I braced myself.

"I'm fascinated. Can't I be fascinated?" He sounded bored and anything but fascinated. "Should I look for my own body double? Maybe if I had one,

I wouldn't be forced to endure—what did you call it, Ms. Ryan? Uncomfortable or unpleasant situations that arise from time to time. Like, I don't know, blind dates, for example."

This suggestion drew a few chuckles from my team. Meanwhile, I held his glare steadily and wished he'd just get it over with.

Mouth morphing from a smirk to a smile, the glint in his emerald eyes became a dazzling twinkle. "You had me *completely* fooled, Ms. Ryan. I really and truly thought you were Ryaine O'Rourke. I can't tell you how much of an impression you've made on me in such a short time."

He's toying with you.

I refused to react. He wanted to play games? I didn't play games.

And I did not enjoy, nor did I tolerate, being toyed with.

CHAPTER 5

BATHSHEBA

"That man is sharp who can say what he wants in a minimum of words."

— ARISTOPHANES, *THESMOPHORIAZUSAE*

Giving Cyrus one last unimpressed look, I turned to the VP of Talent Relationships. "Ms. Wraithington, while I appreciate this opportunity, I feel I must inform you that last night—"

"No, no. Halina is right." Cyrus took a swift step in my general direction, raising his voice over mine but not sparing me a look. "We should move on. None of this is relevant to the situation at hand, no matter how uncomfortable or unpleasant. I am resigned to the necessity of twenty-four-hour guarding of my body. And on that note, what are the next steps?"

Clamping my mouth shut, I held my tongue. For now. But if he made any further taunting remarks, I would tell her and all present what had occurred last night, and then I would promptly hand in my notice, dream job or not.

Wren shared a look with Ms. Wraithington before answering Cyrus. "What I'd like to do from here, Mr. Malcom, is orient the rest of the team on location. We were assured your calendar is open today. I'd like to do a walk-through of your residence, review the schedule with you and your PA, define general expectations—but not necessarily in that order." Abruptly, she adopted an air of contrition. "I understand you were not aware until this morning that any of this would be happening. I want you to know, I advocated that you should be given more time to consider the changes, a chance to meet me and my team before making a decision."

Ms. Wraithington seemed to squirm in place, shooting our team lead a dark look.

Wren ignored it. "Do not feel pressured to accept this without proper consideration. Twenty-four-hour security detail, opening your home to strangers, it's a lot to ask of anyone. I'd like you to be certain. Or, in the absence of certainty, perhaps we could think of this as a trial period of one month."

Cyrus blatantly inspected Wren, sizing her up. "Let me ask you, Ms. St. James, have you read the fan mail Halina told me about this morning?"

"I have, Mr. Malcom. And I've read the analysis provided by the risk assessment team and the FBI."

"The FBI. . .?" Cyrus's gaze widened and flickered to Ms. Wraithington, his voice cracking.

He wasn't aware of the FBI's involvement? I almost felt bad for him. How could the studio expect him to cooperate if they didn't keep him fully informed of threats?

Ms. Wraithington squirmed again, but she also rolled her eyes. "WWS works closely with the FBI on all sorts of matters, Cyrus. Don't be so dramatic."

Expression blank, he asked flatly, "If the FBI is so concerned for my safety, why not come to me directly? WWS isn't the only studio I work with."

"I'm aware. But you are one of many in the DarkLens cinematic universe that require special attention. Your other studio roles aren't garnering you the type and intensity of attention Asmodeus is. The FBI keeps us informed on several of our highest profile talent working on DarkLens projects. As you know, the fans there are . . . passionate."

Features still devoid of emotion, his attention returned to Wren. "What is your opinion of the risk level to my person? Do you feel that twenty-four-hour surveillance is warranted?"

Wren shifted on her feet, widening her stance as though getting comfortable. "First, it wouldn't be surveillance. It would be security. While in your home, you can interact with the other members of your team as little or as much as you like. Make no mistake, you are part of this team—not above it. Our job, yours included, is not to watch you, sir, or regulate your comings, goings, or choices. We are not babysitters or parents, and do not wish to be treated as such."

Cyrus nodded thoughtfully, his gaze moving over Wren with open appraisal. "Makes sense."

"Second, I do not *feel* you are at risk, Mr. Malcom."

These words drew a strangled sound of protest from Ms. Wraithington.

Wren continued, undeterred. "My decisions are not based on feelings but rather on the data and analysis provided by experts. I trust the data experts to do their job. And that means I expect everyone in this room to trust me to do mine."

Yeah. Wren is a badass. I couldn't decide if I was grateful or not for Cyrus's interruption of my confession.

I didn't like that he might use it to toy with me at some future point. The events from last night would be hanging over my head for as long as they were a secret between us.

However, the chance to work with Wren and learn from her might very well be worth any pain and suffering Cyrus Malcom caused.

"Here." Wren pulled a thumb drive from her pocket and held it out to him. "This is for you."

"Presents already?" he murmured, sounding and looking a shade bemused. "I didn't get you anything."

Ignoring his jest, she clasped her hands behind her back. "I've prepared a dossier on each of the team members. I hope you'll feel more comfortable with our presence in your home as well as our presence by your side in public. I'm sure I speak for everyone here when I say we'd like to make this as unobtrusive and as seamless a transition as possible."

Cyrus's gaze flickered briefly to mine—I mean, blink-and-I-would've-missed-it—then redirected it to the thumb drive now in his palm. "Thank you, Ms. St. James. I appreciate the gesture." He put the drive in his pocket, shoulders rising and falling with a deep breath. "Well now. I believe the next step is for us all to reconvene at my abode, is it not?"

Eyes narrowed on Cyrus, Ms. Wraithington nodded slowly. "It is. If that's what you wish."

"Oh. I definitely wish." He grinned suddenly, the abrupt shift in his mood catching me by surprise. Looking positively giddy at the prospect, his gaze settled on each of the team before finally slithering to mine and holding. "In fact, I can't wait."

❄

The plan, as Wren explained it on the way to the elevator, was for us to travel in two armored SUVs to Cyrus's, I mean, Mr. Malcom's house. Three of us would ride together in one vehicle and the other three would ride with him. The two SUVs were loaners from the studio and would be available for our team's use throughout the duration of the undercover term of six months.

But as soon as we made it to the parking garage, Mr. Malcom turned to Wren and said, "You know, I think it would be a good idea for you five to ride together." He indicated to Wren and the other members of the team, excluding me. "Since this is all new and I haven't been seen or photographed with any of you before now, just in case the car is followed, it seems like it would be less likely to raise suspicion if I left the studio with just her." He pointed at me with his thumb. "With any luck, we won't be photographed. But if we are, people will assume she's Ryaine, won't they? And definitely not an undercover bodyguard."

Wren shifted just her eyes to lock with mine, and I immediately felt certain she saw through his shoddy reasoning. She knew something was off between us. I kept my mouth shut and met her shrewd gaze squarely. I also promised myself I would speak to her as soon as possible about last night.

She needed to know, and whatever she decided to do with the information—even if it meant I'd be out of a job—I would follow her lead. If I were her, in her position managing a team of five undercover specialists and a high-profile movie star like Cyrus Malcom, I'd want to know.

"Fine," she said eventually, turning an enigmatic smile on him and handing me the SUV's remoteless entry fob. "I have your address. We'll meet you two there."

"Great," he said, rocking on his heels. "Can't wait."

Looking some mixture of irked and amused, Wren led my teammates to their ride while Mr. Malcom and I walked to ours.

I unlocked the back passenger-side door and opened it for him. "Sir."

He didn't climb in. Instead, he watched as Wren pulled out of the parking spot, waited until they left the garage, then turned to me with a frown. "I want to drive."

My hand tightened around the fob. "Do you have experience with defensive driving techniques—"

"I. Want. To. Drive," he said, his voice low with restraint and something else that sounded sinister. "Ms. St. James said your job is not to regulate my comings, goings, or my choices. And I choose to drive."

We exchanged glares for several seconds until I eventually held out the fob. He was right. Wren had told him and all of us that we would not be regulating his choices, and I had to follow her lead, even if I disagreed with her philosophy at present.

"Here you go, sir."

Holding my eyes hostage, he whispered a soft, "Thank you." But in reaching for the key chain, he stepped into my personal space, his long fingers fully enveloped my hand, and he accepted the disputed device with a slow, drawn-out slide of his palm against the back of my knuckles, the touch sending spikes and tingles of heat straight up my arm. "Now. . ." His eyes dropped to my mouth. "Was that so hard?"

Rallying against the completely inappropriate and bewildering flutters in my stomach, I crossed my arms but refused to step away as I gritted out, "May I make an observation?"

"No. You may not. Sit in the front, please." He turned, leaving me by the open back door, a vacuum of empty space where he'd been.

I shut the back door, careful not to slam it and betray the depth of my frustration. After climbing into the front passenger seat, I shut that door, fastened my seat belt, and folded my hands loosely on my lap, not rubbing the skin of my knuckles where he'd touched me despite how it still prickled.

"Just so we're on the same page," he said lightly, adjusting the rearview mirror and using the control panel on the door to move the side mirrors. "That was you last night, right?"

I did not roll my eyes, but I found I needed to clear my throat of an odd tightness before saying, "Yes. That was me."

"Ah. Good. I wouldn't want there to be any *misunderstandings* between us," he mumbled, the words dripping with sarcasm.

Successfully, I battled a flush of embarrassment and bit my tongue. *I will not explain myself. I will not.*

Pressing the button to engage the engine, he made quick work of pulling out of the spot, his gaze fixed out the windshield. But when he stopped and looked both ways at the garage exit, I spied the severity of his frown and the tense, unhappy lines on his forehead and around his eyes.

I felt . . . a little guilty. Lord knows why. I hadn't done a single thing wrong, and if he wanted to be angry for whatever reason, then I should just let him be angry. Except, he didn't look angry, precisely. He looked disappointed. And upset. And sad.

Which was likely why I felt compelled to offer softly, "Are you sure you don't want me to drive, Mr. Malcom?"

A sour-sounding chuckle left him on an exhale. "Oh, I don't think there's a call to be so formal, Beth. Please, call me Cyrus. After all, as of last night, you're intimately acquainted with some very private parts of me."

Oh. Damn. He was right.

My chest tightened painfully with regret and I closed my eyes. I had done something wrong. In fact, I'd done several things wrong and he deserved an apology. No wonder he was so upset.

I am a thoughtless idiot.

"Mr. Malcom—"

"Cyrus," he growled through clenched teeth.

Forgoing the use of his name, I said my piece. "I am extremely sorry for my behavior last night on the way to my apartment. I feel nothing but shame and regret for my inexcusable actions. I was not myself, but I know that doesn't matter. I—I violated you, and I am so incredibly sorry."

He exhaled another bitter-sounding laugh, and I glanced at him, hoping he'd see I was sincere. "I am ready and willing to accept responsibility for my actions. Say the word and I will resign from my position with the studio. And if you feel the need to press charges—"

He snorted. "Don't be such a martyr, Ms. Ryan. I didn't feel violated last night in the car, and I was happy to be of service, to see you home safely. Even now that I know you're not . . . " I watched his throat bob with a swallow and he flipped on the turn signal, checking his mirrors before merging even though this vehicle had state-of-the-art lane assist technology. Once settled in the new lane, he spared me a quick peek, his green eyes glittering impatiently. "You have no reason to apologize for *that*."

My chest tightened for a completely different reason this time. He wanted to go there? Fine. We'd go there.

"Look, Mr. Malcom, I hate to point out the obvious, but—"

"Do you? Do you *hate* it?"

"But"—I continued, raising my voice—"at no point did I lie to you last night. In fact, I explicitly told you that I was not Ryaine O'Rourke."

"I must've missed that." More sarcasm.

"Yes. We were in the car and I told you, 'I am not Ryaine.' Then you said, 'Who are you?' Then I said, 'Call me Beth.'"

He made a noise halfway between a choke and a laugh. "You've got to be fucking kidding me."

"I am not."

"And you being dressed up, looking like Ryaine O'Rourke's twin, that isn't a lie?"

"When you arrived, if you took a damn second to actually *think* about it,

I was in a hurry to leave because I was experiencing an unexpected drug interaction. I'd planned to tell you as soon as you sat down that—that, if you didn't already know or guess—I wasn't Ryaine. And I had no plans to drink last night, but you sent that bottle of wine and—"

He reared back. "Now it's my fault?"

"No. It's not. I'm the one who didn't read the drug info sheet. I'm ready to take responsibility." I smacked my thigh, wanting this stupidity to end. We were arguing in circles. "I didn't know left from right, up from down, and I was doing the best I could given how I'd been blindsided by—"

"You were blindsided? *You*?" He looked between me and the road, his expression just as furious and incredulous as his voice.

"Yes."

"And I wasn't blindsided this morning when you walked in? How long have you known you'd be guarding me?"

"I found out the very same moment you did." I faced forward, crossing my arms, my stomach empty and uncomfortable. I felt slightly nauseous and probably needed a big glass of water. "They didn't tell me who you were. The packet they gave me protected your identity."

"Oh yeah. Right. I seriously d—" Cyrus began with superfluous mockery, but then snapped his mouth shut.

Peering at him, I found him staring out the windshield, his eyebrows pulled together.

"You seriously what?"

Now he cleared his throat. And he shifted in his seat, his eyes darting to me, then away. "No. I believe you. I—Halina told me as much before you all arrived. I . . . forgot about that detail."

It didn't matter. None of this mattered.

"Look. This isn't going to work." I rubbed my forehead. "I can't guard you if you don't trust me, and you clearly don't trust me."

Dismissing my statements with the wave of his hand, he demanded, "Answer me this: why were you there in the first place? Why did she send you?"

"For the same reason I told you at the restaurant, though I shouldn't have told you." I leaned my elbow on the windowsill and closed my eyes. "Ryaine has bad taste in men. She falls in love with wishing, then breaks her own heart with disappointment. I started going on dates for her the same month I moved out here from DC." My energy was leaving me fast. I hadn't eaten last night, I hadn't eaten this morning. I needed food.

I sensed him stiffen. "You mean I'm not the first person you've done this to?"

"I've never been drunk before, but no. You are not the first. But I never lie."

He was silent for a beat, then said under his breath, "Unfuckingbelievable."

"No," I ground out, tapping into emotional reserves fueled by anger. "No, it's not *unfuckingbelievable*. Do you know what it's like for a woman to date in this town? Y'all out here never say what you mean. It's all lies and schmoozing and seeing more than one person at a time and calling that normal, telling her she's the problem for wanting exclusivity. And then exclusivity never actually means exclusive. Now, whatever. Fine. If that makes you happy, do that. But don't lie about it. Don't gaslight a person and tell her she's not a real feminist if she doesn't want to swing or share her partner."

Leaning forward, I pressed my palms into my eyes. Great. Now I had a monster headache.

"Not a fan of polyamory, eh?"

My temper spiked. "No, no, no. This is not polyamory. Polyamory is totally different." I had opinions about this, and since he'd asked, I was going to share them. "Polyamory is conversations, decisions, trust, and everyone on the same page. This is a bunch of sneaky, manipulative frat boys without integrity catfishing the cake while they eat the pie, and then lying to the pie while they run off to sleep with ice cream. So don't give me that sanctimonious reverse morality BS. Being a liar is never an acceptable lifestyle choice."

The car descended into near quiet, the only sound coming from the tires rotating on the pavement and traffic beyond the windows. My face felt hot with all the oversharing I'd just done. Maybe I'd said too much, made too many of my opinions known, but I couldn't take them back now.

Oh well. What difference did it make if I ranted in his car? I wouldn't know him for much longer.

As grateful as I was now that he'd insisted on driving, I wished I'd quit back at the office. Now I'd have to call a taxi from his place, get back to the studio, pick up my car, and drive it to my apartment. The only thing that made me feel slightly better was the promise of a big greasy hamburger. You better believe I'd be stopping by an In-N-Out on my way home for a pity-party burger.

"So let me see if I have this right." Cyrus broke the silence. "You go on her dates . . . and pretend to be her . . . in order to—to gauge the worthiness of these men?" His words were halting, as though he was thinking through the issue as he spoke. "You lie to protect her from liars?"

"No." I sat back and blinked open my eyes, wishing I hadn't left my sunglasses in my car. "I meet the guys and tell them immediately who I am. Like I said, I don't lie. But I do vet them. They have to get through me first."

"And they're okay with this?" His tone transparently belied his fascination.

I shrugged, not minding his interest. I was just relieved he no longer sounded affronted on behalf of the entirety of Los Angeles. "No. Sometimes they leave right away in a huff. But then, there you go." I lifted my hands and let them drop to my knees with a quiet smack. "If they're not willing to work for her, why should she give them the time of day? And if protecting my friend means I irritate or offend a few supercilious sycophants, then so be it."

In my peripheral vision, I watched his hands tighten and then loosen on the steering wheel, the moment stretching until eventually he asked, "Did I make it past your vetting process?" Again, he sounded honestly curious, not offended.

I turned my head to look at him, marveling at the potent mixture of astonishment and inexplicable irritation swelling within me. "Is that a serious question?"

"Maybe." He pulled to a stop at a red light and twisted toward me, his left eyebrow cocked in challenge. "Based on my performance last night, would I get a second date?"

My lightheaded dizziness meant I was all bumfuzzled. "You mean a first date."

"We already had a first date."

"No. That's not what I—" I shook my head. "You mean a first date with Ryaine?"

He faced the windshield again, making a noncommittal sound. "I simply wish to know, did I pass the test?" Again, it seemed like he was honestly curious.

I stared at him, feeling like I was missing something critical. Was he for real? And why did he care? Here sat one of the most beautiful, desirable, rich, successful people in the entire world, with legions of adoring fans. Granted, many of those fans had contemplated cutting off pieces of his clothing—and his hair—to keep as souvenirs, but still. Why did he care whether or not he passed my screening?

He wants to meet Ryaine, you moron.
Oh.
Well.
That explained it.
"Sir—Cy—Mr. Malcom, I—"
"It's not a difficult question to answer. Yes or no. Do I get a second date?"
A breath left me like a tire deflating and I leaned the crown of my head against the car seat, trying to think.
"It's the dimple, isn't it?" he asked in a solemn voice.
I frowned at him. "Pardon?"
Cyrus smiled and pointed to the freaking adorable dimple at his cheek. "The dimple is why you believe I lack substance."
For those of you keeping count, my chest squeezed for a third time. I felt like throwing my hands up. I surrendered. I could not keep up with his moods. One minute he was withdrawn and upset, then he was thoughtful, the next he was playful and teasing. Whereas I didn't enjoy or entertain rapid shifts in emotion. I liked steady.
If I'd been a boat, I would be a tugboat.
"Fine." I raised my hands, palms out. "If you want to meet Ryaine, I will make that happen. But before you do, know that I will make your life hell if you hurt her. Please be careful with her heart, don't lie to her, don't lead her on. She *will* fall for you like—"
"An anvil off a skyscraper," he filled in, quoting me from last night.
"That's right."
"Because I'm so irresistible." He said this like it was a fact, a mischievous smirk in place.
"Whatever greases your wagon, Mr. Malcom."
He laughed at my turn of phrase, but then corrected me again. "Cyrus." His eyes danced as they briefly met mine. "I really must insist you call me Cyrus, Beth."
I didn't respond, and you wanna know why? He *was* pretty darn irresistible. When he applied himself, to whomever or whatever cause he turned his attention, I felt certain Cyrus would be 99 percent likely to obtain whatever he wanted.
There was just something about him that felt genuine and kind, vulnerable and approachable, even though I knew for a fact—based on how he'd dated and then dropped my stepsister in high school, and based on how he'd taunted me back in the VP's office with such sinister glee—he was probably

just as much of a self-seeking schemer as almost everyone else in this confusing town.

He did see you home safely, though. That was kind. So, there is that.

I closed my eyes, blocking out both him and the thought. "How much longer until we get to your place?"

I'd have to warn Ryaine before they met, she'd be dealing with super-hero levels of charisma and laser-focused sex appeal set to stun. *Bless her poor, sensitive heart. She's doomed.*

He didn't answer straightaway, but I felt his eyes on me. I kept mine closed because I was done. I'd apologized for drunkenly attacking him in the back seat last night. I'd answered his questions as honestly and succinctly as I'd been capable of, given my lack of food and hydration. There was simply nothing left for us to discuss.

"We're nearly there." His voice was quiet, soothing almost, and I felt the SUV accelerate.

Good.

The sooner we arrived, the sooner I could quit and go grab a self-pity burger.

CHAPTER 6

CYRUS

"Under every stone lurks a politician."

— ARISTOPHANES

*B*eth Ryan's eyes had remained closed and she did not speak for the remainder of our short journey up the hill. I exploited her inattentiveness at a stop sign to retrieve my phone and text my chef.

CYRUS

Expect me +6 visitors, incoming. Charcuterie, then lunch. One will require bone broth, water, and Tylenol upon arrival

If I'd remembered my manners at the studio, I would've messaged him long before now. Receiving guests without a proper welcome? Without feeding them? My mother would've been horrified.

Yet more than the potential faux pas of allowing guests to go hungry, Beth's coloring and antagonistic attitude concerned me. She'd rubbed her forehead, temples, and eyes while we'd cleared the air and settled matters to —I assumed—our mutual satisfaction. I suspected she had a headache and the root cause was lack of sustenance.

We passed the other studio SUV pulled off to the side of the road as I approached my gate and my phone vibrated where I'd left it on my thigh. Waiting until I stopped, I glanced at the new message.

BORIS

A little more of a heads-up would've been appreciated

CYRUS

Thank you for your message. Your opinion is very important to us and will be answered in the order in which it was received. Please click here to complete a survey about your experience. If the page doesn't load immediately, please prepare the charcuterie boards and bone broth while you wait

BORIS

You're the worst

I grinned. Sure, that's what Boris *said*. But I knew the text had made him laugh.

Glancing in the rearview mirror, I saw that the second SUV from the studio had pulled up behind us. The proximity key program on my phone automatically opened the gate, and I paused to navigate to the app and indicate that two vehicles would be entering before the gate should close.

I wasn't sure I liked the idea of extending gate permissions for six additional people. Glancing over at Beth, I wondered if it would be possible to limit which of the undercover bodyguards were given proximity key access. I'd be fine with *her* having access. Anyone willing to put themselves through the ordeal of multiple blind dates in service to a good friend was trustworthy in my book.

"Are we here?" Beth sat up, her voice low and scratchy with fatigue.

"We are here." Parking at the far end of the circular driveway and cutting the engine just as the second vehicle pulled up next to ours, I kept my volume low. "Do you want to go lie down? You could use my bedroom."

She started, like my question surprised her. And then she turned her head to look at me, eyes narrowed into slits, mouth a thin line, and eyebrows pulled low. "No. Thank you," she said deliberately, her tone making the hairs on the back of my neck itch.

I stared at her, confused. "What? What is this?" Lifting a hand, I pointed at her face and rotated my wrist such that my finger moved in a circle. "What is this face?"

"It's called a dirty look, Cyrus."

A dirty look? A *dirty* look?

"What? Why? What did I do?"

"I am here for work. I am a professional," she spat.

"And?"

Glancing heavenward, she promptly opened the passenger-side door.

"Where are you going?" I called after her, but it was too late. She'd already exited and walked around the front bumper toward the house.

I tracked her while I fumbled to unclick my seat belt. If anyone should be upset, it should be me. But I wasn't. All was forgiven from my perspective, and I . . . Well. We would be spending a fair amount of time together, after all. I was friendly with all my staff, coworkers, collaborators, and colleagues. As a point of pride, I was basically the nicest person in Hollywood. Everyone knew this.

And this woman was upset that I'd offered her a place to rest?

Intent on following Ms. Ryan and discovering what about my offer could be so entirely offensive, I reached for the door latch. *Spoiler alert: there is nothing offensive about it!*

But then someone opened my door before I pulled the handle. The team lead, Wren St. James, stood there wearing a patient expression. "Shall we, Mr. Malcom?"

My eyes sought out Beth. She'd joined the rest of the team, loitering stiffly by the walkway to the front door in her Oscar de la Renta floral print, cotton summer dress, still looking lovely but also pale. My forehead wrinkled. She needed to eat. I supposed questioning her would have to wait.

I hate waiting.

I sighed. "We shall, Ms. St. James."

Boris, the miracle worker, had already placed several olive wood serving trays of simple charcuterie items in the living room along with bottles of sparkling water, glasses, and ice. I also spotted a steaming mug off to one side, placed on a napkin with two pills.

"Plates and napkins are here." I motioned to the stack of white dishes he'd set on the coffee table. "Lunch will be soon."

Before I could turn to Beth, guide her over to the mug of bone broth, and confront her regarding the administration of unwarranted dirty looks, Ms. St. James stepped in my path. "Mr. Malcom, the time for visiting will have to be later, after we go through the house and are acquainted with the details of the grounds."

"Uh . . ." I surveyed the room, hoping to find supporters for an eat-and-visit-first / tour-later plan.

Several of the women stared at the food longingly but said nothing. Beth Ryan included. Except, unlike the others who'd offered either shy or warm smiles, when she caught me studying her, her features shuttered and grew hostile. *Ridiculous woman.*

St. James gestured toward the staircase at the back of the room. "Do you mind leading the walk-through?"

Apparently, it was up to me to save the day.

Leaning close to St. James, I lowered my voice so that only she could hear. "Don't you think it would be nice for everyone to have some refreshment? They must be hungry."

"Thank you for your thoughtfulness, but they can eat after the tour. Then we can discuss areas of concern with the property."

All right, let me try this.

"But wouldn't eating help everyone focus better on the tour? If they're starving, their minds might wander."

A smile tugged at St. James's mouth. She did not yield to it. "I wouldn't choose anyone for this team who could be distracted by something as insignificant as hunger. Wandering minds won't be a problem."

I leaned a smidge closer and gave this woman the same look I gave my mother when she discovered me sneaking home after curfew.

"Ms. St. James. The thing is—" I sighed, painting on a pained, contrite expression and adding a dash of embarrassment for good measure "—I hope you can understand that, before I lead six strangers around my house, I'd prefer to get to know them a bit?"

Her blue eyes moved between mine, thoughtful, considering. I couldn't tell whether or not she believed me, but I witnessed the moment she decided to concede.

Note to self, my comfort is important to this woman.

"Of course, Mr. Malcom. That makes perfect sense." She turned to the team. "Let's eat and visit before touring the house. And I'll take this opportunity to lay out some general expectations. Does that sound good?"

A collective murmur of agreement filled the room and I returned several grateful smiles. The team grabbed their plates, chatting amicably. Meanwhile, I slowly maneuvered toward Beth, grabbing the mug and pain pills on my way.

The persistent steadiness of her dirty look had me thinking better of the quip sitting on the tip of my tongue. I held out the mug and pills without comment. She glared at me, but accepted both items offered, inspecting the pills first—stamped with the brand name Tylenol—before lifting her eyes back to mine.

The relief I felt as her gaze softened took me by surprise, yet I said nothing. Not even as she nodded her head once in acknowledgment and whispered, "Thank you."

That's more like it.

Something told me not to press my luck, and this was strange because I always pressed my luck. Nevertheless, I gave her a little bow and strolled over to the coffee table for a plate.

"You have a beautiful home, Mr. Malcom," one of the women said, smiling at me amiably across the coffee table. Her long, platinum-blond hair was the most striking thing about her. Although, she also had a nice smile. Very pretty.

This woman was one of the first to be introduced back in Halina's office and thus her name was either Kristina or Nicole.

"Thank you, uh . . ."

Obviously noticing my struggle, she placed her hand on her chest. "Nicole. Nicole Miller."

"Nicole." I said her name with a smile and she blushed, ducking her head. "Thanks for the reminder. I appreciate your patience."

"You know a lot of people, that's a lot of names to remember." This sensible comment came from Kristina. I knew her name was Kristina because she was also one of the first to be introduced and was not Nicole. But I would remember her from now on because of her hazel eyes and how they contrasted with her lovely brown skin. *She has gorgeous skin.* Absent-mindedly, I wondered what moisturizer she used.

"I do know a lot of people," I conceded, selecting apples and strawberries from the trays. I was in the mood for something sweet.

"Maybe we should all wear name tags?" Kristina suggested, looking to St. James who hadn't yet picked up a plate.

"We could." St. James seemed to give the matter consideration before inspecting me. "Would that make you more comfortable, Mr. Malcom? If we wore name tags?"

"I think I'll have everyone's name sorted by the end of the day. You're Wren St. James." I lifted my chin toward her, then shifted my focus to each woman in turn. "Nicole Miller, Kristina B—Bartlet?"

"Barlowe," she corrected.

"Kristina Barlowe," I repeated, then looked at the one with curly dark brown hair. "Mindy Camen?"

"Yes!" Mindy's answering smile was enormous and she immediately flushed with pleasure, lowering the piece of cheese she was just about to eat. She also had interesting eyes, a warm chestnut brown framed by thick dark lashes. When she blushed, everything from her forehead to her neck turned bright red. *How sweet.*

I winked at her, then turned to the woman at my left who'd been quiet thus far. "And you're Tamra Lo."

"I am," she replied with a smile, tucking a curtain of long, shiny brown hair threaded with gold highlights behind her ear. I noted the wedding band on her third finger as well as the diamond engagement ring. *I wonder what her husband thinks about spa days?*

Tamra's gaze met mine briefly. Her lashes fluttered and she looked away. She also blushed, but her cheeks bloomed rosy pink instead of Mindy's flaming red.

Settling in the chair with the best view of the room, my attention snagged on Beth, standing off to one side, watching us all impassively and sipping her broth. I was pleased to see her coloring had improved.

Lifting an apple slice in her direction, I said, "And that's Ryaine O'Rourke—oh! Sorry, sorry. I meant Beth Ryan."

Light laughter followed my joke.

Do you know who wasn't laughing? I'll give you one guess.

Beth's impassivity fell away. Unlike the others, she didn't smile or blush or seem pleased and flattered that I knew her name. No, not my Beth. Her olive green eyes flashed angrily and her full upper lip curled, just a faint curve, but enough to remind me of a snarl.

I grinned, giving into a delighted chuckle as warmth flowed from my stomach to my chest and neck. Perhaps I could get used to dirty looks. Perhaps, coming from Beth, I could even learn to like them. Perhaps they were her love language.

"Now that Mr. Malcom has made the introductions, I do have several housekeeping items to address. I want to make a few things clear." St. James cleared her throat, bringing our attention to where she stood to one side of the room. "Some of you have worked as an undercover specialist before, so you know what this means, the challenges involved. But for those of you who haven't, let me break it down: when you don't look like a bodyguard, people don't treat you like one. They don't know you're carrying when they push you or touch you in order to get to him." St. James pointed at me.

Munching on my fruit and wishing I'd added a celery stalk or two, I did my best to listen along with the others. The general gist of it was: blah blah blah, fans are relentless and determined, blah blah blah, keep your cool, blah blah blah, mob mentality, blah blah blah, be creative in order to maintain your cover and keep Cyrus safe, but if you have to blow your cover to keep Cyrus safe, it's not the end of the world.

"One more thing I want to be explicit about"—she lifted a hand toward me again just as I leaned forward to grab some celery—"he is not your boss."

Everyone's eyes swung to me, then back to St. James as she pointed at herself. "I am your boss. If a client makes a request of you and you're not sure whether or not it's wise, or you don't think it's in the best interest of that client—like, I don't know, sneaking off with him, or letting him sneak off on his own, or sneaking someone into the house who's not on the approved list—don't."

I sat straighter in my chair, affronted by all the references to sneaking. Even though she gave me a genial smile verging on affectionate, I didn't feel at all mollified.

St. James continued. "Cyrus Malcom is part of this team for as long as we all work together. Think of him as a coworker. He is one of you, just as responsible for his own safety as you are."

"Really?" Mindy asked, her cheeks burning with a new blush. "I mean, not that I think you would do this, Mr. Malcom, but couldn't he get us fired if he didn't like working with one of us?"

I opened my mouth to object—first sneakiness, now pettiness? Why all the cynicism?—but St. James beat me to it. "No. Assuming you haven't done anything to breach the terms of your employment, he can't get you fired. If there's a personality conflict, you'll be reassigned. I don't think I have to tell anyone in this room how desperately the studio needs and wants people like us, with our abilities and skill set. Undercover security specialists are in huge demand. So, please, don't hesitate to let me know if you want to be reassigned."

My attention darted to Beth. Her stare was fastened to St. James, but her eyebrows were pulled together in a thoughtful expression. I didn't think I liked that. What if Beth asked for a transfer? My mouth went dry at the possibility. I couldn't have her transferring now. Then she'd . . .

Well, she would . . .

I don't want her to . . .

My hand tightened on my plate. I didn't know why I hated the idea of her transferring. Maybe it was because I felt certain she'd never talk to me again if she transferred. She'd just be *out there*, disliking me for her own mysterious reasons, spreading all that negative energy around. She didn't even know me.

Yeah. That's probably it.

"Likewise, Mr. Malcom has agency and control as well. He doesn't have to do what we ask." Ms. St. James's gaze remained on me, her tone encouraging. "As I said earlier, Mr. Malcom, our job is not to regulate your comings, goings, or choices. We are not here to order you around. If you cannot trust one or more of us, you can request a transfer of those specialists. In fact, you can opt out completely at any time. If you decide to do so, this will not reflect negatively on me or my team, so please do not feel pressured to continue this contract until the end of the term. We'll all be reassigned, no problem."

Her statements sounded slightly contradictory—I was part of the team, I needed to be watched; I had agency, but it was their job to keep me from making bad decisions—which inspired me to also make a statement.

I stood and gave the room a smile. "Thank you for the assurances, Wren —may I call you Wren?"

She nodded.

I continued. "I do not feel, uh, pressured." I set my plate on the table. "If anything, I feel enormously grateful. And I promise to do my best to heed your advice and be a good member of this team. I hope we will never be at odds, and I can't foresee any situation where your goals and my goals don't align."

My statements were met with friendly smiles, with one notable exception.

Unfazed, I went on. "I plan to give you a fair chance here. I will listen to your concerns and I'm open to changing my habits as needed. And I hope, at the very least, you'll give me the same chance." Finding and holding Beth's glare, I added, "I'd like to prove to you that I'm someone worthy of knowing."

It must've been a breathtaking performance of sincerity because a few of the ladies sighed softly.

Meanwhile, Beth folded her arms, her stare unimpressed.

But I'd take it. Unimpressed was still better than a dirty look.

CHAPTER 7

BATHSHEBA

"Even if you persuade me, you won't persuade me."

— ARISTOPHANES

Either it was my imagination, or Cyrus Malcom had been purposefully monopolizing Wren St. James all afternoon, making it impossible for me to speak with her alone.

Between you and me, I had a crap imagination.

For obvious reasons, I hadn't been able to pull her aside during the tour of Cyrus's house and grounds, or when the entire team had reviewed the security system details. When Wren had passed out the schedule, asked us all to review it and bring any conflicts to her attention privately, he'd followed her into the living room. And when she went into the kitchen for a glass of water, he'd followed her again. And when she'd gone to the bathroom, he'd stood outside the door.

It was almost time for me to leave and I still hadn't found a single minute for a secluded conversation. I didn't want to email her or call. This was something that needed doing face-to-face.

So when everyone else packed up to go—everyone but Wren and Kristina, who would be the first pair to stay overnight—I had no choice but to ignore the fact that Cyrus stood at her shoulder like a hovering crow.

Marching over, I opened my mouth to draw her attention when Cyrus stepped in my path and intercepted me. "Ah, there you are. Can you help me with something? Excuse us."

Abruptly, Cyrus pulled me by the arm away from Wren and toward the back of the house, not stopping until we made it to his office. I let myself be pulled, not wanting to make a scene. It was six of one, half dozen of the other as far as I was concerned. I could tell her now, I could tell her later, but I was still telling her.

Once inside, he shut the door and placed his back to it, crossing his arms. "What are you doing?"

I also crossed my arms. "I'm telling her about what happened last night."

He shoved his hands in his pants pockets and peered at me. His suit jacket had been discarded hours ago, leaving him in a suit shirt with his sleeves rolled up. I'd caught both Kristina and Nicole checking out his forearms more than once. Not that I cared. Because I didn't. They could have his forearms.

"Why? Why does she need to know?" he asked softly. "And don't you think it should be my call? I'm the one who was attacked by an octopus in the back of a car and spent twelve hours believing you were someone else."

I cringed at the memory of my terrible behavior last night, but he'd just made my point. "Listen. This is my fault. I know that." I used both hands to point to myself. "Me being here, being part of this team, puts you in a bad situation."

His expression grew watchful. "How so?"

"You don't trust me."

"That's not true."

I plowed on. "I understand why, I do. But I can't guard someone who doesn't trust me, or who is uncomfortable in my presence."

He rocked back on his heels, his gaze growing speculative. "Well then, what if I make you feel uncomfortable too? Then we could both make each other uncomfortable and everything would be even."

"How? By taunting me with what happened last night? By threatening to tell everyone about it and get me fired on a whim? No, thank you."

He straightened abruptly, his frown severe. "I wouldn't do that."

"Oh? Really?" I wasn't sure I believed him after this morning at the studio offices. And this was a problem too, wasn't it? If I couldn't trust him to have my back, how could I guard him?

"It's like you don't know me at all," he said, expression indignant, sounding aghast.

This drew a sharp laugh from me. "I don't know you, Mr. Malcom."

"It's Cyrus, and you could. If you wanted." He stepped away from the door. "Please don't ask for a transfer. Stay."

"I wasn't planning on asking for a transfer. I was planning on resigning."

"What? No!" He drifted closer. "Definitely don't do that. There's no call for that." Cyrus's gaze grew beseeching. "I'm not upset about last night anymore. Truly. Stay. Like I said, if you cause me discomfort, I'll return the favor."

He must've been ten pickles short of a barrel if he thought I'd agree to that. "If you're not going to taunt me with what happened last night, then how do you propose to make me feel uncomfortable?"

"I can be very creative." He winked, setting my teeth on edge. "Leave that to me."

"I don't think so."

"Why not?"

"I have no interest in—" I clamped my mouth shut because I was on the precipice of shouting. My voice had risen in both octave and volume. I needed to calm down.

Turning away, I paced to his desk and back, clutching my forehead. I was usually the calmest person in any room, but this man had sent my temper on an all-expenses-paid tour to frustrationville over the last twelve hours. I needed to settle and find my focus.

Focus.

Bracing myself, I faced him. I was getting better at ignoring how ridiculously attractive he was. This time, his prettiness only slightly registered.

But before I could speak, he lifted his palms toward me and said, "How about—what if I promise to let the matter of last night drop. I'll never bring it up again. It'll be like it never happened."

I glared at him while his eyebrows slowly lifted higher and higher on his forehead, clearly waiting for me to respond.

When I didn't, he said, "Well?"

"I'm not sure I trust you to keep this promise."

"Why wouldn't I? Think about it. This reflects poorly on me too, doesn't it? Do you think I want the rest of my security team to know how you fooled me into thinking you were your famous friend? Think of my reputation as a shrewd and astute expert on human nature. It would be ruined."

"That seems unlikely," I mumbled, hating that he could charm me in spite of myself, which just aggravated me more.

"I promise. You have my promise. I will not hold it over you or taunt you about it or ever bring it up again. But if I do, if I even allude to it in passing, feel free to quit on the spot."

I studied him as he spoke, looking for signs of the earlier performative sincerity he'd donned for the team when he talked about being one of us. I didn't find any.

Pressing his point, he said, "Like Ms. St. James said, this can be a trial period. You can quit the team if I bring it up. So why not stay?"

Chewing on my bottom lip, I felt torn. He was right. If he brought it up, I could quit and I'd be no worse off than I was now. In fact, I'd be better off because I would've had some time and experience with the team and working under Wren St. James.

But it still doesn't feel right to keep it from my team lead. . .

Narrowing my eyes, I tilted my head to the side.

He mimicked me, as though he were my reflection in a mirror. It would've been cute if we'd been flirting, or hanging out as friends, or had any relationship whatsoever other than a professional one—which we did not.

Ignoring his mimicry, I said, "How about this: I tell Wren what happened last night—"

"Beth—"

"And we let her decide what to do. If she fires me, okay. I'm no worse off. If she transfers me, fine." I shrugged. "And if she thinks I should stay, then I'll stay."

"Let me see if I have this straight." Wren—hands on her hips, feet braced apart, standing in front of Cyrus's desk while the two of us stood some feet in front of her—shifted her gaze from Cyrus's to mine. "You—Ms. Ryan—pretended to be Ms. O'Rourke last night for a blind date—"

"She did not pretend," Cyrus interjected, to no one's surprise.

He'd interjected when I'd asked Wren to come with us into the office, he'd interjected when I'd explained what had occurred last night, and he'd interjected when I'd explained my reasoning for telling her now.

Wren sent Cyrus a patient look. "Please, allow me to continue, and do not interrupt."

Cyrus lifted his chin, then nodded.

My phone vibrated in my dress pocket. I ignored it. When I told Wren what had occurred, I'd done my best to keep all feelings out of my recitation of events. Likewise, I'd reported the details, but I'd tried to steer clear of making excuses. As I relived the details of the previous evening for the third time today, I couldn't help but feel renewed guilt and shame for my actions and behavior. I almost hoped she would fire me. It felt deserved.

She started again. "You—Ms. Ryan—pretended to be Ms. O' Rourke last night for a blind date with the full intention of telling the blind date who you were as soon as he arrived. You had no idea the blind date was Mr. Malcom. He was late and sent a bottle of wine. You drank approximately one glass and experienced an interaction with the prescription antihistamines you'd taken yesterday afternoon for hay fever."

I nodded, saying nothing, my hands clasped behind my back.

Wren leaned back on the desk, keeping one foot on the ground, the other dangling and bent at the knee. "Before Mr. Malcom arrived, you attempted to leave. When he did arrive, you realized who he was and explained to him that you were experiencing a drug interaction with the alcohol he'd sent."

Cyrus stirred, drawing my attention to him, and his mouth was open as though he wanted to interject. Ultimately, he did not.

"Mr. Malcom, realizing you were unwell, escorted you home," Wren continued. "On the way, you thought you were dreaming at one point and touched him inappropriately."

"I did not feel violated in the least," Cyrus said emphatically. "Just want to make that clear."

Though she didn't smile with her mouth, when her eyes returned to mine, they were full of mirth. Meanwhile, I refused to feel embarrassed or anything else about it. It happened. Moving on.

My phone buzzed again and I shifted on my feet. Whoever it was, it could wait.

"You have made that very clear, Mr. Malcom. But thank you," she said, folding her hands in front of her and resting them on her lap. "After leaving Ms. Ryan at her apartment, Mr. Malcom was still under the impression that you"—she lifted her chin toward me—"were Ms. O' Rourke. And you didn't realize he was still under this impression until you saw him earlier today at the studio offices. After the meeting in Ms. Wraithington's office, you and Mr. Malcom drove together to his residence. During that drive, he confronted you, the two of you talked through the misunderstanding"—she lifted her voice and glanced at Cyrus before he could interject again—"to Mr. Malcom's satisfaction. He harbors no ill will whatsoever and believes you will make an excellent addition to the team. Do I have that right?"

Cyrus, wearing a small smile, nodded. "That's exactly right."

"Good." Wren also allowed herself a smile and looked at me again. "But you felt it was important that I know what occurred. And now you want me to decide what happens next."

"Whether she is transferred or stays, you mean," Cyrus said. "The only two options are: either she is transferred to a different team, or she stays here on this team. I vote this team."

Wren rolled her lips between her teeth and lowered her gaze to the carpet. My phone buzzed for a third time. Since no one was speaking, the slight sound filled the space and drew all eyes to me.

I cleared my throat before saying, "I'll check it later."

Inspecting me, Wren nodded, then asked, "What do you want to do, Ms. Ryan? Do you want to work on this team? Or would you prefer to be transferred?"

Once I was certain Cyrus wouldn't interject, I said, "There is a third option, Ms. St. James. You could fire me."

Cyrus made a strangled sound, then snapped his mouth shut, his chin falling to his chest. I glanced at his profile, saw his jaw tick and his eyes move in my direction before pointing down again.

Wren's mouth curved upward on one side and her openly assessing stare warmed. "No. I don't think so. You've done nothing to breach the work agreement and your insistence on honesty now tells me I can trust you later. It would be wasteful and foolish of me to throw away skilled, trustworthy people because of a drug interaction."

I nodded, accepting her judgment on the matter, unsure if I felt relieved or disappointed by her verdict.

"So back to my question. Do you transfer and make a clean start with a new client and team where no ancillary baggage exists? Or do you stay and stick it out despite the rocky start?"

I stiffened, then said, "I stay," on reflex. I wasn't someone who took the easy road. Ever. The way she'd framed her question made it clear which path she considered the easier of the two.

"Good." Wren stood from the desk. "That's settled. So unless either of you have anything else, or if you—Ms. Ryan—wish to request changes to the schedule . . .?"

I shook my head. "No, ma'am. But I did want to say—" My phone buzzed again, an obnoxious pest. I reached into my pocket and gripped it, determined to continue my thought. "I want to say, I'm more than willing to work weekends as well as holidays, should anyone need to switch."

"There's no need for that." Her small smile returned and her voice softened. "You don't have anything to prove and you don't need to punish your-self, Beth. You didn't do anything wrong."

A zing of emotion zipped through me, hot and uncomfortable, making my throat tight and my eyes sting. I shoved it aside. "Thank you. But I have no family in the area and it doesn't matter to me which days I work or what shifts I'm given. The offer stands."

Wren considered me, her attention feeling heavier than before. Finally, she nodded slowly. "So noted. If there's nothing else, I'll see you on Sunday for your first shift."

I held her gaze. "Thank you, ma'am."

"You should call me Wren, don't you think?" As she passed by, she placed a hand on my shoulder and gave it a squeeze. "We'll all be working together for the next several months. No reason to be so formal."

Swallowing, I returned her small, warm smile with a tight one before she walked out of the office, leaving the door open behind her and me alone with Cyrus.

I closed my eyes and exhaled a long breath. I understood her logic, but I disagreed with her. I should've read that drug information sheet. I never should have had any of the apology wine. I should—

The sound of hands clapping together once made me flinch and my eyes fly open. Cyrus stood directly in front of me, rubbing his hands together, a giant smile on his face.

"Well, that went better than expected. I think she likes you." He winked.

I schooled my expression. "Mr. Malcom."

"Ah-ah-ah." He lifted a finger. "I'm Cyrus, you're Beth. You heard our boss, no reason to be so formal."

"Whether or not Wren likes me is—" I was cut off by my phone buzzing *yet again*. Growling, I withdrew the phone from my pocket and glared at it. *Santino.* UGH!

"It's okay, you can answer that if you need to." Cyrus stepped closer and angled his head as though trying to peer at the name flashing on the screen.

"No. It's just my—my dumb boyfriend," I grumbled, sending his call to voice mail. I don't hear from him in six weeks and now suddenly talking to me is an emergency?

"You have a boyfriend?" Cyrus took a step back.

"I—yes. I do." It would take too long to explain that I sorta had a boyfriend last month, but that he'd stopped returning my texts or calls, and so I'd thought we were over, but then he'd texted me today asking to visit, and so I did technically still have a boyfriend until I got a chance to break up with him officially.

"Ah. I see."

Distracted, I gathered a deep breath and turned from the room, intent on calling a taxi and leaving as soon as possible.

Today. I'll do it today. The thought was just about as welcome as a porcupine at a nudist colony. But after the day I'd had, what was one more ridiculously uncomfortable conversation?

Oh! Don't forget, you still have to talk to Ryaine.

. . . Sigh.

ACT 2: THE DANCE

CHAPTER 8

BATHSHEBA

"Better not bring up a lion inside your city,
But if you must, then humor all his moods."

— ARISTOPHANES, *THE FROGS*

~Late July~

"*H*eya, Beth. Ready?"

I gave Mindy a friendly smile in response. Climbing into the SUV without comment, I tossed my duffel bag in the back and mentally prepared for another long shift attempting to guard the enigma that was Cyrus Malcom.

Over the last month, the man had proved to be the most complex, frustrating, and unpredictable client (and human) to whom I'd ever been assigned *by far*. Disinterested in his own security, he gave hugs to interviewers, cuddled with random cast and crew on film sets—including my teammates—embraced fans on the street, people in grocery stores, and random dogs literally everywhere. His generosity with his touch and his time made me twitchy and restless.

Didn't he realize someone could be carrying a knife? Or a syringe filled with a sinister substance? And dogs bit people. Did he have no sense of self-preservation?

Making matters even more complicated, he would live stream his planned location *constantly* on social media, which meant we often had crowds to deal with—and a plethora of hugs—whenever we arrived at a public location. Worse, he was always late. ALWAYS. Which meant his rabid fans had even longer to gather and amass before we arrived.

It was one thing to be grateful for one's fandom, but what he did daily, how he constantly gave and gave and gave of himself, was a horse of a different color. Hence why taking the time to mentally prepare now, before we arrived at Cyrus's house, was essential.

Mindy waited until I buckled my seat belt to hand me a cup of coffee. "I had a coffee date and picked up your usual."

"Oh. Thank you." I accepted the paper cup. "I really appreciate it."

My usual was drip coffee, black. It wasn't my favorite—my favorite was a white chocolate mocha cappuccino with almond milk, extra foam, and three shots of espresso—but none of my team knew that. Whenever they asked what I wanted, I asked for drip coffee, black. That way no one would feel bad if or when the order got messed up.

"How was your week?" I asked, setting the cup between my knees, not wanting to tie up one of the cupholders.

She sent me a small smile. "It was good. Missed you last night."

I hummed noncommittally and decided to sip the bitter coffee because that was another thing.

Cyrus treated almost everyone who worked for or with him as a long-lost friend or beloved family member. He'd organized a birthday party for my fellow teammate Kristina last Sunday. Earlier this month, he'd taken over all cooking, gave Boris three weeks off, and hired nurses to care for the guy after Boris had been in a car accident.

My team had been trying to convince me to attend one of Cyrus's Thursday night wine club tastings. Apparently, he'd started the club with his previous security team a few months before we took over, but it had continued after their reassignment. Mindy went no matter if she was working and had told me several times how nice the old guards were. I'd never met the guys as I'd never gone. Being around Cyrus while he was effusively, generously, and genuinely friendly with everyone *except* me was . . .

Well. It was something.

The schedule had shifted and changed over the last few weeks, but I'd never worked Thursdays. Once the dust had settled regarding everyone's special requests, my typical weekly schedule was as follows: A thirty-six-hour shift from Friday evening through Sunday early morning. Then I'd sleep and return to work for two eight- or ten-hour day shifts on Monday and Tuesday. Wednesdays and Thursdays were typically my days off.

That's right. I had the Friday and Saturday night party shift. Every week. I'd volunteered and I never complained.

Leaving the house with Cyrus was nerve-racking but better than the alternative. In public, he flirted like most people breathed, made everyone he encountered feel like they were now best friends, invited random people to spa days, or surfing at Long Beach, or shopping on Rodeo. He accepted drinks from strangers at parties and danced with them in crowded clubs, went home with them after the party ended—at two, three, four o'clock in the morning—to eat pizza and watch cult film classics or just shoot the shit at their townhouses and apartments, no matter how sketch the neighborhood.

All of this meant Cyrus was the most impossible person to keep safe. Guarding him made me want to tear my hair out half the time with all the reckless choices he made. The other half of the time was spent with me on pins and needles, my teeth on edge, my body strung tight as I watched for signs of danger and seemingly everyone else luxuriated in the radiance of his irrepressible bigheartedness and effortless charisma.

Now, just over five weeks into this assignment, sitting next to Mindy in the studio's SUV while she merged onto I-5, I struggled to slip into the right headspace for another night of reckless merrymaking with Hollywood's most popular leading man. Studying the lid of my coffee cup, I questioned whether I would be able to stomach the stress of the coming months.

Every time he accepted a hug from a stranger, my heart stuttered. Every time I had to guide him through a crowd, adrenaline flooded my system. I went to bed each night exhausted and woke up with nightmares where Cyrus ended up sawed in half after scoffing at my pleading warnings to steer clear of some psycho in a blood-spattered ski mask.

Maybe Ryaine would take me back . . . ?

In retrospect, guarding her had been a breeze, even with all the skeevy blind dates. When I'd finally had a chance to tell her about what had happened, Ryaine hadn't been upset about the events of that fateful night, laughing good-naturedly only after I assured her that I was okay and all was well.

Explaining to Ryaine about the disastrous date with Cyrus had gone much better than breaking up with Santino. First, I couldn't get him to answer his phone when I called him back. Then I messaged him and he didn't message back until two days later. When I tried calling him again, again he didn't pick up. Frustrated, I broke up with him over text.

Lo and behold, he'd called after that, asking me to reconsider. I'd been firm, communicated my boundaries—we could be friends but were no longer in a relationship, and if he didn't like it, I wished him well—and ended the call knowing he'd thank me in the long run for being so firm.

Interestingly, Ryaine and Cyrus had met last month. The pair had hung out a few times, danced together at parties and clubs. She'd attended two of his Thursday wine nights, but nothing had come of it. Ryaine was now dating a sound editor named Ransom Mercycut. Despite possessing a James Bond-villainesque name, Ransom was a super decent guy. She'd met him at an industry party about three weeks ago.

Perhaps unsurprisingly, Cyrus had been the one to introduce them.

"Are you wearing that tonight? Or did you bring a change of clothes?" Mindy asked as we crawled through Friday rush hour traffic, pushing her long brown hair over a slim shoulder made even longer since she'd straightened out the curl.

I glanced down at my short jean shorts and white tank top. "No, not this. I brought a few options for tonight, depending on where we go."

"That's a hot look for you. If we go to the beach club, it totally works. Though I'm not sure where you would put your gun."

"Nah. I'm all sweaty. I washed my car this afternoon and didn't get a chance to change. Everything is in the bag." I tossed a thumb over my shoulder, indicating to the duffel bag I'd packed on Wednesday in preparation for today.

"Kristina warned me that only one of the bathrooms is working. Something about water intrusion and ripping out tile."

"Oh." I frowned. "She didn't text me."

"She asked me to let you know. I saw her for coffee just before I picked you up. It happened today."

"I'll be fast if you need to get ready, or you could go first."

"No, no. I already did everything but change and apply lipstick." She sent me a sunny smile and I noticed she'd decided to use the eyeshadow technique I'd recommended for her eye shape.

I grinned. "I like what you did around your eyes."

"Thank you." She winked. "Some sexy gal taught me how to do that."

We both laughed.

"Anytime." I gave her an overexaggerated wink in return. "Let me know when you're ready for cat eyes. You know I do a mean cat eye."

In a very un-LA move, Mindy flipped on her blinker to change lanes. "I do. But I don't think I'm that advanced yet. Baby steps. Maybe when the other two bathrooms are back in commission."

I nodded, chewing on my bottom lip, and wondering if I should've showered at my apartment.

Early on, I'd learned it was wise to get ready at Cyrus's place. He took forever—as previously mentioned, he was always late—and rather than twiddle my thumbs while small birds and rodents gave him a two-hour bath in milk and honey, or whatever he did, I showered and dressed at his house. Even after carefully applying makeup and painstakingly doing my hair, I usually had time to review security logs and updates to the preapproved visitor list and run thorough checks of the security tapes.

Also, on Fridays in particular, I checked in with Boris and Craig to make sure Cyrus's favorite things were stocked and placed where he could easily find them: British *Vogue*, the *New Yorker*, Starburst candy, and a cabernet from a boutique winery in Auburn, California to name a few. I'd assembled a list of his favorites as I became aware of his preferences. It made everyone's life easier if he never had to hunt for his tea or magazine or whatever book he was currently reading (presently, *The Age of Innocence* by Edith Wharton).

And then when Cyrus was ready, we'd all pile into the SUV. Normally, I drove, and I'd spend the next twelve hours—at least—battling high blood pressure and trying to look relaxed.

"Beth."

"Hmm?" I'd been staring out the window lost in thought, so I turned my head when Mindy said my name.

Mindy's hands tightened on the steering wheel as she readjusted her grip. "Are you okay?"

Forcing a smile, I nodded. "Yeah. Of course."

Her gaze darted between me and the freeway. "I know he frustrates you, but—"

"It's fine."

"No, listen. I know he does. He frustrates all of us. But he's such a good guy. He really is." Her voice was soft with affection, like she was talking about her favorite cousin and not her client.

I nodded because I agreed. Cyrus was a really, really, *really* good guy. This had surprised me at first, but now there was no denying it. No one could manufacture the wellspring of constant compassion and tornado of generosity that was Cyrus Malcom. He was truly a marvel of magnanimity.

And yet, at what cost?

Sometimes, after a long night of clubbing or partying, I'd catch his reflection in the rearview mirror as I drove everyone home, and his dazed expression made my heart ache as he stared out the window watching the sunrise. He looked so tired—like bone-deep, soul-deep weary—and I'd get the bizarre urge to yell at him for being so unswervingly giving all the damn time.

I would swallow that urge, content myself with making him a cup of tea when we'd arrive home. Then I'd redirect my attention out the windshield, not knowing what frustrated me more about Cyrus: that his over-the-top generosity made my job almost impossible or that it wore him down and out, exhausted him, yet he seemed addicted to it, unable to stop or willing to take care of himself.

No one but me seemed to notice. Or if they did, they didn't consider it a problem. It was a problem, one I wished I could do something more about, but the last person he would want help or advice from was me. Which was why I'd leave his tea and Starburst outside his room with an anonymous knock, disappearing down the hall before he opened his door.

"It's like Wren is always saying, we aren't his babysitters," Mindy said, turning her head from stop-and-go traffic to inspect me. "Sometimes you have to be creative in order to maintain your cover and keep the client safe. In Cyrus's case, sometimes you have to be *really* creative, put your body between him and other people, that kind of stuff."

I knew what she was referencing because I'd seen Mindy plaster her body to his at a club in order to redirect someone who'd become too handsy or pull him away from a group at a party by his tie, luring him out of harm's way with whispers in his ear and saucy smiles. To a bystander, it probably looked like Mindy—or Kristina, or Tamra, or Wren, or Nicole—and Cyrus were a couple, or hooking up, or something similar. But none of them were. He treated the team like close friends, just like he treated everyone else . . .

But me.

Squirming in my seat, I banished the persistent and useless thought. Point was, Cyrus didn't seem to be romantically involved or interested in anyone, not that I'd personally witnessed so far. The kisses he traded were placed on cheeks and the backs of hands. Public displays of affection were limited to hugs, cuddling, and hand-holding, but—again—with virtually everyone. During my shifts at least, he always slept at home, and he always slept alone.

"If you could just—just relax a little, I think you'd have an easier time of it," Mindy went on, her tone carefully conversational.

"Relax," I repeated, breathing through a spike of unease. I didn't know how to relax around Cyrus, especially not when we were in public and he was so careless about his well-being.

"Yeah. Like, you can dance near him at the club or stand next to him at a party, you know. You don't always have to be the one standing guard at the highest point in the room, sipping on club soda, watching the crowd and all the exits. At least two of us have to be near him, keeping a close watch. At tonight's shindig, one should be you. I'll take the high point."

I turned my face to the passenger-side window, my gaze unfocused on the passing traffic. "We'll see," I said.

We wouldn't see. Wren had decided parties, large events, and clubs required four guards instead of two. Of the four of us who would be working tonight at whatever party he'd been invited to as a VIP guest, I would not be one of the team members dancing or standing near Cyrus.

Just because the worst hadn't happened yet didn't mean it wasn't going to happen. I couldn't seem to effectively get this point across to him. Not that he gave me many opportunities, yet I tried every chance I got. Thankfully, I wasn't the only one on the team who chastised him for making reckless decisions.

That said, I did seem to be the only guard he didn't talk to, unless it was absolutely necessary. I'd never been on the dance floor with him, but somehow I knew—if I accepted the floor as my station for the evening—he'd give me his back all night and pretend I didn't exist.

But you know what? I didn't blame Cyrus. Not even a little. I blamed myself. I'd told him from the get-go that it was a bad idea for me to be his bodyguard. I made him uncomfortable, there was no undoing what I'd done that night in the back of the car, climbing all over him, trying to kiss him, *touching* him.

His avoidance made sense to me, but it also made me the outlier in every group—like I said, even random dogs were embraced despite the biting hazard. But it was especially noticeable compared to how he treated the rest of the team.

Again, I didn't blame him for singling me out. Honestly, I didn't. I was . . . stressed enough already without having to feign friendly disinterest if or when he touched me, and it wasn't just Cyrus's disregard for his safety that had me tied up in knots.

At first, I'd been able to interact with Cyrus while feeling nothing but professional interest (and disinterest). But then, over time and repeated exposure, an uncanny, biological reaction to him had blossomed, built, ballooned. Now my thoughts inexplicably scattered like dandelion fluff on a stiff summer wind any time our eyes met. His ability to temporarily scramble my brain by simply existing was so problematic that, if I sensed him looking in my direction, I avoided his eyes and stared at the handsome cleft in his perpetually stubbled chin.

After every shift of quietly existing in his shadow when everyone else got nothing but sunshine, the tension between us only seemed to increase; the longer we went without speaking, the more stilted our conversations; the longer we went without eye contact, the more charged our glances.

But maybe not to him? I considered this possibility and absentmindedly rubbing my chest. Maybe this discomfort was one-sided? Maybe the eye collisions only felt charged to me? I honestly had no idea.

I did not understand my ever-growing reaction. And so, I ignored it. And him, as much as was feasible given the nature of my job.

I concentrated on protecting him irrespective of how little he seemed to care about his own safety and mental well-being. And since I wasn't a quitter, I would continue to do my job to the best of my ability until the contract ended after the new year.

No matter how frustrating he made them.

"He's taking a nap, I think," Nicole said around a yawn, stretching her arms over her head and standing from the couch as we walked into the room.

"A nap?" Mindy placed her backpack on the floor just inside the living room. "What time did you guys wake up this morning?"

"I think what you mean to ask is, what time did we go to sleep after you left wine club last night? The answer is"—Nicole glanced at her phone—"Kristina went to bed at four and woke up at ten. She left when Wren arrived at eleven. The boys left at noon. Cyrus finally went to bed two hours ago, and I haven't slept."

"He'll be asleep for eight hours at least." Mindy's shoulders rose and fell with a deep breath, and she glanced at me. "So I guess we're not heading out anytime soon."

"I don't know about that. He said he really wanted to go to this party tonight. Did you hear about the bathrooms upstairs?" Nicole asked around another yawn. "Only the one by our bedrooms works. I guess Cyrus's and the other one up there share a wall. There's a busted pipe, water intrusion.

It's all torn up. Boris was the one who discovered it. The water pressure in the kitchen was wonky when he arrived to make breakfast."

"Kristina told me this afternoon." Mindy pulled the car fob from her pocket and spun the ring around her index finger.

"Ah, yes. Craig called her." Craig was Cyrus's personal assistant. "I guess Kristina's dad is a plumber?" Nicole glanced between me and Mindy for confirmation.

I shrugged. If Kristina's dad was a plumber, I had no idea. Of the team, my hours overlapped with Kristina's the least. She liked to work during weekdays and preferred night shifts. For the most part, she worked every weekday night. This was nice because it allowed other people—like me—to work only day shifts during the week. We all appreciated Kristina.

"Yes, Kristina's dad is a plumber," Mindy confirmed. "But he usually only does service calls in the Valley. Where's Wren?"

Nicole yawned again, picking up her duffel bag. "She's in the kitchen getting a culinary lesson from Boris." Wagging her eyebrows, Nicole and I shared a look.

Most of us suspected that Boris was sweet on Wren. Most of us *also* suspected that Wren had no idea, which had been hilarious to watch for the last few weeks. For such a brilliant strategic brain, considerate soul, and wise heart, Wren was oblivious to the effect she had on most men. And women. And, basically, everyone. I'd developed a little bit of a crush on her and I was firmly Team Penis.

"Listen, Tamra should be here any minute." Nicole hoisted her bag to her shoulder. "I'm just waiting for my ride."

Wren had decided early on after witnessing how Cyrus interacted with the public that he needed four of us to work every Friday and Saturday night instead of the typical two. Public events and press engagements also required four instead of two. There had been some talk of adding another two undercover specialists to our team, but I wasn't sure the status of that decision.

"You're not taking the SUV?" Mindy held out the fob to Nicole.

"No. I'm exhausted. I shouldn't drive." Nicole checked her phone again. "If either of you are planning to take a shower, I'd do it now. I let Tamra know about the bathroom situation, but she hasn't messaged me back. She might need it too. And Cyrus didn't say when he'd be up."

"I'll take mine now. Good to see you, Nic." I hadn't put my bag down, so I used my free hand to wave and turned for the back hallway, ignoring the confusing mixture of feelings about the evening ahead.

If Cyrus had just gone to sleep two hours ago, there existed a good chance he'd sleep through the first six to eight hours of my shift. We wouldn't be heading anywhere until 2 or 3 a.m. I didn't know how long this party tonight was supposed to last, but most clubs were closed or closing by then.

Another possibility was that we'd stay here and he would host a small get-together from his approved visitor list. My heart both sank and lifted at the thought.

Those evenings were the least stressful from a safety standpoint even though Cyrus often pushed Wren about feeling restricted by the existence of the approved visitor list. She'd always respond calmly with something like, "You can add anyone you choose, but you have to give us at least one week's notice so we can run a background check. One week isn't a lot to ask. You can wait."

Like Cyrus, she had a magical way with people. With Wren, folks implicitly trusted her and listened to her counsel. Her magic came from being straightforward and blunt, setting boundaries but also being excessively reasonable and gentle about it.

Depositing my bag on the bed I'd probably not have a chance to sleep in until Saturday afternoon, I pulled out my travel bottles of shampoo and conditioner along with my toiletry bag. Through some unspoken agreement, none of us left our stuff in the bathroom we all shared. It had a toilet room with a door, two pedestal sinks, a big, glass-enclosed shower, and no cabinet or counter space. I think we all independently realized that six different toiletry sets for six different people in that bathroom would've been a cluttered, ridiculous mess.

Hair products and bag tucked under my arm, I debated the likelihood of Cyrus skipping an evening out in favor of a small get-together, but then wondered if maybe he'd forgo a gathering completely since two of the bathrooms were out of order. Only ours, a half bath off the living room, and a half bath off the kitchen worked. Pushing open the bathroom door, I wondered—

I stopped.

My heart stopped.

My brain stopped.

Unable to even breathe, I was rooted in place by the mind-melting and life-altering sight of Cyrus Malcom's beautiful body. Completely naked.

But—

But he's—

HE WAS SUPPOSED TO BE ASLEEP!

Also, he was . . . *perfection.*

A sudden, helpless breath puffed out of me at the truth of this reflexive thought.

"Enjoying the view?" he asked lightly, gesturing to his chest, torso, and midsection, Vanna White-style.

My gaze cut to his. Big mistake. Despite the brightness of the bathroom, his pupils dominated his irises, turning his glare virtually black. The intensity of his eyes made his stare feel like a glare. Our usual eye collision this time reverberated through me, a detonation, a bomb going off in my lower stomach, charred shrapnel raining in every direction within me. Inexplicably, my body froze all over again.

While I struggled to unscramble my brain, Cyrus made a soft tsking sound. "Do you have your phone? You can take a picture." His posture seemed completely relaxed, but his lips were curved into a small smile. "Or you could join me . . .?"

I choked and spun away as a pulse of spiky heat pressed forcefully against every inch of my skin. Covering my face with both hands just for good measure, I didn't notice as my toiletry bag and hair products fell to the floor. Instead, I sucked in a breath, my lungs suddenly screaming that they were deprived of oxygen.

GOOD GOD. I'd never seen anything like that. It was—he was—unreal. Every part of him—and I mean every single part of him—was gorgeous. That's what I meant, and that's why his body was unreal. His form reminded me of the magnificence of Greek sculptures, except with a bigger and thicker—

Ahem.

You know.

Speaking of, that was gorgeous too. As mortified as I felt, I wanted to sneak another peek. Just a quick one. Just to make sure it had been real. But I wouldn't. I wasn't a horrible person. I wouldn't take advantage. I was a professional. And even though his entire body was reminiscent of a marble Michelangelo masterpiece, a depiction of the male form too perfect for words, that could only be adequately described using music or—

The sound of Cyrus clearing his throat pulled me from my highly inappropriate and strangely poetic musings about the otherworldliness of his magnificent body.

"I'm, uh, so sorry." Stumbling a step forward because my hands were still covering my eyes, I fought a losing battle against the fierce blush conquering my entire body as my foot connected with one of my hair care bottles.

It wasn't lost on me how overblown my reaction was. I was being ridiculous. I'd seen naked men before. I'd touched naked men. I'd had sex with naked men. So why Cyrus's naked body had turned me into an absurd, blushing, babbling teenage version of myself, I had no idea.

Why couldn't I simply be a normal person around Cyrus Malcom? *Get a grip!*

I forced words out. "I didn't know you were in there—I *never* would have—I hope you know—I wouldn't—I am so . . . sorry."

"Calm down, Bathsheba. Nudity is a natural state," he said, his tone lazy, almost bored sounding. And that just made everything worse for some reason.

"Still," I croaked. "You shouldn't have to show your body to anyone you don't want to. I am s—"

"You're sorry. I know. Bathroom is all yours," he ground out, his bare shoulder brushing mine as he unhurriedly passed.

He walked away.

I listened to his leisurely footsteps climb the stairs. I listened for the telltale sound of his door shutting. I counted to twenty. Once I reached it, I grabbed my dropped items from the floor.

"Beth?"

Whipping up to a standing position, I turned to the left, finding Tamra standing at the end of the hall, her wide, surprised eyes likely a mirror of mine.

"Tamra."

"Uh . . . is everything okay?" Her attention flickered to the direction where Cyrus had just disappeared.

"Yep. Yep. All is well." Despite my years of training and time spent in the field, in that moment, I wouldn't have been able to modulate my voice if my life depended on it.

"Was that—" She cut herself off and stepped into the middle of the hall. "Did you just walk in on Cyrus naked?"

"It appears so," I squeaked like an idiot. Clearing my throat, I finally found the wherewithal to lower my voice. "The door wasn't locked, it wasn't even closed all the way. There's just the one shower. I didn't know he was in there. I thought he was asleep—"

"It's okay. I mean, I was on my way to take a shower too. It could've just as easily have happened to me. He seemed kind of angry, though . . ." Her gaze felt sympathetic but also bewildered as it skated over me. "Don't feel bad. He should've locked the door, or at least closed it."

I nodded inanely, but I felt a little better after receiving confirmation that Cyrus had seemed angry. Which had me wondering, if Tamra had been the one who'd innocently pushed open the door, would his reaction have been similar?

Or was I reading too much into this, his reaction had nothing to do with me, and he was simply . . . in a bad mood?

Tamra gave me a small smile. "Don't worry about it. Go ahead. I'll wait 'til you're done."

"Okay. Thanks," I said, then hurried into the bathroom. I locked the door behind me. I wiped steam from the mirror and stared at my own face, still red-stained with embarrassment.

Perhaps it was self-aggrandizing to think I was the problem, yet I couldn't help but think I was the problem. Cyrus wasn't distant with anyone but me. All this time watching him interact with people—friendly acquaintances, coworkers, strangers—made it painfully obvious: something about me irritated him, and I didn't know how to fix it.

I'd given him space. I'd given him distance. I no longer spoke to him unless absolutely necessary. What else could I do?

I didn't want to contemplate what might happen next, but how could I not considering his anger just now? The embarrassment of stumbling across him naked would be nothing in comparison to being kicked off this team due to a personality conflict with my very first studio assignment if he made a complaint.

. . . *Not* if. When *he makes a complaint.* He should make a complaint.

But if he didn't, there had to be a way to fix this. I wasn't a quitter. I would and could figure this out. I'd make things right for him.

Closing my eyes briefly, I cursed my brain for the image that greeted me behind the darkness of my lids. My eyes flew open, my blush renewed. I refused to allow myself to remember his body, him—no. Just, no. Totally inappropriate. Unprofessional. Wrong. Absolutely not.

And why was I thinking about *that* when my job was on the line?

Swallowing with difficulty, I endeavored to force my muddled and over-heated mind to blank. It didn't work. With every blink, there he was. Standing where I now stood. Steam rising behind him. Towel gripped at his side in one of his big hands. Body glistening with—

Growling, frustrated, and feeling desperate, I flipped on the water and took an extremely cold shower.

CHAPTER 9

CYRUS

"Open your mind before your mouth."

— ARISTOPHANES

~Mid-August~

I didn't know what to do about Beth Ryan.

Unbidden, and yet predictably, my disloyal gaze sought her reflection in the rearview mirror. She sat in the driver's seat, I sat directly behind her, Mindy next to me, Nicole next to Mindy, and Wren in the front. These were our seat assignments whenever we traveled in the spacious studio SUV. If we took a stretched car, Beth didn't drive. She'd sit in the front next to the driver, rarely in the back with the rest of us unless there were logistics to discuss.

Also, she always opened my door for me. Not going to lie, it gave me a thrill each and every time.

Bathsheba Esther Ryan. I liked her name.

Bathsheba. I liked how it sounded even inside my head.

Beth. Even the shortened version held a certain appeal, all the right notes.

Sighing silently, I tore my eyes from the vision of dark green eyes framed by long lashes concentrating on the road. She wore Dior tonight, an impeccable peach confection that had my mouth watering and the rest of me wondering where she hid her weapons. It had a bow at the hip, perhaps there? I hadn't allowed myself a proper look before we left. The color set her skin aglow and her hair appeared gold instead of its usual luscious shade of honey. One quick glance had been too much, but also not enough.

Ugh. Listen to me. I sounded like a bad romance novel. But this inability of mine to form coherent thoughts near or around Beth Ryan continued to confound.

At first I thought the underlying issue was the existence of her boyfriend. This theory had been immediately dismissed. Tamra owned a husband—which was, by all accounts, much worse than a boyfriend—and I didn't have any trouble expressing coherent thoughts with her. Likewise, I knew plenty of women who'd committed. An individual's relationship status had never stopped me from encouraging that person to share and enjoy my company. Then I discovered by chance that she and her boyfriend had split. So there went that theory.

On or around the first month anniversary of our acquaintance, I blamed my mysterious awkwardness on her persistent indifference toward me as anything but a coworker. During our first few weeks working together, she'd made no overtures of friendship, no signs of interest in knowing me beyond a professional setting, no sharing of details about her thoughts, feelings, and personal life. Her answers were succinct and tinted always by her job. She'd been nothing but courteous, polite, professional, and capable.

As an aside, her competence and quiet confidence drove me rather wild. Easily the sexiest thing about her, and this is taking into account her impeccable sense of fashion, the cupid's bow of her bitable lips, the inherent gracefulness of her movements and speech, her adorable turns of phrase I overheard when she didn't realize I was listening, and the perfection of her round, ripe ass.

But I digress.

This particular supposition was also quickly dismissed. Wren, as an example, possessed astonishing competency. It didn't make me wild. Nor had Wren made overtures of friendship outside of work. And yet I'd experienced no difficulty or awkwardness bringing her to my side, discovering what inspired her to laugh, and making her love me despite her vociferous reluctance to cross professional boundaries. She'd crossed loads of boundaries now and was the better for it.

So what was it about Beth Ryan? Why did she make me so confoundedly sappy and stupid?

Presently, my attention glided over Beth's hair, visible beyond the headrest. It fell over her shoulders in long, thick waves, the texture and burnished color in the dark light of the car reminding me of Botticelli's *Birth of Venus*.

UGH! Here I go again! Someone put me out of my misery.

I covered my face and pressed my fingertips to my eyes, rubbing. Undoubtedly, I was attracted to this woman—no surprise there. But attraction had never been my enemy. It had never made me stammer and struggle to find words or worry that the words I ultimately spoke would be all the wrong ones. Attraction, for me, had always been conversational lubricant, made every early interaction easier.

It was the later conversations with the women I desired—the much, much later conversations—that never seemed to go my way.

Shifting in my seat, I indulged in the destructive desire to recall the look on Beth's face when she'd pushed open the door to the bathroom last month, the mortified heat that had crested her neck and cheeks, a mixture of colors that reminded me, ironically, of ripe peaches. She hadn't mentioned the incident since and nor had I. Something had shifted between us, I wasn't sure how to describe it, but her stiff avoidance of me had certainly increased.

Admittedly, it had bothered me for quite some time that I could never stir a blush out of her. Even Wren St. James, master of the universe, had succumbed to a fair shade of rose just one week after taking over my security. I'd complimented her choice in holster. She'd lit up like a Christmas tree. Turns out, she'd designed the holster herself.

That's the key, you see. With those who are world-wise, you had to compliment something they took pride in, something important to them.

In my experience, most people blushed pink when I sent them a smile or a wink. Simply that was enough. But people like Wren and Beth and Lenore Wood—Halina's secretary—didn't. They required finesse.

Lenore Wood had finally given hers to me recently when I'd complimented her multitasking skills. Wren St. James handed hers over when I'd remarked on the impressiveness of her holster design.

But Beth? *Well.*

It's impossible to make any impact on a woman when one constantly finds oneself rendered inarticulate in her presence. Furthermore, it's exceedingly difficult when she won't speak to you or look directly at you.

But she did look at you when she opened that bathroom door, and she blushed plenty then.

I released another silent sigh. First of all, she'd retreated even further into her strong and silent Bodyguard Barbie persona since it happened. And secondly, it had been the wrong type of blush. It wasn't one of pleasure but one of mortification and discomfort. I didn't *want* that kind of response from her. I wanted—

I want . . .

I sighed for a third time.

"So, I was thinking," Mindy said, her cheerful voice breaking the silence. She glanced at me. I gave her a quizzical smile before she went on. "I'd like some experience with crowd visualization and threat detection from the crow's nest position. Maybe Beth could take the floor tonight?"

My eyebrows shot up and my lips parted in surprise. Unbidden and predictably—again—my gaze cut to the rearview mirror. Beth's eyes, still on the road, were huge with what looked like anxiety and she was blushing once more. Still not the right type.

I sent my glare out the window.

"That's a good idea." Wren readily agreed. "And Beth has never worked the floor before."

"But—but it can't be much different than walking him through a crowd," Beth said, her voice higher pitched than usual and reeking of discomfort.

I ground my teeth.

"Mindy needs the experience, and so do you." Angling her body toward Beth, Wren sounded entirely reasonable. She always did. "Working the floor of a club, a room, is a lot different than walking a client through a crowd outside or in a convention space. You're in position longer, there are less exits, you must hold your cover for much, much longer, and you must learn how to gauge threats in your immediate surroundings—which ones are real, which are perceived."

Beth seemed to sink lower in her seat.

Wren wasn't finished. "At first you'll err on the side of caution, and that's fine—so, Cyrus, be patient with Beth tonight if she yanks you off the floor prematurely."

"Expect premature yanking, got it," I quipped.

Mindy smacked my shoulder lightly with the back of her hand.

I made a big show of holding my arm. "Ow!"

"That didn't hurt." She rolled her eyes at me.

"Someone should kiss it and make it better," I pouted, the effect completely lost on Mindy because Mindy was a lesbian.

Not bi. Not pan. Lesbian. Mindy dug females exactly how I dug females, exclusively and with a healthy appetite. We'd bonded while objectifying beautiful women from afar. They'd, in turn, objectified us from afar. All fun things.

Recently however, I suspected Mindy dug Kristina. Last I'd heard, they were supposed to have gone on a beach date today. I hadn't asked Mindy yet whether the date had progressed to her satisfaction as I'd assumed there would be time later. At the club. On the dance floor.

"Okay, friends. Focus." Wren turned in her seat to face us. "Mindy, with time, you'll be able to distinguish between enthusiasm and entitlement on a large scale. Every room has a mood, and it can shift quickly. We'll rely on you to give us that bird's-eye view so Beth can focus on Cyrus. Cyrus, since we're switching things up, let's try to keep your party on the edge of the floor instead of the middle, if it can be helped."

I nodded with all outward dispassion, ignoring the gathering tightness in my chest and elsewhere. Wren continued her monologue, spelling out what could be gained by both Beth and Mindy during their switch in positions. My thoughts were otherwise occupied.

Beth would be with me on the floor tonight. She would be providing security under the pretext of dancing near me, with my circle of VIPs. We might even dance together.

I want that.

I'd like to claim that the ferocity of this thought surprised me. That would be a lie. However, since I'm not above lying to myself, surprise is what we're going with.

Don't give me that look. You and I both know there is no person we lie to more than ourselves.

Facing the window once more, I grappled with the imagery assault. Beth in *that* dress facing me. My hands on her. Her hands on me. Her chin tilted up. Her eyes . . .

Hmm.

She'd have to look at me, right?

No. She's working. She won't be looking at you, she'll be looking for threats.

Too bad I wasn't a threat. Maybe then, she'd look at me.

Don't ask me what made me do it. Thirst? Nostalgia? Bold disregard for my lower gastrointestinal tract? But I ordered a round of Prairie Fires for the table upon our arrival. Naturally, none of my team—oh, excuse me, my *entourage*—imbibed, but the rest of my guests downed the disgusting Tabasco-laced shots like they were ambrosia.

"I've never heard of this drink before. Where is it from?" This question was posed by Gorge Stand who was fighting back tears, his throat muscles still constricting from the shot. Young Gorge was a twenty-something fella who would've All About Eve'd me in a heartbeat if given the chance.

Returning his toothy white smile and raising him a wink, I lifted my third shot and swallowed. It burned like penitence and regret all the way down.

"You forget, dear Gorge, I'm originally from Texas. Tabasco is from Louisiana, but hot sauce goes on everything in the south: eggs, steak, steak and eggs." I glanced at Beth, briefly considering asking her to back me up.

She sat next to me, her eyes scanning the club from our perch in the VIP area and her delicate-looking fingers cupped a glass of bubbling club soda. But her hands weren't delicate. They were calloused. Skillful. Useful in a way mine would never be.

Earlier, I'd tried to catch her eye when she'd opened my door, but she'd studiously avoided my gaze. Don't worry, it was a little game we played: I'd look directly at her, and she'd focus her attention on the vicinity of my chin. So much fun.

I have no idea why, but her chin-focusing irked more than usual. Thus, before she could step back and follow, I'd grabbed her hand. I'd laced our fingers together. And that did the trick.

She'd looked at me then, eyes rounded with obvious surprise and confusion. My heart had done a peculiar thing as I gazed down at her with all the false insouciance I could muster, a painful sort of spasm and sluggish beat occurring in tandem.

"Cy—"

I'd bent forward and whispered something I wanted, "Stay close to me."

She shivered, and I felt her nod as I took advantage of our proximity to inhale the heat of her skin and perfume like a *super* creepy dude. And I would know. I've experienced plenty of super creepy dudes and dames whiff my skin and hair whilst I gave hugs during meet-and-greet events or while in public. Hugs never bothered me. But nothing made me feel quite as slimy as being smelled against my will. And I'd just done it to Beth.

This is what I've become. A smeller.

Presently, disguising a cringe as the aftermath of a Prairie Fire, I leaned back in my seat, didn't overthink my decision to place my arm along the top of the booth behind Beth, and endeavored to listen attentively to the woman on my right. Her name was something like Erin, or Ergo, or Egret. The club music wasn't overwhelming where we sat, but I hadn't been paying close attention when she'd been introduced. Once we filtered down to the floor, where it was loud and dark and crowded, no additional introductions would be possible. Something to look forward to.

I felt the bass reverberating in my chest, but I could also still hear the woman—let's call her Erin—perfectly well while she regaled the table with a fascinating story of ordering at a restaurant in Paris and possessing no grasp of the French language. Though, if I'd been at the other end of the table and not directly adjacent to her, I might've had to lip-read.

Reaching a particularly silly part of her story, she tossed her head back and laughed. I smiled dutifully, wondering if I should order another Prairie Fire or if I'd tortured myself enough for sniffing Beth earlier. As I debated the nature of penitence, I studied Erin. She hadn't blushed yet.

Erin was objectively beautiful in a militantly high-maintenance and avant-garde manner that communicated several facts at once: she chose her clothes based on how she wished to be perceived, not what suited her features best; she relied on color matching—i.e., Erin's teal nails exactly matched her teal Prabal Gurung outfit—rather than complementary colors —e.g., Beth's light pink nails complemented her Dior peach dress which complemented her skin tone and the color of her eyes; and Erin preferred new and novel over classic and chic if the asymmetrical, kitten cutout top and parachute skirt she wore were any indication. I recognized both from the preview magazine sent to me for the upcoming runway season in Milan.

"Parisians are so much nicer than most Americans think. I feel like, as long as you don't assume they can speak English, they'll try to work with you." Her gaze flickered to my left where Beth sat, then returned to me. "Have you ever been? To Paris?"

"I—"

"What am I asking? Of course you have." She laughed, rolling her eyes at herself, then gave my upper thigh a light smack, which ended with her fingers lingering just above my knee.

I could feel the heat of her palm through the fabric of my suit, the grounding weight of it. In my peripheral vision, I watched Beth recross her legs, shifting slightly away from me as she did so. I swallowed around a sudden thickness.

If Beth were any other member of my team, I would've already draped my arm around her shoulders and pulled her close. I'd probably be playing with her fingers by now. But with Beth . . . *no*. I couldn't. She didn't want me to, and I wanted to too much.

Erin's inviting hand on my leg presented a much wiser choice. In truth, it was the only choice.

Removing my arm from the back of the booth behind Beth, I covered Erin's hand with mine and pressed her teal-painted fingers to my leg. "I haven't been to Paris," I said, giving her an encouraging smile. "What were your favorite parts?"

Erin, blushing with obvious pleasure, leaned forward to tell me.

CHAPTER 10

BATHSHEBA

"There is no beast, no rush of fire, like woman so untamed. She calmly goes her way where even panthers would be shamed."

— ARISTOPHANES, *LYSISTRATA*

~Mid-September~

We were in a stretch limo headed into the heart of Chicago, and I was in a bad mood.

Perhaps it was ridiculous of me to air out my bad mood like a wool coat packed in mothballs every time I was near Cyrus—even now, several weeks after the club night from hell—but here I was, more frustrated than my Uncle Spit in a dry county on a Sunday morning. You know, real frustrated.

But this bad mood was a good thing. I wanted to be in a bad mood whenever we were within touching distance of each other. *Trust me on this.*

Despite not wishing to do so, my attention reflexively lifted when Cyrus's charming laugh filled the enclosed space. The almighty dimple on display, he had Mindy on one side and Kristina on the other. Both were curled toward him, their bodies aligned against his, and they were all laughing, watching a funny video on his phone. Some TikToker who dressed up as red blood cells or something. I didn't know and I didn't care.

Well. I sorta cared.

I liked funny videos. But not if I had to enter Cyrus's radius of magical magnetism to watch one. Scowling, I refolded my arms over my stomach and glared out the window.

"Everything okay?" Wren asked on a whisper, drawing my gaze.

Rearranging my grumpy features, I forced a tight smile and replied sweetly, "Everything is just hunky-dory. How about you?"

Her look told me she didn't believe a word I'd said. Either that or she didn't know what *hunky-dory* meant.

I ignored her look and changed the subject. "What time will the interview be over? Craig has it running all the way until midnight, but that can't be right. And when I gave him the final agenda, he said it looked fine, but he didn't fill in the blanks."

"It honestly depends on when we get there. Craig said the producer estimates four hours total."

"Well then, what time is it scheduled?" This was the question no one could—or would—give me the answer to.

Wren's gaze strayed to where Cyrus, Mindy, and Kristina were still giggling, and an affectionate smile pulled at her lips. "I think they wanted us there by ten."

"Ten a.m. or ten p.m.?"

"Ten a.m."

I frowned. "That was thirty minutes ago."

"I know." Her expression flattened somewhat, but her small smile persisted, as though to say, *Whatcha gonna do? Cyrus.*

I huffed a hot exhale and shook my head, so incredibly tired of this always being late BS.

During the last three months, I think we'd been on time to appointments exactly twice. Those two incidents were because I'd purposefully told Craig the wrong times, which he then entered on the calendar and communicated to Cyrus.

Wren did a lot of legwork for our team, emailing us building schematics and maps, details about a location, suggestions for hunkering down if needed or which exit would provide the best chance of an undetected escape. Unfortunately, her legwork only helped if she knew our destination ahead of time, and only if Cyrus didn't change his mind and decide to take us all someplace completely different at the last minute.

These chaotic habits of his stressed me out. I hated being late. I needed structure. I needed to know where we were going and what to expect when we arrived. If the worst happened, I would be expected to efficiently and safely remove him from a bad situation. How Wren, Craig, and Cyrus expected the rest of us to do our jobs under such conditions baffled me.

So at of the beginning of this month, I'd decided to cease caring if Cyrus had a problem with me and subsequently stopped walking on eggshells around him. If I made him uncomfortable, or if what had happened between us that night so many weeks ago made him uncomfortable, or if he'd been angry at me for walking in on him naked in the bathroom, he could've asked the studio to reassign me. No problem. I needed to stop infantilizing him and start treating him like an adult capable of being responsible and making adult decisions. Cyrus was an adult. If he wanted me gone from his team, he could've made it happen already. Case closed.

Also at the beginning of the month, I used my days off to canvass new-to-me neighborhoods and locations for my future shifts. I also made agendas on my own, ordered lists of the places where we'd be going on any given day. I shared everything with Wren and I created informational packets for each of the clubs and house party locations Cyrus frequented on weekends. It wasn't a perfect system, but it helped me feel more in control.

This trip to Chicago was our first detail duty outside of LA. Other than Google Earth, I had no way of staking out the neighborhoods before our arrival. I had hoped we would arrive early, ahead of any potential crowds just in case his unannounced visit to the city had been leaked. Apparently, we would not be early.

Still, prepping the agendas, researching the interior of the buildings, exit points, traffic flow, and mentally running through scenarios during my two days off this week had helped immeasurably.

I was stressed, but I didn't feel unprepared.

"Thank you for pulling together the packet, Beth." Wren placed a hand on my arm and gave me a squeeze. "The interview team knows Cyrus has a reputation for always being late. I'm sure they told Craig ten hoping we'd get there closer to eleven."

Before I could respond with my standard, *It's fine*—even though it wasn't fine—Cyrus announced, "I'm hungry."

This statement drew Wren's attention but not mine. I lowered my gaze to the packet I'd prepared for today, flipping to the schematic of the Fairbanks building and checking the location of the loading dock we'd be using. It was on street level, next to the—

"Is anyone else hungry? Wren?" Cyrus asked.

"I'm not hungry. I had a good breakfast," she said, her tone conversational. "I'm sure they'll have snacks in the greenroom before the interview."

I leaned toward Wren and whispered, "Did Craig triple-check the food list to make sure there is no shellfish?"

Cyrus was extremely allergic to shellfish and Craig wasn't the best at reviewing menus and being diligent about food. I'd stopped Cyrus from eating a dip at a party two weeks ago, knocking a chip out of his hand at the last minute when I suspected it had scallops in it. I'd been right.

He'd taken to calling me "my hero" ever since, getting on my last nerve.

"Yes." Wren tilted her head toward mine. "I looked over it as well. All clear."

"And what about the tea he likes? And the Starburst?"

She lifted an eyebrow at me. "I don't know. I didn't ask about that."

I twisted my mouth to the side. It was no matter, I had extra of both in my bag.

Cyrus waited until Wren and I finished our whispered conversation before continuing his thought. "I had a good breakfast too. But I swam laps this morning and that always makes me peckish. I know!" He smacked his leg, hopeful enthusiasm making his words ring through the car brightly. "Let's go to Al's Beef. Have you ever been to Al's Beef?"

"What's Al's Beef?" Kristina asked.

"What's Al's Beef? Are you serious?" How he managed to sound both horribly offended and over-the-moon happy at the same time, I had no idea. "It's only Chicago's number one Italian beef since 1938, Kristina!"

Despite my bad mood, and the fact that he'd just suggested a major change to my agenda, which would definitely make us even later for the event, I had to press my lips together to keep from laughing at his delivery of this information. Sometimes, Cyrus had the energy vibe of a golden retriever, and it was a Herculean effort to avoid being charmed. This was one of those times.

But I was obstinate. And I had bad-mood inertia to keep me grounded and inoculated against Cyrus's charm. So, no. I didn't laugh or smile.

I lifted my head, glared at Cyrus's chin, and said, "No."

"No?" Cyrus leaned toward me, just a smidge. "No what?"

"We are not going to Al's Beef," I said, returning my attention to my packet.

"What?" he asked, then made a short noise that reeked of frustration. In the next moment, he'd snatched my packet from my fingertips and demanded, "Why?"

I smoothed my skirt over my knees and glared out the window. "Al's Beef is not on the agenda. If you wanted to go to Al's Beef, you should've told us before now. We are not going, we're already late for the interview."

The limo descended into silence. It felt awkward and tense. I did not care.

Cyrus broke it. "Bathsheba, my hero," he said, his tone low and deep and made the moniker sound like a taunt. "If we're going to talk about this, the least you could do is give me the courtesy of looking at me."

"We're not talking about it because we're not going."

In my peripheral vision, I saw him lean closer. "There's no reason we can't go—"

"Yes. There is." I whipped my head toward him and met his lethally alluring gaze for probably the first time in three weeks. But I was prepared. I'd spent every day since that stupid night at the club preparing, building a wall for me to hide behind. The wall held.

He stiffened as our eyes connected, his turning dark, reminiscent of the time I'd walked in on him naked. But I refused to think about *that*.

Snatching the packet back, I spoke through gritted teeth, "It's my job to research all the places on the *approved* agenda, which I have done. I've memorized the layout of every floor in the Fairbanks building where you'll be. I know where all the major exits are, the elevators, the emergency exits, the bathrooms, the loading dock, the broom closets, and any other nook and cranny where someone might hide and wait for you to walk by. I know the traffic patterns in front of the building, the hotel, and seven routes to the airport. I know where the hospitals are, the fire stations, the school zones. I know approximately how long it'll take us to get from point A to point B, depending on the time of day. But what I do not know—since you didn't deign to inform a single one of us until right this minute—is anything about Al's Beef."

Cyrus's eyelids had lowered by half while I spoke and his mouth had hitched to one side. His glittery green irises were now thin halos around black pupils. I couldn't tell if the curve to his lips resembled a smirk or a smile. It didn't matter. I didn't care.

I felt myself mimicking his half-lidded death glare as I said with mock-cheerfulness, "So, no, Mr. Malcom. We are not going to Al's Beef."

I am going to murder him.

"Either his phone is off or he's disabled tracking on my account too."

Mindy showed Wren the screen of her cell as the four of us power-walked down the hallway.

I'd already checked mine, as had Wren and Kristina when we found his short note in the greenroom. Cyrus's avatar was completely absent from the tracking program for all four of us. We'd also called him several times, each attempt going straight to voice mail.

"He's probably at Al's Beef," Wren said, her expression and tone more wry than frustrated as she typed something on her phone.

Not me. I was 100 percent frustrated. Cyrus Malcom, mega movie star and royal pain in my ass, had given us the slip.

I am going to tie him up and torture him until he agrees to stop being a spoiled man-baby.

"No. He's *definitely* at Al's Beef," I mumbled.

Mindy had been the one to discover his note. Apparently, he'd sent Mindy to fetch him a very specific type of sparkling water that the interviewer mentioned was sold in a vending machine on the seventeenth floor. He'd made this request while Kristina was using the bathroom, Wren was wrapping up facilitating a call between the studio and the interviewer, and I was in place on the ground floor, waiting for the limo to return to the loading dock.

The note had read simply, "BRB."

That's right. Cyrus had written, "BRB," as in "Be Right Back."

"Damn it," Mindy muttered under her breath, and I sent her a sympathetic look.

"It's not your fault." I reached for her hand and gave it a reassuring squeeze. "I'm the one who put my foot down, I'm the one who said he couldn't go."

"It's both your faults, and my fault. But mostly, it's Cyrus's fault," Wren cut in, her voice blunt but not harsh. "Looks like there are six Al's Beef locations in Chicago. Let's split up—Beth, catch." She tossed me the keys to a loaner car. One of the producers from today's interview had offered the use of his vehicle when we'd realized Cyrus was missing.

"Mindy, you go with Beth. Kristina and I will take the limo. I'll text you the addresses of the three Al's Beef locations for you to check, we'll take the other three. Check in every twenty minutes by text with a status update."

"Got it." I took a hard left toward the stairway to the underground garage where the producer had said his car was parked, Mindy on my heels. Kristina and Wren continued straight, I assumed toward the loading dock where the limo still waited.

"Come on, let's go." I glanced behind me when I didn't hear Mindy's heels clicking on the linoleum.

She'd taken off her shoes and held them tucked under her arm. I took a second to do the same, and then we were off, jogging down the stairs and out the door. I pressed the remote as soon as we made it to the garage and then heard the chirp of a car alarm. Quickly slipping our shoes back on, we followed the sound and soon stood in front of a Honda minivan.

Mindy snorted. "At least we'll be safe."

I looked at her.

"Minivans are the safest cars on the road for passengers. Instead of an SUV, the studio should bulletproof minivans."

"Yeah, I can just see Mr. Hotstuff pulling up to a club in a minivan," I groused as I walked to the driver's side and opened the door.

Mindy caught my eye as we both slid into our seats, and I gave her a conciliatory smile. "Sorry. I'm just . . . in a bad mood."

"Why are you in a bad mood all the time?" Mindy mumbled the question as she buckled her seat belt. "And what can I do to help?"

I shook my head, only giving myself a split second behind my closed lids before starting the car. "It's—it's nothing. Let's just go."

I felt her eyes study me as I pulled out of the parking garage before she asked, "Are you sure? Being stressed isn't good for your health, nor are month-long bad moods."

I nodded, swallowing around an odd tightness in my throat. She was right. I couldn't go on like this. I couldn't cling to my frustration like a life preserver and hope it would see me through.

Do you want to know the truth about my bad mood? Like a naïve, infatuated teenager, I'd felt incredibly jealous of Cyrus and Ingrid—Ingrid being the gorgeous redhead in the teal outfit—at the club all those weeks ago.

That night, I'd recognized the feeling immediately since I had previous experience with the aching, nauseating burn that had set up camp in my esophagus and the cold, empty sensation in my stomach.

Like the rest of my reactions to Cyrus, this one had also been overblown and had made me feel nuttier than a squirrel's winter stash of acorns. But there it was. I'd been jealous. So. Jealous.

Cyrus had eventually stopped the forward momentum of Ingrid's fingertips by plucking them from his leg and bringing the back of her hand to his mouth. He'd then pressed his lips lightly against her knuckles, holding her eyes like she was the only person who existed. I'd felt my nails dig into the vinyl of the booth on either side of my legs while my brain caught on fire.

I'd been so jealous, I couldn't stop staring at Ingrid's hand and imagining my knife sticking out of the back of it.

Yep. *That* kind of jealous. I didn't stab the woman, obviously. But I'd imagined the hell out of it. And then I'd imagined me stabbing Cyrus's hand, and that's when I knew I needed to get a grip. Avoiding Wren's gaze, I'd excused myself from the table to go switch positions with Mindy.

I'd been, in a word, ridiculous. I'd witnessed him lavish the same sort of affection on Mindy and Wren and Nicole. I'd seen him kiss Craig's hand more times than I could count. Not that any of those details mattered anyway because I had no right to feel jealous in the first place!

But in my defense, I'd been tied up in knots on the drive over too, just as soon as Wren had agreed to switch me and Mindy's usual positions. My immediate reaction to the switch had been excited nonsense, my thoughts veering into the unhinged territory of, *If I'm on the floor with Cyrus, then he'll have to dance with me at some point, even if it's accidental.*

Irritation with myself soon followed for obvious reasons, not the least of which was the fact that I was working. This was my *job*. I wasn't supposed to be excited by the prospect of possibly dancing with my client. I was supposed to be focused on keeping him safe.

But then he'd reached for my hand as soon as we'd exited the car that night, and he'd whispered in my ear, *Stay close to me.*

My insides had turned to jelly. Hot, molten jelly.

The softly spoken command combined with his fingers twisting with mine had cast some sort of spell, I swear. Concerns about professionalism flew the coop and I let him lead me around while images of us dancing together *not* accidentally filled my vision with silly—and sexy—hopes.

BUT THEN, and this is the part that really greases my goose, within a half hour of telling me to stay close to him, he turns his back to me in the booth and gets handsy with Ingrid.

Or rather, Ingrid was handsy with him. They didn't kiss or anything, not that I saw. And they didn't dance together. Cyrus hadn't danced that night, actually. We ended up leaving early and—whatever. It doesn't matter.

He'd encouraged her to touch him. He didn't push her advances away. And so I'd spent the whole night trying to douse the forest fire of inexplicable jealousy in my head and berating myself for being so completely idiotic and irrational.

But the thing is, I should've known. What had I been thinking, huh? That he *liked* me? That there was a cold chance in hell Cyrus wanted to date me? That I'd ever date my client?

Unhinged. That's what I'd been, I'd been unhinged by his magnetism. But I didn't blame Cyrus.

I blamed myself.

Cyrus is a movie star. I've watched anyone and everyone fall under his magic spell over and over. No one was immune. Why had my brain thought a touch of his hand and a whispered request meant anything at all? He touched plenty of hands. He whispered to plenty of people.

The only thing that made me special was that he rarely wished to do either with me.

And I guess that's why I didn't care about the persistence of my bad mood. Staying in a bad mood helped me see clearly. It protected me from his supernatural sexiness so I could focus on my job.

"Turn left there." Mindy pointed to the light two blocks away, pulling me out of my angry ruminations.

I switched lanes so I could make a left, and I saw the sign for Al's Beef at the corner. As soon as I turned, I pulled up to the curb and parked in the thirty-minute load/unload spot.

"Run in and let me know if you see him," I said. "I'll text Wren."

"I see him."

My head snapped up. "What?"

"He's right there, in the window." Mindy pointed toward the storefront, and I followed the line made by her finger.

Sure enough, there sat Cyrus at a high-top table along the window, munching away.

My vision clouded with red. In case I haven't made it clear yet, I had a bad temper. Thankfully, I rarely lost it. I was close to losing it now.

"Please text Wren and let her know," I said. "Tell her we'll meet her back at the loading dock in fifteen minutes or less." I blinked several times and breathed in and out to clear my head while Mindy's thumbs flew over the keypad of her phone.

I gave myself until the count of five to calm down, then I checked my mirror for traffic before opening the door. Smoothing my skirt, I stood from the car, closed the door, locked it once Mindy had exited, and walked unhurriedly into Al's Beef. Studying the intersection, I made note of the bus passing by that had a huge banner ad for *Asmodeus Falls* on its side, Cyrus's face plastered at the center of it.

"Ah! There she is, my hero." Cyrus's cheerful words greeted us as soon as we entered the restaurant.

I scanned the interior, tallied the customers, did a quick threat assessment, made a list of the exits, and kept an eye on the hall leading to the bathrooms.

"I've ordered for you," Cyrus said, standing from his stool at the window. "But where are Wren and Kristina?"

"You ordered for us?" Mindy studied the long, high-top table along the window, likely counting the number of full bags in front of empty stools.

"Of course. Didn't you get my note?"

"Yes. BRB." Mindy looked at me as though to confirm our mutual understanding of his message. "Be right back."

"No. No, no." Cyrus's mischievous eyes slid to mine. Held. His dimple winked at me. Taunting. "BRB meant, Bathsheba Requires Beef."

A short, shocked laugh burst out of Mindy and she smacked a hand over her mouth.

Meanwhile, Cyrus and I swapped stares. His was paired with a friendly grin heavily shaded with rascally delight. Mine was paired with absolutely nothing but quiet rage.

"Oh my God, Cyrus," Mindy said, still fighting laughter. "I don't know what we're going to do with you. You are so—"

"Thoughtful? I know you don't like sausage, so I ordered you a regular beef with peppers and fries. I thought Kristina would like that too, and I got an Italian sausage for Wren. And, Beth, *Mausbär* . . ." Cyrus turned to me, eyes dancing, a satisfied smile still curving his alluring and irreverent mouth. "I ordered you a combo beef and sausage. That's what I'm having, too. It's my favorite."

Despite having no idea what *Mausbär* meant, I was also smiling. Otherwise, I was going to scream at Cyrus Malcom in front of ten customers and four food service workers—assuming no one was in the bathroom. Sometimes, guarding him felt like trying to put socks on a rooster. Not that I'd ever tried, but you know what I mean.

Wearing my hostile smile like a shield, I walked over to the bag he'd gestured to last, picked up his *favorite* lunch, and I strolled to the trash can. And then, turning to face him so he could see my smile, I dumped it in the garbage.

Just like when I'd informed him that we wouldn't be going to Al's Beef because he hadn't requested it be added to the agenda in time, Cyrus's eyelids drooped, his stare growing somehow both cold and hot at once.

"There," I said lightly, dusting my hands together cheerfully. "All done. Thanks so much. Let's pack the rest of this up so we can get going. I'll wait outside."

CHAPTER 11

CYRUS

"High thoughts must have high language."

— ARISTOPHANES, *THE FROGS AND OTHER PLAYS*

~Mid to late October~

"I thought she was going to murder you right there." Mindy wiped tears of hilarity from beneath her eyes and pointed at me. "I mean, how she kept it together, I'll never know. I was honestly terrified for you."

I smiled good-naturedly at Mindy's uncontrollable laughter and swirled the wine in my glass. Mindy wasn't the only one laughing, but she was laughing the loudest.

"What'd you do next?" Brody—one half of my former security detail— stared across the table at me. He might've been on the edge of his seat. Kamar, the other half, had called and canceled, at home with a cold.

"What could I do?" I shrugged at the memory. "I left the restaurant with Beth and Mindy. We returned the borrowed car, Wren picked us up, and we went to the hotel. Then, since everyone had food but Beth, I ordered her delivery of Al's Beef once I got back to my room."

Mindy gasped. "You didn't!"

I nodded, grinning, wishing I could've seen her face when she opened her hotel room door to another bag of Al's Beef. "I did."

She bent over, laughing again. "Oh my God, I did not know that! She never said a word."

I eyed the two unopened bottles of wine in the center of the table. We'd tried the three whites, had opened the grenache about fifteen minutes ago, but the cabernet and the merlot hadn't yet been touched.

"Why'd you do it?" Tamra asked, pulling my attention from the wine.

I met her frank, assessing gaze and shrugged again. "Like I said, everyone had food but her."

"No, Cyrus." She leaned forward, looking at me like I was strange. "Why'd you leave the location like that? You had to know how panicked everyone would be."

My mouth opened. It closed. I scratched my cheek, stalling, and endeavored to ignore the discomfort her question caused. Truthfully, I hadn't realized how panicked everyone would be. No announcement had been made on social media regarding my brief jaunt to Chicago. As such, there were no crowds at the building when we arrived. I hadn't even informed my good friends Rex and Abby that I'd be in town.

Likewise, walking to Al's Beef had been uneventful—a bit of a novelty, actually. It was nice, walking on my own down a city street. I'd missed it.

But mostly I found myself hesitating answering Tamra's questions because I didn't wish to admit the truth: I wasn't sure why I'd left the greenroom. It had been done on a lark, but I couldn't say that. That would make me look frivolous.

In the end, I responded with, "I wanted Al's Beef. It's a local institution." I had wanted Al's Beef, but a craving for excellent Italian beef wasn't the whole reason.

"But you could've ordered it to the interview, or—like you did later—to the hotel. Or if you'd put your foot down, Beth would've been forced to bend. You get the final say, Wren has made that perfectly clear from the beginning. And if one of us doesn't like it, we can always transfer to a new assignment. So why give them the slip?"

Once more, I struggled to answer.

"Being naughty is his love language," Kristina said from her place at my left, her eyebrows wagging at Tamra.

Good old Kristina. She, at least, hadn't been too mad at me.

Wren had been disappointed. Mindy had been bemused. But Beth . . .

I fought a smile at the memory of her livid features, the way her eyes had flashed at mine, the firmness of her words, delivered like commands, her cheeks hot, her neck flushed. Yes, it still hadn't been the right type of blush, but she'd been absolutely magnificent.

"It makes sense to me," Mindy piped up, cutting into my thoughts. "Beth doesn't talk to Cyrus ever, right? Unless it's 'Walk here,' or 'Please wait,' or 'Do you want to take I-5?' We all know this. So, in the limo, Beth *finally* talks to him. I mean, it's the longest she's ever spoken to him—as far as I've seen. Yeah, it's condescending and angry, but it's talking." Mindy picked up her wineglass and lifted it in my direction. "I think Cyrus gave us the slip because he knew Beth would be angry. And if she's angry, she's more likely to talk to him."

Studying my wine, I arranged my features into a mask of angelic confusion to hide the increased tempo of my heart and the twist of discomfort in my stomach. *Uh oh.* What have we here?

Mindy had struck a nerve.

"Why haven't I ever met Beth?" Brody asked. "She's never come to wine club. Why not? The rest of you do."

"That's a good question." Tamra's gaze shifted back to me. "What's going on with you two? What happened?"

"How do you mean?" Further cementing my outward projection of innocent bewilderment, I met Tamra's examining stare.

"She means, why doesn't she like you, boss," Brody filled in, pouring himself another glass of the grenache.

"I think you're asking the wrong question." Mindy placed her gossipy elbows on the table and leaned forward, her voice dropping conspiratorially. "I think what we should be asking is how Cyrus feels about Beth, and why, if he doesn't like being told what to do, he hasn't asked the studio to—"

"She walked in on me naked," I blurted.

The table fell into a stunned silence.

A half breath later, chaos.

I rolled my lips between my teeth, my heart now galloping, but not due to what I'd just said. The blame for my sudden arrythmia rested on the tiny shoulders of that gossip, Mindy, and what she'd been on the precipice of exposing. Perhaps Beth opening door number one to reveal me in my birthday suit wasn't the only topic that would've redirected the conversation quickly, but it was the first thing that popped into my mind.

What?

I panicked.

"Cyrus!" Tamra leaned forward suddenly, her gaze immediately chastising.

"She did. It happened." I lifted my palms up. "I was the innocent party in this scenario, minding my own business, stepping out of the shower. I'd just grabbed the towel, and in walks Beth."

Mindy, now sitting up straight, hit the dining room table with her palm, her eyes hungry for information. "Wait. When was this?"

"July," I said, like it was no big deal. Because it wasn't. It was ages ago. Water under the bridge. I hadn't thought about it *at all*, or what might've happened if she'd agreed to join me. And I especially didn't fantasize about it at night, or while Beth drove us around town and I sat behind her staring at her hair and neck.

Denial. Not just a 2016 film about Holocaust deniers.

"Oh my gosh!" Mindy sucked in a shocked breath, her fingers coming to her mouth. "And you two have been keeping this a secret *all this time*?"

"Calm down. I knew it happened," Tamra said, her admission surprising me.

"You did?" I turned toward her. Now I was hungry for information. "Beth told you? What'd she say?"

"No, she didn't tell me. I was there, I watched it happen. You didn't lock the door or even shut it all the way. It could've been any one of us."

I felt myself deflate. "She didn't talk to you about it?"

"No. She never brought it up after it happened." Tamra shook her head, a small smile on her lips. "Maybe it didn't make much of an impression."

My eyes narrowed. *Et tu, Tamra?*

"She told me," Wren said, immediately drawing my interest.

The security team lead had been quiet for the entire evening, seemingly content to listen and allow me to relate my version of events from the Chicago trip without any added commentary. I'd almost forgotten she was in the room. But now she had my undivided attention.

"When?" I demanded. "When did she tell you?"

"She told me the day it happened. She wanted to make sure I was aware."

Irritation flared in my chest, but I kept my features bland. "Ah. She *reported* the *incident*."

"Exactly." Her gaze felt more watchful than usual. "She's very professional."

"Yes. I know." I struggled against the urge to roll my eyes. *Don't remind me.*

"Well," Mindy said, "there's only one thing to do."

I inspected her before asking, "What's that?"

"Now he gets to see her naked," Mindy replied, earning her a top spot on my favorite person list.

"What?" Tamra shrieked, her lips curled down in distaste. "No, he doesn't!"

"He does. Those are the rules." Mindy sighed at her own statement, sounding resigned.

"And rules are meant to be followed," I added helpfully while nodding sagely.

Tamra slid her glare to me. "Aren't you the one who always says rules are meant to be broken?"

"No. Nope. I would never say that."

Mindy leaned forward, interrupting us. "The rule is, if she accidentally saw him naked, he gets to see her naked. That's the *Friends* rule, as established in 'The One With the Boobies' episode where Chandler sees—"

"I never watched that show." Tamra flicked her wrist as though batting Mindy's argument aside.

"Doesn't matter." Mindy shrugged. "Rules are rules."

"Not for coworkers," Tamra argued, jabbing her index finger at the table. "The show was called *Friends*, not *Coworkers*."

"We're all sorta friends too, though. Right?" Mindy glanced around the room, appealing to each person.

The beseeching in Mindy's gaze made me chuckle, but then Wren caught my eye. Her expression, steady and somber, latched onto mine. I stilled. Her eyes narrowed. My eyes widened. Her eyebrows ticked up.

Hmm.

If I was reading her correctly, she looked displeased. Her stare seemed to caution something like, uh . . . extreme prudence?

Now, on the one hand, I wasn't the cautionary or prudent type. Or I'd never been in the past.

But on the other hand, Wren rarely—if ever—chastised me, though I knew I made her job extremely difficult. She'd always been excessively fair, navigating my antics with patience, creativity, and a certain sanguinity I found calming. She was sensitive to how easily I might feel trapped and confined by a twenty-four-hour security detail. I did feel confined, but only rarely. I credited Wren's even handling, wisdom, and open mind for this experience being tolerable.

Basically, I trusted Wren and her judgment, and if she thought it would be in my best interest to make an outward show of prudence, I would.

"Uh, Tamra is right," I said, still holding Wren's gaze, watching for microchanges in her expression to ensure my words were the right ones. "We are, first and foremost, coworkers."

Wren gave me a subtle nod.

I continued. "We shouldn't be discussing Beth without her being present. It's . . . disrespectful."

Wren glanced down at her glass of water, but she wore a smile. Just a little bitty one.

I breathed a quiet sigh of relief, feeling like I'd passed a test, and glanced around the table.

Tamra looked impressed. Craig seemed confused. Brody was thoughtful. And Mindy wore a frown.

"That's very sweet of you, Cyrus," Kristina said, patting my hand and giving me an approving smile. "And he's right. None of us would want to be discussed behind our backs."

"But we didn't say anything bad about Beth," Mindy protested.

"You called her condescending." Tamra lifted an eyebrow.

"But she was!" Mindy looked to Kristina for support. "I didn't mean it in a bad way. We all love Beth. Beth is the best."

"I know. But nevertheless, a change of subject would be, uh, prudent." I lifted my glass and took a sip, impressed with my ability to feign good judgment while doing improv and making a convincing case for restraint at the same time.

Honestly, I didn't know I had it in me.

Mid-October brought more travel. I'd never enjoyed work travel in the past, and thus avoided it as much as possible. But I found myself looking forward to these fall trips with a surprising level of anticipation.

Trapped together on a private jet or in a luxury home with six beautiful women? Sometimes life is so unfair.

Of course, one of these women—the most beautiful in my opinion—spoke just one or two words at a time, never laughed or smiled at my jokes, and only ever looked at me in order to administer a disapproving glare. But on the plus side, she did look at me. So that's progress, right?

Yeah, no.

I had no chance there.

Surprised by my graceful capitulation? Don't be. What was that saying everyone misattributed to Einstein? *The definition of insanity is doing the same thing over and over again and expecting a different result.*

I am not one of those insane men who believed in toxic concepts such as "wearing a woman down" or "if I'm douchey and pushy enough, she'll eventually say yes out of pity." My mother had been pursued by such men after my father died and the number of evasive maneuvers she'd been forced to employ as a wealthy, beautiful young widow made my avoidance of parasitic Hollywood retinue look like child's play.

Bathsheba Ryan did not, and would never, have any interest in me romantically. I knew it. I'd accepted it—weeks ago at this point—and I'd made my peace with it. That said, hearts are stupid. So are penises. And the main thing (other than being stupid) that hearts and penises have in common is hoping when doing so is the definition of insanity.

I did, admittedly, struggle with her dearth of friendly feelings toward me. I liked Beth. A lot. And not just for her sexy competence and confidence. Sometimes, when she didn't realize I was nearby—or if she did, maybe she forgot?—she'd drop her guard and chat with the rest of the team. On the jet, in limos, in hotel rooms while I read quietly through scripts or checked email. These moments of shameless eavesdropping felt like spying on precious gifts meant for someone else.

Sometimes she'd say something absolutely hilarious, like a colloquialism that felt faintly familiar to me, and I'd have to struggle to hide my laughter.

That man can strut sitting down, mumbled in reference to the actor Tom Low when he'd winked at her for a third time in one night at an industry party.

He's so honest you could shoot craps with him over the phone, cheerfully conveyed while discussing Ryaine O'Rourke's new boyfriend.

Brave as the first man who ate an oyster, said to Craig when he asked her opinion about a particularly bold fashion choice.

When or if she did notice me listening, she'd wrapped those gifts right back up.

I wasn't a bad person. Most people seemed to enjoy my company. I didn't borrow money and not pay it back. I didn't lie . . . much. I avoided topics like politics and religion in polite company. And, since Chicago, I'd been on my best behavior. I followed her agendas, I didn't make last-minute changes, I worked hard on not being late, and I'd stopped live streaming my travel plans.

So why didn't she like me?

Maybe it's my eyebrows.

Frowning, I lifted a hand to my forehead and pressed my index and middle finger to my right eyebrow, feeling the short hairs. "Craig."

"Yes?" He glanced up from his phone.

"Tell me the truth." I stood from the desk where I should've been reading but instead had been contemplating the likability of my eyebrows.

"Anything." Craig perched forward in his chair, ready to be of service.

He also sat at a desk. We were working in the office of a Brooklyn brownstone, our home for the next ten days. This would be our longest stop, a press junket paired with DarkLensCon, the convention associated with all thing DarkLens Comics. A fancy, masked Halloween masquerade would top off the week.

All six of my lovely bodyguards had traveled with us. Presently, Wren lounged nearby on a chaise reading a magazine entitled, *The Circuit*; Kristina and Mindy sat side by side in the window seat playing cards and trying not to be too obvious about their blossoming relationship; and Nicole had just departed the room to make tea.

Tamra and Beth were elsewhere in the house, probably comparing notes about being responsible and hardworking.

"What do you think of my eyebrows?" I let my hand drop. "Do I need a wax?"

"I can get one scheduled for this afternoon." He lifted his phone as though it were a magic wand and, with just a slight nod of my head, he would make my dreams come true within the hour.

"No. I'm just asking. Do I need one?"

"Go on a run, Cyrus," Wren said without looking up from her magazine.

I lifted my eyebrows at her, wondering if she'd be able to detect the movement given my lax waxing habits.

She lowered her magazine, her expression stoic. "You need to exercise. You're too much in your head."

"I worked out for two hours this morning."

She'd been with me. This brownstone had a weight room and gym in the basement. We'd spotted each other.

Wren lifted the magazine into reading position again. "It's been raining all day. You're cooped up. Tomorrow will be busy. You're having guests over tonight. Run on the treadmill or use the rowing machine. Get your excess energy out. You still have plenty of time before dinner."

"Who is this Alaric guy who's coming over tonight with the studio people?" Mindy lowered the cards in her hand to her lap.

"He's—" I tried not to grimace. I failed. "He's an old friend from high school."

"He's the CEO of Point National, was on that Fribb's compilation of the richest people under forty last year, and has been included in TMY's sexiest billionaires directory for the last three years. Don't you read the AV list?" Kristina wrinkled her nose at Mindy, though her question sounded curious and not accusing.

I grimaced even harder at Kristina's description of Alaric. She'd failed to mention he was a bossy son-of-a-bastard (literally) and enjoyed no walks on the beach, dinners in front of his computer with zero candles, and bringing up uncomfortable subjects that were certain to start an argument.

If it—whatever *it* might be—was easy, he didn't want any part of it.

"I read the AV list." Mindy selected a new card from the deck. "But I didn't read Alaric's profile past the short description where it stated he was a friend of Cyrus's from school."

The AV list to which Mindy and Kristina referred was the approved visitor list, a collection of people allowed to enter my abode or gain access to me at events without being patted down or otherwise vetted on the spot. We had one for LA, but Wren insisted we also have one wherever we traveled.

"Cyrus. Go exercise," Wren said, not looking up this time. "You'll feel better for your friend's visit. I promise."

Something about the way she said "I promise" convinced me.

Shutting my laptop, I waved goodbye and made quick work of climbing the two staircases to my room, changing into workout clothes, then taking the three staircases down to the basement. Hyping myself up for a run and doing my best not to dwell on what had occurred the last time I saw Alaric, I walked into the basement gym, and then promptly halted in my tracks.

Beth was there.

I mean, *here.*

In the gym.

Her back was to me. Which meant I was gifted the sight of her hips and ass swaying back and forth in yoga pants as she mounted—er, I mean *climbed* one of the two StairMasters.

I am both ashamed and unashamed to admit I stood just inside the doorway and stared at her bobbing ponytail and body for longer than appropriate—much, much longer—before I realized what I was doing and tore my gaze away.

Okay. Yes. Right. Don't be a smeller.

Shaking out my hands, I blinked around at the rest of the equipment, crossing off options as my eyes settled on each machine.

The treadmill was too small for the length of my legs, I wouldn't be able to hit my stride.

The rowing machine was a full body workout. My upper body needed a rest after this morning's weights.

The elliptical was a pretentious, pestiferous, whiny, bathos of a machine and should be banned from all gyms.

My gaze returned to the StairMaster next to Beth. *Is it hot in here?*

It was. It was hot. I was already sweating and I hadn't moved anything but my neck for the past fifteen minutes. Pulling my shirt off—I couldn't very well begin a workout with pit stains like a charlatan—I draped it over my shoulder and approached slowly, but with confidence. There was *nothing wrong* with me using the unoccupied StairMaster next to Beth.

Two StairMasters resided in this room, a virtual cornucopia of StairMasters for a home gym. And if they didn't want both StairMasters in use at the same time, then they would've installed just one StairMaster. Not two.

Keeping my eyes forward and ignoring Beth's bouncing next to me, I mount—I *STEPPED UP* onto the machine and pressed the On switch. It was difficult to contain my smirk when I heard the faint sound of Joan Jett's "Bad Reputation" blasting from Beth's earbuds. But before I could select my program, I sensed rather than saw Beth do a double take and then fly off her machine.

And I don't mean she left or stepped off of her own volition, I mean she was propelled against her will and fell backward in an aimless, flailing pile of limbs as a strangled, panicked sound of distress emerged just before she hit the ground.

Immediately, I jumped off my StairMaster—on purpose—and knelt next to her prostrate form, unthinkingly grabbing her shoulders to help her up. "Oh my God. Beth. Are you okay? Do you need me to—"

I didn't get to finish my thought. In the next second, she'd launched herself upward and through a complicated and impressively quick series of movements, had my face planted and my body pinned to the ground, one arm around my neck while the other held my arms behind my back.

"What's so funny? And what do you think you're doing?" She panted harshly against my ear, her earbuds dangling at the side of my face blasting Joan Jett. She must've ripped them off at some point.

"Uh . . . Exercising?" I said, not daring to move—partially because she was kinda scary, but mostly because her breasts were pressed against my forearms, her legs were straddling my thighs, and her mouth was extremely close to my neck. I didn't mind this position in the least.

And perhaps it was the position that drove me to choke out, "You could've just asked nicely, Bathsheba."

She paused, clearly confused by my statement. "Asked what nicely?"

"I didn't know you were into choking and asphyxiation play, you kinky minx. I'm happy to oblige."

Aww crud. And I'd been doing so well. *Stupid, insane penis. What a stinker.*

Her arm around my neck tightened, the tempo of her inhales increasing, and either it was my imagination—I have a good one—or she slid forward on my thighs and rocked the apex of her spread legs insistently against the curve of my ass.

"Oh yeah?" she whispered. "Where and when?"

My eyes widened.

My heart tripped.

I held my breath.

But before I could actually think or speak or *do* anything, she let me go with a frustrated-sounding growl. Beth climbed off and strolled out of the gym, not powering down her machine and not sparing me a backward glance, the faint notes of "Bad Reputation" trailing after her.

I knew for a fact she didn't look back. I watched her walk away from my place on the floor, wondering what in the name of Tyche had just happened.

CHAPTER 12

CYRUS

"If it is necessary for us to do anything [in view of peace], direct us and architect."

— ARISTOPHANES, *PEACE*

My mind in chaos, I didn't know what to think.

Flipping on the shower, I stepped under the not-quite-hot-enough spray and stared at the marble tile, reliving the events in the gym for approximately the one hundred and twelfth time.

Had Bathsheba Ryan . . . flirted? With *me*? Is that what that was? Or was that some sort of alpha female warning shot? Or maybe it was both?

How intriguing.

Whatever it was, excitement and worry took turns building their respective fortresses as I quickly showered, struggled to select the perfect attire for dinner, and then contemplated my eyebrows in the mirror.

Perhaps her behavior meant nothing. Perhaps she routinely pinned men to the floor and threatened to choke them. Or perhaps—

No. No more theories. Wait and see.

I scowled on the inside. I hated waiting. I wanted to find her and pester her until she told me what it had meant. I wanted to know now.

Instead of doing what I wanted, I focused on looking my best. As I gave more thought to the matter, tempering of expectations would likely also be wise, most especially since I had no idea what I would say to Beth when I did see her. If the past four months proved anything, it was how wretchedly inept my attempts were at engaging Bathsheba Ryan.

I practiced, mumbling possibilities to myself as I buckled my belt and gave my reflection a final perusal.

"Beth, you look stunning. As always."

I picked up my cologne, marveling at its sudden appearance on my bathroom countertop. I thought I'd forgotten it in LA, but here it was.

"Beth, *terron de azucar*, what have you been up to today? Any strangulations I should know about?"

Holding the bottle slightly away and at an angle, I attempted to achieve both light and comprehensive coverage to my skin and the fabric of my shirt at my neck.

"Beth, I want to ask you about tomorrow's agenda because I respect your opinion and value your time."

Returning the bottle to the countertop, I checked the buttons at my sleeves.

"Beth, *ma choupinette*, I'm starved. Lift your little skirt and sit on my face."

Ohhhh . . . Wouldn't that be lovely?

On a cloud of rapacious desire, my feet winged, I left my suite and attempted to imagine what she might say—what she actually might say to me—if I were to make that particular suggestion.

She'd probably slap your face.

Inexplicably, the thought drew a smile on my lips. Before today, I would never have dreamt of contemplating such a request. But then, I hadn't dreamt of offering her my neck for a choke either.

Oh yeah, about that . . .

The truth was, that offer *had* been a joke. I'd never wanted to be choked and I had no interest in asphyxiation play. In case you haven't noticed by now, I'm basically the opposite of a mullet: superfluous bravado up front, shockingly little intention or desire to back it up.

Still preoccupied by the thought of having my airway constricted by Beth's capable hands and whether or not—theoretically, purely as an academic exercise—it would be something I'd consider if choking facilitated us naked, touching, and in bed together, I didn't see her approach until she stepped in my path.

"Beth!" I stopped short, losing a bit of breath with the surprise of her sudden closeness. "H—hi. How are you?"

Oh yeah. Real nice. Smooth. Classic. You could sell T-shirts with that one.

I didn't face-palm, but I did forget to hide a grimace at my verbal clumsiness.

She didn't miss it either, her eyebrows tugging together as she inspected my face. Taking a step in the wrong direction—which was away from me—her gaze lifted no higher than my chin, and she said stiffly, "Do you have a minute? Can we talk?"

"Always."

Her eyes cut to mine and she held very still, an obvious blend of startled and perplexed swirling over her features. And perhaps a shade of discomfort?

I didn't like that.

Removing myself a short distance to give her more space, I lowered my voice and said, "Anything you want."

Her unease and surprise dissipated gradually, eclipsed by determination. After a prolonged, intoxicating moment of simply staring into my eyes, she tilted her head toward the office where I'd been working earlier in the day.

"Please," she said.

I followed as she turned to lead the way. She selected the corner furthest from the door but didn't ask me to close it as I entered, so I didn't. When she faced me again, I stole scant seconds to enjoy how exceptionally lovely she looked tonight, wearing a classic midnight blue Coco Chanel with a square neck and flared miniskirt. She'd paired it with sinfully high heels and simple pearls—around her neck and at her ears—the sight of which made my mouth water.

Joining her in our secluded corner, I considered speaking the words I'd rehearsed in the mirror earlier, specifically, *Beth, you look stunning. As always.*

Instead, I pushed my hands into my pockets and waited for her to take the lead. I didn't want to push. I wanted her to come to me, if that's what she also wanted. *I hope that's what she wants.*

Inspecting her stiff posture now, I estimated my chances were slim.

Gifting me her eyes once more, she took a deep breath. On the exhale, her shoulders seemed to sag. "I'm sorry," she said, her tone soft and contrite, laced with guilt and shame, her stare suspiciously glassy.

I frowned, immediately concerned, shuffling closer to her. "What's wrong?"

She was sorry? What for? Looking like a dream? Possessing the voice of an angel and the strength of a mini-Hercules?

"I'm sorry I tackled you in the gym and—" Her mouth snapped shut, the muscles at her jaw and temple jumping before she finished with, "And everything. It—*I* was extremely inappropriate. I don't want to add additional stress to our professional relationship, and I'm so sorry."

Professional.

She was distressed and I wasn't sure what to do with that word. It kept popping up. I hated when she used it, or applied it to herself, or when others —like Wren—applied it to her. At a loss, I stared at her and said nothing, wishing I could do something, anything, to assure her that she needn't worry about being professional with me. I didn't want it.

Beth shifted her weight from one foot to the other when my silence persisted but otherwise waited for my verdict with calm stoicism.

Hmm.

"And you want . . ." I said, not knowing I was about to speak until the words emerged. I'd begun the thought, I decided I should finish it. "And you want to be professional? With me?"

"Yes. Obviously."

"Obviously," I rasped around several dusty rocks that had abruptly lodged themselves in my throat. Leaning back on my heels, I absorbed this news. It was old news. Nevertheless, given the events in the gym, disappointment pinged around my chest like a pinball in an arcade machine, leaving little bruises in its wake.

But had I truly expected any different? No. Not really.

Sucking in a deep breath, I ignored the little bruises left behind by the pinball of disappointment. My stupid, insane heart had wished for something impossible.

And yet I told myself this interaction was still good news. Beth was looking at me up close, her gaze open, not shuttered and glaring from behind her fortress of solitude or scowling and impatient across her field of fucks-not-given. She was speaking in full sentences, her voice soft, belying vulnerability. Perhaps, with a lot of luck, she could, one day, possibly, grow to not loathe my presence.

Who knows? Maybe she'd give me an indulgent wave at a red carpet event ten years from now when I caught her eye.

"Hey." Beth shifted her weight again, stirring me from my reflections. "I really am sorry."

An achy, dry laugh tumbled out of me. "You're always apologizing to me," I said, wearing a careless smile. "I wish you wouldn't. I'm never angry with you. You never upset me."

Beth blinked once. Hard. Like I'd just spoken gibberish.

"You're extremely professional," I continued, hoping these words would make more sense to her. "You're exceptional. I respect you a great deal. And you have nothing to be sorry for."

"But I am sorry. So sorry." Staring at me, her chest rose and fell. She shifted a few inches closer. "Listen, I know we got off to a rocky start, and—and we haven't clicked, not like you have with the rest of the team. I blame myself for that. I should've transferred right away given how uncomfortable I make you, and if you want me to transfer now—"

"Wait. Stop." On impulse, I reached out and gripped her hand. "You make me uncomfortable? Why do—why would you think that?"

"Cyrus." She gave me a look like, *come on.*

I mock-mimicked her expression, causing her to huff.

"Fine. You don't feel safe with me," she whispered harshly, her green eyes liquid. "After what I did to you that night, you don't. And I get it."

I choked, no strangulation required. "That is not true. I told you before and I meant it, I did not feel violated or unsafe with you that night. Believe me. And I do feel safe with you now. Excessively safe. Too safe. You take your job and professionalism so seriously, I'm constantly concerned you might start a bodyguard-based religion."

"I don't believe you. Why else—" She huffed again, it sounded anxious, and her gaze flickered to our joined fingers. "Why else are you comfortable with every member of this team except me?"

"But can't the same be said about you?" I hypothesized out loud and then stepped into her space unthinkingly. "You're comfortable with everyone but me."

Perhaps I did it to prove a point, perhaps to test a theory of which I hadn't been fully conscious. I don't know why I took that step. It was a thoughtless movement.

And it changed everything.

I saw and felt her stiffen at my advance, heard her breath catch twice before her respiration increased in speed, watched her eyes widen. Her mouth opened. It closed. Her lashes fluttered. And then—with a fair amount of disbelief—I witnessed a faint blush of pink warm her cheeks. The *right* kind of blush.

Wait a minute.

My eyes moved between hers, searching, searching.

Her back connected with the bookcase. "I—I'm not the one who needs to be guarded. My safety isn't what's important, my comfort is—is—" The breathlessness of her words betrayed her, and my stupid, insane heart couldn't have been more surprised.

My penis, however, was ready to throw a party.

Wait a whole damn minute.

I couldn't believe what I was seeing, and I didn't know where to look first. If any sound existed in the room or beyond it, it faded to nothing as I stared at her, dawning realization striking me like a hammer to the temple.

She wants me.

And not alpha-cave-woman-choking want, or whatever that business was in the gym earlier. This was altogether different, and I would bet my future Best Actor Oscar that her feelings weren't new. She *struggled.*

Dazed, my stunned attention drifted to the necklace she wore. Gazing at the rapid rise and fall of her chest, I had the baffling urge to lower my mouth to her neck and suck one of the pearls into my mouth.

"Cyrus."

My eyes jumped to hers, pulled there by the unmistakable pleading in her voice.

At some point I must've backed her against the bookshelf and filled my hands with her hips. Our bodies were pressed together from thigh to chest. Her arms, however, were limp at her sides.

"Do you want me, Beth?" I asked, craving her response, starving for it.

She closed her eyes, the crown of her head connecting with the shelf at her back. Since she'd taken her eyes from me, I bent and brushed my lips against her skin along the edge of her necklace. She shivered and whimpered.

Fucking glorious.

"Cyrus, please," she said, more breathless pleading fueling my certainty, her hands finally lifting to my shoulders, her nails digging into the fabric there, her palms spreading sumptuous warmth through my entire body.

Was I dreaming? She felt amazing. Her instantaneous responsiveness— just this—felt divine. Her touch heat and heaven. I wanted her hands everywhere.

"Because I want you," I said, sliding my nose along the column of her throat, boldly inhaling her, and grinning when her breath hitched again.

The involuntary sounds of her restraint were beautiful music. I considered saying the other words I'd practiced in the mirror, specifically, *Beth,* ma choupinette, *I'm starved. Lift your little skirt and sit on my face.*

Would she slap me? Or would she obey? I very much wanted to find out.

But then her arms went rigid, and she said, "This isn't serious. You're never serious."

I slid a hand to the small of her back and pressed her body more intimately against mine, wanting her to feel how tremendously serious this was to me. She rewarded me with another sharp inhale.

"You could have me, you know." I kissed the base of her throat, her skin was so hot and soft and *tasty*. "Whenever you want."

She gave her head a jerky shake. "Never going to happen." The effect of her words was ruined as she moaned.

Giving in to the earlier impulse, I tongued one of the pearls on her necklace and therefore the surrounding skin. My hips rolling against hers, I found her hands on my shoulders and peeled them off, threading our fingers together and pressing the backs of her knuckles against the books.

"I'll leave my door unlocked at night," I whispered, just for her. "And I sleep naked. If you wanted, I'd be a very, very good boy for you."

Another gorgeous whimper slipped past her lips, igniting me from the inside. Her entire body vibrated, her small fingers opening and closing around my larger ones where I held her captive. But we both knew I didn't hold her captive. If she wanted, she could have me on the floor in a heartbeat.

I nipped at her jaw and chin, kissing and biting, kissing and biting. Teasing. Tasting. It wasn't enough, not nearly enough. What I really wanted was her mouth, but I needed her to give me something first, more than her body's instinctive responses and involuntary sounds.

I wanted words.

I wanted participation.

I wanted explicit enthusiastic permission.

I wanted her to admit it.

"Say it." I tongued the little pearl adorning her ear. "I want you to say it."

I felt her teetering. I felt her body begin to melt, to surrender, to lean and seek and press. My mouth watered in anticipation and my mind worked through several immediate possibilities should she consent.

I could slip a hand between her legs and touch her, stroke her, make her come with just my fingers. Holding her eyes. Watching her fall apart while she struggled to keep it together would certainly be a cherished memory. I hoped she'd be loud, but I suspected she wouldn't. I suspected she'd be miserly with her sounds, keep them to herself, and not share.

She'd make me work hard for them and reward me sparingly. I couldn't wait.

For maybe the first time in my life, the thought of hard work filled me with delirious anticipation, and I'd just released her hand to slide my palm down the heavenly length of her arm, preparing to put my plan into action just as soon as she said the words, when the doorbell rang.

Beth's eyes flew open and locked with mine, frantic. And that felt like a slap.

Her body became a wall of granite in the span of a single second. She twisted her hand out of my hold and snatched her arm away. Pushing my chest—not forcefully, but rather insistently—she ducked to the side, slipped past, and made it as far as the center of the room before Mindy poked her head into the office.

"There you guys are. We've been looking for you."

Slowly, because I wasn't capable of quick movements at present, I turned toward Mindy's voice, leaned my back against the bookshelf with all the nonchalance of a man with a penis who'd been hastily preparing for a party, and folded my hands in front of my groin.

Mindy's eyes flickered between Beth and me several times, her smile waning. "What's going on?"

"We were—we were just—" Beth twisted at the waist and made a vague gesture in my direction. "We were, uh, just—"

Oh for God's sake.

"Bathsheba, my hero, wanted to review this week's agenda, *again*," I lied, smoothly and convincingly, pitching my tone perfectly between bored and impatient. "You know how protective she is after saving my life from that lethal scallop dip. Mindy, make her stop. I already promised I won't request changes at the last minute." And because I was feeling lucky, I added, "Tell her I will be a very good boy for her."

I'm probably going to hell for that last bit. Worth it.

"Cyrus has been and will be a very good boy for you, Beth." Mindy stepped fully into the office and crossed her arms, leveling her teammate with an imploring gaze. "He's been a dream, recently. Be nice to him."

I watched as Beth twisted her fingers, her hair dancing around her shoulders and back as she nodded. "You're right. Sorry. You're right. He—he has been extremely considerate."

Mindy sent me a proud smile. My heart was beating too quickly to return it, my mind too full of wishes that might be granted if only Mindy would exit ASAP.

But then Beth announced, "I will leave him alone. Starting now."

It required a moment—what with the lack of blood in my brain—but once Beth's words landed, I took a reflexive step toward her. It was too late. She was fast and nimble and escaped the room before I'd managed to put my foot down. For the second time in one day, she left me staring after her, and she didn't look back.

This is hell. . . Still worth it.

"Your friend is here," Mindy said, reminding me I wasn't alone. "He's on the patio. And a few other guests arrived too. The people from DarkLens and WWS, I think. Everyone is waiting for you."

"Oh." I spoke through murk and fog. "Great."

She snorted a short laugh. "You don't sound excited."

I didn't bother to force a smile. I wasn't excited.

Now, I'd have to wait. Wait until small talk ended, wait until appetizers, dinner, and dessert were finished, wait to steal Beth away and finish some version of what we'd started. Or wait for everyone to leave.

How I loathed waiting.

CHAPTER 13

CYRUS

"Hunger knows no friend but its feeder."

— ARISTOPHANES

Beth wasn't on the heated patio with everyone else. Alaric was. And he smirked when he spotted me.

Since the one person I wished to converse with wasn't an option, I heaved a long-suffering sigh dusted with a modicum of self-pity and strolled over to my friend.

He looked at me. I looked at him. I spoke first.

"I hate that tie on you. It does nothing for your eyes, and it's the wrong width for the number of buttons on your jacket."

His smirk stretched into a grin. "Cyrus."

"Alaric."

He opened his arms. I sighed again, but I hugged him. He was a good hugger, didn't give excessive and forceful pats on the back, and didn't mind when I rested my head on his shoulder. He was the right height for it too. And he had nice shoulders.

I'd learned the term *Mausbär* from him. Sophomore year of high school, he'd returned from a summer-long exchange program in Germany with a number of interesting words. Most teenagers collected foreign language expletives for their repertoire. I preferred international terms of endearment.

129

Call a man *tonto del culo* and he'll punch you in the face. Call a man *terron de azucar* and he'll either frown with confusion, back off in fear (and confusion), or blush with delight. What can I say? I'm a lover, not a fighter.

Speaking of lovers, the last time Alaric and I spent any time together, he did nothing but give me *mierda* about my choices in women, which might've been why I was feeling so cranky toward him now. We'd been attending a charity ball with our other close friend from high school, Rex McMurtry. For all you football fans in the audience, yes, that Rex, defensive end for the Chicago Squalls, philanthropist, and cuddly Mausbär. Rex had married another friend of mine just last year and—honestly—they were so nauseatingly perfect together, I'd stopped dropping by their place in Chicago when I visited for work.

"You look great," Alaric said as he pulled away, earning some brownie points.

"I am great," I said, scanning the heated patio, searching for Beth. "How have you been?"

If he said anything but *great,* I was calling shenanigans.

I know I'm not supposed to have favorites, but between you and me, I preferred Rex to Alaric on the principle of the matter. We'd all grown up together and had supported each other through thick and thin. In Alaric's case, his had been the thickest. It's hard to root for someone who's lived a charmed existence and always gets whatever he wants.

Relative to the rest of his life, Alaric's high school experience had been an awkward and unlucky time for him: valedictorian of our class, state championship winning QB of our football team for three years in a row, prom king. *How he suffered.*

Whereas Rex was the strong and silent type, humble and hardworking, a man of few words but many clever ideas. Luck hadn't always been on Rex's side, but he managed to pull through with grace and an attitude of gratitude. He reminded me a bit of Beth, actually. Except their height. He was six-foot-six. Beth would've looked Hobbit-sized next to him.

But I digress.

"I'm well," Alaric said, probably an understatement. "You're in New York for work?"

"Yes." I scanned the other guests present again and gave three or four of the not-Beths waves and smiles. "My job is very complicated and important, I wouldn't want to confuse you with the details."

"Try me." Alaric sipped his whiskey or bourbon or whatever he had in his glass without ice or other accoutrements. Probably whiskey. He'd become a bit of a snob about it.

"Well, let's see." I rubbed my chin and made a show of putting on my thinking cap. "How to put this in language you'll be able to grasp."

A rumbly chuckle shook out of him like spare change. My statement was funny because Alaric was stupid-smart. He'd left Alenbach and gone on to be the top of the class and top of the world in everything he attempted. His accomplishments would've irritated me if I didn't love him so much.

"I've missed you," he said, setting his hand on my shoulder and squeezing it with affection.

I grunted noncommittally but smiled at his dumb, handsome face. "Come on, I'll introduce you to people."

"Only people you like." He hung back and narrowed his eyes at me, waiting for my promise.

"Fine, fine." That would cut the introductions in half. "Follow me."

The DarkLens people were very interested in talking to their counterparts, I mostly left them alone to chat even though there were several I found enjoyable. I avoided the WWS folks, but not because I didn't like them. Their group was comprised mostly of producers who would be *very* interested in talking to Alaric about investment opportunities. They weren't unlikable, simply business focused in this setting and therefore boring.

He already knew Craig and Boris, and so I introduced Alaric to each of my bodyguards in turn, careful to maintain their cover stories. The looks of appreciation sent his way by several of the DarkLens and WWS members were impossible to miss as we completed the rounds. I would've rolled my eyes at how Nicole's had lingered on his broad shoulders, but I didn't want to strain myself.

Beth wandered onto the patio just as I'd finished introducing Wren to Alaric, my heart jumping to my throat at the sight of her. Wren's friendly but ultimately tepid interest in my old friend had been highly amusing—that *never* happened, people typically fell all over themselves with him—so when I escorted Alaric to Beth, I was in high spirits.

Also, simply looking at her put me in a good mood. I loved how she carried herself. I loved her quiet confidence and calm focus when I wasn't actively trying to get a rise out of her. For the record, I also loved getting a rise out of her.

To my astonishment, she didn't avoid my eyes as we approached; to my delight, her cheeks turned the most resplendent shade of peony pink and she didn't look away; and to no one's surprise, my thoughts turned decidedly lustful as I imagined how the color might deepen when I lay her beneath me, spread her wide, and—

"Beth Ryan?" Alaric's guessing of her name drew my attention. He frowned, then smiled, his expression quizzical. He offered her his hand.

"That's me." She slipped her fingers into his for a handshake that felt just a little bit too long. When she reclaimed her hand, she pressed her palm against the side of her glass.

Alaric stepped back, his eyes moving down and then up Beth's body in a movement that took me by surprise, but that looked completely compulsory. If it hadn't looked compulsory, I would've punched him in the face and demanded pistols at dawn.

"Wow," he said, his dark brown eyebrows arching high. "*You* grew up."

I stiffened.

Wait. *What?*

"I—who—you know her? How do you know her?" I demanded.

As he was prone to do, my good friend glanced at me like I was silly. "The same way you do."

I drew myself up. "I doubt that."

"No." He laughed. "It's true."

"Oh, really?" I placed a hand on my hip. "So you're telling me your agent set you up on a blind date with an actress and Beth showed up instead, suffering from a drug interaction that you were partially responsible for since you sent her a bottle of wine as an apology for being late after visiting Vinny Kowfry in rehab?"

Alaric didn't try to hide his confusion. "Pardon?"

"Ah ha!" My index finger shot through the air like a spear between us, a physical representation of having successfully made my point. "See? I didn't think so."

"No, Cyrus. This is *Beth Ryan*." Alaric said her name like it was meant to jog a very specific memory. "Her sister is Gabrielle Morales."

Unease shot down my spine. I remembered that name. "Gabrielle Morales," I echoed. *Sister?* The heated patio was suddenly too hot. *Mierda.*

"Yes. You remember Gabi, right? Tall, dark brown hair. You two dated . . ."

My eyes cut to Beth's. She wasn't glaring at me, but she did seem to be watching me closely, which might've been worse.

"Yes, of course I remember," I said around a very dry tongue, a spreading heat creeping up my neck and cheeks and—

No.

Oh. My. God.

Blushing.

Me. I was *blushing*. From *embarrassment*. I couldn't recall the last time this had happened. Maybe kindergarten?

Clearing my throat of the aggressive anxiety holding an impromptu Tupperware party there, I mustered all the skills I possessed as an actor. "Yes. I remember Gabi," I said firmly. "But we didn't date. We were friends senior year."

Beth continued to study me intently, saying nothing, content to watch me squirm.

How was it possible that I didn't know this? I'd basically memorized the file Wren had given me on Beth all those months ago, but it hadn't mentioned anything of her history before college.

I did remember Gabrielle Morales. She'd been so sweet. A good friend, I'd thought. Then she'd tried to kiss me after we'd gone to the movies, causing embarrassment and awkwardness to plague our friendship until graduation. I suspected it was providence and payback for me. I'd done almost the exact same thing—tried to kiss a good friend I had feelings for—in one of my earlier high school years.

Alaric glanced between Beth and me, a stupid little smile spreading over his big stupid face. "You didn't know Beth was Gabi's sister?"

"I mean . . ." I peeked at Beth, wondering if this surprise reveal was a new providence and payback for some evil deed of mine yet to be committed.

But she was also smiling. At me. Like she thought I was cute. Clearly, I'd entered an alternate universe when I'd mounted that StairMaster this afternoon. I hope I never left it.

"They—you have two different last names and look nothing alike," I said, unable to look away from her smile.

Beth took mercy on me. "She is my sister, but technically she's my stepsister. My dad married her mom."

"Wasn't Gabi's mom one of the lunch ladies at our high school? I remember her being exceptionally kind," I spoke stream of consciousness. The woman had made the most amazing peach cobbler. I used to bribe her with smiles for two servings.

"That's right." Beth's gaze seemed to close slightly and she tilted her chin up. "And my dad was one of the janitors there, on the facilities team, that's how they met."

"Huh." Not caring that my mouth had parted in thoughtful surprise, I stared at her, absorbing all these incredibly fascinating and elucidating details about the woman I—

Uh.

The, uh, woman I, uh . . . Liked. A lot.

"So you two never realized you grew up in the same town?" Alaric gestured to Beth with his rocks-free rocks glass, then to me.

I was about to respond in the affirmative, but Beth cut me off.

"I knew," she said, still watching me. "I knew who he was the first moment I saw him last June."

An odd sort of pleasure unfurled in my chest, sending a new wave of heat to my cheeks. More blushing. This time, I didn't mind so much.

"You did?" A shy smile claimed my mouth, not asking permission before tugging my lips to one side.

"Yes." She nodded, her voice soft, her gaze dropping briefly, like she required a second to gather her thoughts. "I remember you coming to the house, taking Gabi out. You were very memorable."

The interior of my body did a few odd things at her words. There was some swooping. Some contracting. Also heating. But then, suddenly, a drop of my stomach.

"I don't remember you," I croaked dumbly, admitting the plain truth and feeling unworthy.

She tilted her head back and forth, considering this information. Miraculously, she didn't seem upset. "I was twelve but looked ten. I'm not surprised."

I should've remembered her. The realization that I'd met her years ago but hadn't made an effort to remember her felt like losing something crucial, something that required I reassess all my life choices up to this point and make better ones moving forward.

"What is Gabi up to now?" Alaric asked Beth, but I felt his eyes on me.

I knew that look. He was either doing long division in his head or arriving at shrewd, self-serving conclusions.

"Oh, she's married. Works as an attorney in Alenbach, family practice."

I squinted at Alaric.

He squinted right back for a split second, then returned his glorious magnanimousness to Beth. "That's great. Tell her I say hi. And your dad?"

Her expression faltered. "He retired, after . . ."

"Oh, that's right." Alaric's voice dropped an octave. "My condolences."

I glanced between them, obviously missing something. "Condolences?"

"My stepmom died." She lowered her eyes to her glass before adding, "A road trip in Kansas. Drunk driver."

My insides instantly crumpled in on themselves, turning black and cold. *So cold.*

Several seconds passed before I realized both Alaric and Beth were gazing at me with bracing sympathy. I gave myself a mental shake and looked at my empty hands, wishing I had a drink. I knew what they were thinking, or some version of it. These kinds of sympathetic stares were why I'd stopped visiting my hometown.

"I am so sorry," I finally said to Beth, the statement squeezing out of me, knowing from personal experience the words were empty and insufficient but decorum required they be voiced nevertheless.

"I'm sorry for you too," she said, her aching sincerity setting me adrift on a wave of old grief. I really hated grief. It was the worst emotion. So boring and . . . difficult.

"But I wasn't little when my stepmom died. I was, uh—" she paused, took a deep breath, and worked gallantly to appear unfazed "—I was seventeen when it happened, much older . . ."

Than you, was what she didn't say, but we all heard the unspoken words.

I'd been really little. Seven. I'd been in the car with my dad when it happened. I'd stayed in that car for eighteen hours afterward before they found me with him because our drunk driver hadn't stayed.

So boring. So difficult. So much energy required.

An odd sense of being pulled had me drifting closer to Alaric. I couldn't quite manage a swallow.

"You two were close, though?" Alaric directed his attention to Beth while he lifted a hand and settled it between my shoulder blades.

"Yes. She raised me." Beth's gaze flickered between us as Alaric moved his palm in a slow, circular motion on my back.

Instinctively, I leaned closer to my friend, my body seeking the comfort of contact. The connection immediately grounded me, loosened limbs I hadn't realized were tight, allowed me to breathe. I'd been holding air within my lungs in fits and starts. My mouth was dry. I really wished I had a drink. I didn't want to think about this. I wouldn't.

So boring. So difficult. So much energy required.

Seconds stretched during which Beth's eyes narrowed by degrees and she watched us, the silence hovering just on the wrong side of long.

Wanting to bring the conversation back on track, I clumsily asked, "Gabi's mom raised you? What happened to your biological mom?"

Alaric's hand stilled. "Cyrus."

"No, it's okay." Beth's tone was distracted, and she continued to study the two of us with an air of absorption. She eventually answered, "My, uh, biological mom left us when I was four. Wasn't cut out for being a parent, I guess. I barely remember her."

I noted the slight shift in her voice, how it hardened and grew brittle at the same time. It made the hair on the back of my neck itch, poking at the omnipresent restlessness to touch her. I always wanted to touch Beth. Which was why I never did.

But now, watching her eyes dull and shutter while she also smiled—like her mother leaving when she was four was but a passing annoyance—my feet carried me forward an inch. I stopped just in time. The urge to reach forward and force Beth to submit to a hug was strong. But, as I'd learned in kindergarten, forcing people to accept hugs they didn't want was like attempting to force-feed someone cookies by shoving the cookies up their nose—something else I'd learned in kindergarten.

It had been an extremely elucidating year for me. Lots of growth. Big leaps.

Instead of imposing my affection on her, I fisted my hands in my pockets and said, "Her loss," meaning it with every fiber of my fabulous being.

Oddly, focusing on Beth's sad tale made me feel better, as did the small but exponentially more genuine smile she gave me. "Thank you," she said, but nothing more.

Alaric lightly patted my back three times, then let his hand drop. "Hey. How long are you in town?"

"I'm in town until the second of November," I responded automatically, tossing the remainder of my pointless melancholy away and deciding I would have wine with dinner. I liked wine, and I only wanted to have things and do things I liked for the rest of the evening.

"Not you." He sent me a weird look, then turned to Beth. "Beth, how long are you in town for?"

I became a statue. I'm not even sure my cell's mitochondria powerhoused.

"I leave on Halloween," she said, adding with a small smile, "I'm actually stopping by Alenbach for a few days on my way back to LA."

He tilted his nearly empty glass toward her. "We should catch dinner before you go, if you have time."

Thank goodness I remembered myself and halted an expression of outrage as his eyes moved over Beth again, this time in a way that seemed purposeful and not even a little compulsory. The smarmy bastard.

Oh. Okay. So this is how it's going to be?

"I think I'll have whiskey with dinner," I announced before Beth could respond. Placing a hand on Alaric's shoulder, I turned him toward the bar. "Go pick one out for me. Make it good. And I want ice. Don't come back without it. Watch the steps!"

Administering a firm shove before he could react, I turned to Beth and— as there was no time like the present—slid my arm under hers at the elbow, immediately enjoying the heat and press of our connection. Leading her quickly away just in case Alaric lingered, I also debated whether to punch him in the face and challenge him to pistols at dawn if he found us, or simply tell him again how wretched his tie looked.

"I'd like to speak with you about a very professional issue." Only glancing over my shoulder once—just to be sure Alaric wasn't following—I maneuvered into the house.

She stiffened, her feet dragging. "I—I don't think—Cyrus, I don't think that's a good idea." Her voice sounded breathless. "Please. I can't—"

"Nonsense." I lowered my voice and spoke close to her ear. "You excel at professionalism, and this requires a professional's opinion."

Beth shivered, leaning closer, but then halted and pulled her arm from my grip. Perplexed, I let her go.

Eyes rimmed with what looked like extreme anxiety, she rounded on me. "I can't, okay? I can't." Beth shook her head in a frantic movement, gulping in air. "Please. Let's just forget it happened."

The request stunned me, as did the obvious tension and unease in her posture, and the pleading in her gaze. "Beth, *ma choupinette*, I . . ." As usual with her, I didn't know what to say.

I knew she wanted me, wanted this. So why was she fighting it? And why was she so fearful of it?

Craig jumped next to Beth, startling me, forcing me to take a step back. "Na-ah-ah! Where do you think you're going?" His hands were raised, his fingers spread wide as though he might grab me should I dart in either direction. "Boris will kill me if you leave. And Natasha from DarkLens wants to talk multiverse. Halina made me promise you'd make yourself available, and Lenore will never speak to me again if you don't talk to the WWS team. Come on."

I was given no chance to protest, though my mouth opened and closed in an affronted approximation of one.

No longer meeting my eyes, Beth fluidly and dutifully stepped aside and allowed Craig to claim my arm. Turning my head as Craig pushed me like a piece of furniture, I searched for her. She'd disappeared, which meant the evening would be nothing but more odious *waiting*. I dragged my feet, all the way to Natasha, every step I took away from Beth painful.

If she wanted me to leave her alone, I would. But first we were going to talk. I needed to understand what held her back, and why. What was I doing wrong?

Faced with my DarkLens creative team, I fought a frustrated frown, and eventually managed a convincing smile. On autopilot, I accepted their friendly hugs, gathered a deep, bracing breath, and—even though I didn't want to—I behaved like a professional.

CHAPTER 14

BATHSHEBA

"Open your mouth and shut your eyes and see what Zeus will send you."

— ARISTOPHANES

J didn't give Cyrus another chance to pull me aside again after the industry dinner. Nor did he necessarily push me to meet or talk in private the day after that, or the day after that, or during the week that followed. I didn't give him any opportunity. During my shifts, I refused to make eye contact with him and reembraced the necessary habit of only responding with robotic, one-word answers. Avoiding Cyrus during nonwork hours had become my new superpower.

In retrospect, I decided my biggest mistakes last week had been buying him replacement cologne after he'd mentioned that he'd left his behind in LA and lowering my guard and speaking freely when I'd sought him out to apologize. I should've maintained my professional façade. It had been hugely inappropriate to be so candid with him.

But he'd smelled so darn good and when he'd looked at me, I melted.

I'd been living day-to-day for so long, clutching my bad mood around me like a plastic poncho in a thunderstorm, waiting and praying for the downpour to pass. As soon as I'd allowed myself to meet his eyes and talk to him with any openness, I hadn't been able to hide my ridiculous overreaction to his closeness.

I wouldn't make that mistake again.

Hiking my large burlap-and-canvas shopping bag higher on my shoulder, I stood from my seat on the subway and left through the sliding doors. My shift, which started tonight at 6:00 p.m., would end by midmorning tomorrow in time for me to catch my flight home to Alenbach.

I was grateful to my past self for scheduling the trip so many months ago. It saved me from attending the Halloween party tomorrow and having to dress in a skimpy costume befitting one of Cyrus Malcom's stylists.

Cyrus hadn't quite settled back into his old habits once it became clear that I had no intention of discussing what had occurred between us in the office. He didn't tease me, he didn't call me "my hero" as he'd been doing since I'd saved him from the scallop dip, and he didn't avoid me either, like he'd done during our early days working together.

Instead, he seemed . . . I don't know. Both deferential and frustrated? Watchful, respectful, but also quiet and remote. He'd kept saying things like, "Whatever you want, Beth," which in turn made my stomach erupt with butterflies. The way he'd say the words, it didn't sound like he was agreeing to increased safety protocols so much as reminding me that he left his door unlocked at night.

However, he didn't technically push.

It was disorienting, yet I told myself it was for the best. I only had two more months on this contract. If we could coexist like this, I'd get through it without making a fool of myself.

Exiting the subway, I glanced both ways before crossing the street and ducked my chin into my scarf. It was cold. Jack-o'-lanterns lit with candles sporadically dotted the walkways leading up to the brownstones. I only had three blocks to walk.

Today, one week after the office incident—an incident I hadn't reported to Wren because I simply didn't know what to say about it—I'd waited until Cyrus, Nicole, Mindy, Tamra, and Wren had left the brownstone for the last day of DarkLensCon before heading downstairs for breakfast.

I also made sure I was out of the house several hours before they were set to return from the half day of events, opting to use the eight hours off to do some shopping on Canal Street before silencing my phone and catching a movie in Harlem.

On my way back, I'd stopped by a corner shop, my mood improving when I discovered they still had peaches this late in the year. I'd then hopped on the subway so I'd arrive a few hours before dinner. If I wanted to sneak upstairs instead, I could do that too. Slipping in unnoticed wouldn't be a problem as long as I didn't use the front door. The patio and the kitchen used the same code and, assuming I was careful, I could steal silently into one or the other and avoid detection on the stairs by lurking and listening in the hallways.

As I approached the house, my steps slowed. Two police cruisers were parked outside. All thoughts of potentially sneaking in vanished. Picking up my pace, I jogged the rest of the way, entering through the front door just as four uniformed officers were coming down the stairs.

I caught the tail end of one of them speaking, " . . . these fancy assholes. No wonder."

The cops didn't even pause as I walked in, but one of them did wink at me on his way out the door. I glanced around the foyer and found Kristina leaning against the doorframe to the hall, a frown on her face.

"What happened?" I set my bag down and crossed to her. "What's with the police?"

She waved me forward. "Everyone is in the kitchen. I wasn't there, but I guess Cyrus was attacked by a mob."

"He—he what?" My heart lurched and I glanced at the stairs. "What do you mean attacked? Where is he? Is he okay?"

She'd already turned and answered while walking. "He was leaving the Con. A few of the DarkLens people insisted he and Vera Rodrigo—you know Vera, she's the actress who plays the angel—get their photo taken in front of the big sign outside the convention center. Anyway. There's Mindy. She can tell you the rest."

Mindy currently sat at the long table in the kitchen. Quickly scanning the room, I saw not everyone was present.

"Where's Cyrus?" I asked again, conducting another scan just in case I'd missed him the first time. Also missing were Nicole and Wren.

"He's upstairs, resting. He's not hurt, but I can't say the same for his suit." Craig, who had been standing in front of the fridge, shut the freezer drawer and handed a bag of ice to Mindy. "This is for your knee."

The tension in my chest both eased and increased at Craig's odd assurances about Cyrus's health and the cryptic statements about his suit.

Sliding into the empty chair across from Mindy, I asked, "Are you okay?"

Kristina took the seat next to her, reaching for and holding her hand.

Lifting a gaze that looked both weary and shell-shocked, Mindy's hand squeezed Kristina's. "It was a lot. I'm just a little—uh—shaken up."

I noted she had scratches and dirt smudges on her face.

Pulling my bottom lip between my teeth, I glanced at Tamra who sat on Mindy's other side. She seemed to be in better shape, not nearly as shaky.

"Do you mind telling me what happened?" I asked her, hoping my voice communicated that there was no pressure.

Tamra, her frown heavily seasoned with anger, nodded. "Yeah. Those assholes at DarkLens didn't tell us they were taking Cyrus up to the fucking front of the goddamn convention center and force him to stand there, waiting in front of a giant fucking crowd for fifteen fucking minutes while their asshole photographer played with her stupid fucking camera trying to get it to work."

Mindy swallowed convulsively, her hazy focus dropping to the table.

Tamra leaned forward, her dark eyes flashing. "Of course the crowd is going to go crazy! What the fuck did they think was going to happen?"

My heart racing, I glanced at Kristina. She seemed preoccupied with Mindy.

"They all rushed in at once, tearing at his clothes, screaming." Tamra's voice had taken on a deadened quality. "Mindy got trampled at first, but Cyrus got her up, thank God."

"But not before a few people ripped off his jacket, half of his shirt, and someone stole his watch." Mindy lifted her eyes to mine, her voice equally devoid of emotion.

I winced with every cell in my body, a flash of cold dread and fiery fury pulsing within my nerves. "God. Is he—is he okay?" I asked again, not believing their first answer anymore.

"He's okay." This answer came from Wren as she walked into the kitchen, tired lines bracketing her mouth and slashing between her eyebrows. "He's a little banged up—just like the rest of us—but we got him out before things escalated too badly."

"Can't say the same for Vera's people, though," Tamra said, exchanging a glance with Wren. "Those guys took forever getting her out. Nicole had to go back and help."

"Is Nicole okay?" I wished I'd been there. *I should've been there.*

"She took a few in the face." Craig gestured to his jaw and left eye. "But she doesn't have a concussion. The doctor came and left an hour ago."

And I went shopping, silenced my phone, and watched a movie.

My stomach rolled. My hands balled into fists. *I should've been there.*

"What can I do?" I glanced around at my team, feeling restless.

Wren's features softened. "You've already done enough, honestly. That packet you made on the convention center and traffic routes saved our asses. We knew where to go because you'd already mapped out the escape path."

"Thank you," Mindy said, her voice watery. "Really, thank you."

I blinked away stinging behind my own eyes and reached across the table to hold her free hand. "I wish I could do more."

"Open a bottle of wine. Or better yet, whiskey," Tamra said, giving me a smile edged with exhaustion. But then she was frowning again and glancing around the kitchen. "Where is Boris? I'm starving."

"He went to get more food for tonight." Craig, who'd been leaning his hip against the kitchen island this whole time, pulled off his glasses and rubbed his nose. "He said something about making comfort food for dinner instead of salmon salad."

I thought of the peaches in my bag. *Comfort food.*

Already standing from the table, I asked as I jogged from the room, "How does everyone feel about peach cobbler?"

Balancing the tray laden with Boris's comfort food dinner and my peach cobbler against my hip, I started the climb up to Cyrus's room. It was almost 4:30 p.m. I still had over an hour and a half before my shift started and I would technically be on duty. I told myself I would knock on the door, announce that his dinner was outside in the hall, then promptly leave.

That's what I should do. It's not what I *wanted* to do.

I wanted to stay for a minute or two (or more) and make sure he was okay. I wanted to talk to him and get his side of the story. And I wanted a hug—for me, not for him. He had enough people to hug him already. He didn't need me for that.

That's right. He might want something from you, but he doesn't need anything from you other than your professional expertise. The thought was both sad and sobering, a good reminder that although I was tempted to stick around and assure myself he was okay, reassuring me didn't matter one way or the other to him.

As I crested the first set of stairs, I wasn't certain if I'd stick to plan A, or if my impulsive, selfish side would ultimately win out when faced with his bedroom door.

Unlike Cyrus's claim last week about not locking his door, I'd locked my door at night. I'd also been placing a chair in front of it. I knew he wouldn't enter uninvited or try anything inappropriate. Cyrus wasn't like that, not even a little. And why would he be? Everyone was his cuddle buddy; I was certain he'd have almost as many fuck buddies if he asked.

The lock and chair in my room were token gestures for my mental health more than anything, barriers meant to deter any hasty or lusty impulses.

In the middle of the night, when I'd lain in my bed alone, thinking back on his words in the office last week and the light touches of his mouth on my skin, the temptation to test his door and take him up on his offer had twisted like a tornado in my lower stomach. In the end, chanting to myself *Cyrus is never serious* was the only reminder that kept me from doing something monumentally stupid. Not even chastising myself for lack of professionalism helped.

Cyrus was right. I wanted him. I felt like my want for him was severing me in half, I was becoming two separate people against my will. The person I'd always considered myself to be and the person who wanted Cyrus Malcom more than their self-respect.

It was ridiculous. I was ridiculous. But I'd never felt this way about anyone, this reckless, this out of control. There were times over the last month, before we'd come to New York, where I'd caught myself staring at him and his smile, watching his hands, eavesdropping on conversations not meant for my ears where he'd offer support or advice or a compliment just to be kind with no obvious benefit to himself.

He was so kind. My heart constricted with a sweet and sad ache just thinking about his kindness.

Stepping onto the third-floor landing, I turned toward Cyrus's suite, more out of breath than I should've been after just two flights of stairs. My feet slowed as I approached.

I'd been so certain before last week that he'd continued to treat me differently from the rest of the team because of my terrible drunken behavior in the car back in June. I didn't think he was punishing me purposefully. More like, deep down, he didn't trust me. Deep down, I'd never be able to earn his trust.

But then, in the office last week, he'd blown that theory to smithereens. I had to believe, given everything I knew about Cyrus after watching him constantly for months, he would never touch me or anyone else like that unless it was honest, unless he actually wanted me.

Unless this is just more taunting? A new way to get a rise out of you?

I shook my head at the thought, but the notion did leave me feeling conflicted. Cyrus was a good person, a kind person, but he was also free with affection and touch. Hugging and cuddling with another person didn't seem to be a big deal to him, not like it was to me.

I still hadn't made up my mind. Stay or go? In the end, it didn't matter. Just as I drew even with his room, the door swung open.

I froze, gripping the tray, staring wide-eyed at Cyrus as he stared back at me.

"Beth," he said, his eyes moving between mine, full of emotion I didn't give myself permission to label.

He looked tired, a little pale, but otherwise no visible bruises or injuries. Something within me uncoiled and sagged with relief. I'd wanted to reassure myself he was okay. Mission accomplished.

"Hi," I said, now giving myself permission to conduct a more thorough assessment of his person. He wore a black T-shirt, jeans, and no shoes, as informal an outfit as I'd ever seen on him. His arms seemed free of wounds, but I spied several scratch marks around his neck and one on his upper right cheek that I'd missed in my first quick inspection, the sight of which caused a simmering anger to ignite in my chest.

How dare they touch him like that. How DARE they.

"Are you okay?"

His question had my eyes snapping back to his, and I realized I'd clenched my jaw.

Loosening it, I nodded, and managed to speak around my rising temper. "I brought you food."

"Come in." He stepped to the side, holding the door open.

"Oh, no. I wanted to drop this off for you. I don't want to—"

"Is it from Boris?" He backed up a bit more. "Is it salad? I told him I don't want a salad."

"No. It's grilled cheese and tomato sandwiches with mustard sauce, tomato soup, and—uh—peach cobbler."

Cyrus's eyebrows ticked up. "Peach cobbler?"

"Yes." I hesitated, then blurted stupidly, "I made it."

"You made it?" His eyes, which had resembled Mindy's shell-shocked and weary ones upon opening the door, seemed to expand with wonder.

"I did." I fought a blush. "It's a—a family recipe. My mom—stepmom— she used to make it when I had a hard day and I thought . . ."

"Please," he said quietly, his smile soft and so freaking beautiful and earnest, it made my chest ache. "Please, bring it in."

I hesitated. I hesitated so long, I made it weird. Meanwhile, Cyrus watched me, his earnest smile waning as his eyes sharpened.

Just as I was about to insist I allow him to rest, he said, "I hurt my wrist in the scuffle. I'd appreciate it if you'd carry it in for me."

"Oh! Yes. Absolutely. Sorry." I promptly did as he asked, walking past him into the room.

"No need to apologize," he said, his tone distracted.

Once inside, I spun in a slow circle, looking for a clear surface where I could set the tray. The only spot, unless I wanted to put it on the bed, was the top of the dresser along the far wall. I didn't want to put it on the bed.

Carefully sliding the tray in place and ensuring none of the edges were hanging over, my back stiffened a smidge when I heard the door shut. I turned, intent on leaving, but then I stopped short when I found Cyrus standing directly in my path and closer than I'd anticipated. He was holding his wrist.

Daring another peek at his eyes, I blinked. All thoughts of leaving fled when I spied the dazed, wounded look behind his gaze. The change in him was startling.

"Hey. Are you—are you okay?"

His eyes refocused on mine, like he'd forgotten I was there, then they narrowed. "Don't look at me like that. I was perfectly behaved."

"No. I know you were. This wasn't your fault."

His chin angled back slightly, a distrusting, defensive posture, but then he nodded. "Thank you for saying that. The local authorities don't seem to agree."

"What do you mean?"

"I mean . . ." He turned and paced the room, then stopped suddenly. His shoulders lifted and fell. "They're not too keen on doing anything about it, said I should consider my watch lost, and suggested I get better security next time if someone like me wishes to prance about in public."

My lungs seized with anger and sorrow. "Cyrus—"

"Even if Brody and Kamar had been there, even if I'd had a guard of fifty, it wouldn't have made any difference." Cyrus walked tiredly to the bed and sat, placed his elbows on his knees and gripped his forehead in his hands. "There were too many of them."

He sounded so forlorn. The despairing note in his voice had me crossing to where he sat and kneeling in front of him. "It wasn't your fault. This wasn't your fault."

He shook his head, saying something I didn't catch.

"What was that?"

"It was my father's."

"What?"

He leveled me with glassy eyes and his hands dropped. "The watch." His voice broke, his face crumpling. "It was my father's watch."

"Oh, Cyrus." On autopilot, I reached forward and embraced him, held him forcefully—perhaps a bit too forcefully—and smoothed a hand over his hair.

He took a hitching breath, his arms automatically wrapping around me, the tightness of his embrace stealing my breath. I didn't care. The way he clung to me, it felt desperate, like he needed to hold someone and be held in return.

"I'm so sorry, I'm so sorry," I whispered, my throat closing as I heard him choke on a quiet sob.

Cyrus cried, tucking his face into my neck. Not loud, heaving sobs, but silent tears of despair. And the more he cried, the more desperate I felt to do something to those people who'd hurt him. I wanted to hunt them down and make them suffer. I wanted to terrify them how they'd terrified him. I wanted to take something priceless and precious from them and listen to their pleading cries. And then I wanted to find those officers who'd made him feel like this was his fault and . . . and do something bad.

Real bad.

And mean.

Psychological warfare mean.

Maybe I'd burn down their houses and then tell them if they didn't want their houses to burn down, they should've installed a sprinkler system.

The swiftness and intensity of my vengeful thoughts didn't necessarily surprise me. Every reaction I experienced in relation to Cyrus—to his taunting, his rare touches, his smiles, his kindness, his glances—was overblown and absurd. Why wouldn't I have an equally intense reaction to his pain?

After a time, he turned his head, lifting it and leaning back, his arms loosening and his hands sliding to my waist.

"I'm sorry," he said, giving me a self-deprecating smile. Even after crying, he was still achingly beautiful, and his eyes darted over my face. "You're so lovely and I'm being—it's just a watch. I'm fine. I'm not hurt, not really. I don't know why I'm acting this way."

"No. You were *attacked*." My fingers dug into his shoulders. "Your clothes were torn and shredded. They ripped them apart and they took something from you that mattered." Some instinct had me lifting my hands to cup his cheeks.

He looked down at me with his big green beautiful eyes, so open and trusting, but lacking their sparkle. I gritted my teeth against another spike in temper.

Burn their houses down!

"You have nothing to apologize for," I went on, my throat knotted with so much emotion. Overwhelmed by the need to comfort him and avenge him, I leaned forward and gave him a quick kiss on his cheek. "You're perfect," I said, giving him another quick kiss, followed by another. "You're so perfect. None of this is your fault."

His fingers tightened on my waist, tugging me closer. And just as I shifted to give the other side of his face a kiss, Cyrus turned his head, and my lips connected with his instead of the stubble of his cheek.

A shock went through me, a quick intake of breath, an electrified beat of my heart sending lightning to my fingertips. I stilled, not sure . . .

Not sure of anything.

Cyrus lifted his head a fraction of an inch, his eyes colliding with mine, our mouths just a hair's breadth apart.

I felt rather than heard him whisper, "Beth."

I had the sense of being shoved this way and that by strong waves in an angry ocean, the overwhelming push and pull he caused within my body simply by saying my name, just like that, a desperate prayer, a broken plea.

Watching me with a liquid gaze, he brushed his lips against mine again. "Beth, please," he whispered.

I knew this was him asking permission, but it also felt like he was begging. And I wasn't a strong person, not anymore. Not with him.

My eyes drifting shut, I lifted my chin. I held my breath. And I kissed him.

CHAPTER 15

BATHSHEBA

"One's country is wherever one does well."

— ARISTOPHANES, *PLUTUS*

yrus didn't hesitate taking what I offered, like he'd been waiting for years, like he'd dreamt of this and planned for it. How was it possible that this, a simple press of lips, a mutual inhale of breath, fingers digging into my spine, his jaw and neck beneath my palms, could feel so impossibly good?

Pulling me closer still, Cyrus chased me even though I wasn't running. His mouth searching, hungry, seeking, but also so soft. Cherishing, like I and this moment were incredibly precious to him. I felt wanted, so deeply wanted. So deep, I drowned in it. By the time he'd tilted his head and tasted the seam of my lips with his tongue, I couldn't conceive the worth of fighting. Why would I ever want to?

This is what I wanted, his hot, perfect mouth on mine, his hands on my body. I wanted this so much. I don't think I'd even admitted to myself how badly I'd wanted him. One hand sliding lower on my back, the other higher, his massaging fingers seemed to say, *Give in. Please, just give in. Give me what I want. What we both want.*

My body was liquid fire, molded and reshaped by his hands. I yielded to him, completely. I surrendered. And the small, involuntary moan that slipped past as Cyrus licked my bottom lip seemed to flip a switch in him. The hand that had moved higher on my back speared into my hair, grabbing a rough fistful and pulling, causing a sting and forcing my chin up. My mouth opened and he wasted no time tasting me. His growl of appreciation almost distracted me from the hand on my ass, grasping and kneading and making me squirm.

I felt so completely out of control. Hungry for his enthusiastic reactions and eager to give him mine. The beat of my heart could not be contained, it thundered through me, filling my ears as magic filled my veins. Cyrus seemed equally hungry for me, my mouth, my body.

It wasn't until he lifted his mouth and said, "Touch me. *Fuck,* Beth. Please touch me. Please," that I realized I was now horizontal. He'd lowered me to the floor beneath him, and the hand that had been in my hair was pushing up my skirt, sending spiky shivers down my legs and twisting low in my belly.

Nothing in me wanted to wait, so I don't know why the word hovered on the tip of my tongue. Before I could give voice or thought to it, his mouth captured mine again and the hot, perfect, erotic slide of his tongue against mine drove all thought—coherent or not—from my mind.

I wanted this. I wanted whatever he was willing to give me, for however long. I had absolutely no pride, just want. He captured my hand and slid it under his shirt. My fingertips discovered the heat and ridges of his bare skin and I caressed the smooth, hot canvas of him. He sucked in a hissing breath between his teeth, as though the sensations overwhelmed him. His body vibrated beneath my fingertips and my other hand joined the exploration, my nails threading through the sparse hair on his chest, only stilling when his hand pushed up my shirt and pulled down the cup of my bra, palming my bare breast.

Reflex had my back arching off the floor, my knees pressed together, seeking friction between my legs that he withheld by shifting to the side and lying beside me instead of on top. If he'd told me to open my legs, I would have. If he'd commanded me to strip and bend over, I would've scrambled to obey. I felt so needy, strung tight, hot and frantic. I had no defense against this, against him, and the incredible, perfect feel of his lips closing over my breast, tonguing me, sucking me into his hot mouth, groaning deep in his chest and whispering that I was the most perfect thing in the world, as though he was just as insatiable for me as I was for him.

I wasn't aware of the tears sliding down my temples until I felt them roll into my hair. And it was my inability to breathe, to draw enough air into my lungs even though my airway wasn't restricted and my mouth was open, that finally shook me out of the madness.

What are you doing? A voice screamed inside my head. *What are you doing? This means nothing to him. What are you doing?* I felt my face crumple, a ragged sob ripping from my lungs.

Cyrus stilled.

I tried to fight it, this bewildering panic, bargaining with myself that I could do this, just once. I could have meaningless sex with Cyrus, I could. *It doesn't have to mean anything to me either.*

It didn't help.

I couldn't stop crying, and I couldn't fight what I didn't understand. My breath hitched with another sob, the tears coming fast.

"No. Please, no," Cyrus begged, moving over me again, his fingers pushing gently into my hair, his thumbs swiping away my tears. "What is happening? What did I do wrong?"

I couldn't speak, I could barely breathe, and I definitely couldn't think. On instinct, I pushed his hands away and scrambled to my knees, then feet, intent on making a run for it. But I was clumsy and he beat me there, his hand against the door, stopping me from leaving.

"Please talk to me. Please don't leave," he pleaded.

Unable to look at him, I shook my head, swallowing convulsively. Shame I didn't understand rose up to choke me, pinching my lungs and causing new tears while Cyrus stared at my profile and I stared at the door.

"Beth?"

"I can't do this."

He placed a tentative hand on my arm. "Bathsheba—"

I shook him off, snapping, "Don't touch me."

He flinched. I didn't see it, but I felt it, and it pulled my gaze to his. What I saw had me choking back another sob. His big eyes so open with emotion, I had to close mine so I could breathe.

"Please," I said, the word fracturing as soon as it arrived.

Silence fell between us. After ten frantic beats of my heart, I sensed him lean away and remove his hand from the door. Immediately, I opened it, I darted out, and then I ran down the hall to the stairs leading up to my floor. I didn't stop until I made it to my room. Once there, I locked the door and paced, wanting to tear my hair out by the roots.

What is wrong with you?

I didn't know. I didn't know what to do. I didn't understand myself. I didn't understand this desperation, for him and against him. Pressing my fingers to my lips, my body still humming from the heat of his hands, I once again felt like I was being pulled apart, torn in different directions.

It made no sense. Being with him, touching him felt so right and wrong and terrifying. All I knew was that I couldn't continue like this, idiotically giving my heart away with this insane abandon and trust and *feeling* to someone who was never serious.

He was a client, an assignment, a freaking movie star who existed in an entirely different stratosphere, and I didn't know how to stop myself from shoving it in his direction.

Something had to give, or else I felt certain I would break.

"What's this?" Wren frowned at the letter I'd just given her. "I don't understand what I'm reading."

"I'm resigning." Guilt pressed heavy on my shoulders. She'd dealt with so much over the last several hours, and I didn't want to blindside her, but staying was not an option.

When I'd spied the light still on in her room, I'd decided to do it now and not wait until the morning.

Her tired gaze lifting to mine, she asked, "You mean, you want to be reassigned?"

"No. I need to quit the studio. I need to quit because I have not been professional *at all* and I don't deserve to—"

"Hold on, hold on. Calm down." Standing from her bed, she reached for me and tugged on my elbow, pulling me over to a little sitting area to one side of her room. "Come here and sit. Now tell me, what's going on?"

I settled next to her, forcing myself to breathe. To calm down. I could do this. I could be a professional and take responsibility for my actions.

Squaring my shoulders, I said, "I believe my ability to function at the level necessary for this job has been compromised and I can no longer, in good conscience, continue as part of this team. I have behaved in a reprehensible, unprofessional manner, and I do not believe I deserve to hold this position."

"What happened?" Her gaze flickered over me. "Did you and Cyrus sleep together?"

"What?!" I flinched back. "No!" I stared at her, at how unconcerned she'd sounded when she asked the question.

Her calm manner persisted. "Because, if you did, and it was off the clock, off duty, it's not a violation of your employment contract. What you do in your personal time is none of my business or the studio's business, as long as it doesn't impact your ability to do your job."

I—who—*what?*

"Are you seriously telling me you would have no problem if I slept with Cyr—with the client?"

"Like I said, as long as you didn't do it while you were on the clock, it was fully consensual, and as long as it didn't compromise your ability to keep the client safe during work hours, fine by me." She shrugged.

I couldn't believe my ears. "But—but—all the other security agencies I've worked for in the past had human resource paperwork to fill out and a process for any intra-office relationship."

"The studio has that too, for a *relationship*. But we're not talking about a relationship, we're talking about casual sex. If film studios required filed paperwork to track who was hooking up with who in Hollywood, they'd have to hire a thousand new employees."

My mouth dropped open. I couldn't believe my ears. My eyes stung. And in the very next second, I burst into tears.

"Oh no," Wren murmured. Her hand came to my back. "Beth—Beth, it's okay. Fooling around with Cyrus Malcom doesn't make you a bad person. It makes you a person with eyes and a sex drive."

"But this is not me," I blubbered, swiping angrily at my tears. "I—I have —I should have higher professional standards for myself. I—Gah! Sorry. No offense—"

"No offense taken." She patted my back, her eyes shining with affection. "As long as this is consensual, you're two adults. Workplace romances and hookups happen."

I felt the tears well up again along with regret and frustration. "Okay. Maybe it's not unusual or even frowned upon for lines to be blurred here. But, for me, even though things never went that far, I crossed a line with Cyrus and I'm disappointed with myself. I shouldn't have crossed that line."

"Fair enough," she said on a sigh. "In your personal life, you get to decide what lines exist and with whom." Wren stood and paced to her bed. Turning to face me, she sat on the edge of it and placed my resignation letter next to her. "Let me ask you this: would having a sexual relationship with a client outside of work hours jeopardize your ability to protect that client while you're on the clock?"

I sniffled, blinking through tears to bring her back into focus. "I don't think so. If anything, it would make me even more diligent."

Her searching gaze suddenly grew sympathetic as she guessed, "Because you wouldn't have sex with a client unless you cared about them, right? Unless you were in a monogamous relationship with the client?"

I nodded, my chin wobbling.

She grimaced, her stare full of compassion. "Oh Beth. That's never going to happen with someone like Cyrus Malcom. I've worked with *a lot* of celebrities. It's not out of the realm of possibility, but neither is winning the lottery, or getting hit by lightning."

"I know," I croaked, looking at my fingers. I nodded again, unable to speak, my chest hot and achy.

"Do you have . . . feelings for him?" She sounded bracing. "Do you want to be in a relationship with Cy—"

"No," I said firmly, my eyes cutting to hers.

I did have feelings for him, but things would never work between us. Cyrus was chaotic, hugged and snuggled and kissed people indiscriminately, and made me feel hot and bothered and agitated all the time. I wasn't an illogical person and being around him made me feel illogical. I didn't like how good he was at getting a rise out of me. Since Chicago, he'd done it effortlessly. And I didn't like feeling out of control.

"I want to focus on my career right now. I want to do this job well. I want to protect people, keep them safe. That's what I want." Saying the words out loud made me feel a little better, steadier, enough to admit, "I don't want to feel this way."

Wren studied me. "Do you want me to transfer you to a different client?" she asked. "Just say the word and I will. The studio has a long list of people who have requested someone with your special skill set."

I took several deep breaths and considered her offer. With Cyrus, we'd had that disastrous blind date and it had set the tone for everything that followed. Blurred boundaries before we'd started working together.

It would be so much easier to guard someone else, someone new. I could start fresh and put up barriers for myself early on, hold myself to them.

Except, what if I couldn't?

What if the same thing happened with my next client?

"Beth?"

I felt Wren sit down next to me again and I looked at her.

"I'll follow your lead," she said. Her features held no judgment, only concern. "But please know, I do not think you should quit. On behalf of the studio, I'd hate to see someone like you go. You're so good at what you do and we're lucky to have you. But I also think you're being too hard on yourself. I don't think you did anything wrong, definitely nothing that would warrant a resignation."

Sitting straighter, I lifted my chin and wiped away the last of my tears. "I think, maybe, I need a break? I need to take a leave of absence—an unpaid leave of absence—to get my head on straight. But if it's okay with you, I'd like to leave tonight. I already called a friend in the city. I don't think—" I glanced up at the ceiling and heaved a tremendous breath. "I don't think I can be here anymore."

"Whatever you need." Reaching out, she covered my hand with hers and squeezed it. "Let's say two months? You let me know. You can start on another assignment after the first of the year."

"Okay. Thank you." I nodded, feeling . . . not great, but not terrible either.

Mostly, I felt relieved.

CHAPTER 16

CYRUS

"How can I study from below, that which is above?"

— ARISTOPHANES, *CLOUDS*

~Early November~

When I was informed by Wren upon waking on Halloween morning that Beth had requested a leave of absence, quit the team, and left without saying goodbye, did I spend the whole day feeling like a four-hundred-and-eighty-pound lion was sitting on my chest whilst I suffered from habanero- and onion-induced heartburn? Yes. I did.

And did I neglect to attend the Halloween party held in my honor because the thought of socializing felt like drinking a gallon of spoiled milk, and instead went to bed early just to spend the whole night tossing and turning until a plan pulled me out of bed at 3:30 a.m.? Yes. I did.

And did I exfoliate, don my favorite suit, and call in ten favors to secure WWS's private jet to chase Bathsheba Ryan to Alenbach, Texas in order to convince her to return with me to LA so I could do everything in my power to pamper and adore her? Yes. Yes, I did that too.

Don't judge me. I needed to exfoliate, it had been ten days.

Tugging at my cuffs, I gently elbowed Wren. "How do I look?"

She glanced at me, completed a cursory scan, and said, "You look incredible."

I grinned, grateful for the confidence boost. "Thank you."

"The way you look shouldn't be possible in real life. It's the truth and you know it." Wren squinted at the inside of the building beyond the window. "Are you sure you're allowed inside places like this?"

"What do you mean?"

"Won't you, I don't know, get struck by lightning or something?"

"I'm sexy, Wren. Not a pharisee. Jesus didn't have a problem with sexy people."

"Still." She peeked over the wooden pew in front of us, as though she expected someone with anti-sexy-people holy water to be lying in wait.

My eyes were focused forward. Beth hadn't arrived yet, but when I'd talked to Ryaine O'Rourke at 12:30 a.m. LA time, 3:30 a.m. NYC time, after hatching this desperate plan, she'd assured me Beth and her family would attend the November first All Saints' Day Mass at Holy Trinity Catholic Church.

It was a family tradition, apparently. They all attended together every year to light a candle for her stepmother.

Wren settled back in the pew, but she continued to scan the interior of the church beyond the large glass window. I didn't want to give Beth any excuse to be angry with me or complain about a lack of security given the deviation from her agendas, so I brought the whole team along. The remainder of the ladies had dispersed around the building, learning the layout and stationing themselves at strategically important points, or so Wren had said.

Wren sat next to me in the "cry room" of all things—a small, attached space at the back of the church where parents took naughty children who made too much noise. The room was closed off from the rest of the congregation and we were the only people in it for the noon service. It was, she'd said, the most inconspicuous spot. A place where we wouldn't be noticed unless someone was specifically looking for us, but which allowed us to view both the altar at the front as well as the entrance. We'd be able to see Beth and her family enter and where they sat so I could—

Uh . . .

Ahem. I hadn't gotten that far yet. I'd figure it out.

"When are you going to tell me why we're here?" Wren glanced at me, a frown between her eyebrows.

"This is my hometown," I hedged. I hadn't informed her or anyone else why I'd insisted on canceling all my meetings today and absconding with WWS's jet to Texas hill country.

"Yes, I know. But why did we suddenly have to leave New York one day early and take you to your hometown?"

I stared at Wren, pondering, wondering if I should simply fess up so I could exploit her wisdom. I hadn't confessed to anyone about my preoccupation with Bathsheba Ryan. Prior to last week, anything between us had felt outside of the realm of reality.

The intensity of Wren's frown increased the longer I looked at her without speaking.

"Cyrus?" Eyes narrowing a fraction, she leaned back as though to see me better. "What did you do? Are we here to beg for your soul?"

A speaker in the corner made a few crackling noises before clicking on, filling the room with the sounds of the main church.

"No." I cleared my throat. "Not for my *soul.*"

A small sound of amusement slipped past her lips. It also erased some of her frown. "Then what are we here to beg for?"

I twisted my torso and faced her. "If I tell you, you have to promise not to tell anyone else."

"I promise."

"And you have to be nice to me about it—"

Her eyes narrowed again.

"And"—I held up a finger—"you have to be on my side and do everything in your power to help me."

"I can promise everything except the last part."

I wasn't surprised. It had been a long shot.

"Fine." I braced myself. "Beth left so suddenly yesterday, I wanted to make sure she was okay."

Wren stared at me, nonplussed. "What does us being here have to do with Beth?"

"Her, uh, family lives here. In Alenbach." I faced forward again. "Turns out we grew up in the same small town. I just found out last week. Small world, huh?"

I felt Wren's eyes drill into the side of my face while I tried not to squirm.

I had nothing to feel guilty about, and so I said, "Wren, darling. I have no dishonorable intentions."

"Uh-huh."

"I'm merely—" I searched for the right word, finally settling on, "Concerned. I'm concerned for her health and well-being."

In my peripheral vision, I saw her cross her arms. "No. You're merely infatuated with her."

"That too," I admitted automatically. But then I realized what she'd said and I stared at her. "Wait. How could you possibly know that?"

"Are you kidding?" she hissed, annoyance hardening her jaw. "I'd have to be blind not to notice. I'm pretty sure everyone knows, but—if it makes you feel better—no one seems to be gossiping about it."

I tossed my hands up before crossing my arms too. "Fine. Everyone knows. And yet you're too clueless to notice Boris's interest in you."

"Nope. I know about that too. But, as you well know since you're the king of broken hearts, there's a difference between being dumb and playing dumb."

She knew about Boris? "Why would you do that? Why would you play dumb with Boris?"

"For the same reason you pretend half the people you meet aren't enamored with you. Boris has a harmless crush. He'll get over it." Wren gave me a smile that could only be described as pragmatic. But the longer we studied each other, the more sobriety crept into her features. "Listen, Cyrus, it's none of my business, but here's a tip: I know you're used to doing whatever you want, whenever you want, with whoever you want."

"You say that like it's a bad thing."

"You're charming, gorgeous, clever, witty, and incredibly talented."

"Please. Stop."

"But you're also spoiled."

I felt my eyes narrow.

She held them boldly. "You were Beth's first client at the studio. This was her first assignment. Doing a great job is important to her. Being professional is important to her. She is excellent at what she does and she'd be devastated if she were fired. It matters to her. And if she mattered to you, then you wouldn't want to do anything to jeopardize her job or her mental health."

Even though we were still alone in our little cry room, I dropped my voice to a whisper. "How is me being here, or being infatuated with her, jeopardizing her job at the studio or her mental health?"

Wren also whispered, but hers was harsh. "Because she's not going to do anything with or to you without strings attached. And because—"

"Good." I sniffed indignantly, facing forward and eyeing the two men in dresses at the back of the church. One of them was holding a gigantic red book. "Because, at this point, neither would I."

Several beats of silence passed. Sounds from the larger church beyond the window crackled over the speaker. I preoccupied myself by staring at the entrance and willing Beth to appear.

Perhaps I'm a wizard, because a half minute later, she did.

My breath caught and I sat forward, my hand coming to rest on the back of the wooden bench in front of us. She looked so beautiful, and I was so mesmerized by the sight of her in a wool green peacoat and jeans tucked into brown leather stiletto boots that I didn't notice the people with her at first. Not until Beth had walked down the aisle, knelt, then slipped into a wooden pew exactly like ours.

Alongside her sat a man I presumed was her father. Next to him was a boy in his late teens—or maybe a man in his early twenties—and next to him was Gabi. As soon as they were all in the pew, they knelt.

"You're serious," Wren said, reminding me I wasn't alone.

"Yes," I said, not looking at her. I'd never seen Beth wear her hair in a bun before. The honey-colored strands were twisted atop her head, several tendrils had come loose. Now that I knew how soft her hair felt, my fingers were restless to touch it again.

"You know . . ." Wren poked me in the arm. "You have to file paperwork with the studio if you two are in a relationship. Anyone who is employed or contracted with the studio, regardless of whether they work together, has to declare it."

Her statement yanked me from my hair fantasies and voyeurism. I glanced at her. "No. I wasn't aware of that. Thanks for the heads-up. I'll get right on that just as soon as I talk to Beth about how she'd like to handle things."

Wren's lips parted in surprise and she leaned back. "Cyrus. No. Don't do this to her."

"What are you talking about? You make it sound like I'd be an affliction, not a skilled lover at her beck and call, eagerly anticipating her needs. And wants. And whims. And—"

A voice emanated from the speaker in the corner, informing us what day it was, who the presider was, and encouraging us to rise for the entrance hymn.

Everyone beyond the window stood, as did we.

But Wren wasn't finished. "You have to listen to me. Beth is the type of person who needs rules. She doesn't want them, she *needs* them. She needs clear lines and expectations. And in order to succeed, she needs to trust herself that she can stick to them.”

“Would bending some rules be so bad for her?” I watched as the men in dresses lined up when the piano started to play. “I think I’ve even heard you say on occasion that she needs to loosen up.”

“Yes, loosen up, Cyrus. Not abandon her core beliefs, her foundation as a person, what gives her focus and purpose. And think of her career. How is it a good look for a young *female* bodyguard to date her very first client? Especially if it’s you.”

This had me glaring at her. “Wait a minute, what’s wrong with me?”

She glared right back. “You’re mega famous. And you have a reputation for never seriously dating anyone.”

“I have a reputation? *I* do?” The exquisite irony of her statement was not lost on me since I’d wanted to be serious with women in the past, but—as luck would have it—none of them had any interest in being serious with me. Likewise, I’d agreed to the blind date with Ryaine/Beth because I wanted something serious. I wanted . . . someone.

Wren went on as though I hadn’t challenged her statement about my reputation. “If she were willing, if it wouldn’t mess with her head, fooling around would be one thing,” It struck me that this was an odd statement and argument for her to make in a church. “But making it official? Going public? And when you two break up, how well do you think that’s going to go for her?”

I had no witty or clever response to that. Given my track record and inability to hold the interest of my former paramours, a breakup with Beth was inevitable. My stomach soured.

“If you cared about her, you’d put a pin in your plans, whatever those might be.” Wren put a hand on my forearm, her stare imploring. “At least until the studio assigns her a new client, you’d keep your distance.”

I gaped.

Wren glanced at my mouth. “You look like a fish.”

I snapped my mouth shut just to sputter, “But—but you said she’s on a leave of absence until after the first of the year!”

“Yes. So?”

Grinding my teeth, I said nothing because the truth of it made me sound petulant and childish: I didn’t want to wait that long. I’d already waited. I didn’t want to wait months before kissing Beth again. I wanted more *now*, before she lost interest.

Not to mention the very real possibility that she might be with someone else by then.

"We could keep it a secret," I mumbled, troubleshooting out loud. "We'll keep it a secret until a few months after her next assignment."

"No. You couldn't. You have other guards, they would notice. You socialize like it's a biological imperative despite being the loneliest person I know. And if you tried to keep a relationship secret from the studio, she'd be the one who would pay the price when the proper paperwork isn't filed. Plus, it's not really about all that. That's secondary. *She* needs the time."

The first and last bits were true, but I took issue with her middle statements. "Excuse you, Dr. Freud, but how can I both socialize like it's a biological imperative *and* be the loneliest person you know? Doesn't one make the other impossible?"

Over the speaker, the piano music stopped, the singing stopped, and one of the men in their dresses started to speak. We both ignored him.

"Being lonely has nothing to do with whether or not you're physically by yourself, and it has nothing to do with how many surface-level friendships you have," she said, her tone mellowing. "In LA, you're everyone's best friend, but no one is yours."

"That's—" I cleared my throat of a suspicious lump, feeling like I'd just been punched, and stared unseeingly out the window. "That's preposterous."

"Oh yeah? Then try going one week without the distraction of a party or a club. Try going to work and then straight home, sequestering yourself in your room and spending some time on your own."

Keeping my eyes forward, I shrugged. "Sounds boring."

"Being alone is only boring if you find yourself boring."

I glowered despite the danger of wrinkles. "I'm not boring. I'm fascinating and witty."

She slipped her arm through my elbow. "You've tried to fill the need for a deep, human connection with an obscene number of shallow interactions."

"That's where you're wrong," I croaked around a dry throat. Suddenly, my tie felt too tight. "I have no capacity or desire for depth."

Belatedly, I realized one of the men in dresses—who, yes, I knew was the priest—had finished his spiel and the congregation had sat down in their pews. Sitting too, I reached for Wren's hand and held it in both of mine, studying her fingers. She had less calluses than Beth.

I heard Wren sigh next to me as a new voice came over the speaker, announcing the first reading was from a letter from Paul to the Thesapantaloons, or something like that.

"Cyrus, that's nonsense." Wren let me rub my thumbs over her fingertips as she spoke. "We both know that's not true. You have capacity for depth, and you can't love anyone unless you love yourself."

"Please." I snorted half-heartedly. "I love myself more than is healthy, we both know that *is* true."

"Yes. You love yourself, and you should, but you thrive on other peoples' perceptions of you. You never let anyone actually know you."

"What is there to know?" The question slipped out of me, spoken before I realized how it sounded or how much it revealed.

Wren made a small sound of distress, pulled her hand from mine, and lifted her arm as though to wrap it around my shoulders.

Some strange instinct or reflex had me flinching away. I didn't want her to comfort me. I wanted . . . someone else to do it. Specifically, Beth.

Holding my gaze, hers filled with equal parts sympathy and confusion, she lowered her arm to her side. "Despite what you think about yourself, you do have the capacity for depth." Her voice was gentle, her tone careful, and it pissed me off.

Clamping my mouth shut, I curled my shoulders forward and crossed my arms. Why were we talking about this? I'd purposefully avoided therapists for years to prevent these kinds of conversations. The last person who'd attempted this kind of discussion with me had been Alaric. I'd been dodging his phone calls for about a year until last week.

But she wasn't finished. "And if you took some time to know yourself absent all the noise and gushing flattery of people who have no idea who you really are due to the extremely convincing masks you wear, you might be pleasantly surprised to discover the smart, kind, interesting person beneath."

I grunted, only slightly mollified by her praise.

Sliding her a look, I asked, "In the depths?"

"Yes. In the depths." She smiled softly.

I grunted again. "Depths are where you find things like insects and mold."

"They're also where treasure is often buried."

"Who are you, why are you only speaking in fortune cookie riddles, and what have you done to Wren?"

She nudged my shoulder. "I think you're worried that if you don't strike while the iron is hot with Beth, you'll never have a chance with her. I think you're wrong."

Glaring at nothing, I said nothing. The woman on the altar had finished reading and had left her little podium. New music filled the room through the speaker and I cringed at the cantor's struggle to remain on-key.

Wren, however, had no sympathy for me and continued. "I also think you assume that anything between you two will be temporary because you don't think she'll have a reason to stay, in the long run, once she knows you. You're wrong about that too."

"Apparently, I'm wrong about everything." I studied my hands, asking before I could stop myself, "How can you be sure that I have depths?"

"Why don't you take a week—or better yet, a month—spend some time with yourself and figure it out?"

The suspicious lump had ballooned and I found I couldn't swallow.

"What do you say, Cyrus?"

Since I couldn't swallow, I cleared my throat. "You're proposing I spend a month getting to know the depths within myself, assuming they exist. And you think I should wait two months before pursuing anything with Beth."

"I think you should wait three or four months before pursuing Beth. She'll be reassigned after the first of the year, true. But she needs time to settle into the job, build some confidence."

I gritted my teeth. "That's a lot of waiting, and wading through moldy, insect-ridden depths."

"Again, both you and her are worth the wait."

Beth would be worth any amount of waiting, I felt certain of that. *Me, on the other hand . . .*

I straightened my shoulders, leaned back in the pew, and peeked at Wren. "What if she doesn't want me in three months?"

"That's the way the ball bounces, bucko. You don't always get what you want."

I did. Usually. *At least, for a time . . .*

"I'm impatient."

"Then maybe this'll be a good experience for you." She cracked a smile. "Character building."

"You think I need more character?"

"I think you need more endurance. I think you need more resilience and fortitude. I think you need to know yourself better. Whereas Beth needs to prove to herself she can be a professional as she defines it. She needs to find balance in her life."

"Balance," I repeated the word, an odd concept for me, and one I definitely didn't know how to achieve for myself.

Wren patted my back. "If she's so important to you, wait for her, work for her. Like I said, I like you a lot, but you're spoiled. And being infatuated with someone doesn't give you the right to blow their life to hell."

"I wouldn't do that to her." My eyes were on my hands again. "I care about her."

"Then back off. Give her some space. Let her do her job and prove to the studio—and to herself—she can stick to the boundaries she's set. Wait until February or March—"

"Now it's March?!" I blurted.

She spoke over me "—when she's settled into her new assignment, when you've spent some time learning how to be comfortable in your own skin. Then give her a call, invite her to coffee, a no pressure lunch."

March was in forever. It felt like a foreign concept, a theoretical month in the unknowable distant future.

When I didn't respond, Wren tapped me on the shoulder until I gave her my attention.

In return, she gave me a wry smile. "Come on. A little delayed gratification never hurt anyone."

"Yeah?" I didn't return her grin. "Well it feels like it's killing me."

ACT 3: PERSONAL INCENTIVE

CHAPTER 17

BATHSHEBA

"You cannot teach a crab to walk straight."

— ARISTOPHANES

~December~

"When do you go back to work again?"

"Uh, January ninth. Why?" I turned down the Christmas classics playlist I had blasting from my cell phone and lifted my head from where I knelt in my sister's pantry cleaning the baseboards. I'd already cleaned out the pantry, scrubbed down the shelves and walls, reorganized everything with new, better stacking containers I found at an Austin Goodwill, added labels to the shelves, and washed the floor. But I'd noticed this morning that the baseboards were a little dusty.

Gabi frowned at the cloth I held in my hand. "Do you plan to spend all or most of Christmas Eve cleaning?"

I opened my mouth to respond, then realized—unless I lied—nothing I said would be an answer she wanted to hear.

She released a beleaguered breath. "Beth. Come to Jamaica with us. I'm sure we can find a last-minute ticket."

"What? No! Are you kidding? I have a Christmas tree at Dad's place, three gigantic tins of cookies from all our baking, and I made pot pie from

169

the turkey you roasted over the weekend. We already celebrated Christmas all together before Dad and Matías left. I'm good."

"Beth—"

"Will Jamaica have a Christmas tree and pot pie? And where will you even go to mass? Does the resort have a Catholic church?"

"Yes. There is one near the resort. You are being ridiculous."

"I'm not being ridiculous, and even if I wanted to go—which I don't—I don't have the money for a flight anywhere, you know this." I returned my attention to the slightly dusty baseboard, wishing Gabi weren't so tidy. Would it kill her to be more of a slob? "Why is it ridiculous for me to want to do something nice for my sister?"

"My linen closet looks like something out of a magazine. I've never had an inventory system for my cleaning supplies before. You've ironed all my shirts, including my T-shirts, *and* my sheets! Who irons sheets? That's not being nice, that's keeping busy for the sake of keeping busy. And don't you dare go back to Dad's apartment and take a toothbrush to his bathtub again. Come with us. I'll cover the cost. There are other hotels on the island. You could—"

I stood, leaving the moderately dusty cloth on the floor and faced my sister. "I don't want to go to Jamaica. You and Wes need this break. I've already crashed your Thanksgiving with his family and all your Christmas traditions. He's desperate for some alone time with you. Go to Jamaica with your handsome husband."

She stared at me like I was a problem. "Then see if you can get a ticket to Peru. Join Dad and Matías on their trip. I'll give you the money, no problem. It'll be a Christmas present."

Our brother, Matías, would be graduating from college in the spring. He and my dad had been planning this trip to Peru since Matías's freshman year, and I knew how excited they were for their guys-only hiking vacation. I didn't want to trespass on their time together. Plus, I honestly didn't want to go. Knowing myself, my brother, and my dad, I would've spent the whole time yelling at them for taking stupid risks and not wearing enough sunscreen.

"No, Gabi. Now you are being ridiculous. I'm not taking money from you for something so unnecessary. Dad and Matías have been planning this trip for three years. I'm not flying to Peru."

"But—"

"I was planning to spend this Christmas by myself anyway. I'm right where I want to be, doing exactly what I want to be doing."

"Except you were supposed to be in LA working. You told us you'd have to work over the holidays and there was no chance that you'd be able to get the time off. If we'd known over the summer you were going to be in Alenbach for Christmas, we wouldn't have booked this trip to Jamaica."

"Then I'm glad you didn't know." Placing my hands on her shoulders, I turned her away from the pantry and gently guided her out. "Y'all have half an hour before we leave for the airport. Go. Finish getting ready. Have Wes come get me when you guys want to leave."

She growled, spinning around to face me. "I'm so irritated with you."

"Because I want what's best for my sweet older sister?"

"Because I hate the idea of you being here by yourself and I just wish you would stop being so stubborn about absolutely everything! Why don't you go to LA? You're paying exorbitant rent for an apartment you're not using. Spend Christmas with Ryaine or one of those bodyguards you befriended at the studio. The two who came to visit earlier this month seemed so awesome."

"Kristina and Mindy *are* awesome." Not wishing to witness more of my sister's frustration, I scanned her kitchen, searching for small appliances I could clean. "But they're also in the first few months of their relationship and I'm sure they don't want me crashing their holiday. And Ryaine and Ransom aren't in LA, they're skiing in the Alps with a bunch of their film friends."

I didn't add that Ryaine had already invited me to join them in Switzerland, offering to pay my way, first-class tickets and luxury accommodations. I'd declined, obviously. I didn't want to have that kind of relationship with her or set that kind of precedent for myself. I'd worked for everything I had, every dollar I spent.

I already didn't like that my friendship with Ryaine had helped get me the job at WWS. Working for Ryaine, providing a service she'd desperately needed and having her employ me as a contractor was one thing, but I didn't want to be the type of friend who accepted handouts because I couldn't pay my own way. Even if it meant us drifting apart somewhat due to our differences in means, I'd rather have my pride fully intact than be a first-class-flying charity case.

Also, I suspected she wanted to set me up with one of Ransom's friends who was also going as part of their group. Every time I spoke to her on the phone she'd mentioned the guy, a nerdy cinematographer with a master's from USC and a passion for collecting old Hollywood photography prints.

He actually sounded amazing on paper, but I wasn't ready to meet anyone. It wouldn't be fair to him.

Despite not wanting to, I still thought about Cyrus all the time, especially when I didn't keep busy. If I didn't spend my days engaging in physical labor that left me exhausted at the end, I wouldn't be able to fall asleep. Memories of his hot mouth on mine, his grasping, greedy touch, the feel of his perfect body kept me up and feeling desperate. Or his eyes looking at me, his mouth curving into its careless smirk, and his wicked voice saying, "Bathsheba, my hero."

Which was another reason why I didn't want to be lazy in Jamaica or ski or go to LA.

Mindy and Kristina had talked about Cyrus when they'd visited after Thanksgiving. They hadn't asked any questions about my sudden departure from the team, likely sensing I wasn't willing to discuss it, but I knew they were curious. They'd said Cyrus passed along his well-wishes and hoped we'd get together when I returned to LA. This secondhand message through Mindy was why I'd spent two days scrubbing the grout in my dad's shower with a toothbrush.

If I were in LA during Christmas, feeling lonely and bored, I'd probably do something stupid, like seek Cyrus out.

No, much better that I stay in Alenbach cleaning and organizing my sister's house until the last possible minute. My flight to LA was booked for January seventh, two days before my new studio assignment. That felt safe.

"You keep saying Mindy and Kristina wouldn't want you being a third wheel, but you don't know because you haven't asked. Maybe they're also doing a friend-group Christmas, like Ryaine and her skiing friends. Maybe you'd have a great time. You don't always know best, Beth. You get these ideas in your head and it's like you believe if you deviate from your preconceptions or moral compass—even a little—the whole world is going to end."

She was yelling at me now, looking and sounding so much like our mom, I had to roll my lips between my teeth to keep from smiling fondly at her because *that* would set her off for sure.

Leaning my hip against her kitchen island, I crossed my arms. "Go get ready. You can make your case in the car on the way to the airport, counselor."

Gabi growled, her fingers making the universal sign for *I just want to strangle you right now.* "When is living a full life going to matter more than your stupid pride? When will you—"

The shrill sound of my phone ringing cut off her rant and, like a lifeline, I lunged for it, accepting the call without checking the number. "Hello?"

"Bathsheba Ryan?"

I turned away from my sister, trying to place the vaguely familiar voice on the other end of the call. "Yes?"

"Hi Bathsheba, this is Lenore Wood from WWS. How are you?"

My heart skipped a panicked beat, but I did my best to sound untroubled. "I'm well, Lenore. How are you?"

They were going to fire me. I knew their assurances about waiting until I was ready to come back were all false. They were upset I'd taken a leave of absence and were going to let me go, and then—

"I'm also well, thank you. I'm so glad you answered your phone because I have a huge favor to ask, and I'm at my wit's end here," she said, thoroughly diverting my spiral of dread.

"Oh. How can I help?" I rubbed the base of my neck, the adrenaline that had rapidly spiked dissipated just as fast, leaving me in an oddly good mood. Being of service was much preferable to being a burden.

"The reason I'm calling is, your former client needs a security fill-in and, frankly, you're our last hope."

Uhhh . . .

"Is that so?" I asked with all outward calm, my adrenaline spiking again.

"Yes. Cyrus Malcom flew out to his hometown today—he's already in the air—and we were just informed that the contract security detail we had assigned is stuck in Chicago due to the snowstorm. Your former lead, Wren St. James, mentioned that you're already in Alenbach, where Cyrus's family lives. Is there any chance you could meet him at the airport, run interference with fans and press, if there are any, and ensure he arrives at his family's home safely?"

Many emotions rolled through me and I shoved them aside, needing all my brainpower to figure this out. "I absolutely want to help. But what about his team? What about Wren and Tamra and the rest?"

"Yes. Well. Uh . . ." She sounded uncomfortable and I heard a computer mouse being clicked a few times in the background before she continued. "Your nondisclosure paperwork is up to date, so I can tell you that there was a food poisoning incident on the set of Cyrus's new film. Apparently the craft services table served some expired shrimp and oysters. Two of your former teammates are in the hospital and the rest are in no state to guard anyone. It's . . ." I felt her exhaustion from my side of the call. "Frankly, it's been a nightmare."

Cyrus is allergic to shellfish. "But Cyrus, he was okay? I know he's allergic, he didn't have any or suffer from any cross contamination?"

"No, no, he's fine. He only ate food prepared by his chef that day, wanting to avoid—as you said—cross contamination. Thank God he did."

My shoulders relaxed. "And my team? They'll be okay?"

"I believe so, after some rest and recuperation." Lenore's tone grew even more weary. "Listen, I know it's a big ask during your leave of absence, and on Christmas Eve no less. But all we need you to do is pick him up from the airport in about three hours, walk him to the car, and drive him to his family's home. You don't need to stay. All told, it should take you less than six hours, round trip."

I felt myself hesitate. The request wasn't a big deal. A pickup from the airport, a walk through the service tunnels, a drive through Austin to Alenbach—should be easy. But . . . *Cyrus.*

I'd thought—I'd *hoped*—I'd see him sporadically in the future, at events and parties and clubs, while I guarded one of his celebrity coworkers. I'd be on duty during those encounters and we'd have no reason to talk, but I could look at him from afar and, you know. Admire.

You could give him back his watch.

A twisting of discomfort made me lose my breath, followed by two heartbeats of odd panic.

That's right, I had Cyrus's watch. His father's watch.

I hated that it had been taken from him. The memory of his despair and tears haunted me, made my stomach sick just thinking about it.

Also, I'd felt ashamed after abandoning the team in New York and angry about how the police had treated Cyrus. I'd scoured social media, searching for every video and every view of the convention center when the crowd had jumped over the barriers and begun ripping clothes off Cyrus and Vera. Folks recording with their cell phones had posted reaction videos and commentary after the fact, laced with dumbass opinions about whether Cyrus and Vera had deserved to be mobbed by fans and separated from their clothing.

Anyway, enough about idiots on the internet.

One of the videos gave me a clear shot from behind Cyrus for the last half of the incident, right before Cyrus had been whisked away. I'd sent the video to Mindy and Tamra, asking them if they knew which of the frenzied faces might've taken Cyrus's watch.

Long story short, I'd forwarded a still photo from the video to Santino— my ex who worked for the CIA—and sweet-talked him into helping me find the man. He did. I dipped into my savings to take a plane up to New England and pay the perp a visit at his home in Connecticut, and . . . well, let's just say I gave him two options.

He chose the right one, and now I had Cyrus's watch.

Oh, and don't worry about my savings. I was fine and could sell one of my precious dresses if I needed cash. No big deal. But the reason I possessed any savings at all had a lot to do with my unwillingness to spend it flying to Switzerland, Jamaica, or Peru. Big surprise, but I was careful with money, my only splurge being vintage couture dresses. A girl's gotta have her vices.

I'd debated anonymously mailing the watch to Cyrus. That idea had been promptly dismissed. I worried it might get lost in the mail. Ultimately, I'd decided to give it to Wren the next time I saw her. I trusted her to make sure Cyrus received it without divulging who'd found it.

My silence must've stretched a beat too long because Lenore said, "Ms. Ryan, Wren St. James confessed to me that you've still been helping your old team with location specifications and following up on adherence to rider requirements."

My heart seized again. "Not really. Only once or twice, when there was an emergency." I grimaced. That was a lie.

I had been helping. Wren didn't know about it until just recently, and I felt awful about not keeping her in the loop, but it started out innocently enough. Mindy called the week after I'd left and needed some quick specs on a club I'd already mapped out and prepared a packet for. I'd sent her a link to the document's location on our secure drive and hurriedly gave her advice on my preferred escape route, given her description of their location and the situation. She'd messaged me later to say thanks and that my suggestion worked great. I'd thought that would be it.

Tamra messaged two weeks later, close to midnight, said she'd needed me to call Ryaine and ask her for the address of some party in Hollywood because Cyrus didn't have his phone. The address Craig provided wasn't right and no one scoped out the neighborhood ahead of time.

The texts, emails, and calls had continued all through November and December: Cyrus flew home for Thanksgiving and their car was followed from the airport. Cyrus was on location for a week, shooting in Vancouver, and they lost all cell service. Cyrus was on his way to an event in London, they couldn't certify that the menu was shellfish-free, and Craig was too much of a lightweight softy to throw his weight around.

"Hmm. Well, Ms. St. James told me your assistance was more than that, but that's not the issue." Lenore cleared her throat. "My point is, you've been helping, keeping in touch, which means you know what happened during Thanksgiving, yes? The last time Cyrus flew home, when they were followed from the airport?"

"Yes, ma'am," I croaked out, feeling like I'd been caught with my hand in the cookie jar.

"Then you can understand how important it is that he have a guard at the airport and on the road, especially one who knows defensive driving. Your employment file says you have previous experience as a security chauffeur."

"That's right." I lifted my fingers to my forehead and rubbed.

"If it's a matter of money, Ms. Ryan, we are prepared to—"

"No, no. That won't be necessary." My cheeks hot with guilt, I glanced at Gabi. She stood in the center of the kitchen, glaring at me, eavesdropping unabashedly to my side of the conversation. "Of course I'll help. I'm very happy to—to help."

"I'm so relieved to hear that, Beth," Lenore said, her relief palpable. "And you will be receiving a paycheck for this pay period, to account for the back pay owed for your support to the team while you've been on leave as well as for today's shift."

"Really, that's not necessary—"

"Really, it is. Today will be a workday for you, and Ms. St. James has insisted on the back pay for the last two months of support, ten hours per week."

I gritted my teeth. "No. I will not accept it."

Obviously, I wasn't taking money for helping my team with a few emergencies, that was silly. And as for today, I couldn't accept money for ensuring Cyrus made it to his family home safely. I just . . . I couldn't.

"Not up for discussion," she persisted. "We value our security personnel and—"

"I will not accept it. I will only pick up Mr. Malcom from the airport and transport him to his family home if I'm not being paid. As you said at the beginning of this call, it's a favor, one I'm glad to do. And Ms. St. James didn't know about my—my answering questions for the team until just last week. It really wasn't a big deal, and it definitely didn't take ten hours per week."

I listened to Lenore Wood sigh on the other end of the call, pause, and then sigh again. "Fine. No paycheck," she said shortly, like I was the most frustrating person on the planet. *Get in line, Lenore. My sister was here first.* "I'll send through the details for Cyrus's flight, the rental car, and your credentials for collecting him at the private gate area."

"Would it be possible for me to use my own car? Then I won't have to go back to the airport to switch out the vehicles."

"We'll be sending a car to collect you. Text me your address, please. Once we hang up, I'll arrange the pickup for an hour from now."

"Is it okay if they arrive in thirty minutes? I was actually just about to take my sister and her husband to the airport."

Gabi, waving her hands in my peripheral vision, snagged my attention. She mouthed, "What's going on?"

I mouthed back, "Give me a minute," and held my finger up, turning away again before she sent me another glare.

"Of course." This statement was paired with a bit of keyboard clacking on Lenore's side of the call. "After you've dropped Cyrus off at his family home, simply return to wherever you're staying in Alenbach. Text me the address if it's different than where you are now, and we'll have someone pick up the rental. You understand, if something were to happen to Mr. Malcom in your personal vehicle, it might pose a legal issue."

I frowned at that, not understanding how I—a person not being paid by the studio to pick up Cyrus—would be putting the studio in legal danger should something occur in my personal car, but I'd have to take her word for it. My dad's truck, which I'd been driving for the last few days since dropping him and Matías off at the airport, had four-wheel drive. We were supposed to receive a fair bit of snow later tonight, close to midnight. I didn't want to be in a two-wheel drive rental once it started. But if the whole business would only take six hours, then I'd be home long before the snow started to fall.

I'd argued enough and didn't wish to appear difficult, so I agreed. "Certainly. Thank you, Ms. Wood."

"No, thank you, Ms. Ryan." Her tone tempered, softened as she said, "I can't tell you how much your help in this matter is appreciated. The studio will not forget, and we look forward to having you back with us after the first of the year. I think you'll enjoy working with Vera. She's a conscientious and hardworking person, like you."

As frazzled as I was at the thought of seeing Cyrus again, her words pulled a smile out of me. I'd received the information packet on Vera Rodrigo last week, my next client. Again, the term would be for six months. I'd seen her briefly at DarkLensCon and, based on how she interacted with her current team, I felt confident we'd have a productive working relationship. Glancing over her schedule, I'd felt a bizarre mix of relief and disappointment when I didn't see any engagements or overlapping filming schedules with Cyrus. The next movie in the Asmodeus franchise didn't start primary filming for another year.

I'd probably see him at an industry party or at a club, but I could manage. Just because I saw him, didn't mean he'd see me.

"I'm looking forward to meeting Ms. Rodrigo officially. Thank you. I'll text you my address right now and keep an eye out for that email."

"Sounds good. Thank you again, Ms. Ryan. And Merry Christmas."

"Merry Christmas," I said, then ended the call.

CHAPTER 18

BATHSHEBA

"It is from their foes, not their friends, that cities learn the lesson of building high walls and ships of war."

— ARISTOPHANES, *BIRDS*

"What was that about? What's happening?" Gabi pounced on me as soon as I lowered the phone.

Drawing in a deep breath, I began the necessary mental preparations that would see me through the remainder of the day and my upcoming Cyrus exposure. "That was the studio. It seems I will be working over Christmas after all."

Her head tilted slightly to the side. "Oh yeah? Are you flying to LA?"

"No. Cyrus Malcom is flying here." I braced myself for her reaction. She'd known almost as soon as I did that Cyrus had been assigned as my first client in LA because I'd called and told her the week I found out.

Her reaction over the phone at the time had been negligible, something like, *Oh. Yeah. Cyrus. He took me to prom in high school, what a small world. Have you seen his latest movie? It was great. Wes loves the Asmodeus comics.*

The conversation had moved on to family matters and her complaining about a current case she'd been working on, and that was it. I hadn't known what to think about her reaction back in June, and I hadn't pressed her about

179

it, but I'd honestly expected it to be bigger. She'd been so heartbroken in high school when they'd stopped hanging out, her easy acceptance over this past summer felt false, especially after I knew what it was like to be near Cyrus, to be the recipient of his focus, and how devastatingly charming he was.

Presently, Gabi's earlier frustration with me seemed to ebb at this news. "Here? Today?"

"Yes. He's, uh, visiting his family for Christmas." Hoping the comment sounded nonchalant, I watched her closely while pretending to be distracted by my phone, texting Lenore Wood Gabi's home address.

"Oh. That's nice. Mrs. Malcom is really great. She still organizes the gingerbread houses at the community center every year. Is his brother coming into town too? Titus?"

"I have no idea." Continuing my inspection of Gabi, I ventured to ask what I'd been too reluctant to ask over the summer. I now knew Cyrus's version of events—that they'd merely been friends—but not hers, only that she'd cried for over a week. "What happened with you and Cyrus in high school? It seems like you liked him a lot. Did he . . . did he lead you on?"

Her features lightened and she smirked. "Uh, no. Cyrus was a perfect gentleman. I had a crush which he did not reciprocate, but that didn't make me special. Everyone in my year either had a crush on Rex McMurtry, Alaric Weston, or Cyrus Malcom." A little laugh escaped her. "Except Alison Weston. She hated Alaric and anyone who associated with him."

"Alison *Weston*? I didn't know he had a sister. Or are they cousins?"

Gabi made a face. "I mean, technically they're stepsiblings, but they weren't raised together. I don't think they had any contact outside of school."

My confusion must've been obvious because Gabi went on to provide an explanation. "Alison and Sylvia Weston are James Weston's biological daughters. He left their mother when they were really little, like under three, for his current wife—Alaric's mom. He then adopted Alaric as his own and dodged child support payments for Alison and Sylvia until a court ordered him to make the back payments when Alison was, like, eighteen. I think she used the money to pay for college."

"Oh my God. What a bastard. He's so rich, why didn't he pay child support for his daughters?"

"Right? I have no idea. But apparently he treated Alaric really well. He grew up with all the advantages Alison and Sylvia didn't, which is why Alison hated Alaric so much all through school. He got a corvette for his sixteenth birthday and she took the bus to school until she graduated. It didn't help, of course, that he was valedictorian and she was salutatorian. I think she missed the top spot by a fraction of a point because of some grade point advantage for student athletes, which wasn't fair because she had to work after school and couldn't do sports, but he didn't have to work and could do football. Anyway, she couldn't stand Cyrus and Rex by association. And me. And anyone connected with them."

I grimaced at this piece of gossip. "That's rough. I see her point, but it's not Alaric's fault his stepdad treated her and her sister that way."

"True. But Alison . . . I don't know. She scared me a little, you know? Like, she was so smart and angry all the time. I tried to stay out of her way because she was so mean, would just like, eviscerate people in public who tried to mess with her. I remember she once made this girl cry when she teased Alison about taking the bus and not having a car like Alaric." Gabi made a face like, *Whatcha gonna do?* and shrugged. "Anyway, about Cyrus, no. He didn't lead me on, and when he let me down, he did it gently. I can see in retrospect how upset he was about it, like he didn't want to disappoint me. He was really sweet."

Annoyingly, I wasn't surprised by this. Cyrus was sweet. Except with me.

Now hold on, that's not true. Sure, he tries to push your buttons, and is an indiscriminate cuddler who never takes anything seriously, but he's never been mean to you. Not once.

Shoving those inconvenient thoughts aside—I was doing a lot of shoving of emotions and thoughts today—I gave my sister a small smile. "Well, I guess the good news is that you won't have to worry about me cleaning your house over Christmas. I'll be too busy working. Feel better?"

It wasn't a lie so much as a misdirection, and I immediately felt guilty about it. Except, no. I would not feel guilty about this. I could stretch the truth if it meant Gabi would relax enough about leaving me in order to have a good time with her husband in Jamaica. She deserved a break.

Gabi examined me, then said, "I'd feel even better if you asked Cyrus if you could spend Christmas Eve with him and his family."

Gaping, I stumbled over my words before she put me out of my misery by walking over and pulling me into a hug. "Just think about it. You're driving him home anyway and Mrs. Malcom is so welcoming. It's only the three of them in that huge house, I'm sure she won't mind." Gabi leaned back to look at me, not quite letting me go. "You know what? Bring one of those giant tins of Christmas cookies with you. If she invites you to stay, stay."

Searching my brain for an excuse, Gabi gathered my cheeks between her palms and lifted my face. "Listen to me and believe me: people like you. People want to be around you. You don't have to be proving yourself *all the time*. You don't have to be the most useful, industrious person on the planet in order to have worth. You just have to be yourself."

I lightly wrapped a hand around one of her wrists and buried my reflexive expression of doubt before it could surface.

"Beth, my sweet baby sister, you are loved by your family. We want to be around you. People want to know you."

"I know that," I said, trying to smile. I hated it when she did this, when she felt it necessary to speak these statements out loud. I tried to give her the reaction she wanted so it would stop.

It didn't end. She said the words I despised the most because they always made stupid tears sting my eyes. "Your biological mother leaving had nothing to do with you. You were just a kid. It wasn't about you, it was about her. Do you understand?"

I blinked to clear my blurry vision. No one was as persistent or pushy as my sister. "Fine. I'll bring the dumb cookies. Will you stop with the positive affirmations already? I know you love me."

She grinned, kissed my forehead, and then let me go.

My shoulders sagged with relief and guilt simmered in my stomach. Another misdirection and half-truth. I would bring the cookies, but I'd slip them in with Cyrus's luggage along with his father's watch when I loaded his bags into the car. I *would not* give Ms. Malcom a chance to invite me into her big, fancy house.

Picking up Cyrus at a set time and existing in his vicinity just long enough to drive him home was one thing. Spending Christmas Eve in his orbit without a hard time limit, with his high-society mother, in danger of succumbing to the magnetism of his smoldering, mischievous stare while struggling to not make a fool of myself was quite another.

By the time I arrived at the airport and said goodbye to my sister and her husband, I'd almost convinced myself that a few hours of limited Cyrus exposure wouldn't be a big deal. I could handle it. I'd spent the end of June through the end of October guarding him. I knew how to shut down, knew not to lift my eyes past his chin, and knew to respond to his taunting with nothing but flat, one-word answers.

Worst-case scenario, I'd put on that poncho of jealousy again and imagine teal nails trailing up his leg and him leaning into the touch. That memory would certainly do the trick.

I didn't think it would come to that, however. In the past, when I didn't react, Cyrus didn't push. I would simply not react and he'd have no choice but to simmer down. Besides, he'd probably forgotten all about me by now. Seven weeks was forever in celebrity circles.

I might even have to reintroduce myself to him when his plane lands. The thought made me feel both better and worse. I ignored the worse and focused on the better.

As soon as he stepped off the plane and my eyes connected with the profile of his achingly handsome face, I realized I'd been a fool. My body's insides seemed to rearrange themselves at the sight of him, a blast of irrational longing rushing from my chest to the top of my head, tips of my ears, fingers, and toes, and twisting in my lower stomach. Also, I held my breath. Involuntarily.

Breathe, idiot!

Sucking in air, I found enough wherewithal to tear my arrested attention away before he saw me staring at him like he was a donut and I was a carb addict. Or like he was a donut and I was literally any person on earth who enjoyed donuts.

I walked across the asphalt and waited, working on my mask of outward stoicism while he loitered at the plane's open door. Lazily, he began his descent, his movements languid and graceful, confident and careless— exactly like him.

By the time he'd made it down the jet's stairway, I'd managed to wipe my face of any expression by distracting myself with thoughts of Gabi's small appliances and how her stand mixer was in need of a good scrub. *I will scrub the stand mixer so hard and that will be so satisfying.*

Cyrus paused in front of me, his long fingers splayed over the front of his charcoal gray cashmere overcoat. I recognized it from when we'd been in New York. It was a vintage Versace double-breasted overcoat, it looked absolutely stunning on him, and I knew it was incredibly soft and warm just from having held his arm while escorting him from the car into the convention center for DarkLensCon.

"Bathsheba," he said, his voice low but full of something like affection or mirth. Either he was happy to see me, or wanting to taunt me, or both. But then he added a quiet, "my hero," under his breath and my heart lurched toward him.

I swatted it down, shifted my weight from one foot to the other, and asked flatly, "Where are your bags?"

His chest rose and fell, his head lilting to the side like he might try to catch my gaze. I blinked away from his chin and glanced to the left, giving him my profile and squinting at the tarmac. I searched for someone else who might answer my question.

Finally, he shoved his hands in his coat pockets and said, "I have no bags. No need. My mother's home is fully stocked with my clothes and such. I leave things there, for when I'm in town."

Well. There went my plan of giving him his watch back.

I felt the solid weight of it in my coat's inner pocket as I nodded my understanding. Stepping next to him, I slipped my hand into the crook of his elbow, keeping my eyes down the entire time. Instinctively, I knew to the depths of my soul that if I looked at him, the next several hours would be unbearable. Worse, I'd be too distracted to do my job. I wouldn't be able to focus on keeping him safe with the image of his gorgeous, clever, sparkly green eyes branding my brain.

So I didn't. I scanned the tarmac, then gently tugged on his arm. He followed without comment. We'd done this dance a hundred times, him following where I led as we navigated a crowd, or through backstage areas, or down the tunnels of buildings and onto waiting elevators. But it felt different because I *knew* it would be the last time.

I hadn't known in New York the day before he'd been attacked. But I knew it now.

Making note of each person we encountered in the service tunnels, gauging their threat potential and the risk assessment if they approached, my brain also cataloged the feel of his arm beneath the layers of my gloves and his clothes; the ease of his stride; the heat from his body at my side; and the crisp, seductive scent of his cologne. I wondered if this cologne was from the bottle I'd bought him in New York.

And when we reached the car, I'm ashamed to admit I hesitated before opening the passenger-side rear door—just a fraction of a second—saying goodbye to this, and him, and all the silly fantasies I'd ever entertained about us.

Then I did, I let him go, and it was over.

Stepping back, one hand on the car door and the other behind my back, my gaze sweeping the interior of the garage for potential problems, people, and hazards, I waited for him to slide into the back seat.

Instead, he reached forward and placed his hand on the edge of the door I held open, shut it, then walked around me and said, "I'd like to sit in the front."

By the time his words permeated my brain and I'd spun around to object, he'd already opened his own door, climbed into the front of the SUV, and shut himself inside.

Clamping my jaw around the protest I hadn't managed to voice in time, I walked around the back of the car, forcing myself to focus on my surroundings and not the fact that I'd be spending several hours sitting next to Cyrus.

CHAPTER 19

BATHSHEBA

"What can you answer?
  Now be careful, don't arouse my spite,
  Or with my slipper I'll take you napping,
  faces slapping
  Left and right."

— ARISTOPHANES, *LYSISTRATA*

Snow began to fall in earnest as we exited the parking garage. I was glad for the precipitation as it gave me something to focus on and worry about other than the magnetic movie star sitting to my right. Surprised by the huge line of cars leading into the airport as we left—a traffic jam that hadn't been there when I'd arrived with Gabi and Wes—I turned my head to read the flashing sign next to the road.

"They've canceled all flights," I muttered to myself, my brain distracted by what that meant. Gabi and Wes were lucky their plane left when it did.

It snowed in Austin from time to time, usually just a dusting, but where my dad and sister lived in Alenbach, they might receive six inches or more every few years. Except last year, they'd received over a foot in a short period of time. That kind of weather was extremely rare for Hill Country and Austin hadn't been impacted. At least, I didn't think any flights had been canceled last year, but I might've been wrong.

I chewed on my fingernail and fretted. Cyrus remained blessedly silent as we drove out of Austin and took the freeway toward Alenbach. His quiet presence felt oddly comforting in the big SUV. For the most part, he sat perfectly still, his elbow propped up on the windowsill, his hand lightly covering the lower half of his face, and his gaze pointed out the window.

It wasn't until we pulled off the freeway and I felt the SUV drift just a wee bit on the off-ramp that I realized just how heavy the snowfall was.

Cyrus must've been having similar thoughts, because he muttered, "This is . . . this is a lot of snow."

Forgetting the promise to myself to speak only in one-word answers, I said, "Yeah. I read that it would snow today, but—I guess I should've looked up the forecast again. The last time I checked, this wasn't supposed to start until midnight. I assumed it would be a dusting in Austin, like usual." If I'd been given more of a heads-up before leaving to pick up Cyrus and had been less nervous to see him, it would've occurred to me to do another check of the weather forecast.

I flipped on my blinker, frowning at the whiteout in my rearview mirror, and waited until the light turned green before making the right turn.

Several miles down the road, Cyrus cleared his throat, the first sound he'd made in a while. "The most accumulated snowfall in a twenty-four-hour period was in 1929. I believe Hillsboro saw something like twenty-six inches of snow in one day," he said casually.

"Huh." I did not know that. "Really? Two feet in twenty-four hours?"

"Yes." Cyrus, his eyes looking out the windshield, seemed to absent-mindedly fiddle with something in the center console. "I only know this because my great-great-grandfather moved here from Scotland about ten years prior—during prohibition—and was attempting to grow barley in Texas. He was a whiskey maker."

Checking my rearview mirror again and seeing nothing but a curtain of white, I responded distractedly, "Barley? Can you grow barley here? And, whiskey? Why was he making whiskey during prohibition?"

"If you think about it, prohibition was the best time to make whiskey," he said offhandedly. "And some people think you can grow barley in Texas. The family legend is that he succeeded for several years before the snow came and wiped out his entire crop. Feet of snow, such as never before, and the harvest was ruined."

"How did he recover?"

"How do you know he recovered?" Cyrus shifted in his seat while I gradually slowed to a near stop behind the car ahead making a left turn. It was the first car we'd seen since pulling off the freeway.

"Yours is the wealthiest family in Alenbach. They own half the land." Once the car in front of me turned, I accelerated deliberately, not liking how the tires felt slippery on the road.

"But we own none of the businesses. Those all belong to Alaric Weston's father. Or, I guess, his stepfather."

"And you still own the land. The Westons are your family's tenants, right?"

"Yes. The Weston Factory, offices, storefronts, and associated outbuildings sit on our land. Why?"

"It's just . . ." I shook my head. "Never mind."

We drove in silence for several more miles. At one point, Cyrus unclicked his seat belt and I automatically looked at him, ready to protest or demand he wait so I could pull over first. But then I saw he was simply taking off his overcoat, revealing a pair of snug-fitting jeans and a green Henley that came close to the color of his eyes. I snapped my mouth shut. He tossed the coat in the back seat and refastened his seat belt.

I felt his eyes on my profile as he said, "It was getting . . . hot in here."

"I can turn down the heat." I made a vague gesture toward the AC controls. "Or you can if you want, adjust it to whatever is comfortable."

"No. It's not—that wouldn't help," he grumbled, turning his face toward his window again.

Impulsively, I glanced at him and my heart did a flip. Cyrus was frowning. He looked unhappy. This realization filled me with restlessness and a desire to do something about it.

I considered giving him his father's watch now, that would surely lift his mood. It would also lead to him asking several uncomfortable questions I didn't wish to answer. For unknown reasons, it felt essential that he never know I'd been the one to recover his father's watch.

Hazarding another glance and finding him still wearing a frown, I opened and closed my hands around the steering wheel, debated what to do, and glanced at the map readout on the car's cell interface. It was blank.

"Oh darn." Torn, I reached for my phone, but I didn't want to look away from the road. I put it back and asked Cyrus, "Hey, can you check my phone? See if the maps app is still working."

I'd never been to Cyrus's family's house before. I knew approximately where it was situated—the general direction from downtown Alenbach—but not its specific location.

He picked up my phone and glanced at it. "Looks like you have no service. Here. We can use mine." He reached into the back seat and pulled his coat over his lap. Digging through his pockets, he withdrew his phone and unlocked it. In my peripheral vision, I saw him stare at the screen for a beat before saying, "I have no service either. Must be the snow impacting the cell towers. I'll, uh"—he glanced at me—"I'll just tell you which way to go."

"Sounds good," I said, unable to stop thinking that maybe his frown and grumbling meant he didn't want to sit in silence, and that seemed fair.

As a person constantly in motion, constantly surrounded by interesting and important people, I imagined a three-hour car trip with his taciturn former bodyguard wasn't high on his list.

"Do you want to listen to music?" I asked softly. "Or talk radio?"

"No, thank you," he said shortly, shifting in his seat again while he kept on staring and frowning out the window. "You'll need to take a right when you get to Old Whiskey Road."

"You don't want to go through downtown Alenbach?"

"No. I've seen it before." His response was uncharacteristically irritable.

Fighting a bout of nerves, I considered my next question, or whether I should ask a question.

One popped in my head and I wondered if it was too personal. But you know what? I decided, to heck with it. I wouldn't see Cyrus again after today, not in any meaningful way. If he clammed up, so be it. I had nothing to lose.

I waited another mile or so, then asked, "Do you miss it?"

—at the exact same time he demanded, "Why did you pick me up?"

Stiffening at the hostility in his tone, I redoubled my efforts to focus on the road and responded calmly, "I was already here and the studio asked."

I got the sense he was waiting for me to continue. When I didn't, he asked, "That's it? There's no other reason?"

Chewing on my bottom lip, my thoughts drifted to the watch in my pocket. "What other reason would there be?" I hedged, testing the wiper controls to see if it had a higher setting. It didn't. I felt like we were creeping along at this point and we'd be lucky to make it before nightfall.

His eyes still on me, he grumbled something I missed, then asked, "Do I miss what?"

I considered saying, *Nothing, forget it,* but my reasoning for asking the question was still sound.

"Do you miss Texas? Do you miss being close to your momma and all these wide-open spaces? The culture out here?" I went back to chewing my bottom lip, feeling unaccountably nervous. Carefully, I slowed the car and turned onto Old Whiskey Road. This was the bypass road for Alenbach, which was still some thirty miles ahead.

The snow seemed to thicken while I waited for him to answer. We traveled another mile and I glanced at Cyrus, our eyes connecting for the first time since he'd arrived at the Austin airport.

I absorbed the shock of it, breathed through it. Meanwhile, he stared at me, some combination of puzzled and stunned.

Braving another quick look, I asked, "What's wrong?"

"I believe that's the first time you've asked me a personal question directly."

Gripping the steering wheel tighter, I struggled with how to respond, and eventually blurted, "That can't be true."

"It is. What do you know about me?" The question sounded like an accusation. "We worked together for four months and not once—not *once*—did you make any effort to know me. Why is that?"

A hot, spiky feeling pressed uncomfortably outward against my skin. The truth was, I knew more than I wanted to admit. "I—I know plenty."

"Really? How? Are you a mind reader? What am I thinking right now?"

My breath wanted to hitch. I wouldn't let it. I tried to focus on my irritation, not this strange sense that I'd let him down.

"Go ahead," he demanded. "Tell me what I'm thinking."

Glancing at him, I saw a deeply furrowed brow, glinting narrowed eyes, mouth tugged down at the corners, jaw set. Cyrus looked more like his character Asmodeus than himself—a beautiful, surly, smoldering fallen angel instead of a happy-go-lucky sweetheart with too much energy and charisma.

"Well?" Cyrus pushed.

"Well, obviously you're angry with me."

"That's right, I'm angry."

"Fine. Be angry then!" I yelled.

"I don't want to be angry with you!" he shouted back. "I want to be the opposite of—oh shit"—he braced his arm against the dash—"Stop!"

I saw the deer right before Cyrus did. It was huge. Despite my frazzled state of mind and his insistence that I do so, I did not stop. I didn't swerve either, though every instinct screamed at me to yank the wheel to the right.

Did you know deer kill more people than any other animal? Snakes and sharks have nothing on Bambi. Some people think they're cute, I blame Disney for that. They're not cute, they're dumb. If you're unfortunate enough to see them in the road, stop only if it's convenient *and* you spot them from a distance *and* it's not a winter hellscape outside.

But since this one appeared like a serial killer in a snowy slasher flick, I didn't stop. I pressed gently on the brakes, slowed, and braced for impact. It came with a forceful, bone-shaking *boom*. Airbags deployed, filling my face and vision. The jolt of it caused my foot to press harder on the brake—rookie mistake, I should've removed my foot—and that's when the shit hit the fan.

The car skidded, spun, gliding over the frozen asphalt, whirling us in a single, dizzying circle, the back of the SUV sliding off the small country road. And then everything stopped.

For a good long moment, it felt like I had cotton in my ears. I heard breathing first—mine and Cyrus's—and then frantic movements.

Cyrus unclicked his seat belt, his hands pushing the deployed airbags to the side. "Beth, Beth—are you okay?" His voice was tight and panicky.

I released a trembling breath. In my foggy state of shock, I lifted my eyes and noticed the wipers were still going. Beyond the windshield, I watched two more deer cross the road, right in front of our spun-out car, like they were strolling through the sale aisles of a JCPenney.

Stupid deer.

You'd think after watching their buddy get aggressively bodychecked by a giant machine, they would've run in the other direction.

"Bodychecked? What?" Cyrus asked, reaching for my seat belt and fumbling to unfasten it.

Oh. I must've spoken my musings out loud.

This time I heard my voice say, "Nope. Not deer. They witness the murder of their friend and think to themselves, 'Well, I'll just mosey on out there and see what's up.' Brave as a bigamist, stupid as a watermelon."

Cyrus's hands stilled. Suddenly, they were on my face, cupping my jaw, turning it toward him. He pushed shaking fingers into my hair. "Beth. Love, are you okay? Did you hit your head?"

I blinked, pulling his wide, beautiful, frantic eyes into focus. "Cyrus."

"Bathsheba."

I shivered. "I think . . ."

"Yes?"

I'd never admitted it to myself until right now, but the way Cyrus said my full name made me feel almost sinfully good, like he was groaning it and whispering it and telling me a secret. I'd never loved my name before. It was the only thing my biological mother had given me other than half of my DNA and abandonment issues, but I loved my name when he said it.

Cyrus's gaze traveled over my face, then connected with mine, the urgent concern there dwindling the longer we stared at each other. His lips parted, and I wished he'd kiss me. It would feel *so good.* Staring at him now, I thought of his room in New York, kneeling on the floor, his lips brushing lightly against mine.

For a split second, I thought he would. Cyrus leaned an inch forward, his eyes lowering to my mouth. But then he closed his eyes, his jaw clamping shut, and he pulled back, taking the heat of his hands with him. Breathing out, he faced forward.

"Will the car start?" he asked, his tone still shaky, but also sounding odd, like he'd come to a disappointing conclusion.

Feeling like he'd pulled me off a cliff when he pulled away, I glanced stupidly at the steering wheel. I hadn't realized the engine was off.

"Oh. Yeah. Let me check." Pressing on the brake, I pushed the ignition button. It didn't start.

"Put the car in park," he said, his eyes now open and staring out the windshield.

Of course. It had still been in drive.

Doing as he suggested, I tried again. This time, it did start. But when I shifted it back in drive and pressed the gas, the wheels spun uselessly against the snow-covered dirt at the back, and that's when my brain finally woke up.

Startled, the reality of the situation came vividly into focus. *We're stuck. In the middle of nowhere. With no cell service. During a snowstorm.*

I cut the engine, trying to think, but found I needed to speak in order to organize my thoughts. "We should stay in the car, but turn the engine off, and see if anyone comes by. We've got three-quarters of a tank of gas, so we'll turn the car on every once in a while for the heat."

Cyrus nodded, easing back in his seat but not at all relaxed. "Okay."

Glancing at him, I took note of his clothes again, this time paying attention to his shoes. They were beautiful, Italian, and completely useless for walking through the snow.

My Ugg boots weren't much better. *At least I'm not in heels.*

"Put your coat back on. It'll keep you warm. And we should power down one of our phones—mine probably—to save battery."

Cyrus sat forward and pulled on his coat. "You think we'll be here that long? That we'll need to save our cell phone's battery life?" His voice sounded thin and reedy. Maybe he was going into shock?

I allowed my heart a single beat of fear but kept it out of my voice as I said, "No. I don't think so. There's bound to be a car sooner or later. Or we'll get cell service back and can call for help."

This time I didn't mind speaking in half-truths because the truth was, I had no idea. Given how the snow was coming down and that we currently sat on one of the least traveled roads on the outskirts of Alenbach, I didn't know what to think.

Searching for my cell—it had been thrown somewhere during the accident—I said, "Just to be safe, let's turn off your cell's wireless and Bluetooth. And we'll plug it into the car so it charges when we turn the engine on."

Cyrus lifted his phone to comply and his shaking hands gave me pause. I thought about not saying anything, but when the cell slipped from his grip, I acted on instinct and grabbed the hand closest to me, squeezing it lightly. He returned my grip by grasping me with both hands, like I might disappear, or I was the only thing keeping him from floating away.

"Hey, hey now. It's okay. You're okay."

His eyes closed again and he pressed the crown of his head against the seat. "I know. I just . . . need a minute."

"What's going on? You want to talk about it?" I kept my voice light and easy. He'd gone pale and his breathing didn't sound right.

Cyrus gave his head a quick jerk, his eyes screwing up tighter. My worry for him ballooned.

"You know—" I licked my lips, my brain casting around the car for something to talk about, anything that would pull him back from wherever he'd gone, and settled on the lowest hanging fruit. "I hate deer. I hate them. They're basically serial killers. They kill more folks than sharks do and yet no one is making movies about killer deer. Makes you wonder what kind of PR firm they hired. And they're dumb as a watermelon. If a duck had deer brains, they'd fly north for the winter."

Cyrus opened his eyes to peek at me, a short laugh puffing out of him. But it wasn't enough. His breathing still didn't sound right.

For some reason, I was reminded of the dinner party on the heated patio back in New York and that odd moment when we'd traded condolences about his dad and my stepmom. I thought of how Alaric had comforted him. How he'd rubbed circles on Cyrus's back, letting him lean against his body.

With my free hand, I unclicked my seat belt. I tried leaning over the console to get closer while still ranting some nonsense about my hatred for deer, but it wasn't enough. I was too small and the console was too big. He was still shaking, his pupils little dots.

On impulse, I climbed onto his lap, straddled his hips, and yanked him into my arms. I hugged him, rubbing slow circles on his back, and his arms immediately came around my body. He was shaking all over, and I didn't think it had anything to do with the cold.

"And—and this one time, we were taking care of the old Peckerson place, housesitting, you know the old ranch with no horses? We had our dog with us at the time, and this stupid deer was eating something at the fence line. Mind, our dog wasn't leashed—Polly was her name, like a parrot, because Matías wanted a parrot and not a dog, but Gabi and I wanted a dog 'cause we're right and he's wrong—and the deer just kept on eating even though it saw us approach. I think Polly was a little offended, upset that the deer didn't take her presence seriously, give her the respect she was due as a predator, because Polly chased that dumb deer for over an hour, back and forth in front of the fence. It didn't know enough to run away."

Leaning back, needing to see his face, I gathered his angular jaw in my palms and tilted his chin back. He was still shivering, but not shaking as before, and his eyes were open, looking at me.

I gave him a little smile, relief like a sunrise in my chest. "Hi," I said.

"Hi," he whispered, sucking in a deep breath and then releasing it slowly. Eyes on mine, his forehead wrinkled. "Sorry."

"You want to tell me what's going on?" Smoothing my hands along his stubbly jaw, I cocked my head to the side. "Are you in shock? Do I need to continue regaling you with deer anecdotes? 'Cause I got plenty."

The side of his mouth hitched upward, just barely. Cyrus's hands slid from my back to my thighs, shoulders rising and falling with another deep breath.

He seemed to engage in an internal debate for a few seconds before his eyes hooked into mine, sharpened, and he said quietly, "I was in the car. When we were hit, when my father died, I was in the car. I was trapped in the front seat next to him, my legs pinned."

My mouth formed an "O" and my brain worked frantically to process this news while my heart strained to absorb it. I'd had no idea. I knew his dad had died after being hit by a drunk driver, but I didn't know Cyrus had been with him when it had happened.

And why had Cyrus been in the front seat? He'd been seven! That's a traffic ticket right there.

"They didn't find me for eighteen hours. I couldn't leave, I couldn't get help," he went on, his voice sandpapery as his eyes turned pleading. "I don't know if I can stay in this car, Beth."

Stroking his cheeks, I nodded. "Okay, cutie-pie, okay. If you don't want to stay, we don't need to stay."

That right there was a bold-faced lie. We did need to stay in the car. It was our best chance of not freezing to death in the next twelve hours because this snow didn't show any signs of letting up. But those weren't the words Cyrus needed to hear right now. Oddly, at present, I found lying to Cyrus easy as pie.

"I'm not trying to be difficult," he said, making my heart twist.

"I know, sweetie, I know." I threaded my fingers into his hair and lightly scratched his scalp with my nails rather than lean forward and give him kisses like I wanted. "You're not being difficult. You're wonderful and perfect."

He blinked, like I'd said something surprising. But then, with his next blink, his features transformed. His eyelids drooped over lazy-looking eyes and his lips curved into a small, pleased smile that made my stomach—as inappropriate as it was—erupt with fluttery winged creatures.

But you know what? Looking at him close up, at the way his eyes continued to gaze deeply into mine like he was a little lost, I don't think he was aware of his expression. He wasn't putting on a face or slipping into a debonair character. This was just Cyrus reacting openly and honestly to my words.

This *was* Cyrus.

"Beth?" he whispered after a time, his scorching smolder morphing into an expression of amused bemusement.

Realizing my mouth was hanging open, I snapped it shut. "I'm—uh—" Giving myself a quick shake, I let my hands slide from his hair to his shoulders and then cleared my throat. "I'm just thinking, if we don't want to stay in the car, we'll need shelter, right? So, you got any ideas about that?"

This would be his task, something to distract him while we stayed in the car where it was safe and warm. As long as he was distracted and felt like leaving the car was an option, I hoped he'd be able to sit tight long enough for someone to drive by.

But then he surprised the tar out of me by saying, "Actually, I do."

CHAPTER 20

CYRUS

"My gender has no bearing on the question
Whether I'm offering you a good suggestion."

— ARISTOPHANES, *LYSISTRATA*

Snow is slippery. And wet.

These were the thoughts that kept me warm while we crossed the street, abandoning the now stiff deer Bathsheba had murdered with the rental, and traversed the short distance to my great-great-grandfather's homestead. Other than a slight bend to the hood, the rental remained in decent shape with the bumper having absorbed the brunt of Ms. Deerworth's demise.

That said, it was currently half on, half off the road and I suspected one of the tires might've been going flat.

The barn loomed closer than the house, but we wouldn't stop there for long. I needed Beth's superior survival instincts to help determine what we scavenged before continuing to the house.

Glancing at the top of her hat-covered head, a smile threatened. Though it was likely absurd, I wasn't the least bit concerned about surviving the next hours—or days—in the primitive structure built by my ancestor. Beth was the most competent and determined person of my acquaintance. I would put myself entirely in her capable hands, no matter where she decided to place them.

The threatening smile became a grin.

"Why are you smiling?" she demanded, sounding grumpy, her teeth chattering. "It's freezing out here."

"But it's an adventure." I winked at her, my heart light.

She laughed like she did not find me amusing in the slightest and grumbled something unintelligible beneath her breath, saying nothing else until we made it to the barn.

"We can't stay here," she said as soon as we stepped one foot inside. "It's too open to the elements. We'll freeze."

"Of course. This is a barn." Dusting the snow from my hair and shoulders, I faced her and put on a show of mock-offense. "I'm not sleeping in a barn. Who do you think I am? The son of a carpenter?"

The laugh that erupted from her this time sounded completely involuntary. It also warmed her lovely eyes with humor.

"Okay. So, what's the plan then?" She glanced around, hiking her purse higher on her shoulder, her teeth still chattering. "We search for supplies and continue on to the house?"

"Bingo." I strolled to the driest part of the barn, ignoring my cold feet, and set down a mostly empty grocery bag. The bag housed a large tin container of Christmas cookies and nothing else. According to Beth, they were a gift from her sister. I planned to write Gabi a thank-you note. Or perhaps stop by and express my gratitude in person. And if Beth's stepsister wished to absolve me of any lingering high school hurts at the same time, so be it.

Without expanding on precisely what foodstuffs and tools Beth carried, she'd stated her purse contained several helpful items. I'd been in a hurry to abandon the interior of the car and we were losing sunlight. She'd searched the interior of the rental for anything that might be useful while I'd left a note in the front seat with a description of what had occurred and where a passerby might find us. Then, we'd ventured forth.

Presently, placing her gloved hands on her hips, she meandered over to a pile of straw. "This might be useful."

I smirked. "Fancy a roll in the hay?"

She did not smile, nor did she look at me. "Does the house have a bed?"

Not surprised by her lack of reaction to my joke—*okay, you caught me, it wasn't a joke*—I searched my memory for details about the old house and reminded myself not to do that again. There would be no flirting with Bathsheba. "There's a bedframe, but no mattress."

"Makes sense if no one is using it and it's all the way out here. Mattresses can get gross." Beth gestured to the hay. "We can make beds out of this, so we can sleep. It'll be better than sleeping on the floor, assuming the hay isn't rotten or infested with bugs."

She bent to push her fingers into it and I darted forward. "No—no, you don't want to do that. There's likely snakes in there."

Stiffening abruptly, she stumbled back, her eyes rounded. "Snakes?"

"Yes." Searching the barn, I found a hoe, pitchfork, and a few other tools hanging from a wall. "Let me just . . ." Selecting the pitchfork, I returned to the hay and lifted a quantity of straw from the rest, shaking it out and letting it settle into a new pile near the grocery bag. "It doesn't look rotten. We'll sift it first for snakes and creatures. Can you find something to carry it in? Take the hoe with you."

"Why do I need the hoe?" she asked, her eyes huge, her hand moving to her side. "I have a gun. And a few knives."

"Of course you do." I grinned. "But a hoe will be more helpful with a snake."

She grimaced, but then nodded when she saw my logic. Beth moved toward the hoe gingerly, inspecting the walls and rafters as though snakes might drop on top of her.

Hiding a smile, I settled into a rhythm—stab, lift, move, sift—and was on my seventh load of hay when I heard her ask, "There's a bunch of stuff here. How recently was this barn used?"

"Not long ago, maybe five years. The last tenants boarded horses, but the house hasn't been occupied in—oh—fifty years at least. Maybe seventy-five." Not unless you counted me and my brother using it for our adventures.

Growing up, my mother had ensured the structure was sound and the chimney was cleared, so I doubted it was in any danger of collapse. If memory served, and assuming she hadn't made any changes recently, the house was basically one square room, twenty feet in diameter, with a sparse selection of furniture, and not modern by any stretch of the imagination.

For example, the house did not possess indoor plumbing. Water had to be pumped from a well, a well which I assumed was now frozen and unusable. The outhouse was fifty feet behind the main house. But I wouldn't tell Beth this. I didn't want to spoil the surprise.

My mood, already edging toward cheerful, improved further at the thought.

Her hoe in one hand, Beth appeared in front of me gripping several large feed sacks in the other. "I think these will work. If we have to take multiple trips, it'll be worth it to stay warm and off the floor."

"Find anything else useful?"

She crouched in front of the hay pile and began stuffing one of the bags. "Yes, thankfully. First aid kit, scissors, a few buckets, a toolbox with a hammer and a Leatherman, horse shampoo, and—uh—some leather harnesses, rope, and zip ties."

I bit back the urge to inquire whether our evening would include bondage. Instead, allowing my gaze to move over her, I let the thought percolate in my mind, distractedly wondering if she'd be open to something like that. With me.

Not tonight, obviously, but maybe in a few months after we reconnected in LA. Assuming she wanted to reconnect. And things progressed.

That was still the plan, by the way.

I'd been adhering to Wren's prescription of behaviors over the last two-ish months and I'd discovered several surprising details about myself. Some good. Some bad. Some boring. Some absolutely fascinating.

But I'd also reached several conclusions about Beth, the most irritating one being that Wren had been right. About everything.

Which was why, when Beth had appeared at the base of the stairway leading down from the jet earlier today, I'd been so surprised to see her. Overjoyed, but surprised. Lenore at WWS had texted midflight to explain that a security detail would meet me on the tarmac, but not the contract team from Chicago. I'd been given no advance notice that Beth would be my security.

The joy had lasted ten seconds, rapidly replaced by frustration.

I'd been so good. *So good.* I'd left her in peace back in early November and I hadn't reached out to her other than a friendly message sent through Mindy and Kristina. I'd recommended her for Vera's team, told everyone how professional she was—which was entirely true, so no cookie required for that bit—read seven self-help books about knowing thyself, started a journal, and marked the days off on my calendar, counting down until February first.

I'd changed. I'd grown. I'd waded through depths. I'd *worked.*

And there she'd been, standing at the bottom of the stairs, treating me just the same.

"I think that's enough for now," she announced, standing and then dusting her gloves off on her jeans, several feed sacks of straw stuffed to the brim behind her.

Tucking the pitchfork under one arm, I crossed to her and picked up the grocery bag along with as many sacks as I could carry.

"Ready?" I asked, offering her my arm not holding the pitchfork.

She gave me a bemused look and, instead of slipping her hand in place at my elbow, she lifted two bags. "Lead the way."

"Do you like it?"

Beth stood just inside the doorway, her features painted with dismay.

I grinned, finding her discomfort adorable. In fact, in a strange and unforeseen turn of events, her discomfort delighted me. Excluding Beth, I couldn't remember ever being delighted by the discomfort of someone I didn't dislike.

No, no. That's not true.

I did delight in making my childhood friends Rex and Alaric uncomfortable, and my brother, and my mom. But only because I liked them so much.

Huh. Isn't that odd? The people I enjoyed making uncomfortable most were the people I either disliked or liked the most. I made a mental note to write about this phenomenon in my journal.

I'd entered the house first, asking that she stay outside.

When she'd protested, I'd told her, "I need to check for snakes."

That did the trick. Setting her hay sacks on the porch, she'd sat on them and waited for me to search the house. In all honesty, I did need to search for snakes. But I also wanted to check for other animals and their droppings. If she'd found deer poo, she might've suggested we burn the house down to keep warm instead of sleeping inside.

There was no poop. The interior looked exactly like my memory of it, except perhaps a bit dustier.

I'd checked both cedar chests for snakes, pulling blankets out one at a time with the pitchfork and shaking them. Other than the chests, there wasn't much to the space. A huge, old copper tub in one corner by the southeast window currently held stacked firewood, the bottom of the tub protected by a layer of thick canvas. I'd need to empty it to check for snakes.

A woodburning stove near the tub would be used for heating—both the room and water—and cooking, if we'd had anything to cook. A cabinet sat in the other corner; the aforementioned bedframe with no mattress—a single

—had been pushed in the third corner and laid on its side, broken and not usable; and a primitive table shoved against the wall with a bench beneath it took up the last and final corner.

Satisfied, I'd invited her in, and she'd grimaced.

She hadn't yet responded to my question, so I repeated it. "Do you like it?"

"It's great," she said in that tight, suspicious way people do when you ask them what they think about your latest creative endeavor, or whether they like how you've seasoned the steaks with cayenne instead of paprika.

Beth tilted her neck back, examining the exposed ceiling beams and roof. "There's a hole in the roof, just there." She walked to the spot she'd indicated, the corner near the tub. "It's okay until the snow starts melting. Do you think we should patch it?"

"You want to patch the hole?" I lifted an eyebrow at this.

"Sure. I know how." Her gaze narrowed thoughtfully. "Assuming there's some shingles. Or maybe, if I found tin snips, I could cut one of the buckets."

A wave of warmth fueled by admiration and affection washed over me. Of course she would know how to patch a roof. Of course.

"You seem to know how to do everything." I crossed the small room to stand next to her, peering up at the hole, obvious now that she'd pointed it out. "I wouldn't know the first thing about patching holes in a roof."

She glanced at me. "But you know how to check haystacks and abandoned houses for snakes. That's much more important."

I chuckled. "Well, that's different. I used to run around over here, galivanting and playing. Checking for snakes is just smart. But in all my childhood imaginary games, I never had the foresight to be a roofing contractor."

I felt her eyes on me, so I turned my head and gave mine to hers. A moment passed where we looked at each other, over too soon as she blinked away, dropping her attention to the floor and clearing her throat.

"Uh, well, anyway. I don't know if we should waste time on that. We're not going to be here long enough."

"Look outside, Beth." I lifted my chin toward the window above the tub. "Does it look like it's going to stop snowing anytime soon?"

"We could try to walk."

"Walk?"

She crossed to where we'd left the sacks of hay. "When you came out here as a kid, how did you get here?"

I turned so I could watch her movements. "I ran."

"Your house is close enough to run here?"

"Yes, as the crow flies or as a child runs in the summer, it's only a mile and a half. But there's a wide stream in the way that we cannot cross unless we go to the bridge, which is ten miles north."

She twisted her lips to the side thoughtfully. "Ten miles isn't bad."

"Ten miles north, in snow, to the bridge and then ten miles south in more snow to my mother's house."

Her frown was immediate. "Oh." Her gaze lifted to the corner above the tub again and her voice was tight as she spoke, "I guess I'll try to patch that up."

"Fine. We have blankets to lay over the straw just there, and more to cover us tonight. There's also a few beach towels." I pointed at the pile I'd removed from the chests. "But first, I need to empty the tub."

Her eyes snapped to mine, wary. "Planning on taking a bath?"

"Maybe, if—" I stopped myself just in time before saying, *If you'll join me.* Honestly, I wasn't usually this much of a Depraved Daniel, with every other thought a double entendre or an invitation to debauchery.

I mean, I was a Depraved Daniel. Just not typically to this extent.

I tried again. "Maybe. I'd like to start a fire as soon as possible and this wood is dry. But I'm more concerned that it might be an ideal place for a snake to hibernate."

She hurriedly removed herself from the vicinity of the tub. "Oh. Okay. Yeah. Do that."

I didn't want to smile, but I had no choice.

CHAPTER 21

BATHSHEBA

"To win the people, always cook them some savoury that pleases them."

— ARISTOPHANES, *THE KNIGHTS*

*P*lacing the lighter I always carried in my purse on top of the wood stove, I left Cyrus to his pile of wood and ventured back to the barn for the other supplies. While I was there, I wanted to check for any additional tools or materials I could use to patch the hole in the roof. I'd also needed some space from him.

Out here, marching around in the snow, he seemed different somehow. More settled. Calmer. *Sexier.*

I attempted to repress that last thought with a rough shake of my head. It was no use. Despite it being a snowy mess outside, and freezing inside, my internal temperature was all over the place.

Point was, I couldn't imagine a time when I didn't think of Cyrus Malcom as the most erratically generous, unfailingly sweet, addictively attractive guy in any room. I'd been overwhelmed by his proximity plenty in the past. Even here, Cyrus still emanated that same golden retriever energy, but it was more focused rather than chaotic. Something was different with him.

He's more serious.

The thought filled my lungs with prickly heat which I immediately tried to ignore. Engrossing myself with tasks and to-do lists, I searched the barn for nails, finding a box plus a few other items that might be helpful. I loaded everything up in the buckets, using busy work to distract me.

As I carried my survival treasures back, I spotted a stack of roof shingles leaning against the left side of the house, tucked under the roof of the porch. Heartened, I deposited the items from the barn next to the front door and I marched over to the shingles, inspecting them. I kicked the pile. The ones on top crumbled slightly, but the ones several rows down appeared to be usable.

Crouching and swiping snow from my nearly frozen face—I hoped Cyrus had that fire started—I dusted away the disintegrated top shingles, picked up a handful of the ones beneath that weren't quite stable enough and set them to the side, and then selected four from the middle of the stack. And that's when I saw the snake.

I screamed, lurching backward several feet, my arms flailing, and fell on my ass like an idiot. Backing away, completely heedless to the snow wetting my backside, my eyes remained fixed on the diamond-shaped head of the snake lifting from the pile I'd uncovered. It was *looking* at me.

I screamed again just because I could and because OHMYGODTHATSASNAKE!

"What? What is it?" Cyrus appeared, running to where I sat on the ground.

Not looking away from my adversary some ten feet away, I gestured frantically to the serpent coiled on top of the revealed pile.

Cyrus didn't respond at first, and I wondered if he saw it, or if I'd have to spell it out for him.

But then he said, "Beth, other than the cookies, did you bring any food with you?"

What? "Uh . . ." I shook my head, confused. *Why is he asking about food?* "Well, a little." I had Starburst candy and several bags of his favorite tea in my purse. I hadn't removed them after leaving New York. Don't ask me why.

"How do you feel about snake for Christmas Eve dinner?" he asked.

I whipped my head toward him, at a loss for words. But then I blurted, "I don't want to kill it. I just want it to go away."

"Where? Snakes are cold-blooded. It has nowhere to go." Cyrus didn't even try to hide his grin. "I can't believe you grew up in Texas and are this afraid of snakes."

"I grew up in an apartment! Not on a sprawling estate with ranches and farms and wide-open spaces. I'm Texas, not Alenbach."

"You're Texas, huh?"

"Yes. I am Texas. Just not country-Texas like all y'all. Despite growing up out here, I never rode a horse or fed a pig."

"Okay, Texas. What about the Peckerson farm?"

"I told you, that was just land. No horses or cattle or pigs." I looked between him and the diamond head. It was huge, and I thought I could hear the faint sound of a rattle. "Can't we—can't we relocate it?"

"Oh my God, you are so adorable." Now he laughed. Hard. A lovely rumbling sound I'd missed so much, holding his stomach while snowflakes fell on his dark coat and hair, sticking in his eyelashes as his bright eyes looked at me like he was having the time of his life.

My heart went *kuh-thunk*.

"No, *microbino mio*. I'm not relocating a rattlesnake. I'll kill a rattlesnake, but I'm not playing snake real estate agent or attempting to upsell Mr. Rattles on a cozy barn with no pool or view."

Did he just call me a small microbe in Italian?

Whatever. I didn't have time to think about that right now.

Something in me rejected the idea of killing this snake. "Cyrus. . . " I looked up at him, pleading with my eyes, not knowing what to do.

His wide grin faded into a soft, gentle smile while we stared at each other. My heart gave another *kuh-thunk* and I wondered what the heck I was going to do if he kept looking at me like that. Keeping myself busy out here would only go so far. Eventually, we'd be going to sleep and he'd be lying nearby. I probably had a full night of restless pining ahead.

Unless he makes a move. Which, given our history, he might.

I swallowed thickly at the thought. It was a notion I'd been explicitly avoiding since receiving the call from Lenore Wood.

Then again, he could've kissed you in the car and he didn't. Maybe he's not interested anymore.

I used to think, before our very sexy encounter in the office at the Brooklyn house, that he sorta came on to everyone and no one. But after the office and his bedroom, when he'd *very much* come on to me, I didn't know what to think.

So, if he does make a move, what will you do?

Staring at him, at the beautiful sight of beautiful him covered in beautiful snow, I decided Cyrus's gravitational pull reminded me of Jupiter—all its moons, asteroids, and other heavenly bodies orbiting but never able to actually approach without getting burned in the atmosphere.

I'd spent the last two months thinking about the fact that I'd never seen

Cyrus sleep anywhere but in his own room, and always alone. But who knows what he did when I wasn't on duty. He could've done anything on Wednesday and Thursday, or Sunday after I left, and I never would've known. Given how he'd flirted and touched folks constantly, I couldn't imagine he'd been celibate since June.

I sighed, feeling stuck. I didn't want to be just another heavenly body to him, or to anyone. My pride wouldn't allow it. I wanted the hard work, trust, consistency, and respect of an enduring relationship, like my dad and stepmom had. I did not want overwhelming feelings and jealousy every time my man let a lady with teal nails touch his leg. But that's what Cyrus did and who he was. Consistently.

Eventually, he spoke, his gentle words pulling me out of my contemplations. "Look. It's almost asleep now. The exposure to the cold will kill it soon. *Chuisle*, if the circle of life negatively impacts your delicate sensibilities, turn away."

Steeling myself, I dug deep for some resilience. This was a rattlesnake, not a puppy. Cyrus was a movie star, not a regular guy. "No, no. It's okay. I'll. . . just tell me what to do."

His gaze flicked around the porch, settled briefly on a shovel, then returned to me. Walking over, he reached down and pulled me up, holding my gloved hand as he said, "Could you please retrieve the garden hoe? And don't go near the haystack."

"Okay."

Still holding my hand, he gave me one last smile that made me feel like I was drowning and I didn't even mind, then he released me. "Go, *bella*."

I turned, stumbling, my heart heavy and confused—both of which had little to do with the rattlesnake—and walked three paces.

Then I stopped.

Frowning, I stomped on the ground. *Hmm.* Spinning back around, I walked to where I'd been sitting and stomped on that ground.

"Doing a dance in the snake's honor?" Cyrus asked. "Will you teach me the steps?"

Shooting him a look even though it made my heart skip a beat, I crouched and shoved the layer of snow to one side, perplexed when all I found beneath was wet dirt.

I could've sworn.

"I guess. . . never mind." I stood, dusting off my gloves. "I'll go get the hoe."

❄

When I returned with the hoe, my boots covered in snow but still surprisingly dry on the inside, Cyrus was holding a dead snake in one hand and the shovel in the other.

I stopped as he turned, a big, proud smile on his face. "It's much larger than I'd initially suspected. Don't worry, I waited until it fell asleep. Mr. Rattles didn't suffer."

My eyes wide, I gawked at him and the unalived animal. "You used the shovel?"

"That's right." He came closer.

I backed up, because he was holding a dead snake's body. "Why'd you send me to get the hoe if you were just going to use the shovel?"

"You seemed upset by the serpent's impending demise. I didn't want you to witness it."

I should've been numb, but his words paired with his voice paired with how sweetly he was looking at me, made me warm all over, completely caught in his spell.

But then he said, "Don't worry about the head. I smashed it."

I flinched, coming back to reality. "What?"

He leaned the shovel against the side of the house. "They can still bite even after they die, like how turkeys and chickens can flop around after death."

"How do you know this?"

"I spent much of my life on a ranch. A hobby ranch, but still a ranch. We were never far away from our food. Anyway, best to obliterate the head. We'll need to skin it now. May I have one of your knives?"

I went right back to gawking at him. "Do you know how to . . .?"

"Skin a snake? Of course."

Huh. I did not expect that.

A smile danced behind his expression, his green eyes clearly amused by my shock. In fact, he'd been various shades of amused ever since we'd left the car.

"Knife?" Cyrus prompted again.

"Oh. Yeah." I pushed my jacket to the side and pulled a knife from my belt, handing it over to him, hilt first.

"Thanks." He accepted the knife with a smile and a wink. He then walked toward the house with a spring in his step and I stared after him, not sure whether I should stay here and avoid watching him skin a snake or follow and . . . what? Lend moral support? Give him an audience? Applaud?

Clearly, Cyrus wasn't perturbed by murdering snakes, cutting off and smashing their heads, and then skinning them for dinner.

Who knew?

I decided to loiter outside and use the hoe to separate a few shingles from Mr. Rattles's stack. Where it was freezing. And still snowing buckets. But it was also freezing in Cyrus's family's shack, and there were no dead snakes being skinned out *here*, so. . .

Blowing out a breath, I tried to rub some warmth into my frozen nose, wishing I hadn't fallen in the snow earlier because now my butt felt numb.

Oh. Yeah! Wait a minute.

The necessary shingles now separated from the pile, I placed them on the front porch, then I marched over to where I'd been sitting. I stomped on the newly fallen layer of snow. The ground felt different in this spot, more solid and oddly hollow. On a hunch, and promising myself I would stop digging in five minutes and get back to patching the roof if I didn't find anything, I stabbed and scraped the hoe across the earth to loosen the dirt, then I picked up the shovel to dig a shallow hole.

Sure enough, just two shovel scoops later, I hit something. My heart ticked up. Crouching instead of sitting or kneeling, I glanced to the west where the sun would likely set in the sky soon and I used the hoe to scrape away the remaining dirt, revealing what looked like a wooden door, lying flat on the ground.

Employing both yard tools back and forth to remove as much of the dirt as possible, and fighting the heavy, constant flakes of snow working to obscure my progress, I mostly uncovered what looked to be two cellar doors.

The old Peckerson place had a cellar built into the ground like this, but that cellar was set at least two feet closer to the house.

Smiling at the discovery like I'd accomplished something, I debated with myself for the span of three seconds before deciding to ask Cyrus his opinion. Would an underground cellar be warmer than the house? Possibly. I thought I recalled, though I could've been wrong, that cellars remained at a fairly constant temperature, midfifties or sixties, despite the weather outside.

Midfifties sounded downright tropical right about now.

Opening the door to the house, I spoke as I entered. "Hey, so, I think I found a—"

I stopped.

First of all, the shack was . . . not cold.

I mean, it was cold, but it wasn't freezing ant's titties like the outside was. Not anymore. I searched for the source of the heat.

Also, music from the *Charlie Brown Christmas* album seemed to be coming from somewhere.

"It's the wood stove." Cyrus stood at the primitive table, no coat, his shirtsleeves rolled up to his elbows, one of the feed sacks sitting under the snake he'd just—*gulp*—skinned. The knife I'd let him borrow was sticking out of the wood table, blade down, hilt up. Next to the knife was his phone, which I surmised was the origin of the music. He must've downloaded the album to his phone since, last time I checked, we still didn't have any cell service.

Even his shoes were off, leaving him in what had to be wet socks.

Turning from the table, he meandered over to me, keeping his hands away from his sides. "The stove warms things up."

"I feel that," I said on a breath. I had the urge to flee, to march back to the car and lock myself inside. He was too much.

This might be the strangest day of my life.

Cyrus walked past me, and I turned to watch as he dipped his hands into one of the buckets I'd brought from the barn but had left outside the front door. It now sat on top of the hot stove. Drifting closer, I saw he'd filled it with water. Soapy water.

"Snow," he said, reading my thoughts. "I melted it. Thanks for finding the horse shampoo and the bucket."

Ah. So that's where the suds came from. He'd brought in all my survival finds and placed them on the cabinet in the far corner. His shoes were sitting close to the hot stove.

"You're welcome. Uh, so." I rubbed my forehead, trying to remember why I'd come in here without something to patch the hole in the roof. Besides, shingles go on the outside, not the—*Oh!* "So, I found the cellar, I think. But I guess it's a nonissue now." We'd be toasty warm in our little shack if that wood stove kept on working so well.

"A cellar? Here?" Cyrus lifted a disbelieving eyebrow at my words, picking up a towel draped over the side of the copper tub—which was now free of wood—and dried his hands.

"Yeah. It's just outside, where I fell earlier. You didn't know about it?"

"You mean when you screamed and I rescued you?"

I rolled my eyes, but I also smiled. "Yes. When I screamed and you rescued me from a sleepy snake. Anyway, there's two doors. Should we check it out? Or, I mean, it'll be dark soon. We should figure out a way to get some light in here, and I still need to patch that hole, and make the—uh —beds." I glanced at the corner where the tub sat. Since it had warmed inside the house, a trail of dripping water rolled down the wall. If I didn't patch the hole, we'd have a puddle by morning.

"There's candles in one of the cedar chests. I'll take care of the light and the beds. Let's go see this supposed cellar." Cyrus slipped his feet back in his shoes, his eyes bright and excited as he walked past me to grab his coat from where he'd draped it over the sideways bedframe.

"You seriously didn't know there's a cellar here?"

He shook his head. "No. But I can't wait to check it out."

It was a cellar. A small, cramped cellar with a few spiderweb-covered odds and ends, but mostly full of—wait for it—alcohol. Crates and crates of bottled golden brown alcohol with no label.

Cyrus, the adventurer, picked up the hoe and had gone down on his own, claiming it was best for him to go first, just in case there were snakes. I suspected he'd be using snakes as an excuse to go first from now on.

After completing a cursory check for our slithery friends, he'd called me down and I'd joined him. Using his cell phone's flashlight—which felt like a misuse of resources, but then he'd pointed out we could always go back to the car and charge it up—he'd pulled what looked like a sheet off the closest crate and the alcohol had been revealed.

"Merry Christmas to us," he said, grinning like a kid on Christmas as we reemerged from the cellar with four bottles, leaving at least another sixty or more behind, possibly twice that many. I was too cold to count the crates.

I closed the doors as he exited and gave him an incredulous look. "Isn't that stuff poison by now? How long do you think it's been down there?"

"Are you kidding? That's over one-hundred-year-old Malcom whiskey, made from Texas barley, aged underground. This might be the best whiskey in existence." Juggling the whiskey bottles, he grabbed my hand and dragged me back to the house. "It's cold out here. You can patch the roof tomorrow. Come on."

CHAPTER 22

BATHSHEBA

"I was the first to make it understood that reason could undermine the just premises of the good."

—ARISTOPHANES

Upon reentering the house, Cyrus promptly turned on the Christmas music and I slipped outside to patch that hole. It was going to bother me if I didn't.

I then came back inside and used half a bottle of the Malcom mystery alcohol to disinfect the tabletop, despite Cyrus's lamenting protests about wasting hundred-year-old whiskey and how his great-great-grandfather would likely haunt me until the day I died. This made me laugh, because he was funny and because sometime over the last few hours, I'd started to relax.

Yes, I was still completely infatuated with Cyrus. But that was my problem, not his. He'd been a perfect gentleman all day. Other than his one comment in the barn about rolling in the hay, he hadn't made any flirty double meaning remarks, though I was certain a few opportunities had presented themselves. Fact was, he hadn't flirted with me at all. He'd just been himself.

Mariah Carey's "All I Want for Christmas" was our soundtrack while I made my bed and he made his on the other side of the room some ten feet away, close to the table. Our conversation had flowed surprisingly well

213

despite the constant fluctuations in my internal temperature. He made it easy by being funny and sweet, his excitement and good mood were contagious.

After our beds were made, he handed me a shoebox full of candles from one of the chests, then pulled out cookware, dusty utensils, and chipped plates but intact glassware from the cabinet in the corner. He washed all the dishes we'd need in a new bucket—not the snake bucket—of horse soap and melted snow. I skipped "Santa Baby" on his playlist and he laughed at me but didn't say anything about it when I glared daggers in his direction, holding up his hands like he was innocent.

He placed a ceramic crock directly on the burner to boil water and didn't seem terribly surprised when I produced his favorite tea from my purse.

"Where are my Starbursts?" he asked with a twinkle in his eye. "I know you have some."

"I'm saving them for dinner. They're officially rations."

He mock-pouted but the effect was ruined when his shoulders shook with silent laughter.

Meanwhile, I lit four candles and put the rest away. This caused a teasing disagreement. Cyrus argued that we should light all the candles and put them everywhere. I allowed him to talk me into using half, placing them only where we actually needed the light.

By candlelight, Cyrus scrubbed out an ancient-looking cast iron skillet, one that miraculously had no signs of rust. For dinner, he made a whiskey reduction sauce to cook the snake in, scooping off a fair amount of the butter icing from the cookies I'd made and adding it to the pan. I stood near him and the woodburning stove, scrolling through the downloaded music on his phone while trying to warm up my damp backside and drinking my tea. Stealthily, I deleted "Santa Baby" from his playlist and didn't feel guilty about it.

We now sat at the table by the light of at least ten candles, plates of snake, gingerbread cookies, and a ration of Starburst candy serving as our Christmas Eve dinner. He eyed me over the edge of his mason jar whiskey glass, his third pour of the night, and took a sip, smiling happily as he lowered it to the table.

"If not for my panic attack in the SUV, this might've been the best day of my life. Cheers." From where he sat next to me on the bench, Cyrus clinked his glass of whiskey against my mug of tea.

"You didn't mind the snake? Or making your own straw bed? Or using an outhouse?" I turned my body to face him, pulling one of my legs up and bending it at the knee to rest on the bench between us, noticing that "Rockin' Around the Christmas Tree" was currently playing from Cyrus's phone.

My dad and stepmom used to dance to this song every time it came on during the season, and I'd watch them laugh and smile at each other, thinking to myself, *That's what I want.* I missed her, but I also missed seeing my father that happy.

"Mmm, not one bit. But I did rather enjoy *your* reaction to the outhouse," he said around his latest sip, bringing me back to the here and now.

I flattened my expression as best I could. "The seat is freezing."

"Yes. Isn't it." He grinned, humor making his eyes a dazzling emerald green. "Too bad you can't pee standing up."

I sent him a squint, but I wasn't at all upset by his teasing now that I felt certain it was all in good fun. I wondered, if I'd accepted his teasing while we'd worked together as fun instead of thinking it was taunting, would my life have been easier or harder?

Harder. You would've fallen in love with him months ago.

My merry mood fractured slightly at the realization. I didn't know how long we'd be stuck here in this house. I needed to figure out how to coexist with Cyrus without erecting my old walls, but also without falling in love with him.

Hopefully, we'll be rescued tomorrow.

"Are you sure you don't want any?" Cyrus pointed to the four-ounce mason jar he was using as a whiskey glass. "That is the finest, smoothest, most delicious whiskey I've ever had the pleasure of drinking, and the first thing I will do when we depart is call Alaric and tell him about it."

"He likes whiskey?" I asked, working to mentally shake off the melancholy of my thoughts and enjoy this fleeting moment.

I'd likely only see Cyrus in passing after this. If we were rescued tonight or tomorrow, these were our last moments together. I wanted to make them count.

"Alaric loves whiskey. He's an obsessed whiskey snob, always trying to get me to go to tastings."

"So you'll invite him over to try it? Or will you send him some?" Picking up a gingerbread cookie, I took a bite.

"Are you kidding?" Cyrus stabbed his last piece of snake with his fork. "I've been avoiding him for over a year because he's pushy and unpleasant. Unless he stops being a know-it-all and lets me live my life, I plan on drinking my whiskey in front of him for the next fifty years and never letting him have any."

Unable to help myself, I tossed my head back and laughed, even going so far as to smack my thigh. I hadn't tried the whiskey yet, so I couldn't blame my mood on alcohol. The house was warm. The snake wasn't half bad. The tea was wonderful. But it was Cyrus who was responsible.

While I laughed, Cyrus chewed, swallowed, and his smile widened into a grin, staring at me with a sweet, hazy expression. Eventually, my laughter tapered and he appeared to be on the precipice of saying something. Watching him while wearing my relaxed smile, I picked up my cookie for another bite.

The song switched from "Rockin' Around the Christmas Tree" to a Nat King Cole rendition of "Have Yourself a Merry Little Christmas," and perhaps it was strange, but it really felt like Christmas. The snow outside, the warmth inside, Christmas cookies and music, candlelight. As much as Cyrus's company made me feel overwhelmed most of the time, right now and for the last hour or so, I felt comfortable and cozy. Even my jeans had dried.

This was nice. As long as I kept checking in with reality—*nothing good can come from you falling for this man*—it would continue to be nice.

"May I ask you something, Bathsheba?" he said haltingly, taking another sip from his glass.

Swatting away the fluttering in my stomach, I nodded while I chewed. The cookie was still good without the icing.

Cyrus inhaled deeply, his eyes heavy with intensity, and I found myself holding my breath, bracing for whatever he was about to ask.

But then, his eyes dimming like he'd changed his mind, his gaze fell to my plate. "Are you finished with Mr. Rattles? I'm still a bit peckish."

"Of course. Please." I pushed my plate toward him and took a sip of my hot tea to hide my disappointment. The hilarious irony was, Beth from twelve hours ago probably would've been relieved by Cyrus's reluctance to voice whatever potentially big thing he wanted to ask.

That said, Beth from twelve hours ago hadn't sat on his lap and calmed him down in the car, or stuffed feed sacks with hay after he sifted and sepa-rated it, or witnessed his bravery and know-how with snakes, or his boyish exuberance upon discovering his family's hoard of whiskey. Nor had she discovered how his gazes, expressions, and voice weren't weapons he wielded, they weren't attacks requiring diligent defense, but were Cyrus simply being Cyrus.

It had been a busy day, and though I hated that we'd been in a car accident which led him to reliving his worst memory, I couldn't regret any part of it.

Cyrus poked at the meat on my plate, taking a single bite before sighing and reaching for his whiskey. Downing the remainder, he abruptly stood, gathering both his plate and mine. "Well. It's getting late, and you know how I require my beauty sleep."

"Yes, I remember." From my seat at the table, I watched him place our dishes inside the bucket sitting on the floor near the tub, trying not to admire the long, length of him too much, how he moved with such graceful carelessness, and how epically fantastic of a butt he had. Legendary, for real.

He blew out the candles near the cooking space and picked up the towel resting on the tub, turning to face me. "I think I'll just—" he grinned, paused for effect, and then cocked an eyebrow "—hit the hay."

I blinked at him, then scoff-laughed with extreme reluctance because *Ugh* but also *LOL!* He was adorable, there was no denying that.

"You know, because we're literally sleeping on hay." He tossed the towel to the tub, explaining the joke unnecessarily, which just made it funnier.

"Yes, Cyrus. I got it. Nicely done." Halfheartedly rolling my eyes, I chuckled.

"I've been waiting all night to say it, just wanted to make sure it landed."

"Ten out of ten on the landing." I stood from the bench and stretched, leaving my tea where it was. I could reheat it in the morning on the stove.

"Excellent. And we can worry about cleaning these dishes later." He pushed his fingers into the pockets of his jeans. "If you want to use the Malcom whiskey to swish and spit, I left some here by the tub, so it wouldn't be near the stove. Think of it like using a thousand-dollar bottle of Listerine." Cyrus pointed to the bottle I'd used for cleaning and that he'd used for cooking and drinking.

Surprisingly, it still had a lot left, at least a quarter of the bottle, especially considering how liberally I'd doused the table.

"Won't that upset your great-great-grandpa's tender spirit?" I moseyed over to the tub while he walked past to his hay pile covered in blankets.

"He's already haunting you for desecrating the fruits of his labor, what's one more minor offense?"

"Ah, good point. Then I shall swish and spit." Picking up the whiskey, I poured some in his discarded mason jar glass, then swished. Realizing I hadn't thought through the spitting part, I just went ahead and swallowed it.

Cyrus had been right. That was some damn fine whiskey, and I didn't even like whiskey.

There, Grandpa. Happy now?

"What did you think? Of the whiskey?" he asked while I washed my hands in the warm bucket of clean, horse shampoo water.

"It was fine," I teased.

He made a scoffing sound, followed by another even louder scoffing sound. "My illustrious ancestor is rolling over in his grave."

"I thought he was haunting me," I said lightly, which made Cyrus laugh. "I do have a question, though." I bent and picked up the towel Cyrus had tossed into the tub, drying off my hands.

"What's your question?"

"If your great-great grandfather had all that whiskey down in that cellar, why didn't he sell it? You said the snowstorm had ruined him."

"No. I said the snowstorm ruined his harvest. I don't know why he didn't sell the whiskey—I didn't know that cellar existed until today—but I have my suspicions."

"Which are?"

He grinned and his dimple made an appearance. Rather than shield my eyes from the power of the almighty dimple, I allowed myself to enjoy how it gave his roguish face a boyish playfulness.

"I suspect," Cyrus started slowly, "he found oil two years before the snowstorm wiped out his crops and he became quite the respected gentleman of means. I think he hid that whiskey, not needing to sell, not wanting the risk, but not wishing to destroy it either."

"Hmm. Interesting theory." I noticed he'd cleaned out the bathtub. It looked usable. "Hey, how old is this tub? Can you actually bathe in it?" Carefully placing the towel over the edge, I glanced at Cyrus.

He'd already pulled his blanket up to his chest and was using his wool coat as a pillow. I planned on using my down jacket as my pillow.

"I believe you can. I did a number of times when I was little. Be wary, however. Some copper tubs leach lead and mercury into the water. Not that one. I believe my great-great-grandfather attempted to woo his wife with it, and thus ordered the finest quality copper tub available. It's never been moved—" he yawned, covering his mouth with his hand "—because the house was built around it."

I'd walked to the table while Cyrus spoke, blowing out all the candles except for one.

"That okay?" I asked, gesturing to the last lit candle. "It's in a tall mason jar, so I don't believe it's a fire hazard, and I figured it would be good to have some light in here, just in case we need to use the frozen circle of hell that is the outhouse."

Cyrus laughed delightedly while I crossed to my bed and snuggled inside, wearing my smile from the day and all my clothes. It was darker where I slept as his bed was closer to the table.

"Wonderful," he said, and I didn't know if he was referring to the candle or to my description of the outhouse.

Sighing, I tried to settle down, almost at once thankful for the swallow of whiskey when my limbs slackened and my mind relaxed. I wasn't anywhere near drunk or even tipsy, just . . . loose. It was nice, maybe even necessary given the fact that I was sleeping ten feet away from a man I'd been fantasizing about for months.

Just as my eyelids grew heavy, Cyrus whispered, "Beth. Bathsheba. Are you asleep?"

"No." I tucked my hands under my cheek and peered at the darkness. "What's up?"

"I'm sorry for what occurred in the rental car earlier. It's—uh—the issue with my father's accident, how I was trapped in the front next to him for hours. That's why I usually don't sit in the front passenger seat. If I'm not driving, I prefer the back. But I apologize for my reaction. Thank you for agreeing to come here and wait out the snow."

My heart squeezed and I curled my fingers into fists, wishing I could hold him, kiss him, and make it all better. But I couldn't. Touching him now, even a hug or a kiss on the cheek, felt just as dangerous and charged as it had before, but for slightly different reasons.

Instead, I opted to say, "Please, don't apologize. I know how the wounds of childhood cut deepest, last longest, and leave the biggest scars."

"You do, huh? Why do you think that is? Shouldn't time heal all wounds?"

I considered the question, rotating to lie on my back, and answered with the honesty only a shot of good whiskey provoked. "No. Time doesn't heal childhood trauma because it slices into the very foundation of a person before any walls can be built to protect what lay inside. It forms a person, and they cannot be separated from it," I said, and I believed every word of it.

At least, that's how it was with me. As I considered the matter, I didn't think I'd change myself even if I could. I liked being the best at what I did, I valued this innate desire to prove myself, to be valuable in all situations and with all people. I liked being of service, doing the grunt work, and taking pride in myself, my ethics, and my standards. I liked that I refused to settle for less in a relationship when I knew I deserved more, like my father had found with my stepmom. *That's* what I wanted.

Perhaps my biological mother leaving me when I was four had a lot to do with it, with my need to prove myself, with my rigidity and inability to bend and compromise. Gabi was likely also right when she'd said I prioritized my pride over living a full life.

If I could figure out how to live a full life without sacrificing my pride, then I'd be all set.

Good luck with that.

Cyrus's dry, "That's . . . depressing," stirred me from my internal ponderings.

"I don't know." I shook my head even though he couldn't see me. "It feels inspirational to me, to be formed by my childhood, all the privileges and disadvantages and hurt and wins. Just because a flower grows between the cracks of a sidewalk doesn't make it less beautiful. It's just as—or I would say, even more so—pretty because of what it had to overcome to bloom. It's easy to be a rose in a well-tended garden, isn't it? But to be a rose in the wild, or between the pavement of a city street, that's not just beautiful, that's meaningful. And beauty without meaning is boring . . . I think."

I heard him clear his throat before asking, "Are you saying I'm a wild rose? Or are you implying I'm a city rose?"

"I'm saying, I think you're beautiful, Cyrus. And not even a little bit boring."

Cyrus was quiet and his silence felt thoughtful, then he said on a rasp, "I'm so thankful to know you, Beth."

I grinned, closing my eyes as the warmth of his words spread through my body, so sincerely spoken. "I'm thankful to know you too, Cyrus. Merry Christmas."

"Merry Christmas," he replied.

Sighing silently, I tried to go to sleep. I really did. But now I felt restless —good restless, happy restless—and I wanted to keep talking to him. After all, these were our final moments together. I'd never get a chance to ask him questions like this, not with us alone.

So, like a kid at a sleepover, I asked, "Hey. Cyrus? Are you asleep?"

"Yes," came his immediate and not sleepy-sounding response. "Extremely asleep. I've never been more asleep in my life."

I laughed, tucking my chin under the covers and bending my knees to my chest. He was just . . . *so great.*

"What's wrong?" he asked. "Thoughts of Mr. Rattles keeping you up? I promise, he felt no pain."

"No, I was—um—I was thinking." I chewed on my bottom lip, and like earlier, decided *what the heck, just ask.* "Hey, so, you never answered my question from before, when we were in the car right before I hit that dumb deer."

"Bathsheba." He sighed, it sounded like he was disappointed in me. "Must you speak ill of the dead? Fanny Deerworth was a respected member of the Hill Country hoofed ruminant mammal community, always sharing her lichen with those fawns less fortunate, even that hag, Margo Bucknuts. And which question is this?"

My shoulders shook with quiet laughter. Once I was sure I wouldn't laugh out loud, I asked, "Do you miss Texas?"

My question was met with silence, but this one didn't feel thoughtful like before. It felt heavy somehow, so I strained my ears. I couldn't even hear him breathe. I thought about repeating it, just in case he hadn't heard. But he'd heard me, I knew he had.

"You don't have to tell me if you don't wish to," I said eventually.

"No—no, I—I wish to. I do," he stuttered, which was unlike him. When he spoke next, his voice sounded like it had dropped half an octave. "I also wish to take advantage of this opportunity just in case it never presents itself again."

That had me opening my eyes and turning toward where he lay. Even though I couldn't see him clearly, I could feel him.

"The question was, do I miss Texas. And I do miss . . . it," he finally said, thoughtful and slow and deep. "I miss its . . . beauty. It's *so* beautiful, so incredibly breathtaking. And, like you said, the meaningful kind." Cyrus's tone roughened, turned dreamy in the dark. "Honestly, I spend more time contemplating its beauty than I'd like to admit. And its impeccable sense of style. Its quiet grace and confidence. But I also miss how it challenges me and keeps me honest, or tries to."

I held perfectly still, not daring to breathe, my mind teetering on the abyss of his words.

He wasn't finished. "I miss how funny it can be when it doesn't think I'm watching or listening, or when she lets her guard down with me, which feels like the rarest gift. I miss her—*its* honesty, the sayings, the colloquialisms and accent that reminds me of good people, generosity without boundaries, and home. Texas feels like home. And I miss the caring about me in quiet ways, going above and beyond, things I'd overlooked until I took some time to reflect, gestures I took for granted before . . . before we parted ways. And I miss how safe and seen I feel when I'm with, uh, Texas."

A wave of hot tenderness pressed against my skin, radiating outward, and my heart took off at a gallop. Blinking against stupid tears stinging my nose and behind my eyes, I struggled to shut myself down. I couldn't. His words were too invasive.

Then he said quietly, almost reverently, "Good night, Bathsheba," and I heard him shift in his bed, felt rather than saw him turn his back to me while I lay there, burning, pining, swallowing convulsively against hot emotions.

I wanted him. I wanted to be with him, touch him, and be touched by him so badly, and the way I wanted it didn't feel like being torn in two. It felt inevitable. It felt like the moment right before hitting the deer. This was going to happen, no matter how scared I felt. There was no swerving or stomping on the brakes. Not if I wanted to make it through in one piece.

When is living a full life going to matter more than your stupid pride?

My sister's words from earlier in the day echoed in my mind as I slowly and quietly unzipped my jeans, tugged them down my legs. I divested myself of my sweater and bra, hopefully just as soundlessly. Pausing to consider, I removed my shirt and underwear too, but not my socks. That floor was dusty and cold as hell. I didn't want to give myself any reason to second-guess this, because I would regret it if I chickened out. I felt this deeply, an undeniable truth.

If I didn't set my stupid pride to the side along with all my reservations and fears—some valid, some not—just this once, just for tonight, to be with this sweet, wonderful man who so obviously cared about me on some level, I would go to my grave regretting it. Like Cyrus's whiskey-making ancestor, it would haunt me.

Maybe he'd turn me away tonight, maybe—when it came right down to it—he wasn't interested anymore. Maybe I'd be walking back to my bed in two minutes hot with embarrassment, but that would be okay. I had to try. For myself. Because, as absurd as it sounded, I wanted the memory of tonight more than I wanted my pride tomorrow.

CHAPTER 23

CYRUS

"Love is simply the name for the desire and the pursuit of the whole."

— ARISTOPHANES

I wouldn't sleep until Beth did. I couldn't. I heard quiet rustling from the direction of her bed, near-silent tossing and turning, likely unable to get comfortable after my clumsy, ill-conceived confession.

I'd pissed her off. Again.

I did not understand myself, risking the good feelings and trust we'd built today, tainting our comfortable, lovely, adventurous afternoon by being selfish and impatient. I wished I could take the words back. I wished I wasn't so reckless, so impetuously determined to live in the moment without thought of what came next. I'd spent the last two months of my life endeavoring to unlearn this impulse, working to be thoughtful and circumspect with my actions and words.

It had worked. She'd relaxed today, given me smiles, laughed, looked at me. We'd bantered. *Bantered!*

And then I'd gone and spoiled everything like Charlie Sheen giving a prime time interview, or Elon Musk and Twitter, or Kanye West and . . . you know, every day since 2015.

"Cyrus."

My body jolted at the sound of her voice so close. I immediately turned to look over my shoulder.

Beth was there. *Oh no. She's going to . . .* I had no idea. Put me in another headlock? Yell at me? Neither of those sounded terrible given the alternatives provided by my excellent imagination.

"Yes?" Lifting to a sitting position, I faced her.

She crouched next to my makeshift bed, a blanket wrapped around her. She gripped it at her neck with a tight fist, her other hand holding it together at her chest. Thanks to the candle she'd left burning on the table, I could see her form reasonably well, the shape of her lovely features.

"Are you sober?" she asked, the whites of her eyes catching the light of the candle.

"Very. Why?"

The intensity of her inspection increased. "Are you sure? You had the whiskey."

"Sure. I had three ounces over three hours and approximately one bucket of melted snow as a chaser. Why? What's wrong?" I peeled back my covers, ready to do her bidding. "Do you need me to get you something?"

Beth shook her head, then hesitated. I felt it, but I could also see her reluctance in her posture, how she held perfectly still, perhaps not even breathing.

Then she licked her lips. "Cyrus," she said on a faint, breathless whisper, "I want you."

I waited for her to finish the thought, to tell me what she wanted me to do. But then understanding dawned and another jolt of startled surprise seized me. My mouth opened to ask . . . something, clarification probably, or whether this was a dream, and I tracked her eyes as they lowered to my lips. The words caught in my throat. If this was a dream, I didn't want to know.

Beth's hand released its hold on the blanket at her throat and she reached for my wrist, encircling it slowly, giving me ample time to protest or pull away. Her gaze refastened on mine and, holding my eyes, she brought my palm to her cheek, pressed it there, tilted her head gradually and snuggled against it.

My breath caught at the action, my heart leaping heedlessly to my throat, and I found myself staring in transfixed wonder as she slid my fingers down her neck, slipped them into the blanket, and together we pushed the fabric off her shoulder.

Her bare shoulder.

And that's when I realized Beth was naked under that blanket.

Holy fucking shit.

"I want you," she repeated stronger this time, pressing my hand to her skin but holding my fingers light enough that they would fall without my participation. "Do you want me? I don't have a condom, but I'm on birth control, and I don't have any STDs."

I gaped at her, the words stealing the air from my lungs and hitting me simultaneously in my heart and groin. Yes, that's right. The stupidest parts of me. Thus, you must forgive me for staring at her in disbelief and so much fucking hope, worried that if I moved or breathed the spell would be broken.

While I stared stupidly, Beth pulled her bottom lip between her teeth and nibbled on it, her gaze growing uncertain, and suddenly my brain—blood and oxygen deprived due my stupidest parts hogging my body's resources —caught up.

"I want you," I said, the statement not a whisper. In truth, it was much too loud for the size of the room. My fingers curled against her shoulder, begging her to mean this, begging her to stay with me. "I don't have a condom, I don't have any STDs, and I want you so badly, I think I might die from wanting you so much. Please. Let me have you. I will make you feel so, so good."

Her eyes moving between mine seemed to shine despite the lack of light, and she grinned, her bottom lip still caught between her teeth.

If she were still in any doubt, I let action be my consent. Grabbing her by the back of the neck, I pulled her forward and I kissed her, immediately groaning at the hot feel of her lips still separated by her smile. Biting at her bottom lip—because it was mine now—I sucked it into my mouth, licking it, tasting her while I grabbed her and guided her beneath my covers, laying her down, bracing myself on an elbow, hovering both over and beside her, wanting to be as close as possible.

Our mouths fused together. I wasn't going to let her go. And as I shoved her blanket away, my fingers finding nothing but hot, luscious bare skin, I didn't know where to touch first.

This was like being presented with a ten-foot-tall Christmas tree, under which sat hundreds of boxes and packages, each impeccably wrapped in intriguing shapes and sizes. And they were all mine. I didn't know where to start, overwhelmed, and so fucking grateful.

I wasn't certain who the deserving recipient of this gratitude was. Wren certainly, for reining me in and giving good advice. The self-help section of my local bookstore, absolutely. The teenager at the airport in Newark with the blue name tag and surly attitude who sold me my first journal without asking for an autograph or having any idea who I was. God bless Desmond Sullivan, if that was his real name.

Beth, my hero, *obviously* for making this decision, the right one, and how smart she was. So smart. And her parents for raising her. And her grandparents for having sex. And my parents and grandparents for doing their duty so that I could be born, and—

You know what? I was grateful to the whole world. I loved the whole world, every bee in its hive, every bird in its nest, every snake in its roof shingle pile. God bless us, every fucking one.

But I wasn't grateful for clothing. I needed my clothes off. And yet I couldn't be bothered to stop touching her—her shoulders and arms, her torso, stomach, breasts—oh my God, trust me, her *breasts*. Perfection, thy name is Bathsheba Ryan's breasts.

So I said, "Help," against her mouth, rocking against her restlessly, pulling her close, and roughly grabbing a handful of her amazing, round ass, massaging it, hoping she would read my mind.

Miraculously, she did.

Her fingers fisted the front of my shirt and shoved it upward, her hands —just as greedy and grasping as mine—splaying over my stomach, running along my ribs, gathering the fabric of my loathsome shirt and yanking her mouth away in order to pull, forcing me to cooperate for the second needed to remove the odious garment. Free of it, I fastened my mouth to her neck, biting and licking and tasting the sweet heat of her skin, gratified by her labored breathing when my fingers impatiently slid between her legs and into her sex.

"*Fuuuuck.*" I pressed my forehead to her shoulder, my vision clouding with a flash of stars. Hot and slippery, wet. Soft. Tight, so fucking tight. "Do you know how perfect you feel? Flawless."

She gasped, tilting her hips up for my invasion. "Cyrus. I need you. Please."

Her nails trailed down my stomach, the sting of their scratch causing my muscles to tense beneath her fingertips. Before I could catch my breath, she'd unfastened my fly and reached inside my boxer briefs, her movements frenzied. My hips jerked forward, ordered by the stupid head below my waist, gluttonous for more of her capable strokes, and I had to grab her wrist or I was going to come. One more touch and it would all be over, and then she'd never let me do this again, and that was not acceptable. I'd die of remorse and sorrow.

I wanted this to be the first of thousands, if not millions. I wanted infinite sex, fuckloads of fucking, mountains of making love. Or the possibility of it.

Using my grip on her wrist, I twisted it and threaded our fingers, pressing the back of her hand against my wool coat next to her head. Inserting my knee between hers, I nudged her legs apart and climbed above so that I could properly devour the buffet of her body.

I'd been right about her sounds. She was quiet. We were in the middle of literally nowhere in the center of a snowstorm and she held them in when all I wanted was to tease them out. I would. I promised myself I would force screams of ecstasy from her lungs until she was hoarse and exhausted.

First, I needed her skin, unbelievably soft, silk and velvet. *No.* Cashmere. I wanted to see her more clearly, I wanted more light. But pausing even to light candles was not an option. I was so fucking hungry for her, perhaps a little too rough and careless as I tasted her skin, my hands grabbing her hips, her breasts, her stomach, her sides, her back and her thighs. *Fuck,* her thighs.

I wanted them against my arms, squeezing my shoulders. I wanted them wrapped around my waist, ankles locked behind my back. I wanted them gripping my head as the slippery, slick heat of her filled my tongue. I wanted that knowledge of her, to know that no matter where I was, no matter what I was doing, I could lick my lips and remember the taste of her there.

Settling between her legs, I spread her wide, wider than necessary, wanting her open and stretched, encouraging her by caressing her upper legs. Her muscles flexed, bunched beneath my hands, and I said a new prayer of thanks to the god of the StairMaster. I felt her restlessness, the pivot of her hips, searching. She made a whining sound, her body straining and vibrating as I glanced up, gazed at the plane of her torso, the mounds of her perfect breasts.

She lifted her head to look down at me. Unable to help myself, I grinned and winked just before lowering my open mouth to her succulent softness.

A hitching sob, an "Oh God" burst from her as I tasted her body, this sweet, private place, my tongue licking lazily through her slippery center. I wanted to spend hours here, but I felt she was close, her legs shaking and straining against my hands.

I backed off, invading her with just a single, long finger, careful to avoid the lively pleasure button at the apex of her legs.

"Cyrus!" she panted, her calves flexing.

"You're close, aren't you?" I asked, my voice full of smug, male pride. I didn't care. I wanted to torture her. Watch her writhe and squirm and want me. I wanted her desperate. Watching her like this was now my most favorite thing, the only present I wanted in my stocking.

"Please," she said, her hands reaching for me, her nails digging into my wrist, trying to hold me still. Abruptly, she sat up and grabbed the unzipped waistband of my jeans, thrusting her hand inside.

"Wait, wait," I hissed.

She didn't wait. She gave me a rough stroke, then another. Mindlessly, I reached for her, fisting her hair and yanking her head back because I wanted to, covering her mouth and sucking her hot, sweet tongue into my mouth. Forcing her to lie down again, I braced my other hand next to her as she helped divest me of my jeans, me above, her below.

Releasing her hair, I gripped myself, but her hands were already there, closing around my cock. Her breath hitched, a short gasp, and my eyes opened, locking with her wide stare. She cursed. It was filthy, and laced with shock and awe.

Her eyebrows pulled together in a fretful V, then she muttered under her breath, "Oh damn. That's right," as though she'd just recalled something important.

Her reaction made me grin as I pressed myself into her hands. I know most men believe they have giant, monster penises. I did not. I just had a very, very big one. Curved slightly up and smooth and thick all the way around for her pleasure. Yes, I am very proud of my cock, just as all men should be. When you're proud of something, you make an effort to learn how it works.

Rising to my knees, I watched her hands on me, her hands stroking up and down, getting a feel for what would soon be inside her.

A shivery breath left her lungs, her eyes seeking mine, her forehead clearing as concern became determination.

"Are you ready?" I asked, my hands on her hips.

She nodded, eyes fierce, lining me up with her entrance. I pressed forward, breaching her, and she let me go with a gasp, her eyelids fluttering, her hands flailing before falling to rest on either side of her head, like she was some helpless maiden. We both knew that was the furthest thing from the truth, *thank fuck for that.*

She frowned, moaning as I spread her legs wider to accommodate me. I wasn't fully seated yet and I eased forward, watching the shadows of the flickering candle as the light played with her body. And when I filled her to the hilt, her tight, hot, heavenly walls gripping the length of me, my mouth moved with mindless praise.

"Such a good girl, taking me like that. Do you like it, do you like how I fill you up? You're so pretty with me inside you."

A sudden burst of a breath left her just before I moved, withdrawing only inches before I filled her again and again. Needing more closeness, more of her exquisite skin, I lowered my body to hers, never pausing the blissful dance of our bodies. Her hard nipples scraped against my chest and I sucked in a sharp breath through my teeth at the scrumptious friction, wishing I'd spent more quality time with them, making them tender to the touch, abusing them until she whined in pleasure.

Well. There's no time like the present.

Rolling my hips languidly, I bowed my back and lowered my mouth to her luscious breast, toying with the tight bead at the center, sucking it, pinching it between my teeth. Her body began to vibrate again and I quickened my pace, spreading the sensitive area, rubbing against it, hitting it with every thrust.

"Cyrus! Fuck! Oh—fuck!"

Needing to watch her, I lifted my eyes. The crown of her head was pressed against my coat, her throat exposed, her mouth open as though in a soundless scream. But I wanted her sounds. I wanted her words. I wanted everything.

"Tell me how patient I've been, Bathsheba. Tell me how good I fuck you, how good this feels."

"You—you—"

I nipped at her jaw, lowered my mouth to her neck, sucked at her skin. "Have I been good? Do I meet with your approval?"

"Fuck yes!" came her desperate reply, her hands finally lifting to grab my back, her nails digging into my skin as divine, abandoned sounds burst from her. *A symphony.*

I wanted to make this last, but I could feel myself losing control and not caring.

"Look at me," I demanded, my voice low, a scrape.

She did. She gave me her beautiful eyes. I held them for three rapid beats of my heart, vowing to never take the gift of her gaze for granted, then sucked my thumb into my mouth, ensuring her eyes dropped to watch my tongue before sliding my hand down the front of her body and circling the slick bundle of nerves between her legs, tapping and rubbing her in time with my quickened invasion.

A keening sound, loud and pitched high, wrenched from her, her body going stiff and taut except for the exquisite center of her, squeezing and fluttering around my cock. She couldn't hear herself, I knew this for a fact, but I made sure to listen and hear every delectable word, all the *Oh God*s and *Yes, Cyrus, so good*s, waiting for them to taper, waiting for just the right moment.

And then, when it came, when her body grew languid and loose, and she exhaled deeply, I slammed into her roughly. She cried out, her eyes opening in shock, a new wave of pleasure forcing her body to curl forward, her breaths ragged, her thighs wanting to clamp closed. I lifted and, holding her stare, I didn't let her. I used my hands on her knees to force them wide and she came again, her face contorted in confusion and bliss, her chest heaving.

I gritted my teeth in concentration, trying to hold off, hoping for a three-peat, but it was too much. She was entirely too much. She was everything. Giving her pleasure like this, it was everything.

As I came, losing control of all finesse, my vision blurred and fireworks replaced sight and sound. I cursed, hating that it would be over so fast.

But spiraling downward to earth where she waited with open arms, I contented myself with the knowledge that this was by no means our only opportunity. She wouldn't have come to me tonight unless she was all in, unless this was a promise of forever. That's the type of person she was.

And so with these content thoughts on my mind, a certainty of a future with my Beth, Bathsheba, my hero, who'd seen me at my worst, and who had called me meaningful and beautiful, I surrendered to the pleasure of the moment, indescribably incandescent, and one I knew I'd be chasing the rest of my life.

Which in the happy haze of post-orgasm bliss, I felt certain would be spent with her.

ACT 4: BUFFOONERY

CHAPTER 24

CYRUS

"To plunder, to lie, to show your arse, are three essentials for climbing high."

— ARISTOPHANES

Cyrus

I couldn't sleep. I rested next to her for hours, holding her, but I was too excited by thoughts of the future. I fought with myself, wanting to wake her up and make love to her again. But I wouldn't. I'd be very good and wait. Until after sunrise. After I made her a hot bath. Then we'd spend all day in bed, and then I'd make her another bath, and we'd spend all night in bed, sustaining ourselves on Christmas cookies and each other.

It sounded like perfection. A knock sounded on the door just as I was debating how to best heat the water for the tub.

I stared at the ceiling, the noise completely unexpected. I thought it might've been the wind, but then it sounded again, louder this time. Beth stirred and my heart jumped. I didn't want her to wake up.

Carefully, I disentangled myself and lamentably left our cozy pile of blankets. I then wrapped myself in the topmost one and covered her with the rest.

Hurrying to the door, I cracked it open before whoever it was could knock again and came face-to-face with Rex McMurtry's giant form and snow-dotted beard.

"Rex," I whispered, shocked, frowning and delighted, but also smiling and disappointed—not because it was Rex knocking on our love nest door, but because it was anyone at all.

"I was plowing the roads and saw your—"

"Shh!" I stepped outside, tugging the door closed behind me. "First, hi. How are you? Also, *you* were plowing the roads? You plow roads now in addition to offensive lines?"

Rex, being the six-foot-six star defensive end for the Chicago Squalls, had plenty of experience mowing down men twice my size on the football field. And now, apparently, he plowed backroads in Texas on Christmas, like some sort of road-clearing Santa Claus.

It hadn't quite stopped snowing. Tiny, sporadic flakes continued to fall from the sky, but the moon had emerged from between the clouds in the west and currently provided enough light for me to see Rex frown at the door behind me before giving me back his attention.

"You got someone in there?"

"Yes. So be quiet. She needs her rest."

His frown increased. "Is it that forager lady who calls you her *lover*?"

I scowled. "You and Alaric need to stop gossiping about me, and no. It's not Fern. I think you'll both approve of Beth."

"Beth who?"

"Never mind that. Why are you here and not on a football field someplace? Or preparing to be on a football field someplace?"

"My game was on the twenty-third. I'm in town until next Tuesday. And I bought the snowplow last year so Abby and I didn't have to worry about getting stuck at Aunt Sal's again, like we did that first year. I couldn't sleep, thinking about people being stuck in their houses, so I decided to clear the roads around Alenbach. That way folks can get around for Christmas and go to church."

"Yes. I see. That makes complete sense." Except it made no sense if he'd been anyone other than Rex. Trust me, you'd have to know him. This is exactly the kind of thing he would—and apparently did—do.

Here was a man who made millions playing pro football, and yet he worried about the citizens of his hometown being stuck in their houses during the holiday. Classic Rex.

His attention flickered to the door again. "Do you want to wake up this Beth person so I can get you out of here? Or what's the plan?"

"Uh . . ." I hesitated, undecided. "How much do you have left to do? Could you, you know, swing on by in the afternoon?"

I wanted to spend the morning with her, just her, and take some time to settle into this new phase of our relationship. I wanted us to make plans. And I wanted to make love to her again.

He stared at me like I was a fruitcake. "You want to stay out here? Until the afternoon?"

"I have plans," I said, giving him a meaningful look. "And they include the tub."

The moonlight illuminating his face shone a spotlight on his understanding. "You cleaned it out? Of the firewood?" Rex had run around this property with me just as much as my brother had.

"I did." I smiled, my focus turning inward, my mind alight with visions of the future. Beth naked, in the tub, me sitting at the foot of it, giving her foot a rub. I could recite the naughty version of "Twelve Days of Christmas." Maybe she'd ask me to join her, or maybe we'd get dirty again together and—

"All right. Say no more," Rex said, stepping back from the porch. "I'll be back at noon. Y'all need anything?"

"Do you have the ability or the means to pull the SUV back on the road?"

"I might. I'll try to tow it using the plow. Y'all shouldn't drive it though, not with snow and ice on the ground. That vehicle is only two-wheel drive and doesn't have snow tires. I could bring out some chains if you want."

"Yes. Please. Good. Thank you."

He took another step back. "I radioed Teri to come pick up the deer y'all hit. If the snowplow can't pull your car out of the ditch, his truck might. Cell service is still out. That doe is near frozen, the meat should still be good. Shame to waste it."

Classic Rex.

"Splendid. Venison for New Year's." I shifted my weight back and forth to keep warm, my teeth wanting to chatter. "See you at noon?"

"Sure," he said, his eyes drifting to the house briefly. A frown of consternation pulled his eyebrows together. "I hope this lady is good enough for you, not like the other ones."

"Oh for God's sa—I will introduce you, but not at present."

Now his eyebrows jumped high on his forehead. "She'd be okay with meeting your friends?"

"Yes," I said shortly, understanding the source of his surprise. The last two women who'd held my interest resisted meeting any of my friends, not wanting our worlds to become entangled or the responsibility that came with actually knowing a person.

A pleased—dare I say, proud—smile tugged at his typically stoic mouth. "That's great, Cyrus."

"Yes, well." I cleared my throat. "Leave. Go plow something. Speaking of, where's your wife?"

Chuckling, he shook his head and turned, not deigning to answer. His great big legs ate up the landscape. By the time I'd turned back to the door, he was already halfway to the barn.

I have until noon.

I could work with that.

But that meant I needed to get busy.

Beth awoke just after 9:00 a.m., sitting up groggily and pushing her hair from her lovely, sleepy features. I watched from my place at the stove as she blinked around the interior of the house, her eyes meeting mine, growing suddenly large and sober, then dropping to the blanket.

"Merry Christmas," I said, grinning at her deliciously disheveled state. If she'd let me, I'd make love to her just like this, sleepy and loose-limbed, smelling like us and hay and woodsmoke and whiskey.

"Merry Christmas," she said softly, pulling the blanket up and holding it to her chest, her fingers pushing through the hair at her temple. She licked her lips. She swallowed. She cleared her throat. And then she looked at me again, an edge of wariness in her features. "How long have you been up?"

I didn't allow her wariness to bother me. Of course we'd be a little awkward with each other this morning, given the momentous step we'd taken last night.

"I couldn't sleep." Chancing an approach, I brought her a new cup of tea, crouching next to her before handing it over.

Rosy little spots of pink bloomed over her cheeks as she accepted the cup. "Thank you. That was nice of you." Her free hand came back to her hair and her blush deepened. "I probably look like a mess."

"You're gorgeous," I said, meaning it.

A bit of her wariness waned, her lips twisting. "So are you. You look awfully refreshed for someone who didn't sleep."

Picking up her free hand, I turned it over so I could kiss the soft skin of her wrist. "Well, I did lie with you for a while, and that invigorated me. But then I got to work on your bath."

Her attention was absorbed by my mouth on her skin. "My bath?" she asked distractedly.

"Yes." I used my leverage on her wrist to tug her forward so I could kiss her neck. As soon as my mouth closed over the spot beneath her jaw, I felt her body bend and jolt in reflex. I grinned, whispering in her ear, "I want to feed you while I bathe you. Think of it as a Christmas present for both of us."

She tensed, then a burst of a laugh escaped her and she leaned back, searching my face. "Cyrus. You are not bathing me."

"Oh, but I am." I stole a quick kiss, releasing her wrist and standing, walking backward toward the tub since I was unwilling to remove my eyes from the exceptional sight of Beth first thing in the morning. "And I'm feeding you. I will lift the food to your luscious lips and you will eat from my fingers. If I had grapes, I would peel them for you. Come on, it's hot and ready for you." *Like me.*

She'd wrinkled her nose in thought, a confused smile on her lips. "Do you treat all of your sex partners this way?"

I reared back a little, bemused by the term she'd chosen. "Oh, is that what we're calling each other? Sex partners?"

Beth struggled, my question seeming to fluster her. "You know what I mean."

"Well, no. Actually, I don't."

Blinking twice, she gave me a searching look. "Cyrus, I'm not trying to —wait. Hold on a second. I just want to make sure we're on the same page here." She set the mug down on the bench beneath the table and stood, bringing the blanket with her to wrap around her body. "For the record, I do not regret what happened last night."

What an odd thing to say.

"That's good," I responded, perplexed, echoing back to her, "I do not regret last night either."

Her shoulders relaxed and she smiled. "Great. I'm so pleased to hear that."

I looked at her like she was silly but didn't press the issue. If I pressed the issue, it would delay her bath, and the longer she delayed the bath the longer I had to wait to see her naked. In sunlight. All of her. And we only had three hours since Rex would be back by noon.

"May I bathe you? Or at least sit next to you and look at your beautiful body while you bathe?"

Her eyebrows pulled together and a new blush stole over her cheeks. I couldn't read the blush, but I did recognize the protest in her tone when she said, "Cyrus—"

"And you don't have to eat out of my hand if you don't want to, but I would really like it if you did."

"Why do you want to see me naked so bad?"

"Um . . ." Now I looked at her like she was the most absurd creature on the face of the planet. "Is that a real question? Because I'll answer it if it is."

Huffing, her pink cheeks turning a bright crimson, she let the blanket drop. "Fine. Whatever. And you can feed me a lemon bar. Happy?"

"Very," I said, distracted and somewhat light-headed by the blood rushing suddenly southward. Hungrily, I stared at the beauty of her exquisite naked body, her shapely legs, the dip of her waist, the soft curve of her stomach, the elegance of her shoulders and arms, *and ladies and gentlemen, Bathsheba's breasts.* Perfection.

Stopping in front of me, she placed her hands on her hips and lifted her chin. "Okay. Can I get in the tub? Or should I spin in a circle?"

Eyes still on her body, I said, "Spin in a circle. Slowly. One rotation per twenty seconds."

She made a choking sound of disbelief which drew my attention to her outraged features, and I laughed. Stepping forward quickly before she could react, I wrapped my arms around her, sliding my hands over her curves as I did so, because I could, and I would, always.

"You are beautiful, Bathsheba Ryan," I said, placing a light kiss on her nose, happier than I had a right to be.

She held my gaze, a small, soft smile on her lips, but her face was turned away slightly, like she found me unbelievable. "Thank you, Cyrus Malcom. You are too."

I wanted to hold her like this a little—or a lot—longer. In truth, I wanted to bend her over the tub and take her from behind. But the water would grow cold, and I didn't want to waste all my efforts. Sighing, I let her go, my hands grabbing and caressing her body as she stepped away, gallantly resisting the urge to give her round bottom a light smack.

I would never tire of her skin. And when we were alone together at her place or mine, I would insist on Naked Mondays. And Wednesdays. Probably Thursdays and Saturdays too. Might as well add Tuesdays and Sundays in there.

Gripping her hand, I helped her into the bath, gratified to hear her soft sigh as she sat and settled, her back resting against the slanted curve of the copper tub.

"Does it feel good?"

She looked at me through lowered eyelids and nodded. "Yes. It feels fantastic." Her fingers drifted through the water that sat just under her neck. "This is all snow?"

"Yes. All boiled on the stove in clean buckets."

"Thank you." She gave me a funny look, one I couldn't read, but her thanks sounded sincere.

"Anytime," I said, sitting on the overturned bucket I'd placed at the side of the tub so I could face her and enjoy the view.

She held my gaze for a time, but then she dropped her eyes and looked like she was fighting a smile.

"What? What is it?"

"I was just thinking, you should give Alaric a bottle of that whiskey for Christmas."

I reared back slightly. "What? Why?"

"Now I know you said he's pushy, but he's a good friend to you."

"No, he's not," I grumbled, crossing my arms.

"How so?"

"Well, for one thing, he doesn't like my taste in women and has been a bit of a prick about it in the past."

Her forehead wrinkled. "What do you mean?"

"Alaric called the last woman I liked a fruitcake."

Her hands beneath the water stilled. "What? Why? That's not nice."

"He said it was because she'd been fired from every job she'd held, didn't eat anything that hadn't been foraged—BTW, we should call her about Ms. Deerworth before the snow thaws if Teri doesn't get to it first—and refused to label our relationship using any term but *lover*."

A shocked but sincere laugh burst out of Beth. She covered her mouth with her wet hand and her eyes turned apologetic (but still amused). "I'm so sorry. I didn't mean to laugh."

"It's okay. Because you know what? She was fun."

Her hand slipped back into the water, another enigmatic expression arresting her features. "She was fun?"

"Yeah. Fun and interesting. She'd take me on these overnight camping trips and we slept under the stars. She taught me how to forage in the wild, which plants to avoid and which were edible. And I think the reason she couldn't keep a job was because, like me, she has difficulty with time. I understood that about her and didn't hold it against her when she was late."

Beth's eyebrows pulled together, her gaze moving over me. "What do you mean, you have difficulty with time?"

"It . . . gets away from me." I dipped my fingers into the water, swirling the surface absentmindedly, wanting to be connected to her somehow, even if it was just touching the same water. "Hours will pass and it feels like minutes. I've always had trouble being on time." I gave her a self-deprecating smile. "But I'm trying to get better."

"I noticed. Before I—uh—left. You were getting better at keeping to your schedule."

"Good. Because I know it irritates you."

"It doesn't—okay, it did." Now she gave me a self-deprecating smile. "But I didn't understand that it was a difficulty for you, something you struggled with."

Unable to help myself, I reached forward for her foot. She tensed but let me bring it up to the edge of the tub so I could rub it.

Starting slowly, I said, "You assumed it was just me being thoughtless."

"And selfish."

"Ah." I grinned because I loved her honesty.

She wiggled her wet toes. They were painted red and white and were cute. "I'm sorry."

"No, no. I'm sure it's partly that. I am an adult, after all. One would think I'd have this figured out by now."

Her head fell back to the wall of the tub. "So whatever happened to your *lover*?"

I lifted an eyebrow at how she'd said the word with a strange note in her voice, both hard and brittle at the same time.

"Well, my lover escaped LA. Her grandmother died and left her some money. She used it to buy a van and a dog, and now she travels the country living the—hashtag—van life and makes her money as a social media influencer. She also teaches classes on foraging and doing naked yoga in the national parks."

Beth snorted.

My eyes lifted to hers.

She wore an odd expression. Again, something hard and brittle and perhaps also irritated. "So," she said, her voice false and breezy. "Does she arrive to her classes on time?"

Is she . . . jealous? The thought made me smile. *How delightful.*

"I don't know," I answered with honesty. "I don't keep up with her travels."

Beth directed her attention to her hands beneath the water. "Do you miss her?"

"Sometimes." I shrugged, not missing how she balled her hands into fists and how her lips turned down at the edges, the line of her jaw hard and unhappy. I didn't like seeing her unhappy, so I quit my teasing and added, "Especially when I find myself in the middle of the forest in between meals."

"Cyrus!" she exclaimed on a laugh, her eyes bright with reluctant humor, her cheeks pink from the hot water.

The sound loosened something in me, it felt like soaring and falling, and I gave myself two seconds to luxuriate in her accompanying smile before dialing back the feeling, caging it, and locking it away. For now.

Just because we were together now didn't mean I could stop working on being patient. I would need all the practice I could get. Being with her and not making love to her every second was its own kind of torture, a lesson in delayed gratification.

Looking at her from this new mental space, I returned her smile with a tempered one of my own. "Okay, seriously. I do. Like I said, she was fun. But . . ." I glanced over Beth's shoulder at nothing in particular and shook my head. "She wasn't interested in anything permanent. She was clear about that from the start. I always knew she'd leave, and I didn't necessarily have a problem with it because . . ."

"Because?"

"Because why would she stay?" I chuckled at my former self, at my confusion about who I was and what mattered. I'm not saying I had it all figured out now, but I understood better why I'd lived my life so recklessly and for so long.

I felt her gaze, and so I gave her mine. She wore a small, thoughtful frown between her eyebrows, like she didn't understand my words or my meaning.

"Anyway, doesn't matter. And Alaric already likes you, so maybe he'll be in a more agreeable mood the next time we talk. I didn't give him any opportunity in New York to pull me aside. Maybe now that we're together, he'll stop hovering."

Beth's eyes narrowed infinitesimally, like I'd said something incredibly strange, and she pulled her foot out of my grip. In a fluid motion, she brought her knees to her chest and wrapped her arms around her legs, now wearing a bracing frown.

"What do you mean, 'now that we're together'?"

"Well, you know, now that we're—what did you call it—sex partners? Ha. That's how you should introduce me to people the next time Alaric visits. He'd just love that," I said, smiling. But the look on her face made the hair on the back of my neck itch. "Hey. What's wrong?"

She looked positively anxious. "Cyrus, how can you say we're together?"

"What?"

Her chest was rising and falling rapidly, her eyes wide and anxious. "What happened last night, and this now, while we're here, this—this doesn't mean we're together. Or . . . or I thought it didn't? Or what do you mean by together? How do you define that?"

I flinched, blinking like she'd blown dust in my eyes or had just said that we weren't together. A sinking stone of dawning dread fell from my throat to my stomach, shooting restlessness to my limbs as I rejected her words. I stood too fast from the bucket, knocking it over.

"What?" The question fell out of me. "What do you mean we're—what are you talking about?"

She looked just as shocked as I felt. Her mouth moved but no sound came out, no explanation.

Suddenly, I couldn't look at her. It hurt. A lot. My mind frantic, I paced away from the tub, my chest and head hot, too hot. "I don't understand."

"Neither do I," she said. A second later, I heard the water slosh behind me, and when I spun around I saw she'd wrapped a towel around herself, gripping it tightly at her chest. "I thought we were on the same page last night, but let me be clear now. I can't be with someone like you."

I reared back. "What the fuck does that mean?"

Now she flinched, but when she recovered, her jaw was set. "You—you're always flirting with *everyone*. You let people touch you like it's nothing, and you do the same to them. I can't—I know myself. I wouldn't be able to handle that, not with you. I'm too serious and you are never serious."

"I'm never serious?" A hot, dry breath erupted from my lungs. "And yet, here I am, cleaning out the self-help book section and staying home on weekends to journal."

Her gaze clouded with more confusion.

Tearing my eyes away, I rubbed my forehead with both hands. I couldn't believe this was happening. My heart *hurt*, as though she'd reached inside and crushed it.

But you know what? It wasn't her fault. It was mine. *I should've waited. I should have waited until February. I should've wooed her slowly. I should've fucking waited.*

But I didn't want to wait. I'd been impatient. Again.

Laughing once more, I lifted my eyes to hers, but I didn't really see her. I couldn't see anything past my own misery. "The funniest part of this is, I had a plan. A good one. And it probably would've worked. But I fucked it up."

"What do you mean you had a plan?" She didn't sound angry, she sounded like she was at a loss, confused past reason.

I peeked at her through the cloud of my self-recrimination, fighting more laughter. "You know what I realized these last two months, Beth? You want to know what I realized about me? I've been living my life moment to moment, as though any day might be my last. When you watch your father die next to you at the tender age of seven, it's difficult to comprehend that life has permanence."

She stared at me with wide eyes, her features some mixture of distressed and fascinated.

"I've been impatient all my life. I hate waiting. I lose track of time, but it's not because I'm a selfish asshole." Immediately, I made a face at the false words. "Okay, well, yes. It might be a little bit that. But mostly, I don't expect anything to last. Or I haven't. And then I met you."

I paced back to her and stopped myself just before reaching for her. I couldn't touch her, not if what happened between us last night wasn't as monumental for her as it was for me.

"I've been bored and unhappy for years, and I never understood why, until I forced myself to ask the question. I realized, living like tomorrow won't come doesn't challenge me. Living that way means nothing matters, nothing has weight or permanence. I don't want that. So, no. I don't think we're on the same page. In fact, I don't think we're in the same book. Or the same bookstore. Or universe."

She reached for me. "Cyrus—"

I flinched away, not sure I could handle her touching me. Her hand dropped to her side, her chin giving a little wobble. She firmed it stubbornly.

I watched her, hungry for this emotion from her, some sign that I wasn't alone here in hoping for more and that her wobbly chin wasn't some empathetic reaction to my discomfort.

So I asked, "I want to know, what did you think last night meant to me? What are we doing, Bathsheba?"

She pressed her lips together, her eyes pained. "I didn't expect it to mean anything, not when—"

"It does," I said firmly, surprised by the coldness of my voice. "It means something, at least to me. What did it mean to you?"

"I wouldn't have done it—" Her breath seemed to catch, her eyes moving between mine. "I wouldn't have done it if I didn't care about you."

Oh. Well. That hurts like a motherfucker.

I backed away, trying to pull in oxygen after that sucker punch. "Ah, there it is. *Care*. My least favorite four-letter word."

"No, no. Wait a minute." Beth shook her head like she rejected my rejection of her rejection. "Hold on. I *do* care about you. A lot. But this, your claims about this being meaningful and lasting, it doesn't make any sense. If you'd wanted permanence with someone, with me, then why did I spend months watching you touch everyone else *but* me?"

"I didn't touch you because I wanted it too much!" I exploded in a very uncharacteristic demonstration of deep emotion, anger and hurt, allowing it all to rise to the surface only because it refused to behave and stay buried. *She* did this to me. Only her.

And once I started, there was no interrupting the lava flow. "I can't stop thinking about you! Since we met in June, I haven't been with anyone else. I haven't wanted to, I can't even fathom wanting to. I've read seven self-help books in two months. I've explored my depths. They're the worst. I've been so very good, but I want you so badly, I can't think or focus or breathe. And I don't mean just making love to your beautiful body, Bathsheba. I mean, I want *you*. Days and nights, I want them all. Give them to me. Give yourself to me. Because if you don't, I can't know you. I'm sorry, but I can't. I want every last inch of your soul, or nothing."

That last part was a huge bluff. I would settle for scraps with this woman. But she didn't need to know that. Something I'd learned from my copious nonfiction reading was that the first rule of relationships is to ask for the moon. You might get it, and you're worth it. If you don't, negotiate down from there. But if you start by asking for a beach condo in Cabo, you're likely to end up with a van down by the river.

Maybe one day I'd be able to walk away from Bathsheba Ryan's scraps, but today wasn't that day. I'd been working on myself for two months, not two decades.

Beth exhaled a shaky breath. Her eyes had grown suspiciously glassy as

I spoke and her hands where she gripped the towel had turned slightly blue, her knuckles white.

"Cyrus—"

"The moon, or nothing."

Another breath escaped her, this one seasoned with humor, and the sound made me hold perfectly still as hope dared to flutter in my stomach.

A tear rolled down her cheek and, cautiously, she stepped forward. "You have to understand—" Her voice broke. She cleared her throat and started again. "You have to understand, I didn't know any of this. I had no idea. You've taken me completely by surprise here. I need a minute, or a day, maybe."

The misery clouding my thoughts tentatively lifted and I stared at her, in limbo between the possibility of hope and . . . everything else.

"This is a lot. And it's all unexpected. Can you give me time? Can you be patient?"

NOOOO!

"Yes," I said, the word rough, feeling like hot coals in my throat. "Yes, I can be patient."

What other choice did I have?

CHAPTER 25

BATHSHEBA

"Prayers without wine are perfectly pointless."

— ARISTOPHANES

Rex McMurtry kept looking at me in his rearview mirror like I was an apparition, or a cat on a leash.

His lovely, friendly wife, Abby was her name, sat in the front seat next to him. Cyrus was in the back with me, but I sat all the way to one side and he sat all the way on the other, the middle seat between us. The space felt wrong, but I wasn't sure how to traverse it when we had an audience.

After Cyrus's bewildering reveal, he'd confessed that Rex had stopped by in the middle of the night, ready to rescue us. Cyrus seemed prepared for me to be upset at this news, specifically that we'd had the opportunity to leave last night, but he'd opted to let me sleep so we could spend time together in the morning.

I wasn't upset. In fact, I'd been quite the opposite. And that just confused me more.

Abby and Rex had arrived five minutes after noon, helping Cyrus and I set the house to rights, piling all the wood back in the copper tub, putting all the dishes and candles away, folding the blankets, and such. Abby had been a big help, undeterred by manual labor, and we'd chatted about nothing in particular—her pottery studio, my knife collection—as we ferried all the supplies I'd taken from the barn back to their rightful spots.

Rex had seemed surprised by my welcoming attitude, like he expected me to turn my nose up at him or something. I'd looked to Cyrus for some pointers, but he'd been uncharacteristically quiet—while we cleaned, on the walk back to the road, and now in the car ride into Alenbach. It was discovered that the rental had a flat tire, so that wasn't an option. The hastily concocted plan was to drop me off at my dad's apartment and then take Cyrus to his mom's house in time for Christmas dinner.

Rex and Abby had traded a look when I explained that Cyrus and I wouldn't be spending Christmas together as I had alternate plans, but they refrained from making a comment, which I appreciated.

Approximately forty minutes after leaving the old Malcom homestead, Rex pulled his truck up to my father's apartment building. I glanced at Cyrus as he unbuckled his seat belt and exited the car without a word.

"It was so nice meeting you," Abby said, distracting me from Cyrus's hasty exit.

"Yes, you too."

"Now that I know your sister lives in Alenbach, I'll give her a call when we're next in town." Abby smiled. "I haven't seen Gabi in ages."

Turns out, Abby had graduated the same year as Rex, Cyrus, Gabi, and Alaric, but I didn't remember her.

"I'm sure she'd like that. Thanks again for the lift. And, Rex, it was nice to meet you."

"You too, Beth," he said, not turning, giving me just his eyes in the mirror. "And I hope to see more of you *with* Cyrus in the future."

The way he'd emphasized the word *with* struck me as odd, but before I could give it much thought, Cyrus had opened my door, his hand reaching for mine to guide me out. With one last smile and wave, I fitted my purse on my shoulder and let Cyrus pull me from the truck. Then he closed the door.

I turned to him, a strange tightness clogging my throat, and hesitated for just a second. Mind made up, I grabbed his arm and tugged him away from Rex's truck. He let me, following where I went, his features a mask of stoicism. I hated it.

"Hey," I said.

"Hey." He didn't meet my eyes and my heart twisted painfully. I silently cursed myself for all the times I'd looked at his chin instead of giving him my gaze.

I'd meant what I said back at the house. He'd shocked me. I hadn't expected him to want me. Not that way, and not because I didn't think I was awesome. I *was* awesome, but I still couldn't wrap my mind around how we'd fit.

Would he stop flirting with people and touching everyone? Or would I loosen up and figure out how to remove my jealousy poncho? Or would it be some combination of the two? And how would the studio react? And what would people say about me, dating my ex-client so soon after leaving his team?

This last question was the least of my worries. I didn't care so much about what people said, but I was aware the "optics," as Ryaine would call it, would be bad. I'd have to deal with some blowback, but at least my next contract was with Vera Rodrigo and not some smarmy actor. Vera had a reputation for being exceptionally pragmatic and above any Hollywood pettiness. She was also his costar in the Asmodeus movies and Cyrus had spoken highly of her on several occasions.

But first, before I could reckon with any of that, I needed Cyrus to look at me.

"So, I'll call you?" I asked, feeling uncertain and uncomfortably vulnerable. I could handle the uncertainty and discomfort. It was the vulnerability that had me feeling like a mess.

He nodded, his eyebrows pulling together. But then, abruptly, he shook his head. "No. No, actually. I'll call you."

My heart tripped. "You will?"

"Yes. I'll call you February first."

Now my heart dropped. "What?" The question was more air than sound and I shifted closer to him, my hand tightening on his arm. "What do you mean you'll call me February first? Why February first?"

Staring at where I held him, he lifted his fingers and peeled mine away. "You need time."

"Yes, but not a month."

"No, no. I rushed you. I rushed this. You need more time. Then you can settle into your new assignment. We'll go out for lunch in LA, maybe grab a coffee."

"Lunch?" I choked on the word, my heart beating frantically. *What?* Was he . . . had he changed his mind?

Cyrus removed himself one step, then another, finally lifting his eyes to mine once we were five feet apart. They were distant, bracing. "It'll be good. For both of us."

"It will not be good!" I blinked against more stupid tears and rushed forward, wanting to shake him. Lowering my voice so I wouldn't yell, I stepped close and whispered harshly, "Why are you doing this? Are you— are you punishing me? For needing, like, five minutes to process all of this?"

A sad, resigned-looking curve claimed his lips and he shook his head. "No, Bathsheba. This is me trying to be noble."

"Well—" I tossed my hands up so I wouldn't wring his neck. "Stop!"

The first genuine smile brightened his features since he'd seduced me with a bath and threats to feed me lemon bars with his fingers. Cyrus's head tipped just slightly to the side, his eyes warming. "I'm going to miss you."

"You're serious." I couldn't breathe, I couldn't think. *He's serious.*

He nodded. "I'm going to miss you," he repeated, but with a deeper voice this time.

I crossed my arms, clamping my mouth shut. I couldn't fight my temper and him at the same time, and I refused to cry. Looking at him right now felt like hugging a rosebush.

"Will you miss me?" he asked.

"You're a jerk," I hissed between my teeth.

He laughed lightly, but it sounded all wrong. It sounded sad, not like him at all.

We stared at each other. Well, I glared. Meanwhile, I got the sense he was looking at my face in order to memorize it, the action making my heart beat faster and my temper spike all over again.

For some reason, I thought about the afternoon my mother had left, probably because it had been the week after Christmas. I never thought about it, ever. But now, looking at Cyrus, it flooded back, the memory clear and sharp and cutting.

She'd packed her bags and hadn't looked at me when she'd walked out the door, the sound of the screen snapping shut sounded like a gunshot. I'd banged on the screen door, calling for her, crying, begging her not to go. She didn't look back. She got in her car and left. And that was the very last time I saw her.

So, no. I wouldn't be begging Cyrus Malcom not to leave me. I wouldn't beg anyone. They wanted to leave, fine. I refused to ask him to stay. I absolutely refused. I'd promised myself a long time ago that I'd never be that little kid banging on a screen door ever again, asking the person leaving why they didn't love me or want me enough to stay, wondering what I'd done wrong.

But then before I knew what I was doing, emotion compelled me to whisper brokenly, "Please. Please don't do this. Please, I just need a day to catch up. That's not unreasonable. Please don't—"

He stepped forward, grabbed the lapels of my jacket, and captured my mouth with a sudden, searing kiss. Immediately, my arms wrapped around him, because I didn't want to let him go. I didn't understand why he was doing this. The fear I felt, the uncertainty, it felt like it would swallow me whole. I was drowning in it.

So I poured all my want and pleas into the kiss, sliding my tongue against his, tasting him, savoring him, while a frantic little voice in the back of my head warned me that this would be the last time.

That this wasn't *see you later*.

This was goodbye.

"Are you drunk?"

Glancing over my shoulder from where I sat organizing my vinyl records, I blinked until Wren St. James came into focus. When she did, I said, "No. But I'm trying to get there."

And then I frowned. Wren St. James was *inside* my apartment.

"Wait a minute. How'd you get in here?"

She tossed a thumb over her shoulder, looking cool as a cucumber. "Didn't you hear us knocking?"

"No. As you can see." I gestured to the speaker dock for my phone on my desk and the angry sounds of Queen Bey's "Lemonade" reverberating in the room. "I am throwing myself an angry girl party. So I will ask you again, how'd you get in here?"

Wren walked over to the speaker and pressed the Off button, likely so she wouldn't have to shout to be heard. "Ryaine used her key when you didn't answer."

That had me sitting straighter. "What? Ryaine is here?"

The last time I'd talked to Ryaine, I'd been crying like a fool. And then I'd shouted and cursed like a sailor. I hadn't called or talked to her since, I'd been too embarrassed.

"Yes. Man, you two really look alike. I thought she was you at first." Wren strolled around my room, looking at my tidy shelves and the pictures on my walls. I'd just dusted both this afternoon.

"We get that a lot." Standing from the floor, I picked up my glass of vodka—just vodka—and walked to my bed, setting it on the nightstand so it wouldn't spill.

Wren turned, her eyes conducting a quick survey of my person before she wrinkled her nose. "Beth. When's the last time you took a shower?"

"I don't know. It was this week," I said flatly, sagging down on the mattress. I wasn't drunk, but I was feeling loose and chatty, which was the danger zone. I needed to keep my mouth zipped. I doubted I would.

"What's gotten into you?" My former team lead shook her head.

I glared at her. "He won't return my calls. Or my texts."

Her shoulders seemed to slump slightly and I winced at the look of sympathy in her gaze. I knew that she knew I was talking about Cyrus. And you know what? I didn't care. *Where is my sense of professionalism now? HUH?*

"I know." She gave me a subtle, compassionate nod. "Ryaine told me the whole story."

I stiffened. "What?" Now I was mortified and tipsy, heat unfurling uncomfortably in my chest. It was one thing for Ryaine to know my shame, it was quite another for Wren to be aware. We might work together again someday. "She didn't tell you, did she? Please say she didn't."

"She did. She's worried about you. So am I."

"I'm fine. I'm just—you know—heartbroken," I said on a bitter laugh. "But it's fine. Really. On the upside, I've learned to enjoy the taste of vodka, cleaned and organized my entire apartment, and now I can give myself a pat on the back for being right all along."

Her expression flattened. "No."

"Yes," I hissed, abruptly angry with myself for the seventeenth time today. "I knew better. I kept telling myself not to do it, not to fall for him, and then I did. I should've listened to myself. This is all an affirmation of sorts that I should always trust my instincts and never, ever, ever trust anyone."

"You're never going to trust anyone?"

"Well, no one who looks and acts like Cyrus. And, to be on the safe side, definitely not actors. They get paid to lie, the really good ones get paid *a lot* to lie. And Cyrus is a really good actor." I'd tried to keep my voice even, but resentment had squirmed its way into my words.

"He wasn't acting with you, Beth. He cares about you."

I grimaced.

Oh man. *Wow.* Now I sorta knew how it must've felt when I said similar words to Cyrus on Christmas Day, like someone had reached inside my chest and took an ice pick to my heart. No wonder he left me.

"*Care*," I echoed bitterly. "There's my favorite four-letter word."

Before Wren could respond, a knock sounded from the doorjamb and Ryaine poked her head in. Sometimes, looking at her was like looking in a mirror. Not today. She looked great. I looked like the underside of a shoe.

"Can I come in?" she asked softly, giving me a sweet smile.

I waved her in. "Come on in, Benedict Arnold."

Her smile didn't waver. In fact, it turned even more affectionate. "You need to talk to someone who's good at this stuff, and we both know that isn't me."

"What are you talking about? You and Ransom are awesome together."

"That's one good experience after *years* of making huge, awful mistakes." Ryaine sat down next to me and gathered my greasy hair in her hands, pulling it back from my shoulders.

"How do you two even know each other?" I pointed between Wren and Ryaine.

Wren, resting against my desk, gave Ryaine a small smile. "I thought she was you at a New Year's party last week. I went over to say hi, and that's when I realized who she was."

Ryaine tugged on my hair a little, encouraging me to look at her. "And then we got to talking about you—"

"Oh no." Covering my face, I flopped back on the bed, pulling my hair from my friend's grip. "You mean gossiping."

I'd told Ryaine the whole story. The *whole* story. Because tonight wasn't the first time I'd been drinking since I'd returned to LA after Christmas, frustrated and angry because Cyrus wasn't returning my messages. According to my phone, he wasn't even reading them.

"Beth. You have to pull yourself together." Wren crossed the room and sat next to my prone form, giving my leg a smack.

"Hey!"

"Get up. Take a shower," she ordered. "And then plan your attack. You are so much better than this."

"Attack? What attack? Haven't you been listening? He's not even reading my messages. He won't call me back. He said he'd call after February first, so we could grab a fucking coffee!"

"Okay, okay," Ryaine said soothingly, likely recognizing my flash of temper for what it was, a countdown to a full-blown explosion.

"And you're going to accept that lying down?" Wren poked my side.

"That's not the Beth I know. The Beth I know, when she makes up her mind about something, nothing gets in her way."

"He said I needed space."

Wren lifted an eyebrow at this. "Do you need space?"

"Now? No. Before? Yes."

She nodded, like this was all extremely simple. "Then explain that to him."

"Again, how can I do that when he won't speak to me?" I sat up, feeling like we were talking in circles. Launching myself from the bed, I paced my bedroom. "I am so sick of myself, you know? It's like, I don't have any pride anymore when it comes to him, and I don't even care. I just—I just *want* him. And I don't want to wait. I feel like, if we wait, I'll get angrier and angrier, then I won't trust him to stay because it's so easy for him to keep away. Does my thought process here make any sense? How can I trust him to stay with me if he can leave me like that, with no contact planned for five weeks?"

"Your thought process does makes sense." Ryaine nodded, her gaze supportive.

"If it makes you feel better, he's miserable," Wren singsonged while studying her nails.

I stopped pacing and stared at her. "What?" My throat went dry. "You're still working with Cyrus?"

"I signed a second six-month contract to continue leading his team." She glanced up, a small, knowing smile making her eyes bright.

My mouth dropped open.

Ryaine bounced on the bed. "See? This is why I told her! She can get you in!"

"Get me in?" Flummoxed, I glanced between the two of them. "Get me in where?"

"His house," Ryaine said, like breaking into my former client's house—or my maybe-boyfriend-on-pause's house—with the assistance of his lead of security was perfectly acceptable.

"I—I couldn't do that!" . . . *Could I?*

Wren shrugged.

"Wren!"

"What? I just told you, he's miserable," she said, like this justified every-thing. "And not like before, not when you left the team. He was driven then, determined to read every self-help book published in the last year. Now he just broods. He's scaring my new team. They think he's mean."

"What?" I gasped. "Cyrus isn't mean! He's adorable! How is that possible? What is wrong with your team?"

"He exercises a lot, like he's training for the Olympics. He took up boxing lessons. Boxing, Beth! Nothing is right. Everything irritates him. He never leaves the house except to go on a run or to the set for work. No more wine club nights. Gone is the cuddly, friendly Cyrus from before, and in his place is this flat, angry imposter. When I tell you he is miserable, he is miserable."

I stared at the thrice-vacuumed floor of my apartment, absorbing her words. *My poor sweet Cyrus.* "Well, this might make me an awful person, but at least I'm not the only one suffering." And yet knowing he was suffering too did not make me feel better.

"This is what I'm trying to tell you." Ryaine scooched forward on the mattress. "Wren and I compared notes. You have to be the one to reach out, he's not going to do it."

"He's obsessed with this idea of waiting until February, which I think might be my fault." Wren stood again, shoving her hands into her pockets, her expression abstract. "Back in November, I encouraged him to back off, give you space, and work on himself. I threw out February as an arbitrary date, just to give him something to focus on."

"Should I wait? What's a few more weeks in the scheme of things?" I could hear in my voice that I was trying to talk myself into this, into waiting, as a reasonable, practical course of action.

But now the thought of waiting made me feel even worse. I didn't want Cyrus to hurt needlessly, like I was. Neither of us should be going through this.

Preoccupied, I sat in my desk chair and looked at Wren for advice. "What do I do?"

"Go to him. Make him listen." Her tone was soft and wise. "I'm sorry this has to fall to you, but—I don't know—I think it'll be good for you."

"What? Why?"

"Cyrus needed to learn patience. He has. He's learned it too well." Wren paused, considering me, then asked, "What do you think you need to learn, Beth?"

I stared at her, feeling certain she already knew the answer but wanted me to get there on my own. I racked my brain, discarding the obvious response because it was scary. I'd basically begged him not to leave me, and he'd left. Yes, it was only for five weeks, but it wasn't the time that was the issue, it was what the five weeks represented—that he could and might leave me whenever he wanted and not look back.

"Beth." Wren was suddenly in front of me, and she tapped my bare foot with her shoe. "You know what you need to do."

Swallowing down my fear, I nodded. "I guess I do."

"What? What does she need to do?" Ryaine leaned forward, placing her elbows on her knees, her eyes bouncing between us.

Wren looked at me and I filled in the blank, the words tasting like acid on my tongue, "I have to be vulnerable."

CHAPTER 26

BATHSHEBA

"Youth ages, immaturity is outgrown, ignorance can be educated, and drunkenness sobered, but stupid lasts forever."

— ARISTOPHANES

Sneaking into Cyrus's house, into his bedroom, stripping naked, slipping under his covers, and handcuffing myself to his bed sounded like a good idea at the time.

Actually, no. That's a big, honking lie.

It hadn't even sounded like a good idea when Ryaine, Wren, and I hatched it over vodka, and it felt like an even worse idea now.

I'd brought his father's watch, irritated with myself for forgetting to slip it in his coat while we'd been trapped together in Texas. I wasn't planning on giving it to him as some grand gesture. That felt manipulative.

I'd simply placed it in the drawer of his dresser—not the left one with the handcuff key and his ties, the right one with his socks—leaving it on top where he was sure to see it at some point after I left. No matter what we decided between us, I didn't want the return of the watch to impact his decision. It never should've been taken from him in the first place and didn't really have anything to do with me.

And, inexplicably, him knowing I had anything to do with the watch's return filled me with a strange panic I didn't understand.

"Oh my God, why am I doing this to myself?" I groaned, covering my face with my free hand. Pulling my fingers away, I eyed the left top drawer of his dresser again.

This felt like a mistake. Worse, it felt like a really scary mistake.

There'd been times in my life when I'd been brave, throwing myself between a client and a perpetrator with a gun or a giant fist. While guarding Ryaine, I'd disarmed three men with knives during a signing event. They'd just wanted to "scare her a little." I'd severed fingers and I didn't feel badly about it.

In those moments, I'd been focused and certain, clear about my mission, and determined to see it through. That's how I viewed and related to bravery.

This didn't feel like bravery. This felt like waiting to get my teeth kicked in. This felt like being stupid on purpose.

If he wanted to see you, he'd message or call. He hasn't even read your texts. Don't bang on this screen door. You can wait for him to come to you, you can—

The sudden sound of his voice made me freeze in place. My heart jumped, trying to leave my body.

Oh my God. OHMYGOD!

He sounded angry. He was snapping at someone, saying rough words, reprimanding them. I thought I heard Craig's meek voice, I might've been wrong. I couldn't hear much because blood was rushing between my ears, deafening me with dread.

The doorknob moved, turned. The door opened. He stepped inside. The bed didn't have a footboard to speak of, just two posts at the corners. I had an unobstructed view of his angry frown and the dark, frustrated look in his eyes. He didn't see me. I held still like a rabbit, not knowing what to do. Maybe I could hide under the covers and he'd never know I was here.

But then his stern gaze lifted and I braced for impact.

BOOM.

I held my breath, not knowing what my face was doing because he did a double take, halting mid-movement, his green eyes bulging almost comically.

"What—"

"Before you say anything, you have to hear me out." I lifted my unbound hand, my voice reedy and high. I didn't sound like me. Which I guess was appropriate, since I wasn't acting like me either.

"Are you . . ." He blinked, the stern set to his jaw relaxing, his forehead clearing. Cyrus's eyes flicked from my bare arm handcuffed to the rail of his bed to my hand pressing the sheet to my chest. "Did you handcuff yourself to my headboard?"

"I did," I said, sounding prim and superior. I tried not to roll my eyes at my own audacity, like he was the one who'd been unexpected. "And only I know where the key is, so unless you want to explain to someone why I'm in here, handcuffed naked to your—"

"You're naked?"

"Yes, under the sheets I'm—Cyrus—what—"

He promptly walked over to the foot of the mattress, picked up the blanket, and tugged it off, leaving me in just the sheet. His eyes flared and he reached for the sheet, trying to remove that as well.

I fisted the thin white fabric and gripped it closer to my chest, which made it pull taut between us. We engaged in a tug-of-war for several seconds. "What are you—we need to talk! What are you doing?"

Despite my best efforts, he managed to yank the sheet out of my grip and his eyes flared again, wider this time as they moved over my exposed body.

Holding an arm over my breasts, I sighed. "I came here to talk to you."

"Did you?" He sounded dazed and distracted, his gaze sliding up my legs.

"Yes." I drew my knees up and crossed them at the ankles.

"That's cute." His hands were at his waist, unfastening his belt.

My heart jumped to my throat as a spike of heat pulsed through me. I tried to sit up and away from the pillows, but the handcuff at my wrist prevented me from moving too far. "Listen, just listen. I don't want to wait. I want you to stop being noble and I—"

"Done." Cyrus pulled the belt from its loops and placed a knee on the bed, reaching for one of my ankles.

I kicked out at him, not allowing him to grab me. "Done? What do you mean 'done'?"

"I mean, done. We won't wait and I'll stop being noble. I was rubbish at it anyway."

His words surprised me so much, my leg went lax. "What?"

Cyrus made quick work of claiming my ankle and using it as leverage to tug me down the bed until I lay flat on my back. "My dearest love, do you think I *want* to be noble where you are concerned?" His words were rushed and he made a tutting noise. I watched his face as he spoke rather than what he was doing with his hands, his belt, my leg, and the left post at the foot of the bed. "I want to be ignoble. I want to be filthy and dishonorable and do absolutely nasty and wonderful things to your body all the time. I want to follow you around like a puppy on a leash and bite everyone's hand but yours."

What the heck is he talking about?

"Puppies are terrible on leashes. They need to be leash trained."

"Oh! That's sounds fun." His eyelids drooped, his expression entranced. "Let's start tonight."

"Cyrus, you—I—but—but you left me!" Forgetting my nakedness, I hit the mattress with my free fist. Meanwhile, apparently unconcerned by my outburst, he gently plucked my other foot from the bed and pulled his lose tie from around his neck. Cyrus's fingers sliding up the back of my calf was a distraction, but I was determined, we needed to settle this. "You left me in Texas. And you told me we had to wait until February first to see or talk to each other. And then, when I tried to call you, you wouldn't pick up, you wouldn't call me back, or text me back—"

"I blocked you."

I gasped, stung, my vision tunneling on his handsome face as it filled with hurt tears. "You—you blocked me?"

His gaze flickered to mine. He grimaced and returned his attention to the right bedpost, his voice soft as he said, "If I heard your voice or read your messages, I would've caved immediately. It had to be no contact."

"But you're caving now?" I croaked out.

"Precisely." His eyes blazed a trail from my legs to my hips, my stomach to my handcuffed arm.

An incredulous laugh exploded out of me and my words were screechy with disbelief as I demanded, "Just like that? Just like that, you're okay with us seeing each other now?"

"Oh yes." Unbuttoning the cuffs of his suit shirt, he rounded the bed, his intent gaze never settling until it rested on the arm next to me on the mattress. His eyebrows drew together like it was a problem.

Hot frustration tightened my chest and I let my head flop back, glaring up at the ceiling. "You've got to be kidding me."

"Why so angry?" he asked lightly. I heard his nightstand drawer open and close before his long fingers circled my free wrist.

"I came here to convince you."

"So? You did." Something soft brushed against the inside of my wrist as he slowly lifted it toward the headboard.

"So I've been tied up in knots, Cyrus!" I growled, closing my eyes against the threatening sting. "I was so devastated when you left, and you wouldn't even talk to me about it, and so I came up with this plan to force you to listen to me, and—"

A series of clicks had my eyes flying open and I craned my head up to discover he'd handcuffed my other wrist to the headboard. But unlike my heavy-duty metal cuffs, he'd cuffed this wrist with a fur-lined pair.

My stare cut to his and I found a slow smile blooming on his features. "Hello," he said, his green gaze sparkling.

I frowned at him. "You handcuffed me to your bed?"

"You handcuffed you first." I felt his fingers draw slow, sweeping lines on the inside of my forearm before sliding down to my shoulder as he knelt beside the bed. "I simply followed your lead."

I gave him a flat look. "I'm upset with you. Don't think that—that—ah!"

While I'd been glaring at him, his big palm had smoothed down my front, over my breast, stomach, to cup my sex. Instinctively, I tried to bend my knees. I could not. Lifting my head, I found what I'd suspected earlier, he'd bound one ankle to the left post using his belt and the other to the right post using his tie, my legs spread.

A sound of outrage quickly became a moan as his mouth closed over the center of my breast, his hot tongue laving against my nipple.

"You—you—"

Cyrus's fingers parted me, and his middle finger filled me with a single, smooth stroke. He groaned. "Can't wait to be inside you," he said between wet kisses against my chest. "It's the only thing I've been able to think about for months."

"M—months?"

"Let's get married," he said, his mouth moving against my nipple.

"What?"

"Let's get married—you naked except for a veil, and then we'll fuck on a beach in Bali for the rest of our lives."

He was making me hot, so hot. I couldn't think. But I knew this wasn't what I came here for. Or rather, it wasn't the main reason I was here.

"Cyrus! Listen to me!"

"I am. Speak. Just please don't ask me to stop." He added another finger to his invasion. "I'm so hungry for you. I'm starving."

My legs shifted restlessly. I could close my thighs, he'd left enough give with the bindings, but my body wouldn't obey. I was being dragged under, losing myself to his touch, which was likely why my next words arrived without forethought, "You don't get me if you're just going to leave me again."

As the words settled around us, Cyrus stilled. Several seconds passed, and I heard myself breathing, but he remained completely silent. Opening my eyes, I glanced down at him, found him hovering over my chest, his eyes unfocused, moving as though reading a hefty internal thought.

His fingers left me just as his gaze collided with mine. "I'm so fucking sorry," he said, the words rough with remorse.

The tension when out of my body and I let my head fall back to the mattress. I sighed.

In the next moment, he'd climbed over me, one knee between my legs, the other next to my thigh, his hands on either side of my head as he stared down at me. "I can't believe—I can't believe I didn't think about—Beth." Cyrus kissed me. Like our last, this felt desperate. But this time, it was him pouring all of himself into it, hungrily stroking my tongue, his teeth nibbling at my lips.

"I'm sorry," he said, over and over.

If my hands were free, I would've slid my fingers into his hair and gently pushed him away. But they weren't, so I couldn't. Instead, after returning his kiss for a time, I turned my head and sucked air into my lungs.

"Please forgive me. I'm so stupid."

"You're not stupid. You're stubborn. I get it, I do. But I can't have you leaving me to prove a point, not even to yourself."

"Yes. Obviously, yes." He nodded, lifting himself up on all fours again, his eyes searching my expression. "What can I do to make it up to you? Do you want to tie me up?"

I pulled in a breath, and with it, bravery. The normal kind, not the hand-cuffing-myself-naked-to-a-bed kind. "Promise me you'll never leave in anger, or for any other reason. I can't handle . . . it."

"Deal," he said at once. "You don't have to worry about that. I would never want to." As he spoke, his gaze drifted, his eyebrows pulling together as though overwhelmed by the sight of my body beneath him. "What else?"

I loved it when he looked at me like this. I loved it. How his eyes heated with want and plans, like he couldn't stop looking, like he hungered for me like he'd just said. It didn't feel addictive, it felt essential to my very survival.

Okay, sooooo, that's addiction.

I batted the thought away, deciding I was okay with being addicted to him.

Licking my lips, I whispered, "Cyrus."

Immediately, his gaze cut to mine—still hot, still full of plans.

"Yes?" he asked, like he was waiting for orders, more demands to satisfy me.

My heart thundered, my blood whooshing between my ears again, this time for a very different reason.

I lowered my gaze. "Your mouth."

"Yes?" he said again, his lips curving, like they enjoyed my attention.

"I want it."

"It's yours." He leaned forward to kiss me.

I shook my head. "Not there."

Eyes alight with happiness and mischief, his smile spread, his devastating, almighty dimple winking at me. He looked wonderfully wicked.

My stomach fluttered, heat twisting low in my stomach. With one last long stare, Cyrus slid down my body, moving his knees between my legs.

"Is this part of my punishment?" he asked, his eyes on the apex of my thighs, his fingertips a light touch trailing down my stomach and over my hips. "Because this feels more like a gift."

"I can think of something else as a punishment instead," I said, falsifying bravado.

"You wouldn't dare." He lowered to the floor, kneeling at the foot of the bed, his elbows and torso still on the mattress.

Before I had a chance to respond, he caressed his hands around my thighs, encircling them with his arms, and placed a hot, wet, open mouth kiss at my center, his tongue skillfully sliding upward to reveal and lick my clit.

I tried to bend my legs, but my ankles caught. A spike of strange pleasure shot through me at the knowledge that I couldn't move but at the same time Cyrus was mine to command.

He hummed and our eyes caught, his were smiling, gazing at me like my reactions fed something within him. He was so good at this, his tongue and lips lapping at my body, truly exceptional. And when he slipped two fingers inside me, my legs jerked again, that same spike of wonderful frustration making me moan.

"If I'm very good, can I fuck you?" he asked, his voice dark.

And just like that, I was on the edge, because Cyrus wasn't dirty talking, he was honestly asking, like we were having a conversation about his performance and what he might get for it, and it made me so wild.

"If you're good—" My breath caught, hitched as he quickened his pace. Licking my dry lips, I forced myself to finish the thought, "If you're very good, I'll tie you up next."

He cursed, his lashes flickering, like I'd just said the magic words, and I felt myself hurtling toward the end, cresting that peak way before I was ready. My legs searching for purchase and finding none, the helplessness only served to speed and increase the intensity of my release. Everything twisted tight. My body tensed and the last thing I heard was Cyrus groan, sucking my clit into his mouth, his tongue a vibrating pressure, his fingers in my body hitting just the right spot and at just the right pace.

Slowly, so slowly, I fell back to earth, my chest heaving as I labored for air. I felt him kiss the inside of my thigh, brushing his lips back and forth against my skin as though feeling me with his mouth.

"You're so soft," he said, his voice full of lusty wonder. "I want to lick every part of you. I want to touch you everywhere at once."

A small laugh left me at his nonsensical words, but I understood what he meant. Our first time together had been incredibly intense for me. I'd felt more like a passenger than an active participant, and not in a bad way. I hadn't worked for those incredible orgasms, and the second one had taken me by complete surprise. I hoped he'd let me return the favor. I hoped he'd let me tie him up and tease him, stretch out his pleasure, and make him come when he least expected it.

The tie at my ankle loosened, then the belt. Bending my knees, I opened dazed eyes and watched him draw even with me, his gaze on mine as he opened the drawer next to the bed and withdrew a key. "*Chuisle*, these are for mine. Where's yours?"

I couldn't stop my smile. "What did you just call me? You've said it before."

Eyes on the cuffs, his grin looked secretive. "Something wonderful," he said as he reached forward and unlocked the fur-lined cuff. He tried his key with my cuff, but it didn't work. "Where's your key?"

Drawing my knees up, my eyes on the unforgiving metal around my wrist, I said, "In your top dresser drawer."

He tossed his key and the fur cuff into the open nightstand drawer, closed it, and crossed to the dresser.

"Aren't we using that?" I asked, glancing at the nightstand, referring to the fur cuff he'd just put away there.

"I want to hold you first, I want to run my hands over your body and pet you. I'm really only interested in BDSM for the aftercare. And then you can have your wicked way with . . ." he trailed off as he opened the dresser drawer.

I lifted my head, frowning at his pregnant pause, but then I realized which drawer he'd just opened. *Oh. Yikes!*

Scrambling up to sit against the headboard, I quickly tried to arrange my features but didn't know what I wished to communicate. I hadn't expected to be here when he found it, I hadn't wanted to be. It still felt essential that he not know I was responsible for returning the watch.

Should I lie? Or simply express surprise and allow him to think whatever he thought? Or . . .what should I do?

Don't lie. Why would you lie? That's foolish.

I didn't get a chance to decide. Cyrus turned, holding the watch, his eyes on me, and any plans I might have made would've been pointless.

"How?"

I winced.

"Bathsheba."

Groaning, I gave up. "I'm sorry. I didn't mean for you to find that. Yet. The key is in the other—"

"How?" he demanded again, his voice cracking, his eyes an entire universe of emotion.

"I tracked the guy down, okay?" I felt oddly defensive and antagonistic. "After it happened, I looked through all the videos, found the guy, sent an image to a friend who works for the government, and got an address. I flew to his house. I got the watch. It's no big deal."

"You got an address." He drifted closer; his mouth curved in a soft, awestruck smile; his eyes captivated even as a tear rolled down his cheek. "It's no big deal, she says."

Tugging my arm against the cuff holding me hostage—my cuff, the one I'd snapped into place all by myself—I sighed, feeling more trapped now than I had before.

"How long have you had this?" he asked quietly. "When did you find it?"

I didn't want to tell him. Telling him felt scary.

"Bathsheba. Please."

Grumbling, I finally admitted, "I've had it since November. I just needed to figure out how to return it to you without you finding out it was me."

He placed the watch on the nightstand with tremendous reverence and sat next to me on the bed, his body angled toward the headboard, his eyes never leaving my face. There he sat and stared at me. I felt that funny feeling again. The one where I got the sense he was about to say something big, like at the homestead after dinner on Christmas Eve. But he didn't speak. He simply stared. Smiling.

I grew restless, sometimes meeting his eyes, sometimes not. It felt over-whelming, how he was looking at me. Too much.

Unable to stand it, I blurted, "What do you want me to say?"

"How about, 'I love you, Cyrus. I'm in love with you. I've been in love with you since November.'"

I pressed my lips together and tried to swallow. I couldn't.

He looked like he wanted to laugh. Instead, he said, "Here, I'll go first. I love you, Bathsheba. I'm in love with you. I've been in love with you since the first moment I saw you in your green vintage Vera Wang, slurring your words and regaling me with the details of your rash. You are the only one in my heart."

He didn't touch me with anything but his eyes and words, and when I returned my blurry gaze to his, his eyes were glassy. There were no more tears from him, only certainty.

I blinked. My chin wobbled. I tried to firm it. It didn't work.

"Your turn," he said softly, looking so smug and delighted.

I both loved and hated that he was right. I'd loved him, had been in love with him, for months. That's the real reason I hadn't wanted him to know I'd tracked down his watch, what I couldn't admit to myself.

Obviously, I loved him.

"Bathsheba," he said, his voice teasing. "I'll wait all night. Blame your-self. Loving you has taught me the art of patience."

"Fine!" The word exploded out of me. "I love you, Cyrus," I growled through a waterfall of stupid tears. "I'm in love with you. I've loved you since *before* November, and it scares the shit out of me because if you break my heart or leave me, I might murder you. Happy now?"

An immense grin on his beautiful face, dimple revealed, eyes shining like jewels, he nodded.

Cyrus reached for me, tugging me forward by the back of my neck, and just before his lips met mine, he said, "Yes, *my hero*. I'm so very, very happy."

EPILOGUE

CYRUS

"Wise people, even though all laws were abolished, would still lead the same life."

— ARISTOPHANES

*B*eth's father looked over at me, his eyes narrowing just slightly before he crooked his finger.

Gulping, I leaned over Beth's lap to obey, turning to give him my ear.

"I was nervous my first time too," he whispered, his hand coming to my shoulder to give it a squeeze. I lifted my head, glancing at him, and he cupped my jaw to give it a little pat, gazing at me with affection. "You'll do great, son. Remember, slow and clear. And enunciate."

I nodded, returning his encouraging smile with a tight one, not necessarily wanting to hide my nerves but also uncertain if I could.

I had no idea why I was so nervous. I'd never experienced this kind of jittery, unsettled feeling when performing in front of an audience, large or small. A church full of people who were about to line up and do exactly what I planned to do wasn't precisely an audience. We were all in this together, I supposed. We were all here for the same reason. We were comrades who'd never spoken, yet with a shared experience.

Straightening, I rested my back against the pew and stared forward, not really listening to the priest as he described what would happen next. Beth and her family had filled me in on the particulars when they'd offhandedly asked if I wanted to join them for All Saints' Day Mass. It had seemed like a good idea at the time, but now it felt . . .

"You okay?" Beth's hand squeezed mine, drawing my gaze.

Her smile was small and compassionate. "You don't have to go. I can say his name for you."

"I'm not scared," I said, lying. I was scared.

Why am I scared?

Depths.

Ooooohhh yeeeeah. Those.

Gathering an expansive breath, I lifted her hand and turned it, brushing my lips against the inside of her wrist. I adored how soft her skin was here. Raw, warm silk. The insides of her elbows, the backs of her knees, the tops of her feet, soft little gateways to heaven.

Something I'd learned about Beth over the last year was that she was extremely greedy and possessive about my touches. Something I'd learned about me during that same time, was that I felt the same way about her. I still showed affection toward my friends, but only people she knew well and with whom she had a level of comfort. This, as it turned out, was also my preference.

For my part, if anyone appeared to be enjoying her hugs and cuddles too much, I'd developed the habit of sitting between them and cuddling them both. It made her laugh, and I loved her laugh. I would do almost anything for it.

That's a lie. I'd do anything, not almost anything.

"It's time," Gabi whispered, pulling her purse onto her shoulder. My hand spasmed where Beth held it and I shared a quick smile with Beth's sister, an understanding passing between us.

I liked Gabi. She was my best ally and often took my side against her sister.

Beth had extended her contract for another six months with Vera, and I fully expected her to extend it for an additional six months come January. They worked marvelously together. However, to my chagrin, the studio often asked Beth to also work additional shifts on an ad hoc basis and as a consultant for major events like cons. Her services were often in demand by many of my colleagues and their security team leads.

This vexed me. I loved that she was so successful. I hated the lack of time together and her exhaustion after work. We were still working on balance.

When Beth worked too much, or too hard, or pushed herself beyond what would be reasonably expected of even the most dedicated employee, I could count on Gabi to fight that battle so I didn't have to quite as much. Gabi was the bad cop to my good cop, and that suited me fine. I was so much better at playing good cop.

I looked magnificent in the uniform, I think you'd agree.

Beth had consented to move in with me just two months ago and I credited my lack of pushing as the reason. However, I missed her apartment. Even though she'd never acquired a coffee table. Her furnishings came with her, of course. I loved her eye for design and space.

I suddenly found myself standing, filing out of the pew, my mind still on Beth's lack of a coffee table. At the end of the row, Beth held me back to allow her sister to join Matías and Mark. We walked behind, shuffling our feet, waiting our turn. I studied the architecture of the interior, comparing it against the vast cathedrals I'd visited as a youth in Europe during my few years of boarding school. Those churches had felt like museums. This one felt like a community center in comparison, humble but purposeful.

Facing forward, I realized with some surprise that Mark was next. In fact, he was just about to speak into the microphone held by the priest. I blinked, understanding that I would be next.

I'm next. I'll go next. He'll go, then me.

"Gloria Morales," he said, speaking slowly and clearly and annunciating beautifully. Beth's mother's name echoed in the church, bouncing off the walls and taking on a life of its own.

Jeez. I have to follow that performance? He was flawless.

I watched Mark Ryan and the priest share a small smile, and then Gabi, Matías, and Mark walked forward. They would each select a thin candle from the basket, light it using the Easter candle, and then use that flame to light one of the thick, white pillar candles that had been placed on tables in front of the altar in remembrance of Gabi, Matías, and Beth's mother—Beth considered Gloria her mother—and Mark's wife.

But I didn't see them do this. They'd explained what would happen, but I didn't get a chance to watch their progress. It was my turn now, my turn to say my father's name. And then I'd be lighting a candle, for him.

My eyes on the priest as I stepped forward, I gathered a shaky breath, forcing the air in and around an inexplicably tight throat. He smiled at me with encouragement, placing the microphone in front of my lips so the whole church would hear, just like he'd done with everyone else.

But unlike everyone else, when I opened my mouth, no sound came out.

And that's when I realized, this would be the first time I would say my father's name out loud since the accident, since he'd died next to me. My eyes burned, my heart raced, my airway threatening to close.

The priest's forehead wrinkled in concern, his eyes urging me to speak and asking me if I was okay at the same time.

I couldn't. I simply couldn't. And just when I was certain a black hole had opened beneath my feet, Beth leaned forward, took the microphone from the priest, and said, "Cyrus Wallace Malcom the third," slowly and clearly and annunciating beautifully. It bounced around the church, taking on life, and I marveled at the sound of it even as I struggled with my own inability.

Taking my arm, Beth put it around her shoulders and led me forward, lifting a hand to the center of my back and rubbing a slow circle between my shoulder blades. I followed where she led, her soothing touch a lifeline. I watched as she lit one of the thin candles, then passed it to me. She lit another for herself.

Guiding me to the tables with rows and rows of flames representing loved ones lost, she took her time, then tilted her head and whispered, "How about that one?" She pointed with her wick, voice soft, thoughtful, steady as another name was said behind us. "I think that's a nice one for your dad."

I lit the pillar candle she'd selected, watching the wick sputter before a strong flame took over. It danced, shifted, flickered. Beth also lit a pillar, whispering under her breath, "For Cyrus and his father."

Beth extinguished her feeder candle, placing it back in the basket. Gently, she took mine and did the same. Then we returned to our aisle while more people spoke more names and lit more candles. She held my hand when we walked single file down the pew but returned my arm to her shoulders again as soon as we sat, then placed a gentle kiss on my jaw.

I looked at her, not ready to speak but wanting to apologize. Her sweet smile beamed back at me, from her eyes and from her lips.

"Hey," she said. "I'm so proud of you."

This statement fractured my daze and I squinted at her, my tongue loosening. "What for? I couldn't say it."

"No." Her gaze dropped to my lips. "But you wanted to. You wanted to remember him." Beth's olive green irises lifted once more, held mine. "And you did remember him. We did."

I stared at her and realized she was right. This was big for me. Huge. Growth. Leaps. Bounds. *Progress.*

As I smiled, her attention lowered to my lips again, and she smiled too. "Ah. There it is," she whispered, like this, my smile, had been what she'd been waiting for all along. She loved me. And that, too, had taken on a life of its own.

An intangible life we couldn't see, like a candle, or hear, like a voice. But Beth's love felt more real than anything I'd ever known. Quite suddenly, I wished we weren't in a church. I wished we were alone. In Bali. Or anywhere, just as long as it was just us and she was naked. Those were my only requirements.

Oh yeah, and the moon.

But I had that already because she'd given me herself. And I intended to do everything in my power to keep her. Despite where I was and who I was with, my thoughts strayed as they were prone to do, several delightfully debauched possibilities occurring to me at once that would ensure Beth's continued satisfaction as my "sex partner" and, quite frankly, the love of my life. I eyed the collection envelope and pen in the pocket of the pew, wondering if I should jot down some quick notes. I decided against it.

Jesus may have harbored no ill will toward sexy people, but I felt fairly certain he would frown upon what I had in mind.

The End

Scan me to receive new book updates and news from Penny!

Scan me if you'd like a signed copy of this or any Penny Reid book!

AUTHOR'S NOTE

In case you couldn't tell while reading the book, Cyrus is one of my favorite characters of all time. He was SO MUCH FUN to hang out with. I suspect you can look forward to bonus scenes in the very near future.

Thank you to my editor, Iveta, for being a rockstar. She's *my hero*.

Until next time, happy reading.

<3 Penny

ABOUT THE AUTHOR

Penny Reid is the *New York Times*, *Wall Street Journal*, and *USA Today* bestselling author of the Winston Brothers and Knitting in the City series. She used to spend her days writing federal grant proposals as a biomedical researcher, but now she writes kissing books. Penny is an obsessive knitter and manages the #OwnVoices-focused mentorship incubator / publishing imprint, Smartypants Romance. She lives in Seattle Washington with her husband, three kids, and dog named Hazel.

Come find me -
Mailing List: http://pennyreid.ninja/newsletter/
Goodreads:http://www.goodreads.com/ReidRomance
Facebook: www.facebook.com/pennyreidwriter
Instagram: www.instagram.com/reidromance
Twitter: www.twitter.com/reidromance
TikTok: https://www.tiktok.com/@authorpennyreid
Patreon: https://www.patreon.com/smartypantsromance
Email: pennreid@gmail.com …hey, you! Email me ;-)

OTHER BOOKS BY PENNY REID

Knitting in the City Series

(Interconnected Standalones, Adult Contemporary Romantic Comedy)

Neanderthal Seeks Human: A Smart Romance (#1)

Neanderthal Marries Human: A Smarter Romance (#1.5)

Friends without Benefits: An Unrequited Romance (#2)

Love Hacked: A Reluctant Romance (#3)

Beauty and the Mustache: A Philosophical Romance (#4)

Ninja at First Sight (#4.75)

Happily Ever Ninja: A Married Romance (#5)

Dating-ish: A Humanoid Romance (#6)

Marriage of Inconvenience: (#7)

Neanderthal Seeks Extra Yarns (#8)

Knitting in the City Coloring Book (#9)

Winston Brothers Series

(Interconnected Standalones, Adult Contemporary Romantic Comedy, spinoff of
Beauty and the Mustache)

Beauty and the Mustache (#0.5)

Truth or Beard (#1)

Grin and Beard It (#2)

Beard Science (#3)

Beard in Mind (#4)

Beard In Hiding (#4.5)

Dr. Strange Beard (#5)

Beard with Me (#6)

Beard Necessities (#7)

Winston Brothers Paper Doll Book (#8)

<u>Hypothesis Series</u>

(New Adult Romantic Comedy Trilogies)

Elements of Chemistry: ATTRACTION, HEAT, and CAPTURE (#1)

Laws of Physics: MOTION, SPACE, and TIME (#2)

<u>Irish Players (Rugby) Series – by L.H. Cosway and Penny Reid</u>

(Interconnected Standalones, Adult Contemporary Sports Romance)

The Hooker and the Hermit (#1)

The Pixie and the Player (#2)

The Cad and the Co-ed (#3)

The Varlet and the Voyeur (#4)

<u>Dear Professor Series</u>

(New Adult Romantic Comedy)

Kissing Tolstoy (#1)

Kissing Galileo (#2)

<u>Ideal Man Series</u>

(Interconnected Standalones, Adult Contemporary Romance Series of Jane Austen Reimaginings)

Pride and Dad Jokes (#1, coming 2023)

Man Buns and Sensibility (#2, TBD)

Sense and Manscaping (#3, TBD)

Persuasion and Man Hands (#4, TBD)

Mantuary Abbey (#5, TBD)

Mancave Park (#6, TBD)

Emmanuel (#7, TBD)

<u>Handcrafted Mysteries Series</u>

(A Romantic Cozy Mystery Series, spinoff of *The Winston Brothers Series*)

Engagement and Espionage (#1)

Marriage and Murder (#2)

Home and Heist (TBD)

Baby and Ballistics (TBD)

<u>Pie Crimes and Misdemeanors (TBD)</u>

<u>Good Folks Series</u>

(Interconnected Standalones, Adult Contemporary Romantic Comedy, spinoff of The Winston Brothers Series)

<u>Totally Folked (#1)</u>

<u>Folk Around and Find Out (#2)</u>

<u>All Folked Up (#3, TBD)</u>

<u>Three Kings Series</u>

(Interconnected Standalones, Holiday-themed Adult Contemporary Romantic Comedies)

<u>Homecoming King (#1)</u>

<u>Drama King (#2)</u>

<u>Prom King (#3, coming Christmas 2023)</u>

<u>Standalones</u>

<u>Ten Trends to Seduce Your Best Friend</u>